TAZMAND

Jack Murphy

Bloodstone of Cardemont - Bk1

Cover design by Tom Brown

For Richard I

CONTENTS

Title Page

Copyright

Dedication

Chapter One   1

Chapter Two   35

Chapter Three   53

Chapter Four   69

Chapter Five   95

Chapter Six   120

Chapter Seven   147

Chapter Eight   177

Chapter Nine   201

Chapter Ten   221

Chapter Eleven   252

Chapter Twelve   272

Chapter Thirteen   299

Chapter Fourteen   319

Chapter Fifteen   338

Chapter Sixteen   358

About The Author   379

CHAPTER ONE

First Reckoning

Heart racing, Iphigenia rests her forehead against the wall and takes a moment to compose herself. *Remain calm. Look normal. Remember who you are.* She takes a deep breath, stands up straight and raises her voice loud enough to be heard on the other side of the door. 'Attend me!'

The door opens instantly, revealing the sentry to her bedchamber; a young man, no older than she is herself, dressed in the uniform of a house guard. He bows to his duchess then straightens, touching the tip of his sword to his helmet with a soft clink. 'Your Grace?'

He's a new one, Cardemont though, one of my own. Not Kareshian, not shadokin. Still, can I trust him? She is trembling and digs her fingernails into the palms of her hands to quell her nerves. The sharp bite of it helps. 'I will rest a while. Admit no one. That means anyone, until I order you otherwise.'

The guard nods. 'Yes, Your Grace.'

'And send word to His Grace, the Duke, that I will join

him within the hour.'

'Yes, Your Grace.' The guard starts to close the door, then hesitates, looking anxious.

Iphigenia glares at him. 'What?'

'Apologies, Your Grace.' He glances behind her, scanning her chamber. 'It's just that you seem. You look. I mean... is all well?'

'Why wouldn't it be?'

'You seem out of sorts, Your Grace. It's just...'

'Everything is perfectly well. Attend to my command!'

'Your Grace, I-'

She turns her back on him in dismissal. 'Do not presume to question me!'

'Of course, Your Grace! My apologies.'

Iphigenia hears him closing the door, and only then allows herself to relax. She lets out a long breath and feels the hard knot between her shoulders soften a little. Trusting that the abrupt tone in her voice and manner will ensure his strict obedience, she moves swiftly towards a large tapestry that hangs on a far wall. It is a rich and detailed representation of a woman bathing two small children in a woodland stream. A happy memory, she thinks, allowing herself a moment of calm to enjoy the image.

I must pull myself together. There is much to do and little time.

She pushes the heavy fabric of the wall hanging to one side revealing the smooth stone blocks beneath, then reaches down and raises the hem of her dress to extract a small key from her garter. Feeling along the texture of the stonework with her fingers, she identifies a tiny keyhole and, despite her hands trembling, manages eventually to place the key in the lock. She turns it until she hears a soft click. A crack appears, as a hidden spring mechanism activates to release a section of the wall. She pushes firmly and squeezes through the emerging gap to the top of a narrow, winding flight of steps.

Making haste, Iphigenia removes a candle from a nearby sconce and lights it with sparks from a small firesteel, before carefully starting to descend the stairs. She keeps the candle low before her so she can see where to place her feet. The smell of damp is strong. A scuffling noise focuses her attention on a small dark shape scampering over her foot and the brush of clammy rat fur against the fine silk of the stocking covering her ankle. She ignores it, careful not to trip.

As she descends the steps, she recalls the time the duke first showed her this secret staircase. It had been only four years ago, before she became his wife and prior to the invasion of Cardemont by the imperial armies of Karesh. *Is it truly only four years since we wed? So much has happened since; so much has changed.* She had been fourteen years old when expected to move into the castle for the couple of months preceding their wedding - the usual custom. She had been given the highest room in one of the castle's two turrets as her personal chamber. One night, she sat alone at her dressing table making final preparations for bed, when the duke had appeared miraculously, out of nowhere.

He had done nothing improper; simply walked towards her as she watched him reflected in her mirror and, standing behind her, he had leaned forward and kissed the top of her head. How handsome he had been, blonde and athletic. At sixteen, he was only a couple of years older than her. He had become duke young, when both his parents had died unexpectedly in a hunting accident. As the new ruler of Cardemont, he had been expected to marry quickly, and he had chosen her from a host of young women from the noblest families of Cardemont.

The young duke had revealed the secret staircase to Iphigenia and shown her how to access it. It led from her chamber directly down to a hidden room, built centuries before by one of his ancestors. He had given her the only key so that he could never again enter her chamber without her permission and, for this, she had started to trust him.

She reaches the base of the staircase and enters a windowless and narrow chamber, with curved walls that follow the line of the base of the turret. Her candle flame flickers as she moves, revealing glimpses of rich tapestries and gilt-framed paintings hanging on the walls. Ornately carved wooden furniture, draped in thick furs with cushions decorated in gold and silver thread still occupy much of the space.

Being in a hurry she only half notices her surroundings, remembering instead how the duke had insisted that the chamber be comfortable for their early courtship - somewhere for them to meet and not be disturbed - and, to please her, he had arranged for these luxuries to be installed in secret by trusted servants. Once married, court routine and the rigours of government had taken over their lives; they had little time to be together, let alone visit this private sanctuary. Then of course the war came, followed by the occupation.

Most of the paintings are now eaten at the edges by mould, as are the furs. The furniture is still solid enough but much of it has discoloured in the damp since the room has been abandoned and now, no amount of polishing would eradicate the bloom of mildew.

Iphigenia crosses to the far side of the chamber, to an area that is well-lit, clean, dry and newly furnished. A welcoming log fire burns in a grate and before it sits an elderly female servant. Her head is bent backwards, resting on a cushion, her mouth open wide, snoring gently. Her hand rests on the side of a cradle, which it would seem she had been rocking before dozing off. She is wearing heavy oilskins as if prepared for a journey in harsh weather and, as a consequence, she looks hot, her lined and wrinkled face red and glistening with sweat in the firelight.

Iphigenia peers into the cradle and staring back at her is a baby boy, wide-awake with clear blue-green eyes and a broad, toothless grin. For a moment, her shredded nerves relax and she forgets all else. She smiles back and starts to rock the crib as tears trickle down her cheeks. The servant wakes immediately, sensing the movement of the child's bed.

'Your Grace! Oh, My Lady! Forgive an old woman her weakness,' she starts to say; flustered at being caught asleep on duty. She stands up too quickly and is forced to sit down again, equally quickly, as the heat combined with the weight of the oilskins makes her dizzy. 'I got all ready and dressed-up to go out of the castle as you ordered, and the heat must have sent me off on a doze while I waited for you.' She wafts a clean baby's napkin in front of her face in an attempt to cool off. 'I didn't dress little Lord Derron as I didn't want him suffocating or being uncomfortable but, it will take me no more than a moment to get him ready.'

'Good.' Iphigenia wipes the tears from her face with the backs of her hands. 'You should be ready to leave within a half of an hour. I must return to my chamber immediately, so I need to know that you are sure of your instructions?'

The old woman nods. 'I am, Your Grace. I will wait until you and the duke have quitted the castle with Prince Orlando. All attention will be fixed on you as you all proceed to Golden Square. I will leave here through the back gardens of the castle and take Prince Derron to-' she stops suddenly and looks behind her into the darker parts of the chamber.

Iphigenia smiles. "There is no one else here but, you are right to be cautious.'

'To the...' she hesitates again, fearing to reveal the location out loud. 'To the pre-arranged destination. One of the Coenobites of the Order of Ra will meet me there and take him into their charge.'

'If all goes well, you will be back here within a couple of hours and no-one will be any the wiser.'

'Yes, Your Grace,' the woman nods, her face set in grim determination. 'You can count on me sure enough.'

Iphigenia smiles. 'I know I can. May the gods be with you and protect you.' She takes the servant's wrinkled hand gently and places a leather purse in it. 'Give this money to the coenobite.' The woman stands still for a moment, clutching the purse. She appears to want to say something but, seems uncertain how to phrase it. 'What is it?'

'Oh, nothing, Your Grace it's just...'

'Yes, go on?'

'Well, it's those coenobites,' she blurts out. 'Can we trust them? They go 'round all secretive like. No one knows where they come from or what they get up to. Meant to be a religious bunch and yet they carry swords and get into all sorts of scrapes and carryings-on. Some say they practice majick and that don't seem very righteous, let alone lawful, to me, if you don't mind me saying. I just don't know if it's a safe place to leave a baby that's all and-'

'Enough!'

'Your Grace, I just-.'

'I have known the order since I was a child. They served my father well and they will do the same for Derron. I would trust them with my life and with that of my child. They will make him safe and...' Iphigenia's voice trails off as she stares at her son.

'My Lady?'

'They will need to Prove him. There is no other way.'

The nurse stares at her mistress then takes a deep breath and nods. 'Yes, Your Grace, I know you know what you're doing. I didn't mean anything by it. I hope you will forgive me speaking my mind.'

'There is nothing to forgive.' Iphigenia's tense facial muscles relax into a sad smile. 'You are a loyal servant and you do well to be honest with me.'

'Thank you, Your Grace.'

'Just follow my instructions and all will be well.'

The woman nods. 'Your Grace.'

Turning from the old woman, Iphigenia bends once more to the crib. 'Farewell my son. My undying love goes with you.' She kisses her baby's forehead then stands and hurries to the foot of the steps. Without turning around, she issues one last order to the nurse. 'I must hasten to my bedchamber to prepare for the Reckoning. Ensure you get word to me of your success the instant you return.'

The nurse bows her head. 'Yes, Your Grace. As soon as I get back.' For a moment she watches the duchess hurry up the steps then, she takes the baby Derron out of his crib and wraps him in a fur-lined blanket.

He starts to wail.

#

Iphigenia sits motionless at her dressing table. Oblivious to the cold and drizzle blowing through an open window, she gazes out over Cardemont, her shattered city. Beatrix, her lady-in-waiting and oldest friend, arranges her mistress's hair.

'It is all broken,' the young duchess murmurs aloud.

'What's that, Your Grace?' Beatrix concentrates as her practised fingers continue to coil her mistress's auburn mane into a silver net strung with black pearls. 'It is hard to see clearly what I am doing by this light. The evening is drawing in and twilight is deepening. There are too few candles lit and they flicker and spit so in the chill breeze.'

Iphigenia ignores her, continuing to stare through the window. Purple clouds drift slowly from the west, releasing their rain, drenching the shattered buildings of her scarred and plundered metropolis. The great river ripples like a silver-grey ribbon, thin in the distance and becoming ever wider as its waters, swollen by the increasing downpour, flow past the castle. The remains of immense marble bridges protrude through its surface in chunks like broken teeth, whilst hastily made wooden walkways and floating pontoons now address the needs of the populace as treacherous links between the banks.

This evening, each crossing is packed with people making their way to Golden Square, their heads covered by cloaks and coats for shelter against the elements. Far below her tower, they shuffle in slow lines. Tiny, they swarm like ants in their thousands amongst the wreckage of what once was the wealthy trading city of Cardemont. Some start to ignite torches as evening draws in: little pinpricks of light spark and remain burning. Others blink a moment, then disappear as the rain extinguishes them.

She thinks of her own ancient castle: sizeable sections of it are now rubble, the rest of it pitted and scarred by repeated mortar attack. Of its twin turrets, one has been mutilated to a stump, the other, at the top of which she now sits in her bedchamber, survives entire but only just: an arthritic finger, pointing stubbornly towards the darkening sky.

'I did not hear you well, Your Grace. I am distracted by the wind and wet coming through the window, along with the noise made by the crowds. Should I close it perhaps?' Beatrix moves to do so but, Iphigenia gives an imperceptible shake of her head so the girl, although shivering, stops and leaves it open. She takes the opportunity, however, to light some more candles before returning to her work.

The duchess shivers and heaves a loud sigh. 'Broken. Everything.'

'Broken, Your Grace?' Beatrix continues to coil her missstress's hair. 'What do you mean?' Again, there is no further response, so she pauses in her task and tries once more, less formally, to encourage her mistress to speak to her. 'Iphigenia?' She leans forward so they can see each other clearly reflected in the mirror. 'Please talk to me.'

The duchess gazes at Beatrix, noting her young, fresh face marked all down the left side by a large purple birthmark. Her light blonde hair usually a mass of unruly curls is bound into a net. An earnest look of concern creases her usually smooth forehead and is equally reflected in her clear blue eyes. So different, Iphigenia thinks, to her own eyes, hazel-green, usually bright and alive themselves but now glazed like a ruffled pond and sad, a cruel pain evident in their depths. She raises her fingertips to her lips, usually full but now somehow thinner and fixed in a humourless smile. Her skin, always pale is more so; it now has a dull, lifeless pallor, with more recently acquired lines and creases around her eyes.

Iphigenia lowers her hand and turns back to the window. She still says nothing, preferring to listen to the lazy rumbling of thunder in the distance.

'My dear,' Beatrix continues. 'I am worried about you. You've barely slept or eaten anything substantial for days. I have never known you like this. So washed-out and thin. Your skin is ashen; translucent almost to the point that I can see through to the bone.'

Iphigenia closes her eyes and breaths deeply. She knows Beatrix is worried for her but, what can she do about it? *What can I tell her? So many heavy secrets. So much at stake. I cannot, dare not. I shall not burden my oldest friend.*

Exasperated, Beatrix crouches lower, squats and, placing one hand on her lady's shoulder and the other on her lap, tries again, looking up at her. 'Why won't you speak to me?' she begs. 'We used to share everything.' She turns her head briefly to look behind her and peer into the darker recesses of the chamber. She knows the room is guarded but, she needs to reassure herself no-one else is spying from an unlit corner. Shadokin spies are everywhere. 'What troubles you? I know it is something more than the Reckoning, and that is fearful enough. You know you can talk to me about anythi-'

'Enough!' Iphigenia snaps at last, pushing her friend's hand off her lap, a little more harshly than intended. Startled, Beatrix stands. Iphigenia takes another deep breath pauses, then exhales to steady her nerves. 'Enough,' she says again more gently. 'I will finish my hair myself.'

'Yes, Your Grace, of course. I apologise, I-' Beatrix looks chastised, her eyes turning towards the ground. Her face flushes and the birthmark deepens in colour to an angry blood red. The young woman in the chair is her friend but, Iphigenia is also her duchess.

Iphigenia sighs. 'You have no need to apologise old friend.' She takes over the complex assembly of her hair. It feels heavy, damp with air-chilled perspiration. 'What I must do, I must do by myself. And I, alone, will face the consequences – good or bad. I would not involve you in it.'

Beatrix crouches by her mistress once more. Her young face is pained with concern, her large blue eyes starting to tear up. 'But what, by all the gods, is it? What consequences? I know you fear something more than today's ordeal but what? Why the secrecy? We have always trusted each other. Why won't you share with me now?'

Iphigenia finishes arranging her hair. She glances at her lady-in-waiting and at last smiles looking, briefly, more like her old self. She clasps her friend's arm and gives it a reassuring squeeze. 'I would keep you safe my dear. Please do not ask more from me. Not today.'

'Keep me safe? From what? We have been close since childhood, sharing everything or, so I thought. You looked after me, protected me from my persecutors when they mocked me.' She instinctively touches the swollen discolouration on her face. 'I can look after you now. I would do anything for you, you know that. I-' Beatrix is interrupted as the door behind them opens and they hear the metallic clink of the chamber guard's sword tapping his helmet in deference to somebody important.

'Time already?' Iphigenia mutters. She leans forward on her stool, placing her hands over the tight corset restricting her stomach to quell a sudden swell of nausea.

Beatrice grasps her friend's shoulders. 'Stay strong,' she whispers.

A snake's hiss of satin robes swishes across the stone floor accompanied by the thud of a wooden staff, as someone crosses in the room. Iphigenia sits up straight. her eyes flashing a subtle warning to Beatrix to keep quiet. She does not turn immediately, instead she busies herself in front of the mirror, unnecessarily applying more powder to her face.

The visitor stops the required distance behind her, and gives a gentle cough, like a frog croaking. Iphigenia takes her time to turn, first glancing at Beatrix and offering her a weary but reassuring smile. 'Thank you, my dear. You may go.' She knows Beatrix is concerned and confused but is relieved to see her manage to remain expressionless, as she leans down to kiss her lightly on the cheek. Years of training at court have taught them both the value of keeping their facial expressions neutral, their emotions well hidden. Beatrix leaves without another word. She glances back briefly then exits the chamber, offering the visitor a formal incline of her head on her way out.

Despite the breeze through the open window, Iphigenia's nose is assaulted by the oppressive scent of patchouli and jasmine oils blended with thick musk; the unmistakeable, perfume-drenched odour of Osmand, Grand Vizier and Chief Advisor to her husband, Duke Anthony.

She continues to keep her back to the visitor, fully aware that this will be considered discourteous. *Good! Let him wait and learn his place.* Relishing the cool air blowing through the window, she takes a deep breath. She is mindful to keep her face impassive and her posture rigid as her mind careers in a myriad of directions all at once. *I need time to think.* For the thousandth time she considers every possible option but, she can find no imaginable alternative. Her plans cannot be altered now. It is too late: she must steel herself for what is to come.

Osmand's voice interrupts her reverie. 'It is nearly time, Your Grace,' he announces, a slight edge of impatience accompanying his nasal whine.

'Already?' She keeps her back to him as she fidgets with an ornament on her dressing table.

'Indeed, Your Grace. Are you ready?'

Iphigenia does not answer immediately, continuing to stare at the purple rainclouds suspended like bruises against the slate sky. *I wonder how long until the real storm breaks?*

The grand vizier coughs again. 'The duke requests your presence in the Great Hall. He has your son, the young Ne-Duke Orlando with him. They are ready to depart for the Annual

Reckoning.'

She takes another deep breath of fresh air to quieten her thoughts before turning on her stool, at last, to face him. She is careful to keep her face expressionless as she studies the man standing in front of her. Osmand is dressed from head to toe in emerald-green satin. His robes trail across the floor behind him like a lizard's tail and every bony finger sports at least one ring.

By the Gods - has he broken into a jewellers shop? If so, he has emptied it. Iphigenia allows herself a mocking laugh. In her head only - outwardly, her face remains perfectly impassive.

He also wears an enormous turban, also green and far too big for his head, in the centre of which is displayed an orb of heliotrope. This stone is the size and shape of a goose's egg, deep viridian green in colour and shot through with veins and spots of blood red that pulsate as they catch and refract the light.

She has always wondered about his age. He is old, she thinks. In his sixth or seventh decade, probably older. It is hard to tell. He is excruciatingly thin and tall with a deep stoop of the shoulders and upper back. His face is pinched, tapering to a pointed chin that matches his hooked nose. His eyes are an anaemic grey, lacking any discernible depth of colour and, consequently, any hint of emotion. She notes the sickly pallor of his skin and the thin, lipless line of his mouth, which points downwards at either side in a permanent look of disdain. He leans heavily on a staff of brutally twisted ebony and encased in his vulgar green robes, he reminds her of a locust.

Next to him stands a cat. It has short legs and a fat stomach that drags on the floor. Its orange fur looks greasy;

14

standing out from its body in stiff spikes, as though it has been rolling in something sticky. Iphigenia regards the animal with obvious distaste. The cat, in return, squints at her through half-closed eyes; it appears to be smirking.

'You are looking radiant, Your Grace.' The vizier offers a superficial bow. 'Rarely have I seen black worn with such confidence by one so young. A daring choice, might I say? It would usually signify deep mourning.' As she does not respond, he continues. 'May I also wish Your Grace many happy returns for today, on her eighteenth birthday?'

Iphigenia offers a slight nod then turns to look again out of the window, keeping her back towards the unwanted intruder and busying herself by aimlessly rearranging objects on her dressing table. 'I have been watching the people out on the streets,' she comments, at last. 'They walk through the rain to Golden Square to do their duty. Within the next hour I shall accompany the Duke to do the same.' Her voice sounds detached and dull.

'Indeed, Your Grace,' Osmand replies, yawning behind his thin fingers. He glances around the chamber, squinting in the dim light, seemingly more interested in its furnishings.

'How can the people contain so much grief?' Iphigenia murmurs to herself.

'The people?' He smiles. 'Oh them. I would not pay them much heed. The masses feel very little you know: they work, they eat, they get drunk, they breed, they sleep, they die. It is their function. They are...' he pauses momentarily, wafting a bejewelled hand in the air, searching for the right word, '... livestock.'

The duchess, careful to keep her face averted, cannot

help but give a quiet gasp. She closes her eyes and grimaces. 'These are my people. Along with my husband, I am their ruler and their servant. One day, Grand Vizier, I predict that the dam will burst. The bovine insensitivity you speak of will be stripped away to reveal an underlying resilience; they will rebel.'

The grand vizier pauses before replying; a warning edge creeps into his reed-like voice. 'If anyone else were to express such an opinion, it could be viewed as sedition. I would remind Your Grace that they are performing their duty to the new order. Any insurrection would be viewed by Karesh as treason against the emperor and dealt with accordingly.' He smiles and his tone becomes silky once more. 'However, the brave and selfless fulfilment of your own obligation today will be an example to them all, I'm sure.'

Iphigenia manages to control the escalating emotion in her voice. 'I am resigned to it. I will do what is required.'

'Oh yes, Your Grace. I am sure of that.'

Iphigenia feels momentarily threatened by his words. *What does he know? What have his spies told him?* She does not respond. Feeling unsettled, she remains still for some time until Osmand is forced to gain her attention by giving another affected cough.

'Oh, Vizier. I had almost forgotten you were here. You may leave.' She waves a hand casually over her shoulder to dismiss him but does not turn.

'Yes, Your Grace. But before I withdraw, the duke requires a response.'

Iphigenia tries to control herself but, finds it impossible not to betray her irritation. 'Tell my husband that I shall be ready on time and will join him presently. Now, you may go!'

Osmand does not move and Iphigenia does not miss this act of understated insubordination. His refusal to retire immediately once dismissed reminds her to be careful; this over-perfumed scarecrow is a powerful man. Ostensibly, as Grand Vizier of Cardemont, he is a servant of her husband, the duke and should follow his orders. But, since the siege and occupation of Cardemont by Karesh, he is also now an employee of the empire, having been given the official position of regional governor by the Kareshian emperor himself. Osmand is the duke's servant in name only and everybody, not least Iphigenia, knows it.

I must tread more carefully. I make my personal distaste for him too apparent. Stay calm! I must not do anything to give him an excuse to exercise force against the duke for treason.

Iphigenia's fingertips absentmindedly brush across the front of her dress, where she feels a small hard lump; a vial of poison, hanging from a chain around her neck and secreted under the fabric. She moves her hand quickly back to her lap. *Patience... for a little longer at least.*

Osmand has still not left. She turns, at last, to face him, her tone tense but polite. 'Is there something else?'

'Nothing, Your Grace,' he murmurs, smirking. 'Nothing... immediate.' He looks over at his cat, which is reclining on a sofa. It has one leg raised into the air and is licking under its tail noisily. 'Come Facinorous. We shall leave Her Grace to finish her toilet.' He calls for the guard to let him out and, at last, turns to leave.

The cat, taking its time, flops from the divan, stomach first, onto the floor to plod after its master, all the time leering at Iphigenia through half-closed eyes. The door closes and they are finally gone.

Relieved to be rid of the vile pair, Iphigenia opens all the windows as wide as they will go to rid her chamber of the stench. She is glad of the cold wind that penetrates the thin crepe silk of her dress and is thankful for the rogue drops of refreshing rain on her face. The candles in the wall sconces sputter but remain alight.

She looks once again over the cityscape. Amongst the teeming mass of civilians, she notices some Kareshian soldiers, the Shadokin. Although tiny from this distance, they are easy to spot by their green and black striped turbans. Under the direct orders of Osmand, they patrol the capital keeping order. She has heard reports that many, while off duty, drunkenly wander the streets as if they own them, casually bullying unfortunate citizens for money or food and even forced sexual services. This evening they are herding civilians on their way to Golden Square; they use long batons to prod, poke and even hit, to force them to hurry up. Fearing for their lives and those of their children, the citizens of Cardemont do as they are told.

As their duchess, she feels powerless to help them and imagines, at night, how they huddle awake under their bedclothes anticipating the echoing march of shadokin boots. How they hear the sound of hammering on doors, the crash of shattering windows, the screams and cries of people being dragged from their homes and how they must groan with guilty relief when the boots pass, silence returns, and they recognise it is not their turn – not this time anyway. She is not immune from the same fear herself. *I must never be complacent.*

No-one is safe.

She knows that these terrors are carefully nurtured by the authorities, led by Osmand as imperial governor. He ensures the Kareshian law of occupation is mercilessly enforced: fresh 'traitors', men women and even children, are brought out of the prisons every evening and burnt publicly in iron cages, suspended over fierce bonfires. She has witnessed this too many times. Duty forcing her to attend with her duke.

On the mornings after the fire cages, she has helped often, alongside mothers, fathers, brothers, sisters, sons and daughters to dig out, with their bare hands, the charred bones that remain, which may be collected for burial. All except the skulls, these are retrieved by officials and piled onto an ever-rising mountain of blackened eye sockets and grinning, yellow teeth. It grows daily as a monument, a reminder to all citizens of the penalty for disobedience to the new order.

She considers how quickly, and how thoroughly, everything can change: this is what remains of Cardemont since its defeat, occupation and assimilation into the Kareshian Empire only two years ago.

Finding that she is weeping, she dries her face with a shawl and fills her lungs with the evening air. She relishes the perfume of the amaranth blossoms that grow abundant and wild along the streets and up the walls of every building of the city, releasing their fragrance into the rain. These flowers have always grown in Cardemont. Once they bloom a deep and vibrant crimson, their colour never fades, even after dying. Each year they bring new life to the metropolis but, on this cold, spring evening, the broken buildings look to Iphigenia, like they are drenched in blood.

She starts to shiver, closes the window, crosses the room to the door and steels herself to perform her duty.

#

The main doors to the castle swing open as the Duke and Duchess of Cardemont emerge on foot into heavy rain. Escorted by Osmand and a retinue of retainers and assorted servants, they join the thousands of citizens on the wet streets in their reluctant march to Golden Square. Pages grasp staffs, suspending a waterproof canopy above the heads of the ducal party, whilst others carry spluttering torches to light their way as the evening grows darker.

The duke clasps his infant son, the Ne-Duke Orlando, heir to the throne of Cardemont, close to his chest. Iphigenia walks next to her husband, her head leaning against his shoulder, her hand resting protectively on her child's head, stroking his downy, red hair. Beatrix walks behind her mistress, carrying a small bag of items necessary for the care and comfort of the ne-duke. The citizens of Cardemont grow silent and the crowd parts to make way, showing deep respect for the royal couple as they go, like their people, to surrender their child to the new authorities.

On arrival, the duke and duchess are guided by Osmand to their allotted position: a dais has been erected for them in the centre of the plaza, especially for the occasion. They climb a short flight of steps on to the platform.

'We are to be on show then Grand Vizier?' Duke Anthony comments.

Osmand takes his position on the stage next to them.'So

your people can witness you perform your duty to the New Order, Your Highness. It is, after all, the first Annual Reckoning. I felt sure you would both wish to lead your people by example.'

The duke and duchess decline to respond. Iphigenia stands erect in the hazy glow of the torchlight. The deep black of her dress, her bare head and the glassy stare of her eyes would be fitting for a funeral. In contrast to the sombre fabric, her face is pale and haggard with exhaustion. She grips her husband's arm. To the crowd it appears as if she needs to keep herself from collapsing yet, in truth, it is the duke who requires the support.

Duke Anthony is dressed in military uniform. He chose it to project the impression of a firm resolve to his subjects but, he no longer wears it well; the ruler of Cardemont has lost much weight through ill health. The jacket hangs across his narrow shoulders as if he were a boy wearing his father's clothes to play soldiers. His thin neck and angular head stick out of the large collar like a tortoise peeking out of its shell.

Iphigenia regards her husband. She remembers before the war started with Karesh, he was strong, fit and every inch a young duke. Now, though barely twenty years old, he resembles an old man. Worry has lined his face beyond his years, his eyes sink deeper in their sockets and even his once thick mop of blond hair is silvering and thinning.

Thousands of citizens are waiting in the square, herded like cattle into wooden pens. Many have already been there for hours; standing in the rain and mud while more families continue to arrive from throughout the dukedom. Officials in Kareshian-style orange gowns and turbans – the 'quotamasters' - take the names of all the citizens, ticking them off extensive lists.

Watching the quotamasters at their work produces a range of conflicting emotions in Iphigenia: most native citizens would rather die than ally themselves with the enemy but a minority, whether from fear or greed, possibly both, compete fiercely for these administrative positions. Quotamasters have the responsibility of recording the births of all children during the preceding year. They then have to decide which babies will be given up to Karesh and which can remain with their families. Some are forced to take the job others, however, want to benefit from the favours afforded by their new masters and, under normal circumstances when not every child under a year must go, there is great potential for handsome bribes. A corrupt quotamaster can grow rich.

'I never thought to see so many of my own people working so eagerly for the empire.'

Osmand nods his head. 'Yes indeed, Your Grace. It is wonderful to see how eager they are to perform their duty and uphold the law.'

'Not *our* law.' Iphigenia mutters.

'As a matter of fact, Your Grace. It is *your* law-'

Iphigenia raises an eyebrow. '*My* law? You no longer consider yourself one of us then? No longer Grand Vizier to the duke?'

'Of course, Your Grace. Merely a slip of the tongue. I am, as always, loyal to His Grace but, it is difficult to balance my role for him with my new responsibilities in Kareshian government. I meant to say *our* law. The laws of Karesh are now ours, as they are for all territories fortunate enough to be welcomed into the empire. A challenging period of adjustment for all of us I grant you but, there you have it.'

'Adjustment! Karesh has already taken most of what we have; our food; our grain and livestock; wool, textiles; bullion from the treasury. Even our art and books and now they take our children.'

Osmand shrugs. 'Well everyone has to pay tax, even me. Assimilating Cardemont into the empire has cost money - lots of it. Our emperor has a right to recoup some of his losses. Surely you see the sense in it?'

Iphigenia's emotions override her caution.' And children, Grand Vizier? What right does the emperor have to take our children?'

'Yes, the children.' Iphigenia detects the hint of an eye roll. 'A shame Cardemont's birth rate was so low this last year or you could have kept some.'

'Our birthrate was low because of the war. The war *your* emperor made on us!'

'*Our* emperor, Your Grace. *Ours*. Not just mine. And there was no war. Cardemont was assimilated. Integrated into a bigger, better-'

'Your so-called *assimilation* was not of our choosing and it has cost us dearly!'

'Yes, well let's not get dragged into word-play; we'll just go around in circles and, besides, I would not want to have to chastise you for anything that might begin to sound treasonous. Wouldn't that be a bore? Let's just agree to disagree shall we?'

With great restraint, Iphigenia remains quiet for some time. She watches events unfold around her as children are taken from their families until, eventually, her emotions get the better of her. 'But all the babies Grand Vizier. *All* of them!'

'Yes indeed, Your Grace. Unavoidable this year, I'm afraid. To reach the required quota, all infants under a year old must be given up to Karesh. And no exceptions, even for the nobility. As I said, the low birth rate.'

'I am aware of that.'

'Of course you are, Your Grace. Although, look on the bright side. From next year, get your birth rates up and your quota will diminish: you will only have to provide a fraction of newborns, perhaps as little as a quarter.' Osmand attempts, unsuccessfully, a friendly smile. 'Not so bad eh?' Iphigenia feels too sickened to reply. 'And I can assure you, your people will be left with more than enough food and necessary supplies.'

'Only enough to keep them just about alive and able to work.'

Osmand looks shocked. 'Not at all, Your Grace! The very notion! I would estimate a bit more than that. Karesh wants to ensure it looks after all its people.' Iphigenia is about to reply when Osmand cuts her off. 'Anyway, I think that's enough chit-chat for now, don't you? Let's get the job done and we can all go home.'

Iphigenia is about to reply but thinks better of it and bites her tongue. She stares out into the rain and watches the scene playing out before her. Mothers and fathers grasp small, wriggling bundles close to their chests. Brothers and sisters, grandparents, aunts and uncles stand nearby crying, their tears mingling with the rain, their shouts and cries drowned by thunder. They have been told what to expect but there is much confusion and disbelief amongst the growing throng.

Beatrix places a reassuring hand on the duchess' shoulder. 'Stay strong,' she whispers into her ear.

'Strong!' Iphigenia hisses back, turning to look directly at her friend and careful that Osmand cannot hear her. 'These are my people. They are hungry and brutalised, and I can do nothing to help them. Their spirits are worn after a year of war, followed by half a year of survival in a city under siege and a further half-year of brutal occupation.' Beatrix does not reply. 'They are strong, I am not! Giving up their children is the final thrust of the dagger into the pulsing heart of the land. Our land. We are powerless.'

She stops and Beatrix removes her hand when Osmand speaks. 'Why is it taking so long?' He looks around, bored. 'You!' he snaps in his nasal tone, pointing the heel of his staff into the crowd. A quotamaster looks up from a ledger he is studying, not sure if the Kareshian governor is pointing at him. 'Yes you!' Osmand squawks again, getting irritated at having to repeat himself. 'Come here.' The man approaches the ducal party at full speed, slipping and almost falling in the mud. 'Attend to us at once. We do not propose to remain out in this filthy weather a moment longer than we have to.'

'Yes Eminence, straight away!' The man bows low, opens his ledger again and instantly starts to prepare the necessary paperwork.

'Who is this man?' Iphigenia asks. 'I do not recognise him. Where is the usual quotamaster with responsibility for the castle? Why is he not attending us?'

'Hm, what's that, Your Grace?' Osmand murmurs as if he has not heard properly.

'This quotamaster. I do not recognise him.'

'Oh him,' he continues vaguely before she can repeat the question. 'Oh, the usual one will be along presently I'm sure.' A mean smile stretches his lips. 'I believe an alternative duty calls him... elsewhere.'

Iphigenia feels uneasy. She studies Osmand's skeletal features closely, attempting to read the meaning behind his amused expression. *I cannot, under any circumstances, trust this man.*

Looking beyond him, her attention is caught by the ever-increasing mound of burnt, grinning human skulls, piled in the distance, near the fire cages. To many it acts as a monumental warning to those who would oppose the Empire, to others it is a shrine to those in Cardemont victimised by the occupying forces. The larger skulls are gruesome she thinks but the smaller ones; the ones that had once belonged to children make her stomach lurch to her throat.

She looks at the man she considers responsible for this atrocity; she stares at Osmand as he peers into the rain, seemingly oblivious to the pain and suffering surrounding him. Then she glances down and her attention is caught by Facinorous, Osmand's cat, sitting behind his master under the shelter of the canopy. It stares back at her for a moment before closing its eyes in disdain and bending its neck forwards to lick the sticky, orange fur on its plump belly.

The rain is getting heavier. Thunder continues to rumble, closer and louder. Flashes of lighting can be seen occasionally in the distance. Hundreds of torches hiss and sputter in the downpour. Families stand in their allotted pens, desperately clutching their young offspring as if holding them tighter might prevent the inevitable. Quotamasters walk amongst the pens offering the head of each chosen family a large gold-coloured star. They are instructed to hold the wooden stars high enough above their heads to be plainly visible to the shadokin, Kareshian soldiers who will come to take the children.

Iphigenia's heart crashes against her chest as she watches the soldiers walk amongst her people. Her eyes struggle against the impulse to release tears. Many of the men and women of Cardemont scream and resist the shadokin as their babies are torn from their arms. Some are knocked and pushed to the muddy ground. Some fight back and are summarily killed, their children taken anyway. Most just stand hopelessly in the rain; crushed and numb. They stare blankly at massive wagons that roll into view and are loaded with the cargo of tiny, screaming infants.

Iphigenia continues to resist the urge to cry. She can sense Osmand's occasional scrutiny but, she will not give him the satisfaction of seeing her lose control. She feels the wasted muscles of the Duke's arm tense under the fabric of his jacket as his grip tightens on their infant son. His once handsome face, now pinched and thin, remains rigid. She notices the small muscles around his mouth tighten as he grinds his teeth. His green eyes blaze with ill-concealed fury and she understands completely the effort it is taking him to maintain control.

Staring at the monstrous wagons, she realises with dawning horror that her son is soon to be a passenger in one of them. Dozens upon dozens of small cages rest on top of each vehicle. Every one, weatherproofed with waxed canvas flaps, is just large enough to contain one infant. The citizens of Cardemont observe, powerless to intervene, as shadokin queue by the wagons, waiting to hand the confiscated babies over to the care of old women who sit high up on each wagon..

These women, known as wagon nannies, hoist the infants up onto their laps as if they were nothing more than small sacks of potatoes, waiting to be peeled and boiled. Without ceremony, they stuff the infants into fleece bags which tie at the neck to keep them dry and warm and then lock them into the cages. Each wagon, once filled to capacity with freight, is pulled away by a team of powerfully-built buffalo along Silver Avenue and out of the city. The wagon nannies sit amidst the wailing, wriggling bundles and ignore the pandemonium generated by the grieving parents left behind. They light their pipes, pull their greased coats tightly about them and settle down for the long journey ahead; they have seen and heard it all countless times before in many other lands assimilated into the empire.

Osmand stands on the dais surveying the activities taking place around him. He wrinkles his nose in disgust and looks bored until his attention is caught by a small group of people who are fighting with a pair of quotamasters. A woman in the group has been thrown to the ground and is crawling in the mud, crying. Blood is pouring from a cut in her head. A man, presumably her husband, is being held back by other family members as a quotamaster, his orange turban lying in the dirt where it has been knocked off, tries to take down the man's details in a damp ledger book. The other quotamaster is gripping a small baby in his arms and heading towards one of the waiting wagons whilst, at the same time, attempting to shake-off some young children who are clinging to his robe.

The grand vizier snorts in contempt. 'I simply do not comprehend the incompetence of these people. I could have had apes trained to do a better job!' He sees a servant standing close by and pokes him between the shoulder blades with the heel of his staff. 'Get the names of those two quotamasters. I want them flogged in public for incompetence and, while I think about it, get some soldiers to arrest that entire family. They can go into tomorrow's fire cage. Not the baby obviously. That can still go on the wagons. Not wasting valuable stock.' The servant bows, then hurries off at once to carry out the orders.

Osmand turns to the duke and duchess. 'My sincere apologies for the delay; you will not have to wait much longer.'

'Waiting is not a problem,' Iphigenia replies through clenched teeth. 'If it means I can keep my son with me I would be willing to stand here forever.' She watches, horrified and powerless as the family and quotamasters are dragged away by shadokin.

As Osmand watches his orders being carried out, a thin smile curls the edges of his mouth. 'Your Grace will have other children in the future I'm sure.'

'I will never birth another child just to give it away. I would prefer to die now.'

'That is an interesting attitude, Your Grace. You know that if one of your subjects expressed that point of view, he or she could be relegated to a fire cage. We cannot have people refusing to provide children. It is disloyal to the emperor.'

'Why haven't I been given a gold star to hold up?' Duke Anthony asks, interrupting. His voice sounds weak but resolute. His eyes look glassy, his stare vacant.

'I beg your pardon, Sire?'

'A gold star Vizier. Why haven't I got one? All the other heads of families have.'

Osmand gives a bemused snort. 'I hardly think it necessary Your Grace,' he replies, looking astonished. 'Everyone can see you clearly enough. It is hardly needed, let alone fitting, for the duke of Cardemont to hold up a gold star.'

Duke Anthony turns and stares at Osmand, his gaze now clear and intense. 'If all the other fathers must hold one then so shall I!'

The grand vizier holds the duke's stare briefly, one quizzical eyebrow raised then shrugs his shoulders. 'As you wish.' He turns to a servant and hisses an order. The servant runs over to a near-by cart and retrieves a gold star. He brings it back and hands it to the duke who, like the other citizens of Cardemont, raises it above his head with his left arm, his son still cradled securely in his right. Iphigenia notices Osmand raise his eyes towards the sky and mutter something under his breath.

At last, the quotamaster picked earlier by Osmand is ready. He approaches the duke.

'Your Grace, it is time. I must take the Ne-Duke Orlando.'

Duke Anthony says nothing as the man tentatively takes the baby from him. He and Iphigenia watch without expression as their son is carried to a waiting wagon and handed to an elderly wagon nanny. The woman takes Orlando and places him on her lap. The child cries a great deal but, the wagon nanny does nothing to comfort him. He then howls in sudden shock and pain as she takes a small metal poker from a red-hot brassier and places its glowing end against the inside of his left wrist. A tiny plume of sizzling smoke erupts from the infant's soft skin and Iphigenia lets out a brief scream as if she too has been branded. Beatrix grasps her arm, to prevent her falling. Duke Anthony, suddenly animated, turns towards Osmand in a fury. 'By all the gods Osmand, what is that damn bitch doing to my son?'

'An unfortunate formality, Your Grace. Just a tiny mark,' Osmand replies as if nothing out of the ordinary has occurred. 'Something indelible to make sure we don't lose him amongst the masses. It is in the shape of an amaranth. I thought you might be pleased to have your national flower chosen.'

'How dare you-' Duke Anthony is about to say something more when he is interrupted by Iphigenia who, with tears of pain glistening in her eyes, flashes him a warning look.

'But none of the others are being branded,' she remarks to Osmand.

'My point exactly, Your Grace. Something to single him out, make sure we can keep an eye on him, you understand. He is no ordinary baby after all and he has no ordinary parents. We would not want to lose sight of such a highborn child in the future, just because he is lucky enough to be going to serve the great empire of Karesh. I want to make sure he is, how should I put it…well looked after.'

Well looked after. Well looked after. Osmand's words echo inside Iphigenia's head as she considers their implication. She realises that whatever Osmand means by *well looked after*, at least her son is to be kept alive and, while he lives – even in a foreign land - there is hope. Yes, there is always hope. Osmand could have arranged to have Orlando killed, or just lost amongst the others but, he has chosen to keep him alive. Why? It is not just, as he says, because of Orlando's noble birth; Osmand would not spare a child just by virtue of its high-ranking blood. No, there is more to it, but what?

The duke and duchess watch as their son is unceremoniously fleece-bagged and locked in a cage by the wagon nanny who appears indifferent to his cries of pain and confusion. The immense wagon then trundles away through the rain. The wails of Orlando, Ne-Duke of Cardemont, are swallowed amongst the hundreds of others crying and screaming around him.

Osmand yawns and looks down at his feet, giving a disapproving look at the mud spattering his silk slippers. He attempts, unsuccessfully, to wipe it off with the butt of his ebony staff.

'Time to return to the castle,' he announces unexpectedly. His thin voice can only just be heard over the combined noises of screaming and crying people, wagons, snorting buffalo, pouring rain, intermittent thunder and howling infants. Iphigenia and Anthony do not move. They cling to each other and stare at the departing wagon that has just swallowed their child.

The grand vizier turns and snaps at them, irritated. 'I must insist Your Graces. Back to the castle – now!" He signals to a nearby group of shadokin who immediately form a protective ring around Osmand and the duke's party, pushing any citizens who happen to be too close out of the way. Facinorous snarls as a soldier almost treads on him. Osmand barks an order at the soldier to pick the cat up and carry him. Facinorous, as he is being lifted, snarls again and gives the soldier a malicious scratch across the back of his hand. The soldier grimaces at the pain but remains silent, aware that Osmand is watching. He carries the growling animal without complaint.

Iphigenia and her husband, as if waking from a dream, look at each other for a moment and then turn to head back to their empty home. Iphigenia thinks about Orlando and then, more furtively, of their other, secret child, Derron.

'At least he will be saved,' she whispers to her husband, looking into his eyes, knowing he is thinking the same thing. He responds with a short, stiff nod and an attempt at a pained smile. Then, without warning, he stumbles forwards onto his knees in the mud. A gasp erupts from the surrounding crowds and the ducal party comes to an immediate halt. Beatrix moves towards the duke to assist him but, Iphigenia waves her away as she stoops herself to help her husband. He leans his full weight on her arm and, after some stumbling, regains his standing position. He stares ahead and, with his wife's assistance, starts to trudge his way back towards the castle.

Osmand barely grants them a scornful glance. Seemingly impatient to be dry and warm, he signals the pages carrying the canopy to hurry. Iphigenia staggers under her husband's weight as she tries to keep up. She feels her arm bruising from the tightness of his grip but, keeps her posture erect and proud; she will not be seen to be beaten. Her sons will live – one in slavery and the other in exile but, both will live. She has to believe that. The royal House of Cardemont will survive. It will exist for centuries after Osmand's scrawny body has putrefied to slime in its grave. And, if the gods allow, she will - one day - see both of her children again.

With each heavy step, she wills her heart to shrivel. She is no longer a mother; her children have been taken. She has no need of a warm-blooded muscle to pump her blood. From this moment her heart will be cold, black stone. She wills it to feel nothing – nothing but revenge. *He burned my baby. He seared the innocent flesh of my child.* She does not cry, she will never cry again. All her thoughts, emotions and energies are now channelled in one direction - her hatred of Osmand. The vial of deadly poison still hangs around her neck but, now it is destined for someone other than herself.

I shall live long enough to ensure Derron's safety and then Osmand, you will die by my own hand. You will die before I do – by all the gods I swear it!

CHAPTER TWO

Library

Tazmand woke in a panic and sat up. Sweating, heart thumping, he looked around the dormitory in the dim light. The other boys appeared to be sleeping soundly under their thin bedsheets, which was a relief - at least he wouldn't get it in the neck again for waking them up with his shouting.

His sheets were in a mess, twisted, wound and knotted in between his legs and around his neck and, feeling hot and clammy, he climbed out of bed to untangle himself. He took the opportunity to cool off and glanced over to the exit, noting that the nightwatchman on duty was also fast asleep at his post by the door. Big relief! No whipping from him then.

Dawn was creeping through the windows, and it would soon be time to get up. There was no chance of getting any sleep now, so he thought about dressing and going to the latrines to wash, getting a head start on the others but, in the end, decided to take some time to order his thoughts, climb back in to bed and wait for the bell.

He lay down and, pretty quickly, his breathing began to return to normal. After a day's hard work in the library, he had always slept well. Over the last couple of months, however, since reaching his fourteenth year, his rest had become relentlessly disturbed by confusing dreams and terrifying nightghasts. This was not the first time he had dreamt about the castle with the duchess and the babies and the wagons and the skinny man with the big turban and the ugly cat but, he had never before experienced it in so much detail. It seemed that each time he had this dream, it lasted longer, became more vivid. It was really getting on his nerves and, more importantly, interfering with his rest.

He could not settle, so sat up again and peered around. He felt groggy, his otherwise clear, green-blue eyes felt dry and bloodshot and his hair, usually a messy blond mop anyway, would be in more chaos than usual. He rubbed at the sticky grit at the corners of his eyes then spat in his palms and attempted, unsuccessfully, to smooth his hair down. There was never enough time to both get washed and eat before work, so he would rather spend less time at the washing and more time doing the eating before work if he could.

He yawned loudly, then stretched out his arms and arched his back, attempting to ease the tender muscles. His back and neck ached terribly; standing at the top of a ladder all day shelving books was great exercise but, it did take its toll.

It was getting lighter. Early sunlight had started to seep through the cleaner gaps in the otherwise filthy skylights overhead, giving an orange glow to the stone walls of the room. He watched Dharma, his best friend, fast asleep on his back in the next bed and listened to his gentle snoring. The ample mound of his stomach rose and fell under the covers, the close-shaved stubble of his head looking like an over-sized gooseberry. Not that Tazmand had ever tasted anything as exotic as fruit but, he had seen it eaten by privileged visitors to the library and was desperate to try some. All the other boys appeared to still be sleeping too and, as there was no one to talk to, he lay back on his rag-filled pillow, yawned again and absent-mindedly scratched at an itchy scab caused by a flea bite on his scalp.

He sighed and stared at the ceiling, attempting to remember the details of the dream. Fragments drifted through his memory like soap scum on bath water; small segments floated together to converge for a moment into larger islands before stretching, separating again and drifting away. Some seemed to make sense and others made none. Although he usually remembered a lot when he first woke up, the images always faded quickly.

He tried to piece it together now, before he forgot again: a duke, a duchess, a ruined castle, babies, wagons, that bloke with the big turban, name's gone again... Where was all this coming from? Oh yes, that sticky looking cat, nasty soldiers, erm... and that was about it. It all seemed so familiar, but why? And why did he keep dreaming it again and again? He scratched the itchy scab too hard, and it came off, wedged under his fingernail. He aimed it Dharma's head, flicked it and missed.

Bored now, he thought about how much he would love some more sleep. No chance of that. He was tired all the time nowadays anyway. It was really getting on his nerves and, it was proving dangerous being up a ladder all day. The least lapse in concentration could cause an accident - either to him, if he fell, or to Dharma, if he should drop a heavy book on him, pushing the ladder below. He would be in for a serious whipping if a book got damaged. It really did not stand thinking about.

He stretched his arms again and yawned, squinting towards the dormitory time candle. Its dim flame flickered in a far corner of the room, its cheap tallow spitting fat and belching black, acrid smoke up the wall. It had burned down six one-hour marks since he had come to bed; it would be only a matter of minutes before the bell summoned him...

As if on cue, the harsh clanging of the bell signalled time to get up. Though he was expecting it, Tazmand still jumped. 'Pangbats!' No matter how many times he heard that racket every morning it always jarred his nerves. 'Already?' he groaned aloud to himself, not moving. He felt worn-out and there was no time now to catch-up on much-needed sleep.

Noise and activity erupted around him as Dharma and dozens of others jumped out of bed. Work started by next bell. Robes were hastily thrown over heads, feet jammed into footwear, beds hurriedly made and faces sprinkled with water from a bowl at the door.

'Hurry up Taz,' Dharma shouted, pulling Tazmand's sheet off him before racing for the exit with the rest of them. 'It'll be your own fault if you miss breakfast.'

Tazmand groaned again and sat up. He was famished. Also, he did not want to risk yet another whipping for being late. He jumped out of bed, threw his robe on, flicked some water at his face and raced for the door. 'Wait for me Dar!'

Tazmand balanced precariously near the top of an extremely tall iron ladder, fifteen metres above the ground. Clutching a stack of books under one arm, he stretched the other as far as he could above his head to slip a volume into place on one of the highest shelves.

He was just about to position another, particularly bulky, volume when he heard a sudden crack, followed by a loud ripping noise from high above. He jammed his mouth to the communication tube running down the length of the ladder and bellowed, 'dodge!' Then, instinctively, tightened his grip on the remaining books, bent his knees, held on with his free hand and pressed his stomach closer to the shelves to increase his stability.

A dark shape plummeted from above through the shadows and whistled a hair's breadth past his ear. He tensed as he felt the rasp of dry canvas against the side of his face accompanied by a rush of stale air. The ladder wobbled violently beneath his feet as he heard the missile clang once, twice, three times against the metal rungs on its inevitable descent. He knew exactly what it was, a decayed chunk of wood about twice the size of his head.

He shut his eyes and held on tight. If he lost his balance now, he could expect a quick plunge, followed by a crunching death on the marble floor a long way below. He made a mental note to wear his safety harness in future, even though it felt restrictive and made his job harder. Eventually, the ladder stilled and, as usual, he was lucky. He prayed to the gods that

Dharma had heard his warning and that the projectile had missed him at ground level.

His throat was parched. It was hours since he had had any water and his tongue stuck to his lips as he whispered down the tube. 'Are you all right?' There was no answer. 'Dharma!' he hissed more forcefully. 'Dharma, can you hear me?'

After what seemed like for ever but, was only in fact a few seconds, a shaky voice responded. 'Hello?'

Tazmand breathed a sigh of relief. 'Dharma. Thank the gods. You managed to dodge?'

Another longish pause.

'Yes, I'm all right Taz. It bounced off a rung just above my head and landed a few feet away. Thanks for the warning. Scary though!'

'Good. Give me a minute to get myself sorted.'

Relieved his friend was safe, Tazmand got back to business and checked his books for dents or torn pages - any damage would be sure to incur a whipping. Thankful to see they were all fine, he placed them safely back in the moveable basket attached to the ladder, rearranged his tangled robe and wiped the sweat out of his eyes.

Grime clung to his hair, irritating his scalp and making that bloody flea bite, where the scab had come off, itch like crazy. Nothing much he could do about that. He would just have to bear it, and gave it a good scratch. He then pinched each nostril in turn and did his best to blow out the accumulated dust. This he immediately regretted, as the smell of mouldy leather, decaying parchment and bird droppings made him feel nauseous and the dust, constantly in the air, made him want to sneeze. Sneezing and throwing up at the same time, especially whilst up a ladder - not a good thing. He managed to hold off from doing both, for the time being anyway.

Feeling more organised, he glanced upwards towards the immense dome of thick glass that capped the library's central chamber. Once, apparently, it had been as clear as crystal but, the age-old build-up of grime now ensured that everything was shrouded in permanent dusk. It was always a job to see anything clearly in the gloom but, he could just make out remnants of gigantic blinds, clinging to the dome like vast, black cobwebs.

Hundreds of years before apparently, they had been white, designed to protect the books from the blinding light of the desert sun. Now, after years of neglect, they hung rotten and useless and often dangerous as bits regularly wrenched loose and fell. All that protected the books from the glare now was the thick dirt which, Tazmand had to admit, worked pretty effectively.

He watched as the dark silhouettes of birds and bats flitted like elusive phantoms amongst the remains of the ragged blinds. Over the years, they had entered through gaps around the edges of the roof and bred in the rafters. They liked to swoop without warning to hunt on the prolific vermin that inhabited the labyrinth of bookshelves below, plump rats and beetles being their favoured prey. Sometimes the larger birds even caught the odd cat.

Dharma's voice bellowed from the tube, cutting through his reverie. 'Taz! What are you doing? What's happening up there? Are you all right?'

'Yes, I suppose so-'

'You suppose so! Are you hurt? What-'

'No. I'm all right. I mean I didn't get hit! I'm fine!'

'Thank the gods. Then what are you doing? Daydreaming again?'

'Dar, stop shouting - you'll get us whipped. I can hear you perfectly well if you talk through the tube in a normal voice.'

'Oops, sorry, forgot,' Dharma whispered back, now barely audible. 'That's the second fall we've dodged this month. It's just as well you're used to it. Anyway, are you ready yet?'

'Just taking a breather.'

'Are the books safe?'

'Yeah, the books are fine.'

Tazmand heard Dharma give an audible sigh of relief. 'All right but get on with it. It's been a bloody long minute! You've been ages.'

Tazmand screwed up his eyes and peered around. From the top of his ladder, he had an excellent vantage point, despite the gloom. He could just make out a shadowy landscape of hundreds of circular metal bookcases. The largest, where he was, followed the outer wall of the huge building, with each bookcase, perfectly concentric and impossibly high, becoming gradually smaller until the one at the heart of the chamber surrounded a central desk. This was where the divines sat, ruling everything that went on in the library like spiders at the centre of a web.

Hundreds of little black dots moved about around, up and down and over the bookcases, like termites. These were the grunts getting on with their work, shelving or retrieving books. Shelvers like Tazmand crawled up and down tall ladders. Pushers, like Dharma, gripped the bases of the ladders and moved them back and forth along the bookcases via tracks on small, well-oiled wheels.

Dharma's voice piped up the tube again. 'Taz. Are you ready now? I'm starving.'

Tazmand did not answer immediately. He was thinking, casting his mind back to when he and Dharma were seven years old and had left the municipal nurseries to come to the library. At first, they had worked as undergrunts at menial tasks but, as soon as he reached eleven, he had been promoted to 'pusher'. Having just had his fourteenth birthday he had been recently promoted to 'shelver'. Being allowed to choose his own pusher, he had selected his best friend Dharma.

'Tazmand!'

'All right Dar, don't shout!' Tazmand resumed shelving the books. 'Get ready to push the ladder to another section. Just a few books left to shelve then we'll get some food.'

'Okay. But hurry up or the refectory will be shut!'

'Hold on a moment. I need to get comfortable.'

Tazmand adjusted his long, black robe, pulling the back hem up and forwards between his legs and tucking it into the front of his belt, forming a sort of makeshift pair of pantaloons. Just as he was finishing, a white shape swooped past his face. He let out a gasp and toppled backwards, grabbing the ladder with both hands just in time to break his fall.

Dharma's voice shot up the tube. 'What's wrong now? I felt the ladder wobble! Are you all right?'

Tazmand paused and steadied his breathing. 'Fine. Just an owl hunting.'

'Just a -? Oh is that all? Just a bird that almost cost you your life. I will never understand how you shelvers cope with being up there.'

'Just be thankful you're not an undergrunt any more or you'd still be scrubbing the floors and cleaning out the latrines.'

Dharma mumbled something that Tazmand could not hear. He ignored him and pulled a book out of the basket. 'You know you ought to get over your fear of heights,' he whispered down the tube.

'For the love of the gods, don't start all that again!'

Tazmand smiled at his friend's expected outburst. 'If you ever want to get a promotion to a black robe that is,' he continued.

'Will you give it a rest Taz! Seriously. You know a black robe is the last thing I want. You're welcome to yours. I don't want one. I'm more than happy staying down here; grey suits me just fine. Just shut up about it.'

'But I don't get it Dar. Where's you ambition? How can you be happy just pushing ladders for the rest of your life?'

'Easily. I've told you before, stop going on about it.'

'I know but I can't believe you wouldn't want to be a divine one day. Cushy life at the top in charge of the library, plenty of nice food-'

'Just shut your mouth and tell me where to push to.'

'Tazmand ignored him. 'And imagine being allowed to read! Imagine being able to read.'

'Your dream Taz, not mine. Reading is overrated anyway. It would give me a headache.'

'But there are so many books here Dar; think of all that

knowledge waiting to be discovered.'

'Please Taz, give it a rest. I can recognise my numbers and I know all the colours of the library sections, and that's all I need to do my job. Just get the books shelved when they come in and fetch them when they want them. Easy!'

'Yeah, and what about when you're older?

'There's hundreds of new books coming in every month Taz. There will always be work.'

'It's physical stuff Dar - you can't do it for ever. What will happen then? I'm just worried.'

'Not interested. Happy where I am. Anyway, what about you? I thought you'd hate to be an overgrunt, bullying everyone. You've said so often enough.'

'True Dar but, you've got to be overgrunt before you can get higher up. One day, I want to wear purple – be a divine.'

'Wish you'd make your mind up. I thought power wasn't your thing.'

'It isn't but I want to be able to read and only the divines can do that.'

Dharma snorted and pointedly changed the subject. 'I'm hungry. So would you please hurry up?'

Tazmand knew his friend well and just how far he could push him before it resulted in a major sulk for the rest of the day, so decided to leave it there - for now. He peered at the spine of the book. 'All right, push the ladder over to orange sector twelve, and put some effort into it.'

Dharma, glad for an end to the subject, responded immediately and put the entire strength of his squat body into pushing the tall ladder. Tazmand held on tight as he felt it lurch into action, running along its track rails.

'Whoa, slow down!' he hissed suddenly.

'What is it?' Dharma pulled back bringing the ladder to a shuddering halt.

'Small window.'

'Oh, for the sake of the gods Taz? You've looked through that window a zillion times!'

'Just back up a little bit so I can have a glimpse. Please?'

'Are you serious? You're doing my head in today.'

'Pleeeease?'

Dharma muttered something unintelligible before heaving an overly-loud sigh. 'All right, but just a few seconds. I really, really, really need to eat.'

'I know. I'll be quick. Promise.'

Grumbling loudly enough to ensure that Tazmand could hear him through the tube, Dharma moved the ladder back a couple of feet. This particular spot was Tazmand's favourite in the entire library; at the highest level of his ladder was a tiny window hidden behind a row of large books. He moved two of the books off the shelf and immediately, a shaft of bright sunlight hit his face.

He rubbed the ancient glass with his sleeve for about the thousandth time and absent-mindedly shook his head to flick the dust out of his blond fringe. A crease of intense concentration settled above his nose as he squinted through the grimy windowpane and shielded his eyes with his hand until they had adjusted to the glaring sunshine outside.

Below lay a wide thoroughfare that bustled with activity. People thronged the street. Groups of men, sporting colourful turbans and ornate robes, stood idly engaged in conversation whilst others jostled past in a hurry to cross the busy thoroughfare. Women, their faces draped in mysterious veils and wearing elaborate headdresses, ambled slowly in the heat, stopping now and again to admire objects in windows and fanning themselves to cool off.

Some figures, many of them children, dressed in plainer clothes, their wrists encased in metal bands in various colours, carried packages, following the women and waiting for orders to either wait or move along. Others, also with wristbands, pushed heavily laden handcarts filled high with provisions. Their heads were bowed low with the strain of their work but, they were forced to look up constantly, in case they collided with one of the enormous wagons pulled by lumbering buffalo that also shared the street. More difficult to avoid were the chariots that would suddenly appear, as if from nowhere at high speed, drawn by beautifully groomed horses, throwing up clouds of sand and dust into the crowds and stopping for nothing and no one.

Tazmand noticed that many of the handcart pushers were followed closely by overgrunts. He winced as he saw the length of a whip land on a back and absent-mindedly rubbed his own shoulders, remembering the countless number of times his skin had tasted the sharp sting of leather.

Tearing his eyes away from the people below, he looked upwards. The silhouettes of immense glass, stone and metal buildings towered against the intense light of the sun. He stared into the distance, lost in thought, wondering what it would be like to get out there, just once, just to have a look.

These were the only sights outside the library he had ever seen. This was all he knew of Karesh city or the world outside.

'Don't even think about it,' Dharma's voice echoed quietly up the tube. 'I know exactly what's going through your head.' Tazmand turned away from the window and, temporarily blinded, blinked a few times to adjust his sight once more to the interior gloom.

'There must be some way out-'

'No, there isn't! I can't believe you are thinking about it Taz! No one has ever left the library. Even if you wanted to, there is no way out. I don't know where the exits are come to think of it. Don't want to, particularly. And even if I did, they'll be guarded.'

Tazmand sighed and did his best to ignore his friend, who was busy working himself up into a fully-fledged rant. He replaced the books, concealing the window and plunging his face into darkness once more.

'Dharma, calm down. I'd only want a bit of a look around. I know there's nothing for us outside but, there is so much to see. It would be interesting just to have a quick scout about then come back. Don't you think?'

'No I don't!' Dharma could scarcely keep his voice below a loud yelp. 'Taz, even if you got out, they would take one look at your gold wristbands and know you belonged to the library, send you straight back and you could wave goodbye to any promotion. Bang goes any chance you would ever have of becoming a divine. You would never learn to read - ever!'

'But Dar-'

'La, la la...' his friend began to sing. 'I'm not listening and I am not talking about it any more. I can feel another headache coming on, which, I might add, is as a result of lack of food. Come on, hold tight. We've got hardly any time to finish off now. I'm not risking missing the refectory just so you can daydream about stupid, pointless things.'

With reluctance, Tazmand did as he was told; he held tightly to the top rungs whilst Dharma pushed on. As he felt the ladder move underneath him towards the next section, he could not stop thinking about what life must be like outside. He imagined himself as one of the people he had seen. Standing on the street, in the sunshine discussing whatever it was that people outside the library might talk about.

He was not sure exactly why he wanted to go out so much. But he did know it was not just curiosity; he had been thinking about it every day since he had first found the window and something small, deep inside, was niggling at him to go and take a look.

#

'By the gods Taz, I am so starving,' Dharma's voice echoed up the ladder tube. 'And hurry up. I'm sick of asking!'

Tazmand smiled and muttered quietly to himself as he prepared to descend. 'Don't you ever think of anything besides your stomach?'

'Ow!'

He froze when he heard the sharp cry of pain. He placed his lips to the tube. 'Dar, what's happened?' Receiving no response he peered below but, could see little. 'Dar, are you all right? Can you hear me?'

He went further down the ladder and stopped about five metres above ground level, holding tightly to the rungs. He could just distinguish the outline of a corpulent figure in what appears to be a dark-brown robe, standing over his friend, holding a whip. He knew immediately who it was - an overgrunt and a bully with a personal grievance against him and an immediate dislike of any of his friends.

'Sash, leave him alone!' The words left Tazmand's mouth before he thought to stop himself. He cringed inwardly, cheeking, or talking back to an overgrunt, or any superior, was a serious offence, and could easily incur a range of punishments, not least of which was a random whipping. On top of that, he had shouted in the library. Another punishable offence.

The overgrunt looked up towards the voice, narrowing his already beady eyes to get a clearer view through the gloom. 'Now who might be up there?' he said in a loud whisper. 'I bet it's my old friend Tazmand. Am I right? Certainly sounds like him. Long time no see and how nice to hear you, even if a bit loud. Why not come down so we can talk properly?' The loathing in his voice oozed through his words like pus seeping through a bandage.

Reluctantly, Tazmand descended further, stopping about a metre above the older boy's head. Able to see Sash more clearly now, he noticed that he had put on weight since his promotion to overgrunt; the lithe body of the shelver he had once been was now engulfed by a new covering of flesh. Probably because overgrunts did no manual work at all; they just spent all their time bossing grunts and undergrunts around. They got better food and the only exercise they ever got was with their whipping arm. He was also sporting a turban, which meant that he had reached the age of sixteen.

He studied his face for any indication of his mood. Sash's

mouth remained fixed in a strained smile but, his small, rat-like eyes displayed no emotion, resting in his chubby face like two black currants nestled in a bed of raw pastry.

Dharma sat on the floor nursing his left arm. Tazmand gave him a quick *are you all right* look. His friend signalled back that he was.

Tazmand started to try and reason, 'listen Sash, we've nearly finished our quota and-'

'I beg your pardon?' The overgrunt looked astonished. '*Sash*? I am an overgrunt and you *will* show due respect.'

Tazmand bit his lip; he needed to tread carefully. 'Sorry, I mean, Gruntmeister Sash. We just want to finish our shift and get back to our quarters before we miss lunch. We've almost finished in record time. I apologise for cheeking you just now-'

Tazmand was interrupted by a loud crack from Sash's whip as it flashed past his ear at lightning speed and hit something behind him. This was followed by a soft thud as a grey rat about the size of a small dog fell from a shelf into the soft carpet of dust on the library floor. All three of them watched the animal as it writhed in pain, a deep gash across its belly. Blood pumped from the wound and its tail flicked from side to side mixing it with dirt into a viscous paste. It squealed piteously.

'For the sake of the gods Sash – I mean, Gruntmeister - finish it off!' Tazmand gasped, looking directly at the overgrunt. 'The poor thing is in agony.'

'Oh I think I'll leave that to you,' Sash glared back, a cold glimmer in his tiny eyes. 'You're not very good at finishing things off I seem to remember. But, I suppose even you deserve a second chance.'

51

The older boy coiled his whip, tucking it into his belt and turned to go, his long robe whipping-up a cloud of dust as he moved away. Dharma noticed that Sash walked with an exaggerated limp.

'I'll see you two again later,' he added ominously, without bothering to turn around.

Tazmand did not waste time; he took a few more steps down the ladder then jumped, landing squarely with both feet on top of the squealing animal. He heard the squish of flesh and sinew under fur and felt the crunch of delicate bones through the soles of his boots. He looked at the sticky mess that had only recently been a living, breathing creature. Blood had spurted from its burst stomach and continued to soak into the thick grime on the floor. He heard Dharma throw up violently, and then there was silence.

Tazmand stared at the remains of the rat. He felt sick and wanted to look away but, something about the sight of the blood transfixed him. His eyes widened unnaturally. All he could see was red, deep ruby red. He became dizzy as the noises and sights of the library around him started to fade. He could vaguely hear Dharma's voice as a reverberating whisper somewhere nearby. Or was it far away? He could no longer tell.

He started to feel himself fall then, he saw the castle again.

CHAPTER THREE

Betrayal

A t about the same moment that the duke and duchess emerge from the castle's front entrance to proceed to Golden Square, a small door opens discretely at the rear of its surviving turret. The plump figure of Derron's nurse, cloaked and hooded in her heavy oilskins, slips silently out into the rain and obscurity of the evening gloom.

Once in the castle gardens, she makes her way between weed-infested flowerbeds and across wet, overgrown lawns to the outer, defensive wall which, despite having suffered heavy mortar attack, still stands. She produces a large key from within her waterproof wrappings, unlocks an old metal door, peers through it cautiously until satisfied that no one is about, then steps out into a wet alleyway, carefully re-locks the door, and melts hastily into the shadows.

Cardemont's Old District sprawls from the perimeter of the castle wall right out towards the far eastern edge of the city. A rambling tangle of alleys and narrow streets twist erratically like tree roots through a warren of buildings.

Quality stone houses for the rich lean against the backside of the ancient castle, jostling uncomfortably with lesser structures; meaner mud brick dwellings and rudimentary, low-level huts made of tin, canvas and wood.

Knowing the area well and mindful of lurking dangers, the nurse moves into this dark labyrinth, negotiating sudden intersections, looming potholes and meandering passages without the aid of any illumination, save for the intermittent flashes of lightning overhead.

As she hurries on her mission, she considers how much the Old District has changed. It had been founded by itinerant workers immigrating to the famous trading city looking for employment during its heyday. Slowly, over a great length of time, more settlers had arrived and added to it in an ad hoc fashion. Not so long ago, it teemed with life but, now it is silent save for the wind rattling the odd loose shutter, the driving rain and the occasional rumble of thunder. Most of the dwellings have been deserted and the shanty structures sit abandoned and slowly decay, their inhabitants frightened off by war and the whispered fear of having their children stolen.

She pushes against the wind and rain and heads in the direction of a small group of stone dwellings far enough away from the castle to ensure some privacy. They sit in the oldest part of the district, isolated amongst a clump of willow trees. As she nears her destination a powerful gust of wind rips back her hood. A crack of thunder reverberates overhead and a sheet of lightning reveals her red startled face. She closes her eyes against the sudden glare, bows her head against the wet and continues walking.

Fifty paces behind her another figure, also dressed in

oilskins, jumps into the concealing shadows as the lightning flashes. The figure has been following the woman ever since she left the castle, pausing and squatting every now and again to place something carefully on the ground.

The nurse lets out a satisfied grunt as she finally reaches her destination and pushes her weight against an unlocked door. She enters to find herself in a dry, dusty room. Breathing a sigh of relief, she uses her back to slam the door shut against the weather, then wastes no time in removing her wet outer garments, allowing them to fall to the floor. She produces a small bundle wrapped in a white fur-lined blanket that she has been carefully carrying in her arms.

'There now my dumpling. Safe and sound.'

With loving hands she lifts a corner of the blanket to reveal the face of Derron who is sleeping comfortably in the warmth. The nurse places him on a bed in the far corner of the room then pulls a curtain over the only window, making sure there are no gaps where light might shine out. A long, deep rumble of thunder trails off into the distance.

'Sounds like one of the gods has got as bit of tummy trouble eh?' she chuckles tickling the baby's stomach. He is awake now and gurgles back, as if sharing the joke.

In the dark, the old woman opens a cupboard and pulls out some candles which she lights and places in holders already positioned around the room. She looks about, checking that everything is undisturbed and as it should be.

'I used to live here with my mum and dad. Nice to see nothing's been touched,' she continues to prattle to Derron, keeping him calm and hoping he won't make any noise. 'Not long now precious fairy,' she croons, kissing his forehead. 'Safe soon, once the coenobite comes to get you my little prince, my darling. What the-'

Without warning, the door flies open accompanied by a wild influx of rain and biting wind, which blows out all of the candles but two. The tall figure of a man enters and slams the door shut quickly.

The nurse is shocked but, remains silent and waits to see what will happen. Keeping her eyes fixed firmly on the intruder; she picks up Derron and clutches him to her chest. The man pulls his hood down and undoes the front of his oilskin coat revealing an orange turban and matching uniform underneath. The woman recognises him immediately; he is the quotamaster assigned to the castle. They stare at each other for some time but say nothing.

At last, she breaks the silence. 'What do you want? What are you doing uninvited in my parent's house? Why aren't you at Golden Square with the others?'

The quotamaster takes a moment to answer. 'You m-m-must give up the child to the R-reckoning,' he says, peering at the floor, avoiding her eyes.

'What by all the gods in the afterplace are you talking about?' The nurse points at Derron. 'You mean this baby? This child belongs to a neighbour. It was not selected for the quota as it is well over a year old as any idiot can see. He is-'

'He is Derron, twin brother to N-Ne-Duke Orlando, son of D-Duke Anthony and the Lady Iphigenia. He was t-taken from his m-m-mother's bed immediately after his birth ten m-months ago and hidden by you in a secret chamber at the castle. His brother, born at the same time, was then presented to court by the duke and duchess as their only child.'

The nurse stares at the quotamaster with undisguised astonishment. Appearing lost for words, her mouth opens and closes a few times like a fish gasping for water. Eventually gathering her wits, she tosses her head back and laughs. 'I haven't time for your fairy tales my man. What rot! Where did you ever get hold of such a stupid tale-?'

'D-d-don't try and deny it. I am on d-d-d-direct orders to bring him b-back.'

'Orders? Who from?'

The quota master does not reply.

The old woman looks aghast at the quotamaster. She realises that lying is going to be pointless. 'How can you know this?' she says at last. 'It was only me and the parents present at the birth. No one knows about him. His identity and his existence have been the most closely guarded secret.'

'I know only because I have been told by the grand vizier himself. I mean the K-Kareshian g-governor.'

'Who? Osmand? That vile skeleton! How could he possibly-?'

'You sh-should know better than to ask,' the quotamaster hisses, looking around him nervously, as if the walls were listening to their conversation. 'Lord Osmand has w-ways of f-finding things out. It is said that he knows all our s-secrets. That he knows when even a mouse farts in the castle kitchens. His s-secret police are everywhere. Anyone could be one. N-n-now please give me the child. I do not w-want to do this but, I have n-n-no choice.'

'N-n-n-no choice!' the nurse laughs out loud, cruelly mimicking the man's stammer. 'No choice? I suppose you had no choice when the invaders came and raided our lands then sacked our city. You had no choice when all our best men and women went off to fight and die, when the Shadokin violated us and burnt our buildings. Oh you had a choice all right, you and the rest of the scum that decided to side with the enemy. You make me sick. You certainly knew which side your bread would be buttered on.'

'You don't know what you are t-talking about. It's n-not that simple. I have a wife, children. I have a duty to look after them-'

'What about your duty to your country? To your duke and the rest of your countrypeople?'

'I am only one m-m-man. What g-g-good could I be against a whole army?'

You're not a man. You're a-'

'I will n-not discuss this with you any m-m-more!' the quotamaster shouts. His eyes fixed firmly at a spot on the floor, unable to meet the nurse's outraged glare. 'He m-must go to the Reckoning. It is the direct order of Osmand. The child must be t-t-taken as proof of the duke's crime of harbouring an unlicensed infant.'

'The duke's *crime*?' The nurse looks astonished. 'Osmand would not dare accuse the duke!'

'Believe it or not as you wish m-madam but, Duke Anthony is to be arrested as soon as the Ne-Duke Derron is returned to c-c-c-custody.'

'Why did he leave it so long? If Osmand knew of his existence, why didn't he take the child from the tower long ago?'

'How sh-should I know? I cannot speak for the governor's motives.'

'And what of the duchess? Is she to be arrested also?'

'I have n-no idea. All I know is that if I don't get this infant back and ready for the wagons, I will d-d-dis d-d-disappear in a puff of smoke along with my wife, her mother and my children before t-t-tomorrow morning, all crammed into the same f-fire cage.' The man looks up at last, his eyes pleading. 'Please give him to me.'

The nurse's grip tightens on Derron. He squeals with discomfort. 'He cannot be added to the quota. He must be hidden,' she hisses through clenched teeth. 'I am here to meet a representative from the Order of Ra. One of the coenobites is coming to get him. Once they have charge of him he will be safe.'

'Give me the child, M-Madam. I will n-n-not ask again.'

She clasps Derron closer to her chest and scrutinises the man. 'You know who he is, don't you.'

'Of course, I just t-told you. He is Derron-'

'No, not his royal title you fool,' she hisses, cutting him off mid-sentence. 'I mean who he really is.'

The quotamaster looks around at the walls again in case there might be someone or something listening and says nothing in response.

'I thought so,' she says. 'He has the Mark!'

At these words the quotamaster's eyes widen involuntarily.

'Yes indeed. You know the significance as well as I,' the nurse watches him carefully to gauge his reaction. She then pulls back some material to reveal a livid red birthmark in the shape of a star on the baby's left upper arm.

She talks quickly and quietly, looking often towards

the door as the sound of heavy boots marching in the distance mixes with the lashing of the rain, the roaring wind and distant thunder. Shadokin are not close enough for concern she thinks but, too close for comfort all the same. The quotamaster's attention is drawn towards the sound of soldiers also.

'Superstitious d-drivel, Madam,' he says. 'He has a birth m-m-mark. So w-w-what? Many babies are born with them. My wife has one similar on her leg. It is of n-no sig- no significance.'

'You look uncertain all the same quotamaster and your speech impediment seems to get worse when you are nervous, or lying.' She is distracted by the sound of boots getting closer. 'They come in the dark like wolves howling for their prey,' she mutters aloud, as if quoting from an old story or proverb. She turns back to the man. 'If shadokin take him he will never have the chance to discover his true destiny, never receive the necessary training. Cardemont will be doomed forever unless the coenobites can care for him and Prove him.'

'The coenobites? That bunch of itinerant beggars. Surely you jest? Thay are little less than a joke.'

'I had my doubts also but, they are not what they seem. I-'

'Will you sh-shut-up w-woman and hand him over to me now,' the quotamaster replies in an agitated whisper, looking towards the door and shifting his weight nervously from one foot to the other as if desperate to urinate. He steps further into the room, coming closer to her. 'If we don't hand him over n-none of us will have the opportunity to reach our t-t-t-t-true destiny. We'll all be hanging by our thumbs from the city walls by order of Osmand. Those of us who aren't roasting like suckling pigs in a cage, that is. Now, for the last time, g-give him to me.'

The nurse's face expresses nothing but scorn. 'Make me!'

'Wh-what?'

'You heard. Make me.'

'I do not want to use force, Madam.'

'I do! Come anywhere near me and I'll kill you!'

The quotamaster, suspicious, looks her up and down in the weak candlelight, scrutinising her for concealed weapons. 'L-look, just hand him over woman. We don't n-need to get violent.'

'Stay away!' she shouts, raising her voice despite the danger of discovery. Then, calming herself, she looks directly into the quotamaster's eyes and whispers one word, 'Bloodwielder.'

The quotamaster looks uncomfortable, shuffling his feet and staring at the little clouds of dust being kicked up from the floor by his boots. He says nothing but, his lips move silently, as if muttering to himself.

The nurse continues. 'Yes, I thought so. You know exactly what I'm saying. It could be him. It could-'

'You know nothing!' he blurts out suddenly, moving towards her and shaking his clenched fists directly in her face. The nurse takes a step back and her look of fear at his outburst seems to bring him to his senses. He looks ashamed and his anger dissipates. He lowers his fists and regards her haggard features for several moments before letting out a low sigh and continuing in a calmer tone. 'Please. I have no choice. His n-name is now registered on the w-w-wagon lists. I put it there myself today under the eye of Osmand. He w-watched me do it. What can I do? N-n-nothing. Bloodwielder or n-not. Whatever or whoever he is or m-might be, there is nothing either of us can do now to s-s-save him. He must be taken to the wagons.'

'But we *have* to save him.'

'We will be killed for it you m-m-mad old crone.'

'What of it? We will die and your wife, your mother-in-law and children will die but, in return, he will be saved. One day he will bring Karesh to its knees. Be a man for once and do something that you know to be right!'

The quotamaster looks towards the floor. Then he looks up, straight into the nurse's eyes and for a brief moment she senses that he will change his mind and help. That moment is lost, however, when the door is savagely kicked open once more. A violent gust of wind blows out the candles and whips up clouds of dust from the floor. The nurse instinctively shields Derron with her body by gripping him tightly in her arms and turning away towards the back wall.

Two soldiers stomp into the room. One, a young private, carries a flaming torch. The other is older and wears a strip of silver braid across his chest to denote the superior rank of sergeant. They both wear the black and green striped turbans of shadokin. The quotamaster shields his eyes from the sudden glare of the torchlight. The private slams the door shut and the sergeant points his gloved finger imperiously towards the woman.

'How old is that infant?' he demands, his tone harsh yet controlled.

The nurse says nothing, keeping her back to the soldiers. She turns her head to look at the quotamaster, pleading with her eyes.

'Answer the sergeant you old slut,' shouts the younger soldier. He is skinny and his face is covered in large, red pimples. His uniform is brand new. 'And turn round when you are addressed by a shadokin.'

The nurse turns to face them.

'He is almost a year old Your Honour but, he is sick and feeble, hardly worth your bothering with-'

'Shut-up hag! Don't volunteer information that hasn't been requested,' the young private shouts, again unnecessarily loudly. His voice reaches a high-pitched squeak at the end of the sentence and he coughs in an attempt to cover it up. He then brandishes his torch around for no apparent reason, other than dramatic effect.

'You,' the sergeant says to the quotamaster, ignoring the private. 'You're wearing the uniform of a quotamaster. Why hasn't this infant been taken? You know this year's quota has no exemptions. If it's under one year old it goes in a wagon. It would seem that this one is in the wrong place.'

'I was just about to b-bring him Your Honour,' replies the quotamaster, throwing an appealing glance at the nurse as he tries to prize the crying child from the sanctuary of her arms.

'No, he's nothing but a tiny bairn. I won't let him go,' the nurse screams. She tries to sound defiant. Her hold on the child becomes tighter, squeezing his small bones and making him wail with discomfort.

The sergeant narrows his gaze on her face and starts to advance towards her. 'I never repeat an order,' he whispers. The younger soldier moves forwards also, copying his superior and holding the torch in front of the nurse's face so his sergeant can see her more clearly.

'I won't give him up. I can't. He is my charge.' The nurse steps back until she feels the unyielding surface of the wall behind her. Her eyes stare back at the sergeant's. They start to water, as they remain open unnaturally wide, like a terrified rabbit caught in a snare. They sting from the acrid smoke of the torch. She tries to reason with the man. 'Please, you can just ignore this one and take another. They are all the same surely. One won't be missed. Look,' she says as she remembers something and fumbles at her belt for the purse given to her by her mistress, 'I have money. A large sum for a soldier; more than a lifetime's wage. Just take it and go. No-one need ever be any the wiser.'

She holds the purse out to him, her outstretched arm trembling. Her other arm clutches the child in desperation. The sergeant's eyes move briefly from her face to the money purse then back to her face again. His mouth curls up at the edges giving the impression of a grin but, his eyes display no gentleness.

'Are you m-m-mad woman?' the quotamaster gasps. 'Give him the ch-ch-child.' He directs a plea to the sergeant. 'She d-doesn't know what she is saying Your Honour. Please ignore the ranting of a d-d-deranged old woman.

The sergeant ignores him and the quotamaster looks aghast as he sees the man draw a long knife from his belt and clench it in one hand. 'No!' the quotamaster gasps. 'This was n-not part of the agreement. It is not n-nec-n-necessary. She will see sense. Just let me t-talk to her for a moment.'

Hearing his words, the nurse turns to look at the quotamaster. *Agreement?* Her mouth forms the shape of the word but, no sound emerges. Her eyes look sad and questioning as recognition of the quotamaster's betrayal registers in her face. 'You did not need to involve these animals.'

Without a word, the sergeant extends one arm holding the knife towards her throat. His other arms reaches out to gather the child. His face is close enough to the woman's now for her to smell the stench of his rotten teeth. Her head moves from side to side in a slow, sweeping motion and her body involuntarily jerks with fear as her eyes are drawn to the approaching blade. At the feel of cold metal pressing against her throat, her head stops moving and her eyes fix rebelliously on the sergeant's. All fear is gone. She snorts through her nose then spits a wad of green phlegm directly into his face.

'This child is the Prince Derron, twin brother of the Ne-Duke Orlando and son of Duke Anthony and the Duchess Iphigenia. He is to be taken straight back to the castle. If he is harmed you and your young sidekick here can expect a painful roasting in a fire cage.'

The sergeant gives her a cold smile. 'I know who he is.'

In one slow and practiced movement, he draws the sharp edge of his dagger smoothly across the pink, wrinkled skin of her neck. The quotamaster looks on in impotent horror as his eyes chronicle the scene in front of him: the sergeant's impassive expression, the old woman's spit still clinging to his cheek, her startled eyes, the private's ill-concealed look of shock. All are branded on the quotamaster's memory in a silent, frozen moment.

At first, time appears to stand still and there is utter silence. A thin, red line appears across the woman's neck; as if an invisible hand has drawn it with a scarlet crayon. Then, the tableau before the quotamaster unfreezes. The child can once again be heard to wail as the woman's body crumples like a limp rag doll to a sitting position on the ground, Derron still clutched in her arms. The red line grows wider and becomes a slick of gushing crimson running down her chest, soaking her dress and bathing the child's head and body in a baptism of blood.

Crouching on his haunches, the sergeant takes his time as he wipes his blade clean on the hem of the nurse's robe. He inspects the blade, running his thumb across the length of it slowly then, after a moment's contemplation, looks up at the quotamaster who is staring at the now lifeless body on the floor. The sergeant looks in the same direction.

'Shame that,' he says. 'I don't like to chastise unless there is need'. He looks back at his blade, contemplating its keen edge. 'I'm glad I find no need to chastise you, Quotamaster,' he continues without looking up. 'You performed your duty well, leading us to her. We could see the luminous pebbles you placed on the ground easily in the dark. I will send in a favourable report to Lord Osmand. Your life will, in all likelihood, be spared.'

'What about m-my wife and family?'

The sergeant shrugs. 'Dunno. You'll have to talk to the governor about that.'

The quotamaster continues to stare at the dead body. The woman's face is bloodless; her blue-white skin is a stark contrast to the red gash in her throat. Her glazed eyes gape at him, sightless as a fish lying on its marble slab at market. They accuse. They also seem to plead for the life of the infant who sprawls on her chest, wriggling in its gore-saturated garments and crying.

Still crouching, the sergeant uncurls the woman's dead fingers and takes the purse of money. He stands up, pushes it into his pocket and turns, grinning towards the private.

'Perks of the job boy. You're fresh out of training but, you'll learn once you've been soldiering for any length of time.'

The young shadokin swallows hard and tries to smile at his superior. He seems incapable of speaking and the attempted smile turns into a grimace. He looks pale and shaken, although desperately attempting to look tough.

'Don't worry;' the sergeant says, misunderstanding the younger man's scowl and clamping a heavy hand on his shoulder. 'You'll get a share of the money.' He re-sheaths his knife and, without looking back, starts to walk out of the house. 'Quotamaster do your job. Put that brat in a wagon.' Just before reaching the door he stops, realising he has forgotten something and turns back to hand an object to the quotamaster. 'Oh yeah, I almost forgot. Take this and make sure it's used.'

'What is it?'

'What does it look like? It's a branding iron.'

'I d-don't understand. Why would-'

'Brand the child. Inside right wrist. The governor says to make sure it goes nice and deep. Remember, inside right wrist. He was most specific and don't leave the city. He will want to see you.'

The sergeant walks out into the rain, followed by the private, who turns back to look and gives the quotamaster a nod as if reinforcing the sergeant's order but, he evidently lacks his earlier bravado, as his face is ashen and he looks like he might be sick. He runs out after his superior covering his mouth with his hand and the room is plunged immediately into darkness.

The quotamaster re-lights a candle and inspects the brand in the dim light. He notices the design of the amaranth bloom, the emblem of his homeland, and starts to weep.

After a while Derron starts to cry for attention. The quotamaster dries his tears and takes the infant out of the lifeless arms of his dead nurse, wiping what blood he can from the child's face to ensure he can breathe.

He holds Derron in his arms and looks down at the woman's face. 'It isn't my f-f-fault! What could you expect of me,' he shouts at her. 'They were going to k-k-kill my family unless I helped them. My whole family was to b-b-burn. Don't stare at me like that!' He pulls her oilskin coat from the floor and throws it over her body, making sure to cover her face. 'No time for prayers now. Forgive me. The g-gods f-forgive me,' he mutters, half to himself and half to the corpse as he hurries to follow the two soldiers out of the room and into the pouring rain.

CHAPTER FOUR

Daniel

He senses he is moving or, rather, floating. It is dark, his vision swamped by a crimson flood that undulates and swirls around him like the strong currents deep below the surface of a river. The images that had been so vivid a moment ago now blur, merge then dissolve; the nurse and the baby escaping the castle, the man with the stutter, the soldiers, the murder. The murder! He has a moment of panic as he remembers the woman's throat being cut. The baby covered in a gush of her blood.

Tazmand's first instinct is to swim, take some control. He doesn't know if he can swim though, and he is tired, so incredibly tired. Anyway, where would he swim to? And it is so warm and peaceful here, so quiet, so why bother? Disoriented yet strangely calm and relaxed, he gives in to the force that envelopes his body and awaits whatever might happen next.

At the whim of the current, he feels his body move but, he has lost all sense of direction until he sees, or at least senses, a dim light in the distance. It is only a pinprick to start with but, slowly it grows bigger, and ever bigger. At the same time, he feels like he is moving upwards, although he can't be sure until, eventually, his face breaks the water's surface into moist, warm air. He gasps, inhaling deeply, even though he does not remember having needed to hold his breath.

Now he is floating on his back. He is still tired but his breathing is relaxed and he feels comfortable. Everything is quiet. *How long have I been here?* The water is warm, as is the air above although there is no sun. There are no clouds, no sky. No daylight. There are no stars or moon either. He has no sense of time. There is nothing to see above him except a red haze.

He hears a noise and looks sideways, staring across the water's surface into mist. There is no horizon. No reference to give any sense of space. He thinks he can make out a vague form, however; a figure approaching in a boat. *That's a very small boat, with a very small person in it. Or is it a big boat and just a long way off?* As the vessel gets closer, it does, indeed, become bigger and more distinct. Sitting in it is a normal-sized, yet painfully thin, man wearing an over-large turban. Tazmand sees his face. A stern countenance, thin and mean with cold, colourless eyes. He recognises the man. *Oh, it's you!*

Next to the man sits the fat, orange cat. Tazmand can just see its head poking over the top of the hull. It shows no interest in him, preferring to stare down into the water. *Probably looking for fish*? Tazmand feels like he might giggle but, stops himself, sensing he ought to be serious really.

The boat is getting closer and closer. The thin man smiles, as if they know each other, but it is a cruel grimace more than a smile Tazmand thinks. Then he reaches out, his long sleeve trailing in the ruby waters and beckons Tazmand with his finger. Tazmand reaches a hand towards him in return, then stops when he hears a sound.

A muffled voice shouting in the distance, calling his name. *That's not the man speaking; it sounds a long way off . Sounds familiar. Why do I recognise it?* Gradually, the shouting gets closer, louder, and Tazmand feels someone gripping and shaking his shoulders.

#

'Wake up! Taz, are you all right? Hello? Tazmand answer me!'

'Er, what?' Tazmand heard his own voice as though it was someone else's. 'What's going on?' He opened his eyes, his vision clearing to reveal Dharma's round, concerned face peering down at him.

He was lying flat on his back on the floor with Dharma kneeling over to him. He sat up carefully with Dharma's help, his head throbbing, feeling exhausted and confused.

Dharma let go of his shoulders, stood up and started bouncing up and down with excitement. 'By the gods Taz, you missed all the hullabaloo. There's been an 'upheaval', if that's the right word. People are saying it was an earth tremor, a temblor. Everyone's been running around in a panic looking for shelter. Only there isn't any, so lots of people have been knocked out by books falling on their heads and it-'

'I fainted?'

'Yes you did. Anyway, it only seems to have affected this sector but, it was really frightening - the temblor, I mean. I tried to wake you but, you passed out so suddenly-'

'Dar stop gabbling.' Tazmand raised his hand. 'I've got a

71

headache.' He took a deep breath and shook his head, trying to wake up. 'I fainted?'

'Yeah. Out cold. One minute we were standing looking down at the squished rat. The next minute, there you were lying in the dust. That's when the rumbling started.'

'Rumbling?'

'Must have been the sight of rat's blood that made you pass out. Might have been the guts too. Made me feel queasy too I can tell you, what with my sensitive digestion and-'

'What rumbling?' Tazmand looked around, still groggy. 'Dharma slow down, you're not helping my headache.'

'Sorry but, it was all so sudden. You missed everything. Just at the moment you fainted, the floor started to shudder and then the bookcases were all vibrating and books started falling off the shelves. Some of the ladders even came off their rails and Dukka, you know, that stuck-up shelver? The one with the squashed nose, like his face is permanently pressed against a window?'

Tazmand massaged his temples. 'Dar, just get to the point.'

'Well, he fell off his ladder, almost from the middle rung and apparently he's got a broken arm and collar bone. One of the girl pushers – don't know her name - got her veil stuck in a ladder wheel when she fell over. Professional hazard I suppose but, it seems that she's all right apart from a cut on her forehead. A couple of minor injuries reported by some others, nothing too serious. Which is pure luck, if you want my opinion, and just goes to prove the danger I'm always talking about...'

Dharma, still animated, continued to babble as Tazmand

looked around at the mess. In the gloom, he could see that there were books in various states of disrepair all over the floor, hanging off ladder rungs and shelves. Many were torn, spines dented and pages folded over and creased. A few people were wandering about holding bruised and bloody heads. Some were limping and the usual sombre stillness of the library had been replaced temporarily by anxious chatter.

Overgrunts with flaming torches moved quickly, issuing orders to clear up the books and using whips to restore order and quiet. Thank the gods we can't be blamed for a temblor thought Tazmand; if the earth shakes then it's the fault of the gods – nothing to do with him or Dharma. No floggings this time hopefully; no harsh ones anyway.

Dharma's voice was still droning on.

'What's that?'

'I said are you all right? You seem leagues away.'

The image of an old woman's throat being cut flashed across Tazmand's mind. He closed his eyes and rubbed them furiously, trying to clear it from his thoughts. 'I'm fine. Just thinking. I went a bit dizzy.' He took a deep breath and shook his head to clear it. 'Hey anyway, how's your arm?

Dharma looked bemused. 'Arm?'

'You know, from Sash's whip?'

'Oh that! I'd forgotten all about it in the excitement. Not every day you get a temblor.' Dharma inspected the hurt area of his arm. 'It is a bit sore still actually. Now you mention it.' He gave it a tentative prod.

'Well stop poking it then if it hurts!'

Dharma ignored his friend and sighed. 'Oh well, at least he didn't draw blood this time.'

'He's a sadistic bully Dar. Just because you were a bit noisy and he heard you.'

'Taz I hope you don't get into trouble. Sash can be such a pronk and he's bound to want to get even with you for cheeking him.'

'Don't worry about it. I can handle him.'

Dharma was quiet for a moment as he looked around. 'Taz,' he said at last slowly, temporarily forgetting about his arm. 'This entire area is covered in fallen books.'

'Yes,' Tazmand replied, looking around too. 'It is.'

'You were lying on the floor. Right in the middle of all the commotion and yet not one of them landed on you.'

Tazmand looked at Dharma. 'Yes,' he repeated.

'Odd.'

Tazmand shrugged. 'Lucky I suppose. Anyway, I notice you didn't get hit either.'

'No, that's true.' Dharma paused for a moment, offering his friend a speculative look. 'Now I come to think about it, I'll tell you something else that's weird.'

Tazmand stood up and brushed down his clothes with his hands. 'If you must.'

'Who's ever heard of a temblor confining itself to such a tiny area, especially just one specific sector of the library? It doesn't make sense.'

Tazmand looked around again and noticed that the devastation only extended as far as the end of that section.

He adopted a breezy tone, obviously not wanting to talk, and certainly not wanting to think, about it. 'Weirder things have happened I suppose. Come on. Let's go and eat before they start forcing 'volunteers' to clear up the mess.'

'Yes but-'

'Oh come on Dar. I thought you said you were hungry.'

'Yes I know but, don't you think it's a bit strange-'

Tazmand did not answer as he looked around at the clutter. He was thinking about his dream, trying to remember it all. Piece it together. Why was he dreaming suddenly and repeatedly of these people? The duchess, her babies, the nurse and that awful scarecrow with the big turban – what was his name? He massaged his temples but couldn't remember. His head felt full of wool. Why did his mind play tricks, make him think bad things about Karesh like the baby wagons and the fire cages? The real empire would never be so cruel. Would it? The emperor was a benevolent ruler; he only invaded other countries for their own good; where people could not look after themselves.

Dreams are weird things; they rarely made any proper sense, mixing up things from real life with other stuff and none of it is ever quite right. He decided not to think about it any more.

'Come on Dar, let's go.' He threw his arm over his friend's shoulders and steered him in the direction of the refectory.

'And you are going where?' a stern voice hissed from behind them. They turned round to find Sash staring at them. He held his whip poised for use.

Dharma gave a weak smile. 'Food?' he replied hopefully.

Sash shook his head and tutted. 'I don't think so. No one eats until this mess is cleared-up.'

Dharma looked horrified. 'But, I'm ravishing-'

Tazmand poked him with his elbow.'Ravenous.'

'Ravenous.'

'Don't argue Dar.' Tazmand took his arm, all the time keeping a close watch on Sash, especially at his whip. 'Come on, the quicker we get on with it, the quicker it's done.'

Sash stared at them until they returned to their ladder and started picking up the fallen books, then waddled off towards the refectory.

#

The long tables in the refectory were crowded. Metal spoons screeched against tin plates as hungry grunts of every level of importance gulped their food. Wooden benches scraped the stone floors as people came and went and everyone shouted, partly to be heard over the noise, although mostly to make up for the silence imposed during long working hours in the library. The din was amplified a thousand times as it ricocheted off the smooth limestone walls and spiralled and echoed high into the vaulted ceilings above.

Tazmand and Dharma had managed to clear up the fallen books quickly, making it just in time, and grateful to be sitting in front of their bowls of tepid, grey bean soup. A hunk of black rye bread and a tin cup of vaguely warm, pale yellow tea were the sole accompaniments. It was the usual unappetising slop served up to grunts but, there was plenty of it, and they wolfed it down hungrily.

Dharma finished eating first and sat quietly. He was used to the din going on around him and well able to ignore it. Besides, being conscious of his delicate constitution, he was always careful to give his food plenty of time to digest and he was happy just resting and listening to the gossip going on around him. Most of the talk seemed to be about the mysterious temblor and those who had experienced it were thrilled to be able to relate it to those who had not. He smiled to himself, pleased in the knowledge that he had been at the centre of the drama yet, at the same time, feeling unsettled. *What had just happened? How do you get a temblor happening in such a small area? Why had Taz fainted at that precise moment? Why had he fainted at all?*

Dharma was worried. He watched his oldest and closest friend, sitting across from him, still eating, his face fixed in his usual frown of concentration. He made light of it but, he dreaded the day that Tazmand might get his promotion. Once that happened, they could be separated. Bound to happen, if Dharma didn't go for promotion too. They might never see each other again.

They were the same age and had been together the entire time since the nurseries. But, that's pretty much where the similarities stopped. While he was short, dark and stocky with brown eyes and a complexion like milky coffee, Taz was taller, slimmer, more athletic, pale-skinned, green-eyed and blond. Not that all that mattered. What did matter was that Taz was ambitious and he was not. Taz wanted adventures and he definitely did not. Taz was brave and he, well he had his moments but, generally, bravery wasn't his thing. He worried too much to be brave. Taz was more intelligent and thought things through before acting. He was more impulsive - did things without thinking. But, all that was all right because as long as they were together, they looked out for each other, protected one another.

And he was worried too about what was going on with

his friend at the moment. Apart from the fainting, Taz wasn't sleeping well. He thought Dharma didn't notice but, he did. And what about Sash? Why did he have it in so badly for Taz? And now this temblor thing.

Dharma tried not to show it but, all in all, he was really, really worried.

His thoughts were interrupted by a sudden ruckus on the next table. Several grunts were shouting and waving their arms and others were bent double with laughter, as a particularly large owl had swooped down and stolen some bread. Most birds were scared off from the refectory by the din, preferring the safety and quiet of the central chamber. Although, a few braver ones did circle or perch in the refectory rafters, waiting for any opportunity to swoop and scavenge food.

Dharma laughed then let out a thunderous belch. 'I'll never get to sleep after all those beans. Not with the wobbly state of my innards,' he shouted above the noise.

'Doesn't sound like I will either.' Tazmand took a spoonful of soup. 'Not while we share a dormitory. Make sure that wind just comes out of the top end tonight please.'

Dharma smirked. He wanted to talk more about the temblor but, decided to change the subject. For the time being anyway. 'So, what did Sash mean when he said you weren't good at finishing things off Taz?'

Tazmand glanced anxiously around the table. 'Dharma! Keep your voice down. Someone might hear you.'

'It's all right, there's no one listening; I checked. So?'

'So?'

'So, did something happen between the two of you at

some time and, if so, why don't I know about it?'

'You could say that,' Tazmand muttered, stuffing a large chunk of soggy, black bread dripping with soup into his mouth.

'Seriously? Why don't I know about it? We've always done everything together and you've never mentioned anything before.' Tazmand continued munching his bread. 'Taz! What happened? Tell me.'

Tazmand shrugged. 'All right, don't get all airy. It isn't that interesting anyway. Something and nothing.'

'Well, it is not just something and nothing to Sash. He's mad as a box of angry crabs and he's holding an obvious grudge.' Dharma winced and rubbed his arm, deciding to remember once more how sore it was. 'I've always thought he's just bad-tempered and mean to everyone. Well, I know he is but, he seems particularly miffed with you.'

'How's the injury?'

Dharma gave a dramatic sigh. 'It's actually incredibly painful. I will have to take the next shift carefully in case I do it permanent damage.'

'Very wise.'

'Sash?' Dharma prompted. 'Stop avoiding the subject.'

'Oh him.' Tazmand pushed his empty bowl away, checked around to see if anyone was listening, then stood up and moved around to Dharma's side of the table so he could lower his voice. 'Well, if you must know, it was about three years ago when you and I both became pushers.' Dharma leant closer to his friend so he could hear better. 'I was allocated to Sash who had been a shelver for a while already and you went to push for that stuck-up girl.'

79

'Oh her! Don't remind me.' Dharma raised his eyes to the ceiling. 'Rude? Anyone would have thought she was a divine the way she bossed me about.'

'Well, if it is any consolation. Sash was worse. As you know, I was his fifth pusher. The previous four had all ended up getting injured.'

'Well of course I know the rumours. Some people said he dropped heavy books from the top of his ladder on purpose, aiming for their heads.' Dharma's voice was getting louder with excitement.

'Keep it down!' Tazmand hissed, having another furtive look around the table. It was empty now apart from some older, female grunts gathered at the far end who were engrossed in their own conversation, their veils lifted with one hand to allow their other hand to spoon soup into their mouths. 'We could get into serious trouble if people hear us talking about this.'

'Well, you know it's probably true as well as I do.' Dharma hissed back. 'What about that boy who died? Don't you think it's just a bit suspicious that Sash was at the top rung of his ladder and it was one of the largest and heaviest books in the library that he dropped? Must have come down at some speed.'

'Dar you must keep what I'm about to tell you secret or we will both be in trouble. Promise me.'

'Of course I promise. I can't believe you need to ask. Discretion is my middle name. I would never-'

'All right, don't get huffy.' Tazmand paused for a moment and looked around again before continuing. 'You are right. I'm sure Sash did cause that boy's death on purpose.'

Dharma took a sharp intake of breath. His eyes as wide as saucers. 'I knew it!'

'I had only been his pusher for about a week when the *accidents* started.'

'Accidents?'

Tazmand had a gulp of tea. 'I found myself having to dodge falling books. Just one or two to start with. Nothing unusual but, the number soon increased. If I shouted up to Sash to ask him to be more careful, he would just laugh and tell me it was my responsibility to either dodge or catch them. Said it would be good practice for when I became a shelver and had to deal with the birds and rotten chunks of blind.'

Dharma gave a low whistle. 'So, he killed that boy on purpose.'

'I don't think he set out to kill him exactly.' Tazmand thought about it for a moment. 'It was more of a game to him which went too far. And when the boy died because of it, Sash just didn't much care. I don't think he has much respect for life.'

'I can't believe you didn't tell me about this at the time.'

'I didn't want to worry you. Anyway, as it turned out there was no need.

'No need? I'm your best friend. I-'

'Do you, or do you not, want to hear the rest of the story?'

'Well of course I do! But-'

Tazmand ignored him and continued. 'After pushing Sash for a couple of months I became pretty wise to his tricks. I learned not to rely on him for any advance warnings and to keep a sharp lookout for anything falling, books or anything else. After a while he seemed to get bored and stopped his tricks all together. I think he realised that I wasn't falling for it anymore. A few weeks had gone past since he had tried anything nasty, so I started to relax.'

'You thought he'd given up?'

Tazmand shrugged. 'As I said, I thought he was bored with it. I knew we would never be friends but, I thought we could get on with our work together. Anyway, one day we were filling the shelves as usual and we were in a hurry to finish our book quota on time, so I had been doing some high-speed pushing. Using some real muscle. You know what it's like.' Dharma smiled with professional appreciation. 'I was exhausted, so Sash called a break.'

'A break. Really? Since when has Sash done something nice for anyone?'

'I know, I know, I should have realised something was up. But I was caught off guard because, while I was taking a breather, I had no idea that Sash was busy loosening the screws on the book cage.'

Dharma gave an alarmed squeak. 'What the-'

'Then he shouted down that we should set off again, but slowly. His plan worked instantly; the cage detached from its moorings and came crashing down the ladder.'

'How did you survive that? Was it full of books? It would have caved your head in! You should be dead!'

'Sash made a stupid mistake; he had not tucked his robe between his legs and the cage snagged it.'

'No!'

'He got dragged down straight after it. Of course, I heard him screaming before I knew the cage was coming at me. I brought the ladder to a stop. Sash was squealing like that rat earlier on. He had jammed his leg between two ladder rungs to prevent the fall and had twisted it completely out of its hip socket. He was dangling there just on the strength of tendons and sinews. The robe was still caught in the cage which was dangling just above my head. His hip socket was bearing the weight of the lot. I moved out of the way quickly, just before the cage ripped the material and came crashing to the ground.'

'It's a miracle you weren't both killed.'

'As it turned out, as well as the dislocated hip, he also had a nasty gash in the side of his head and a broken collarbone. He was in a bit of a mess.'

Dharma stared at Tazmand, his mouth hanging open in astonishment.

'Now, here's the weird bit,' Tazmand continued. 'Loads of unshelved books had fallen to the floor and, though he was in obvious agony, he kept screaming at me to finish off the shelving quota. He may have been in pain but, he was terrified of losing any future promotion if we didn't get the books finished for that shift. I told him to forget the books, it was more important to get his injuries treated. He used a load of bad language and kept shouting that we had to finish. He was in no fit state to do it but, he just wouldn't listen.'

'Shouting in the library,' Dharma gasped in astonishment. 'And all those damaged books too – not to mention the broken cage!'

'Well, as I said, he was in a lot of pain. I got him to the infirmary, and they agreed to treat him because of his excellent past record. I didn't have time to look after him and get the rest of the books shelved in time by myself, so I left them. As it turned out, Sash still got his promotion, again because of his good record. He just had to wait a bit longer. Neither of us got seriously punished – just a few lashes; it was considered an accident. But, Sash cannot bear the idea that I refused to do what he told me to. He also resents the fact that the incident did not affect my eventual promotion to shelver. He ended up in the infirmary for three months while I was appointed as pusher to someone else. So, no great harm done – thank the gods. He has had pain in his hip joint and a severe limp ever since and, though it's obviously his own fault, he blames me.'

'But, it was his fault. He caused his own injuries and you saved his leg, probably his life. He should thank you.'

'He doesn't see it that way Dar. He believes that I caused the accident because if I had been squished like he planned, he would have been OK and I would have been dead or, at least badly injured. He thinks that I'm to blame for his disability and his pride is injured by the fact that I refused to carry out a direct order. He hates me and now that he's an overgrunt he has the power to get at me.'

'And your friends,' Dharma murmured, thinking of how often Sash had punished him.

Tazmand shrugged. 'Friends too, I'm afraid. He could have done more to punish me today. I'm still not sure what he's waiting for.'

'What a twisted sh-'

'That's an interesting tale youngster,' a deep, male voice commented suddenly from the other side of the table.

Tazmand and Dharma jumped in alarm. A man, whom neither of them had noticed arrive, sat opposite them, only a couple of feet away. He had apparently been listening to

Tazmand's story and he was wearing the brown robe of an overgrunt. His whip lay coiled on the table like a sleeping snake.

#

'My name is Daniel.'

Dharma's eyes widened in terror. Tazmand's jaw dropped. Where had this man appeared from? Their area of the table had been vacant since Tazmand had moved only a minute or two ago, and they had not noticed him sit down.

The overgrunt stared at them both for a moment then let out a loud, good-humoured laugh at the obvious panic apparent on both the boys' faces. 'Fret not lads. This Sash bloke sounds like an awful pronk, and nasty too, so I wouldn't dream of punishing you for gossiping about him.' The friendly twinkle in his eyes seemed to indicate that they should not worry.

Tazmand and Dharma looked at each other in complete bewilderment. They had never met an overgrunt that was this pleasant and informal before. And certainly never one who used words like 'pronk'. They were still too taken aback to respond, so they said nothing.

'And your names are?' Daniel prompted eventually.

'Oh um, I'm Tazmand. I'm a shelver and this is my pusher, Dharma. Sorry, I meant to say, Sir. Sorry, I mean, Gruntmeister.'

Still unable to speak, Dharma gave the man a feeble wave.

Daniel inclined his head in greeting and, noticing his

long beard had dipped into his soup, pulled it out, replacing it with a spoon. 'Pleased to meet you both.' Dharma saw that there were chunks of pink meat in Daniel's soup, a privilege granted to overgrunts. 'Hope you don't mind if I return to my repast but, I am ravenous and due back on duty in two quarters of the hour.' He sucked the end of his beard to get all the soup out and gave the boys a big smile. 'Waste not want not eh?' he shouted and then started eating in earnest; he made a great deal of noise as he slurped the grey liquid off his spoon with enthusiasm. 'Just let me finish-up and then we can have a chat and get to know each other eh? Cannot eat and talk at the same time; it gives me terrible wind.'

Dharma gave Daniel a sympathetic nod and, still too shocked to speak further, the two boys watched the man as he ate. He looked old Tazmand thought. Very old. Could be thirty, maybe forty or fifty, even sixty or seventy. Maybe even more? It was impossible to tell. He had deep, crinkly wrinkles under his bright blue eyes but, he gave the impression of being full of vitality. He wore a large, brown turban that was wrapped badly so it perched on his head like a wonky bird's nest and grey wisps of hair stuck out from underneath it. Tazmand could not help noticing that Daniel had the largest nose he had ever seen. It looked like he was wearing it for a joke, and it had purple veins creeping across it like the tracks left by insects in the dust in the library. The lower half of his face was covered with matted hair, which cascaded down his front in a long, dirty-grey beard.

'Oh sponk-bags,' Daniel tutted. 'Spoons, cutlery – all a complete waste of time, just gets in the way of serious eating and makes consumption tediously slow.' He slammed his spoon on the table, lifted the bowl to his mouth and gulped down the rest of the soup. 'A fine beany banquet my new friends. Jolly satisfying,' he pronounced once finished, rubbing his stomach and letting out possibly the longest, most thunderous belch the boys had ever heard. 'Oops, pardon me.'

Tazmand was fascinated by the soup that had not quite made it into Daniel's mouth. It was dribbling down his tangled beard over bits of other food that had obviously dried there from previous meals. Some of the soup had made its way down as far as the front of his robe, which was similarly encrusted. As his gaze moved back up to the old man's face, their eyes met. Daniel's were twinkling and laughing under his wiry eyebrows. Tazmand wondered what the old man might be thinking. They could still be in big trouble.

'So boys, how long have you both been in the library?' he asked, breaking the silence.

'Seven years,' Dharma replied, at last finding his voice.

The old overgrunt nodded slowly with a knowing look in his eyes. 'Came straight from the nurseries I suppose?'

'Obviously,' Tazmand replied. 'Hasn't everyone?'

Daniel laughed, regarding them both with a good-natured smile. 'Of course not. Some slaves get shunted around all over. Depends on what they're good at and who needs what.'

'Slaves?' Dharma asked, obviously surprised by the word. 'What do you mean, *slaves*?'

'I have been in lots of different work areas,' the old man continued, ignoring Dharma's question. 'I have been all over Karesh actually. I worked in the city stables for a while, then the vineyards and then, er, let me think. Oh yes, did a bit of well digging out amongst the dunes in the desert regions followed by a spot of buffalo milking when they sent me back over to the arable plains. Injured my back trying to push a buffalo up a ramp into a wagon. Stubborn beasts, buffalo.

Then got sent back into the city where they gave me a desk job in the treasury, just filing by numbers you understand and eventually got promoted to teaching assistant at a school. Was just starting to learn to read when they sent me to this here library a few weeks ago. Swapped my blue wristbands from the city school for these gold library ones. Terribly glamorous, aren't they? Itchy though; can't get underneath them for a good scratch.'

'But, what do you mean *slaves*?' Dharma insisted.

'You can read?' Tazmand exclaimed.

'How old do you think I am?' Daniel asked, ignoring both the boys, and lifting his head up so they could get the best view of his face.

Dharma and Tazmand looked at each other. They had never been asked a personal question like this before, especially by a superior. It unnerved them. Dharma nudged Tazmand with his good elbow indicating that he should make a guess. Tazmand raised his eyebrows and shook his head.

Dharma turned to Daniel. 'I'm rubbish at guessing ages, Gruntmeister Daniel. Taz is really good though.' He turned to his friend. 'Go on Taz, give it a go.'

Tazmand gave Dharma his best *I'm going to get you later* look then turned to Daniel. 'Erm, about forty years old?' he lied, pitching the estimate low and hoping that it would prove to be taken as a compliment.

It seemed to work as Daniel looked delighted. 'Ha ha. Good guess boy but way out. I am a lot older. A lot!'

'Gosh!' both boys said at the same time, trying their hardest to sound, and look, surprised.

Tazmand changed the subject. 'You said you could read, Gruntmeister?'

'No, lad. Said I started to learn. Hardly got past the alphabet before they shifted me here and had to curtail the lessons.'

'*Slaves*, Gruntmeister Daniel,' Dharma insisted, sounding impatient. 'What did you mean?'

Daniel raised his eyebrows in vague surprise at the question and ran his hand down his soup-covered beard. He studied Dharma for a bit then sighed. 'Well young man, what do I mean by slaves? Hmmm. I suppose what I mean by the term is something along the line of human beings, owned by their masters, put to work and not paid. Human beings who are not allowed to do anything or go anywhere without permission, not allowed to make their own decisions. Treated and owned like a farmer owns cattle.'

'So, are you a slave then, Gruntmeister Daniel?' Dharma asked.

'That's right,' Daniel replied, tucking into his bread and spraying small, black crumbs over the table. 'And just plain 'Daniel' will do. Forget the Gruntmeister. All right?'

Tazmand and Dharma stared tab the man, bewildered by his strange behaviour.

'But, you're a...' Dharma began but gave up as his confidence failed.

'I'm a what?'

'You are an-'

'What Dharma means to say Gruntmeis-, I mean Daniel,'

Tazmand interrupted. 'Is that you are an overgrunt in the library. You are in charge of us, and we aren't slaves so how can you be? If you don't mind me asking that is,' he added, attempting to sound polite.

'Bless me!' Daniel shouted, looking hugely amused and spraying breadcrumbs straight into the boys' faces without seeming to notice. 'You are slaves! Of course you are. Don't be daft. What else do you think you are…or aren't for that matter.'

Tazmand and Dharma gave each other a doubtful look. Tazmand knew he and his friend were both thinking the same thing; this person is crazy but, how could that be if he is an overgrunt? Mad people do not get promotions – well not obviously mad people anyway. Mind you, there was Sash, of course…

'Well,' Tazmand started, being careful to articulate slowly, as if for a child. 'We are grunts. I am a shelver and Dharma here is my pusher.'

'Very nice for you both, I'm sure,' Daniel replied. 'But, all those fancy titles are just more words for 'slave'.' He took a long swig of tea and started to gargle noisily. Some other people, who had just come to sit at the table, looked over in his direction.

'But Daniel-' Tazmand started to say. Daniel raised his hand to silence him.

'Boys. Now listen. You think you are not slaves. Is that right?' Tazmand and Dharma glanced at each other, nonplussed. 'You are both young but, let me ask you a few questions. You do not have to answer, just listen if you prefer. Are you allowed to leave the library? I mean have you ever been outside the library into the City?'

The two boys shook their heads to indicate 'no'.

'Do you get paid for your work?'

They shook their heads again.

'Are you allowed to do any work or activity other than those prescribed by the overgrunts? Will you be punished if you do not do what you are told?'

As Daniel asked each question, Tazmand and Dharma did not reply, just shook or nodded their heads, or shrugged.

'But Daniel,' Dharma said, confused. 'We are lucky to be here. Working in the library is a privilege. We are well looked after.'

'Who says?' Daniel asked.

'Who says?'

'Yes. Who says working in the library is a privilege? Who says you are lucky?'

Dharma thought for a moment. 'Well, everyone does. We have always been told so. All our lessons when we were younger taught us about Karesh and how blessed we are to be members of the empire. Outside Karesh the lands are hostile places, full of savages who fight each other. They kill and eat children and take each other as slaves. It's just common knowledge.' Getting flustered, Dharma turned to Tazmand, looking for some support. 'That's right isn't it Taz?' Tazmand stared at the tabletop and said nothing. 'Here we are protected, fed, looked after. We are educated and if we work hard we are promoted. Why would anyone want to leave the library?' Dharma persisted. 'They would get into trouble and then never become a divine.'

'Well now Dharma,' Daniel replied. His piercing blue eyes glanced at Tazmand and he paused for a moment to give serious consideration to the question. 'I think you've just put your finger on the nub of what slavery is all about.'

'What do you mean?'

'I mean, young *slave*,' Daniel said, emphasising the word, 'that slavery is essentially a state of mind. If you believe you are a slave, then you will be one. Once you decide no longer to be one, then you break your chains and you become free.'

Dharma gave Daniel a particularly vacant look. 'Chains?'

'He doesn't mean real chains Dar. Do you Daniel?' Tazmand said.

'No Tazmand, I don't. Sometimes you can't see the chains that bind you. There are many things that tie you down,' Daniel said kindly. 'Like reliance on the library and desire for promotion, for example. Or, perhaps just a person's lack of interest in the outside world.'

'What is out there?' Tazmand asked a little too loudly, suddenly animated.

Daniel gave him a penetrating look. 'Freedom Tazmand. Freedom is out there. You might want to try it some time.'

Tazmand looked down at the table, suddenly nervous that he had revealed too much of himself to this stranger.

'But what about the child-eating savages?' Dharma exclaimed, looking terrified. 'It's all very well being free but, I wouldn't want to have to meet a savage or be eaten by one for that matter. We are much safer here where it's civilised, and people know how to behave properly.'

'Savages,' Daniel repeated the word to himself with a private smile on his face still looking at Tazmand. 'You boys get cartloads of books coming into the library every day. Is that not so?'

'Yes of course,' Dharma said.

'Where do they all come from?' Daniel asked.

'Come from?' Dharma said, looking nonplussed. 'Well, that's obvious. They come from...'

'Yes,' Daniel said being encouraging and giving Dharma some time to think about it.

'Where do they come from? They come from...they come from...' Dharma could only give a weak smile as he realised that he had no idea; he had never thought about it.

'I know where they come from,' Tazmand said suddenly, remembering his dreams, although not daring to believe they might be true. 'From the lands that become part of the empire.'

Daniel gave Tazmand a surprised look. 'That's right. They come from the countries where all your so-called savages live. These are books taken from the savages.' Daniel was silent for a moment to let this information sink in. 'Have you ever heard of a savage who can read, let alone write a book?'

Tazmand and Dharma exchanged a confused look. Suddenly, there was a noise as a young grunt who had just entered the refectory, dropped her food tray on the floor. They turned in the direction of the commotion and clapped and whistled with everyone else, as was the custom. The young grunt was embarrassed as she knelt on the floor to clean up the mess. Tazmand turned back to ask Daniel some more questions only to find that he had gone.

'Giant pangbats!' Dharma gasped. 'He's a fast mover for an old bloke.'

Tazmand looked around the huge room to see where Daniel could have gone. 'But, we only turned away for a moment. How did he shift so quickly?'

'He was bonkers,' Dharma said.

'He didn't even say goodbye.'

'Yes Taz, I thought the same thing. How rude.'

'Who was he?'

They both scanned the refectory but, there was no sign of the elderly overgrunt.

CHAPTER FIVE

Eye of Horus

I phigenia paces the floor of her private chamber, her clothes damp from her trip to Golden Square, her shoes still spattered in mud. She has dismissed Beatrix, her lady-in-waiting, her fresh clothes remain untouched, laid out ready for her on her bed. A bath of now lukewarm water stands unused in front of a blazing log fire. The window remains open but, she ignores it, preferring to shiver under her wet clothing. She sits for a moment but cannot rest and starts pacing again, wringing her hands in nervous anticipation. Where is she? Where is she?

Only an hour ago, upon their return to the castle from attending the Reckoning Iphigenia and Beatrix had supported the duke to his quarters where, exhausted, he had collapsed at once onto his bed then proceeded to toss and turn in a feverish stupor.

She continues to pace across her chamber. *My poor dear Anthony. All will be well. But, where is she?*

Assisted by Beatrix, she had undressed the duke, placed

him under the counterpane to ensure his comfort, then had waited anxiously until the court physician arrived to tend him. He had been given a strong sedative then, as soon as it took effect and she was convinced her husband was out of danger and sleeping comfortably, she left him to be tended by Beatrix. She had hurried back to her own chamber to await the return of Derron's nurse, and news of his safe delivery to the coenobite.

Where is she? Iphigenia is about to summon her guard to ensure he has not denied admittance to anyone and sent her away when, abruptly, her chamber door opens. Her heart leaps in her chest. 'Is it done?' she shouts towards the door. A moment of hope is brutally crushed as, without ceremony, Osmand enters.

He has changed his robes from vivid green satin to black silk, studded with grey crystal beads. The sombre material highlights the sallow complexion of his skin and he has a suspiciously smug expression on his face. As he approaches her, the train of his robe scuttles along the floor behind him, the beads sounding against the stone like the claws of a pack of scurrying rats. The large green and red heliotrope nestles, as usual in the centre of his turban, in its bed of a freshly wrapped black silk.

Facinorous waddles in behind his master then moves, as fast as he is able (which is not very), to the open window where he proceeds to sit as still as a statue, staring at a small sparrow that is sheltering on the sill from the rain.

'Is what done, Your Grace?' He turns his head and looks at her bath. "Oh, forgive me, I have interrupted your toilet. I assume you thought I was your maid. Was she running an errand for you?'

Iphigenia has a momentary premonition of disaster; nausea overcomes her, and she finds it hard to breathe, as if a mouldy blanket has been placed over her head and tied around her neck with a tight cord. She fights the feeling away and forces herself to sound reasonably normal. 'What do you think you are doing?' she asks in her most imperious tone. She modulates her voice carefully, not without effort, to appear confident and to camouflage the real fear and repugnance she feels at the sight of him. 'These are my personal rooms. How dare you burst in unannounced? You overreach your authority Grand Vizier. Leave immediately!'

Osmand leans on his staff and offers the duchess the shallowest of bows. 'Do excuse my presumption, Your Grace. I bring important news which I thought best delivered to you in person and... in private.'

'If you must. I would appreciate it if you would deliver it quickly and then leave. I am tired and, as you can see, I have not yet changed.'

'Of course, Your Grace. I will go as soon as you wish.' He pauses to examine his fingernails before continuing in an affectedly casual manner. 'But, you must realise that the sooner I leave, the sooner your husband will be arrested.'

'The duke – arrested? Don't be absurd. What are you talking about?' Her legs feel weak. She feels like she has been punched in the stomach and crosses to her dressing table to sit, then starts to remove her jewellery. Her hands tremble and her stomach turns somersaults. *What, by all the gods, is going on? Where is the nurse? Where is Derron?*

'I mean madam that as soon as I leave your chambers, I

will have no alternative but to perform my most loyal duty to the emperor and have your husband taken into custody.'

'Take my husb-?' Iphigenia gives a wary laugh and stares at the reflection of Osmand's face in her mirror. 'Have you completely taken leave of your sanity? Perhaps the power of dual roles as grand vizier and Kareshian governor has gone to your head and it is has swelled to now truly fill that abnormally large turban. He is the Duke of Cardemont. He is your master. You owe him fealty and complete obedience. He cannot be arrested by you, or by anyone.'

'Are you quite sure of that?' Osmand continues in an irritatingly serene manner.

'Of course, I am sure.' Iphigenia does not feel nearly as confident as she tries to sound and feels suddenly cold. She picks up her hairbrush then places it down again without using it. *Derron, my son. Are you safe? Where is that nurse?* Her hands fidget, picking up small bottles and toiletry implements then putting them down again pointlessly. Osmand watches her discomfiture with obvious pleasure.

'And what, Madam, if he has been found guilty of high treason to the New Order of Karesh? What then?'

'High treason? He is the duke! What court has been in session to find him guilty?'

'I do not need a court. I am Kareshian governor, and I have incontrovertible proof of his subversion.'

'You are lying!' Iphigenia spits the words at Osmand, turning on her stool to face him and allowing him a glimpse of her true loathing.

At the sound of Iphigenia's raised voice Facinorous turns lazily to see what is going on. Immediately losing interest, he returns his full attention back to the bird.

'Be careful how you speak to me Iphigenia. I do not take kindly to accusations.' Osmand remains calm. He smiles knowingly whilst his voice holds a threatening edge. The fact that he has breached protocol and used her first name is not lost on either of them. She decides not to comment on it and regains some of her well-trained composure. Standing up, she walks towards the tapestry on the wall. One of her hands moves towards her neck: her fingers caress the vial of poison through the material of her dress as she stares at the picture of the two children being bathed.

'And his treasonable offence is what exactly?' she asks eventually, keeping her back to him.

Seeming to enjoy the duchess's discomposure, Osmand does not respond immediately. Iphigenia feels a rush of blood to her cheeks, along with a surfeit of excess moisture to her eyes, promising imminent tears. *He's enjoying this. I won't cry. I won't give him the pleasure.*

'Your son will be well on his way to Karesh by now,' he says at last, continuing to stare at her.

'What? What of it? We handed him over at the Reckoning and I cannot get him back so why do you taunt me? It is done. Don't change the subject or dangle me like a fish on a hook. What is my husband's imaginary offence, of which you have so called proof?'

'No my dear, you misunderstand me. I am not talking of your son Orlando.'

'What?' Iphigenia splutters, confused. She turns towards him, unable to breath, her muscles rigid. 'Not Orlando? What do you mean?' *It cannot be. Surely?*

'I mean your other son.' Osmand looks directly at her, his usually colourless eyes now as hard and dark as obsidian, 'I mean Prince Derron.'

Osmand holds her gaze for a few moments more, then looks casually towards the tapestry. Iphigenia's blood turns to ice. Sweat trickles down her back. She feels faint.

'Derron?' she whispers; her lungs hardly provide enough air to get the words out. She notices, in her peripheral vision that the bird has disappeared from the windowsill. Facinorous stares at her, a thin trickle of blood oozing down the orange fur on his chin.

'Yes Iphigenia. Your secret child. Derron, twin of Orlando. Only not really that secret at all. Did you seriously think you could hide him from me? I have known of his existence since his birth,' Osmand hisses. His facade of cool indifference has evaporated; his face is now a twisted mask of distain and pent-up fury.

'I don't know what you are talking about,' she mumbles weakly. Her legs feel like jelly as she stumbles forwards. Her hands grip the dressing table, accidentally sweeping her toiletries and bottles of scent to smash on the floor as she sits down.

Osmand throws his staff to the ground; his scrawny hands clutch the duchess by the shoulders and turn her back round to face him. He grasps her chin and tilts her head back, standing over her and glaring down at her tear-stained features.

'You both thought you were so terribly clever. You, the proud Duchess of Cardemont, from one of the oldest noble families and your weak-minded husband. You aristocrats make me sick; everything handed to you on a plate while you walk around staring down your noses at the rest of us.' He lets go of her and walks away in disgust.

Iphigenia realises there is no point in further pretence. The muscles of her throat constrict but, she manages to force the words out. 'Why did you wait so long?'

The grand vizier walks towards his cat and stoops briefly to stroke its head. 'Because I needed to be completely sure of my evidence; it was necessary to wait until you made a move and tried to spirit the child away for good. I knew you would make your move sooner or later. You are so ridiculously transparent; I need only look at your face to tell exactly what you are thinking.'

Iphigenia says nothing. She remains at her dressing table and stares blankly into the mirror. When she does eventually speak again, her voice is dull and hollow. 'Is Derron well? Has he been harmed in any way?'

'Yes, perfectly well...for now.'

A sob of relief suddenly erupts from her chest and she gulps for air. 'Thank the gods! That is something. And his nurse?'

'Oh her – she's dead. Her throat was cut by soldiers when she refused to hand over your son.'

'Yes, I can imagine she would have put up a good fight.' The duchess bows her head momentarily. 'She was loyal and brave. I send my thanks and blessings to her in the afterplace.'

'I suppose you could see it as a mercy killing; she would have had to go to the fire cage otherwise.'

'By the gods Osmand, couldn't you have just turned a blind eye? What difference does one child make to you? You could have let him go!'

'Do you consider me stupid? *Just one child!* I have done my research. I have heard of your prophecies. Apart from being a royal and second in line to the ducal title, he was born with the mark of some so-called saviour or other. The Bloodwielder you call it, I think?' He walks back towards her. 'Every culture, every religion has one, you know. Everyone's looking for salvation from something, someone to help them. It's all rubbish of course. If you want to be saved, do it yourself.'

'How can you possibly know all this? Who has told you?'

'About the prophecies? Don't be ridiculous, they are common knowledge. Fairy tales told to children.'

'I mean how could you have known about Derron's existence? Nobody knew except the duke, his nurse and me. It is just not possible.'

Osmand's mouth twitches at the corners. Iphigenia realises he is smirking. 'Your naivety would be attractive if it wasn't so pathetic. I have various methods of obtaining information, My Lady.'

'Then tell me how!'

Leaning forward, he strokes her cheek. 'All in good time Iphigenia.'

She pulls her face away from his emaciated fingers, feeling sick at the sight of the dirt-encrusted fingernails.

'I did not think you were the sort of man who would take much notice of religious superstition Osmand.'

'You are right, I'm not and I don't. I know of course that the prophecy is nonsense but, I also know that it makes him even more dangerous than his brother. People love to believe in predictions and fate and all that nonsense so my dear, in the eyes of some, that could make him a potential leader. He could be a messiah; if the wrong people got hold of him, he could be manipulated and used against Karesh. More importantly, he could be used against me.

'No, I want him somewhere away from here where he can do little harm. But, somewhere I can keep an eye on him. And...' Osmand pauses and stoops to press his face against Iphigenia's neck where he takes a deep breath of her perfume, 'I want you as well.' His tongue flicks out of his mouth like a lizard and licks her skin. Iphigenia flinches away from him, shuddering with disgust.

'My husband is to be arrested for harbouring his son from Karesh; both my children are now Kareshian slaves. Everything that means anything important to me is gone. I will kill myself before I come to you.'

'No you won't.'

Iphigenia laughs uncertainly. 'You sound sure of yourself Grand Vizier.'

Osmand stands up straight. His eyes narrow, they penetrate the duchess like maggots digging into cheese. 'Yes my dear, I am.'

'And just how do you think you will stop me?'

Osmand does not answer her directly. Instead he smiles and asks, 'do you want to see your sons Iphigenia?'

'My sons? When?'

'Now my dear. You can see them right this moment.'

'What?' She looks frantically about the room, as if expecting to suddenly see them appear. 'Are they here in the castle. Are they still in Cardemont?'

'No, but I can show them to you.'

Iphigenia stares at him, her forehead creased with confusion. 'Why do you take pleasure in taunting me? You offer me a confection, yet I dare not eat it for fear that there will be a sharp blade hidden at its centre. I don't understand.'

'Of course you don't my dear.' Osmand smirks, taking a short dagger out of a pocket. He giggles as she shrinks back. 'Don't worry, My Lady. I don't intend to use it on you.'

He pushes the point of the blade into the palm of his left hand allowing a pool of blood to collect, then, with his other hand he reaches up and undoes the clips that keep the heliotrope in place in his turban. Looking intently at Iphigenia, he places the stone in his hand, allowing it to sit in his blood. The young duchess watches this operation with growing apprehension; she doubts the man's grip on sanity.

'Do not be concerned my dear,' Osmand whispers closing his eyes and murmuring a few words she cannot hear under his breath. 'Regard the Egg.'

'Egg?' Iphigenia realises he means the green stone. Reluctantly, she does as she is told and looks at it, with little interest at first as nothing happens. Before long, however, she notices the grand vizier's blood, which has been trickling through his fingers onto the floor, reversing its direction; it starts to ooze upwards, soaking into the stone, as if being sucked into a sponge. She continues to stare in growing revulsion as the red veins that form a network within the stone begin to throb; they thicken and pulsate like throats, gulping the liquid. Osmand keeps his eyes closed, a look of intense concentration across his face, mumbling words in a language she has never heard. Facinorous gives a discontented yowl and flops off the windowsill. He waddles as fast as he can

104

to a low divan and, with effort, squeezes his bulk underneath it.

An odour pervades the room. Iphigenia cannot identify it but, it seems vaguely familiar; it reminds her of freshly dug earth on a damp day mingled with the smell of burnt hair. It makes her feel sick. At the same time, a crackling, buzzing energy charges the air, like the chamber was filled with invisible, whining mosquitoes. Iphigenia feels her hair floating about her head as if she was under water. Osmand's face has become as white as chalk. Beads of sweat trickle down his forehead and his hand, which has a tight grip on the heliotrope egg, is trembling uncontrollably.

Slowly, darkness begins to emanate from the stone. Iphigenia stares at it in disbelief. It engulfs Osmand's hand then radiates outwards into the surrounding air like an oil slick on water. She continues to stare as it grows larger. To start with it is like dense mist or shadow but, soon she realises that it is not a tangible essence at all. Rather, it is a hole, an absence, like someone or something has taken a chunk of air away and not replaced it with anything. As she looks at it, she feels like she is peering into a deep, black cavern.

At first it is formless, shapeless. Then, slowly, it changes, manipulating itself into a form resembling the dark figure of a man. Iphigenia stares in terror at this thing that is there but not there at the same time. The figure looks towards her. It has no visible features save for a muted glow of pulsating red light in the centre of the area where its forehead should be. It has no eyes, yet she can sense that it sees her.

Iphigenia gasps, horrified. 'What, by all the gods, is it!'

Osmand opens his eyes and gives a tired shrug. 'A

servant. Nothing more.'

A deep sigh emanates from the figure, like a hiss of vapour. 'What do you require of me Philodox?' The words are so elusive that Iphigenia cannot be sure if she has heard them with her ears or just sensed them in her head. All the same, the profound power of the voice resonates deep in her chest.

'My name is Lord Osmond at this time.' He appears exhausted. 'Show her the Cardemont princes,' he pants, wiping sweat from his forehead and pointing at the duchess. 'No, on second thoughts just show her one. We do not want to over-indulge her.'

The figure does not respond. Osmand looks furious and raises the egg above his head. 'Heed my command. Do it now. I compel you!'

The figure still does not react immediately, as if resisting. Eventually, it gives a hiss and moves towards Iphigenia enveloping her in its shadowy arms, stifling her startled scream. She is plunged instantly into darkness. She screams again but, no sound escapes her lips or, the sound escapes but, is stifled, even from her own hearing by the blanket of shade that engulfs her. She is cold; the air is damp causing her to shiver. Then, slowly, the intense, black gloom begins to dissipate, transmuting to paler grey. She is able to distinguish a light gleaming in the distance; a small pinprick that is growing bigger. Or is it approaching closer? She is disoriented and cannot tell.

She hears Osmand's voice. 'Proceed towards the light.'

'Where am I?'

'Do as I say Iphigenia. You will remain safe if you do what I tell you. Go towards the light.'

She does as she is told; she approaches the white glow. But, as she gets closer, it becomes unbearably bright, forcing her to shield her eyes with her hands.

'Go into the light.'

'It is so cold. I don't know where I am.'

'The light Iphigenia, go there if you want to see your son.'

She hesitates for another instant, then steps into the brightness. Instantly, she finds herself standing on the boards of a rolling waggon. She recognises it as one of the massive baby waggons that came to Golden Square. Before her sits an old woman, wrapped in oilskins and smoking a pipe through a face covering of thick, brown gauze. *Is she the one that branded my son?*

Anger flares through her and, without thinking, she goes to rip the veil from the woman's face so she can better see the monster who scarred her son but, her hand goes straight through her, as if she was made of nothing but air. She hears Osmand laughing somewhere nearby, although she cannot see him. Then she hears his voice. 'You have entered the realm of the spirits, Your Grace. You are a ghost.'

'I am dead?'

'Yes, but only temporarily.'

'You have killed me?'

'Not at all my dear. I have simply invoked the powers of the world of the dead and gained their permission for you to travel in spirit through their realm. Your earthly body is here in the room with me.'

Iphigenia is not worried at all that she might be dead but, she does have a jolt of concern about her body being left alone and unprotected with the grand vizier. *Spirit? No, a dream surely. Has he drugged me?* The waggon jolts as it passes over a large boulder or some other obstacle. She staggers slightly, managing to her balance, and her thoughts return to her surroundings. She looks about her at the passing countryside, nearby trees rustle and sway in the wind, mountains rear towards the sky far away beyond the acres of fields on either side of her. She feels the rolling movement of the huge wagon beneath her. Although she feels the rain fall on her, she is not wet and the chill wind no longer makes her feel cold. Then, she becomes aware of the crying of the hundreds of babies that surround her in their cages. She savours their unmistakeable smell, sweet milk and soiled nappies. Even the scent of their skin pervades the overwhelming odour hanging in the air of wet hay along with the dung from the team of lumbering buffalo pulling the wagon. *But then… it is all so real…*

Eventually, her attention returns to the old woman who, sheltered from the wet weather by a small canvas sheet tied above her head, is making sucking noises with her toothless mouth as she sits and now chews a wad of tobacco. 'Where are my sons?' Iphigenia attempts to grasp the woman's shoulders but, it is useless, her hands may as well be attempting to clutch smoke. Frustrated, she screams into the air. 'Where are they?!'

She receives no response for some moments. Then she hears Osmand. "One of them is there Iphigenia. Look for him.'

'Why should I believe that these images represent the truth? What if this is an elaborate trick?'

'Because My Lady these are not images. What you see and hear is real because you are there or, at least, your spirit is.'

Iphigenia looks around her again. He is right, it is so vivid and somehow, in her heart she knows that she is there. Really there. *This is no dream. Where is he?*

She spins in a circle, looking, searching; so many little babies are squalling and kicking inside their fleece bags. She wants to hold and comfort them all but, she must find her son. Each time she attempts to unlock a cage to have a closer look, her fingers melt through the bars. Then, she sees Orlando. She recognises her son immediately; his little, round face is peeking through a loose section of canvas that is flapping in the wind. He cries gustily and he is alive! Iphigenia desperately wants to pick him up but, try as she might, she is unable.

She screams in frustration when, without warning, her surroundings vanish abruptly, the darkness returns and, when it clears, she finds herself back in her chamber with Osmand who looks utterly worn out. Facinorous has emerged from under the sofa and is brushing his greasy fur against his master's legs, purring loudly.

'Where is Derron?' Iphigenia demands.

'In another wagon.' Osmand's voice is frail with exhaustion.

'I want to see him too!'

'Another time, not now.'

'I want to see him now!' she demands but is cut short when Osmand slaps her hard across the face. Iphigenia is too shocked to respond. She is conscious of nothing except the sharp stinging on her cheek and raises her hand to feel the tender patch of skin.

'You will see him when, and if, I allow you to and not before.' Osmand's voice is calm and controlled, although

Iphigenia notices a fleeting scowl cross his features. He regains control of his temper quickly and smiles. 'Now my dear, here is the pact. Your husband will be placed under castle arrest as I said but, he will be allowed to live – for now. Both of your sons will be permitted to live and grow-up under the protection of Karesh. They will be safe, and they will live Iphigenia. Did you hear me? They will live. Or, at least, they will do so as long as you do as you are told. I have the power of life and death over all three of them, and over you. Do you understand?'

'Yes, but-'

'Yes, but what?'

'How do I know Derron is still alive? What proof do I have?'

Osmand thinks for a moment, a grim smile stretching his lips. 'Well, you have my word for it.'

Under other circumstances Iphigenia would have been tempted to laugh. 'Your word-'

'Think of it this way my dear. If I had wanted to kill him don't you think I would have done it a long time ago? A secret child with no proof of his existence and no formal paperwork for me to fill-out if he disappeared. No, My Lady, he is much more valuable to me alive, just as his brother is. Because with them both alive, I have complete control over you.' Iphigenia can think of nothing to say. She simply gapes at the man.

'You are mine now Iphigenia and, because you are mine, you will kill neither yourself, because I do not permit it, nor me, obviously.' He stares meaningfully at the bulge below the material at her neck, the small vial of poison. 'In fact, you will remain very much alive. And if I should die under, shall we say, 'mysterious' circumstances, I have left orders for both princes to be killed and your husband to be taken to Karesh and tried for treason. If he should manage to survive the journey, that is. I hope that is clear. You do understand, don't you?'

Iphigenia, still too astonished by all that has happened to argue, closes her eyes. 'Yes,' she whispers.

'Oh, and one other thing,' Osmand taps her cheek to regain her attention, 'just in case you decide not to take my advice seriously, do not forget I will be watching you.' He strokes the heliotrope meaningfully with his thin fingers as he replaces it in his turban, clicking the clasps back into place. 'I can see you when you rest in your chamber, whilst you are dressing or,' he pauses, 'even when you descend that secret staircase to your special, secret room to see your little, so-called, secret baby.' He stops and raises his hand to his mouth. His eyes widen as if shocked at his insensitivity. 'Oh dear! So sorry, I forgot. No more secret baby is there? Just an empty cradle.' His expression hardens and he chuckles. 'I can go wherever I wish. I can watch whomever I please. Don't forget it.'

'The stone!' Iphigenia gasps.

'How perceptive of you. Yes, the Egg. Whenever you think you are alone, just remember that I am probably standing right next to you, watching you, listening to your every word. You will remember that won't you?' Iphigenia does not answer immediately. 'Won't you!' Osmand repeats more forcefully, raising his hand as if to hit her again.

'Yes.'

'Yes, *My Lord* would be a more appropriate response, don't you think. I am now, after all, the one in charge.'

'Yes, My Lord,' Iphigenia hisses through clenched teeth.

She can taste blood in her mouth from where he slapped her before and cut the inside of her cheek against a tooth.

'Very good my dear,' Osmand purrs, patting her on the head like a dog. 'Really a most satisfactory meeting.'

#

On the morning of the second day after the Annual Reckoning, Osmand sits alone in the audience chamber of Castle Cardemont. The rain, at last, has stopped and sunlight pours through tall, stained-glass windows, casting a multitude of colours across the room. He lounges on the ducal throne (now renamed the 'Governor's Throne') and prepares to receive the wearisome line of supplicants that arrive day after day to entreat him for help and advice or ingratiate themselves by offering bribes. All in all, it is a tedious responsibility, he thinks, but unavoidable. He is, after all, both Grand Vizier to the duke as well as Kareshian Governor and the day-to-day duties of running a newly occupied realm will usually get in the way of more important things.

Doing his best to ignore the sound of muffled voices coming from the other side of the doors at the far end of the chamber, he is deep in thought, regarding a statue situated a few feet away. It is a newly commissioned, life-sized marble representation of himself and, in his opinion, not that bad. Facinorous, his cat, is curled-up on a velvet cushion at his feet, sleeping after a heavy breakfast. He is purring and passing wind simultaneously.

With little warning, one of the large double doors opens and a uniformed herald enters to announce the first petitioner. With the door open, the clamour of voices increases dramatically. Osmand rolls his eyes and grimaces. *Sounds like I'll be here a while. No surprise I suppose, after the Reckoning.* He yawns then signals with a bored wave of his long fingers for him to continue.

'The Castle Quotamaster,' the herald bellows in a loud voice, before standing to one side to admit a tall man in matching orange robes and turban. The herald leaves the room, closing the door, once more reducing the hubbub to a muted murmur. The man approaches and kneels before Osmand, shaking violently with nerves. He shades his eyes from the light and attempts to ignore the noxious fumes emanating from the vizier's cat. Osmand ignores him and returns his attention to his statue.

The quotamaster remains quiet for some time before giving a polite cough. 'Your orders G-grand Vizier, I mean L-lord Governor?' he stammers.

'Hmm. What?'

'Your orders, Sir?'

'Orders?'

'About the n-n-ne-dukes?'

'Oh them.' Osmand is annoyed by the interruption but, recognises that he ought to make a decision about the future of the two boys. He says nothing further, keeping his gaze firmly fixed on his statue.

The quotamaster takes the vizier's silence as permission to continue talking. 'They are both safely on their way to K-K-Karesh, Your Eminence. M-messengers report that the two n-ne-dukes are hardy and well and are expected to survive the rest of the j-journey. They eat regularly and the w-wwagonnannies reports that-'

'Yes, yes, yes I know all that,' Osmand interrupts, obviously irritated. 'I've seen them.'

'Seen them?'

'Yes, seen them,' Osmand murmurers, distracted.

'How c-c-could you-?'

Osmand ignores the man's query. Then asks abruptly, 'left or right?'

'Eminence?'

'Left – or - right,' he repeats, enunciating the words slowly, as if explaining something to an idiot. 'Of the wall-hanging?'

The quotamaster still looks confused. 'The statue, you ninnyhammer; which side of the arras? Left – or – right?' He waves his bejewelled fingers languidly in the direction of the sculpture.

'Oh, the st-statue Eminence.' The quotamaster shrugs his shoulders. 'Um, perhaps the r-r-right?'

'The right you say. Hmm, in that case I shall leave it on the left.'

'If you don't m-mind me broaching the subject again, Your Eminence. The n- n-ne-dukes?'

'What? Oh, by the gods what about them? Can't you see I have other things on my mind?'

'Y-yes Eminence but, you asked me to keep you informed. They have b-b-been branded so we can keep a track of them once they arrive in Karesh, but I still do not know what s-special orders you m-might have for them once they are there. I need to t-t-tell the authorities what to do with them.'

'Special orders? I don't have any as it happens. Just put

them through the usual process. They are to have no special treatment. They will end up wherever they end up.'

'But Eminence, excuse me for s-seeming ignorant, I thought we were to k-k-keep a special eye on them.'

'I am k-k-k-k-keeping a special eye on them,' Osmand spits at the man, cruelly imitating his stutter.

'You have employed other s-s-spies Eminence?'

Osmand's eyes half close in a knowing manner and his hand strays subconsciously towards his turban to stroke the heliotrope. 'Hmm, you could say that I suppose.' His eyes open fully again, and he stares at his frightened servant. 'My methods of surveillance are none of your business. As long as I know they are both in Karesh and that they are not causing any trouble that is good enough.'

'Y-yes Eminence.'

Osmand turns his attention back to his statue. 'Good enough for now anyway,' he murmurs.

'Yes Eminence. I can assure you b-b-both ne-dukes D-Derron and Orlando are safely on their way to Karesh in the w-w-wagons.'

'Oh yes, Prince Or-lan-do.' Osmand repeats the young ne-duke's name absent-mindedly. He stretches out the syllables into a long, nasal whine whilst he continues to stare at his statue. 'Orlando's the older one, isn't he? He's not of any significance. I don't suppose I care much what happens to him. If he were to die, I can just tell the duchess that they are both well and she won't know any different. But Derron, the younger one, he's very much a different matter. I have a use for him yet and it definitely suits my purpose to keep him alive. I will be keeping a close eye on him.'

'Y-yes Eminence.'

Osmand turns at the sound of the quota master's voice, as if startled. 'Are you still here?'

'Yes Eminence, of c-course. You have n-n-not dismissed me.'

'Well buzz off then. You're dismissed. I'm busy and you're getting on my nerves.'

'Yes Eminence.' The quotamaster still does not move. He fidgets nervously, rubbing his hands together as though cold. Osmand ignores him, returning his attention to his new statue. The man coughs.

'What is it?' Osmand shouts, turning to him obviously annoyed. 'Why haven't you gone yet?'

'My w-w-wife and children Eminence and my mo-mo-mo-mother-in-law.'

'What about your mo-mo-mo-mother-in law?'

'You have not yet rescinded the order for them to be taken to the fire cage. I have done what you commanded. I have-'

'Oh, is that what you're standing there wittering about? Yes, yes, all right. Give me the document.' Almost crying with relief, the man hands the release paper to Osmand who signs it brusquely then lets it flutter to the floor. 'They are free to go, as are you. Now shove off before I change my mind!'

The quotamaster picks up the paper and makes a low bow, thankful to be leaving. As he turns to go, he notices the grand vizier's cat has woken-up. It has a languorous stretch on its cushion and then sits up slowly, opening its jaws in a wide yawn. As its lips peel back the man cannot help but notice the glint in the bright sunlight of sharp metal teeth and the brutal scars left by stitch-marks to its gums.

'Tell the man on the door to let the next one in,' Osmand shouts after him.

'Y-y-yes Your Eminence.' He hurries away, clutching his valuable paper and breathing a huge sigh of relief.

#

Tazmand knows he is dreaming. He is in a fitful, half-sleep. He wants to wake up fully but, feels like he is stuck in it against his will. *Why can't I just open my eyes?* The throne room, the ugly cat, the nervous quotamaster are gone. He is suspended in water. It is freezing cold and dark. Not warm and comforting like the last time. The currents are strong, he has no control over his direction, and he is losing his ability to keep his head above water. *Am I drowning? Can I die in a dream?* These thoughts are worrisome but, he feels strangely calm. His body is numb from the cold. So cold that he cannot feel his limbs. He is unable to tell if he is moving them or not. *Am I swimming or floating?*

His head sinks beneath the surface. He feels the water creep over his face, the bitter cold squeezing his head like two giant thumbs bursting a pimple. The blood pumping through his temples seems to expand in his veins as if turning to ice. His lungs begin to feel on fire with the effort of holding his breath and total blackness envelops him as he continues to sink. Still he does not feel panic, just resignation.

Just as he thinks he will never reach air again, his face breaks the surface once more. Breath explodes from his lungs and, as he desperately sucks fresh air in, his head goes under once more and his mouth fills with water. No, not water, with something much thicker and stickier, something with a metallic taste that makes him gag. Once more, his head pops above the surface. He coughs up some fluid and takes some proper breaths. The intense cold has gone. He is getting warmer. His muscles relax and some feeling returns to his feet and hands. His senses turn sluggish and his movements lethargic as the gluey liquid envelops him like warm treacle. He is too sleepy now to be concerned or surprised but, at least he can feel his body, and he is able to move his arms and legs enough to keep afloat, allowing the current to guide him. The darkness around him has lifted to a dusky pink and he can see around him a bit. The water has turned a deep red, his surroundings a gloomy mist.

After a while of aimless paddling, a sound drifts towards him over the water; it sounds like someone far away laughing. *That's annoying!* The laughter grows slightly louder, and he can see a small, dark shape in the distance, gradually growing bigger. *Is it someone, or something, swimming?* It gets closer and Tazmand can see, eventually, that it is a small boat. He hears the rhythmic splashing of oars against the water. *Oh, a rowing boat.* He thinks he can see a figure sitting in it and watches it drift closer and closer towards him, until it stops nearby. Tazmand manages to stay afloat by kicking his feet and swimming with his arms but, the liquid is thick, and he feels it cling to him, still trying to suck him down. The effort is wearing him out. The boat is so close that all he can see is its wooden hull. He wonders if someone has come to help him. *Hello.* He tries to speak but, he is not sure if he made any sound. He tries again, *Hello!* A figure leans over the side of the boat and seems to peer down at him. At first, it is just a silhouette with no discernible features, then the mist clears slightly and he recognises the shape of a man in a large turban. He can just about make out a face. A lean face with pale, colourless eyes and a thin line for a mouth. It is the man from his dreams, Osmand. *Help me!* The man does nothing. He is grinning. In fact, he is laughing.

Tazmand's anger flares; he is drowning and this man is making fun of him and not trying to help him to safety! He summons-up his last ounce of strength; he thrashes around in the water or blood or whatever it is and tries in vain to reach up to the grinning, cackling face. This makes the man laugh harder. Tazmand's strength eventually gives out and, at last, exhausted, he gives up and allows his body to go limp. He takes a final, deep breath as warm fluid creeps across his face and blocks his ears so that all he can hear is the thudding of his own heart.

The last thing Tazmand sees through the crimson veil is the man beckoning him with a long, bejewelled finger. He tries to lip read but, can't tell what the man is saying. 'Come' and 'north'? Or at least that's what it looks like. Tazmand continues to hold his breath as he sinks. Another figure joins the man to peer at him over the edge of the boat; a large, round, furry face with a mocking sneer and sharply pointed, metal teeth, the face of the cat. Both faces eventually vanish as Tazmand sinks deeper and deeper. At last, he is forced to let go of his breath. He tries to scream but, blood pours into his mouth and deep into his lungs.

His surroundings turn black.

CHAPTER SIX

Skylark

Tazmand woke suddenly and sat up in a panic. 'I can't breathe!' His cry echoed around the dormitory as he gulped for air. His thin sheet was drenched in sweat. Dream images of drowning in blood flashed in his mind.

'Shut up!' a voice shouted from another part of the dormitory, followed by someone else coughing. 'Some of us are trying to sleep.'

He lay down again and remained still, doing his best to quieten and slow his breathing, hoping he had not disturbed anyone else, particularly the nightwatchman who might come to check on the noise. 'Only a dream, only a dream,' he repeated quietly, as he focused on slowing his rapid heartbeat. It was beating so hard he was amazed the noise of it had not woken up half the dorm.

After a while, he started to feel calmer so tried sitting up but, felt immediately queazy. His head was spinning, so he closed his eyes and remained still, taking several more deep breaths until, eventually, he felt well enough to open his eyes and look around the dormitory. He glanced towards the time candle and saw that only two hour marks had passed since he had come to bed.

'Blimey, it's still the middle of the night,' he muttered to himself. 'Hours yet 'til the work bell goes off.'

He looked around. Weak moonlight pushed through gaps in the filthy skylights, giving a blue-grey glow to the bare stone walls. He saw Dharma, snoring as usual in the next bed and, as far as he could tell, all the other boys now appeared fast asleep. He lay back down, stared up at what he could see of the moon through the dirty window, and tried to remember the details of his dream. Once again, it had been so vivid, as if he were actually there but, the details were fading quickly.

Who were these people and why do they insist on haunting me? I feel sorry for that duchess and those poor babies. But, please stop! I need some rest. Oh, and that creepy mist-ghost or demon or whatever it is, coming out of that egg thing. Weird! Just too weird.

Probably just a result of badly digested food, he reasoned but, all the same, he wished they would go away and haunt someone else. Let him get a decent night's sleep.

Speaking of sleep, Tazmand thought, there was no chance of that now. He was wide awake so decided to not even try. Instead, he lay with his eyes open, looking up towards the skylight and forming the shapes of animals out of the moonlit clouds he could glimpse through the few patches of clear glass. A small cloud passed across the window, looking like a rabbit. Then, as it drifted, it changed shape, stretching into a longer animal which Tazmand thought might be a mink or a mongoose then it changed to an elephant.

He sighed, wondering what these animals might look

like in real life. He had seen pictures in books but, that wasn't the same. The only real creatures he had ever seen were the birds and bats that got into the library through the holes in the roof and the insects and rodents that scurried across the floors and nested behind the books. Oh yes, and now that ugly cat in his dream.

Of course, he wasn't meant to look in the books – that was forbidden. But, they all did it, or most of them did. Sneaky flicks through the pages at break times, ooh'ing and ah'ing at all the pictures of weird and wonderful things and wondering what they were. There were the animals, of course, and also rivers and forests. Having never seen a real tree, Tazmand had to wonder if forests really existed. And as for oceans – vast bodies of water as far as the eye could see, with ships on them. Really? Probably made up, half of it, he thought. But, even so, wouldn't it be amazing to see them if they were real.

Dharma interrupted his reverie by muttering something aloud, then yapping a few times before turning onto his back to start snoring again even louder. He often made noises in his sleep, so Tazmand took no notice and returned to his thoughts of foreign places and things. He sighed as he realised that he would probably never get the chance to see any of them.

Until recently things had been simple. Nothing interesting or weird ever happened. The library was his life. He wanted to become a divine, learn to read and that would be that; he would then be content. Now everything was changing, things all happening at once. His dreams were driving him crazy and making him feel really unsettled and then there was that weird overgrunt Daniel popping up out of nowhere and going on about slaves. And now, what about that temblor? It was all making him feel restless and besides, he could not shake off the feeling that there was something he should be doing. If only he knew what it was?

As he was mulling these thoughts over, he realised that he needed to visit the latrines. He got out of bed quietly, making sure not to wake the others, put on his threadbare dressing gown and regulation cork slippers, and walked quickly and quietly towards the door. He was expecting the usual routine of asking permission from a grumpy nightwatchman to be allowed out but, when he got to the dormitory door, there was no one on duty. He stood still, feeling at a complete loss. This had never happened before and, frankly, he did not know what to do.

All his life, everything at the library had run like a well-oiled shelving ladder; things were ordered and predictable. His stomach did a little dance and his brain went numb. He had been trained never to do anything without permission. Should he call out? No, he would wake the others. Perhaps he should just wait around by the door until the nightwatchman came back. Not an option, not without wetting himself. He was bursting but, if he left the dorm without permission, he could get into serious trouble.

As Tazmand considered his choices, he approached the door and absent-mindedly tried the handle. It turned and the door creaked open, just a crack. It was unlocked! He jumped back, his hand leaping off the metal handle as if it was red-hot. He looked around to see if anybody had seen him or heard the door make a noise. No one had woken up. It was all clear - not a sign of anyone else around. He pushed the door open a little bit more. It creaked again, louder this time but still no one woke.

He peeked into the corridor beyond. Empty.

'Hello,' he called softly. His voice echoed briefly along the stone walls. There was no answer. Tazmand had one last look behind him to make sure no one was awake to see him, then ran down the length of the passage, as far as the latrines. After relieving himself and washing his hands, he returned quickly to the dorm where there was still no sign of the nightwatchman. He was about to go back to bed when the thought struck him that this was a once in a lifetime opportunity: the nightwatchman was missing and Tazmand thought there couldn't be much harm in just having a little look around. If he got caught, he would just have to say he was on his way to the latrines. After all, it wasn't his fault there was no one on duty to give him permission. Or he could pretend to be sleepwalking. *What's the worse that could happen? Actually, let's not go there. The worst could be pretty nasty. Just do it!*

He stopped thinking, turned around and headed back the way he had just been. This time he carried on past the boy's latrines and followed the corridor down as far as the refectory then on to the grunt's entrance to the library. His heart hammered in his chest. It felt strange: he recognised the corridor well, having been up and down it every day for the last seven years but, he had never been here alone or at night. It looked different. Usually the corridor was alive with other grunts and various staff going about their duties. Now it was deadly quiet with just the moonlight filtering through the high windows, reflecting his shadow against the pale stone walls.

He felt exposed. If someone were to come along now there was nowhere to hide and he instinctively kept close to the wall, as if it would provide some sort of protection.

He thought the scuffling of his cork-soled slippers against the hard floor sounded awfully loud and tried to walk more quietly.

Before he knew it, he had continued around a bend into a new section of corridor, one that he had never seen before. He stopped in his tracks and let out a deep breath at the seemingly endless stretch of white wall ahead of him. All of a sudden it occurred to him that he had just crossed the border of his known world. For the entire fourteen years of his life, he had lived and worked exclusively in either the area of the library complex restricted to grunts or in the city nurseries. This was somewhere completely new, and definitely out of bounds.

What was he doing? If he got caught he would be... What would he be? He considered for a moment that he wasn't sure what would happen to him. Sure, he had been punished before with thrashings for minor offences but this...this was really serious, and he didn't actually know what sort of penalty he might get for this level of disobedience. He had heard of other grunts disappearing after committing a serious crime but, he had never questioned what they had done or where they might have gone; he had never dared.

He considered his options. Go back to the dormitory now and go to bed before the nightwatchman returned or, go on down the corridor and see what lurked at its end. More than likely there would be nothing too exciting to find but, on the other hand, would he ever get this chance again? While he was still considering his choices, he found that he was running, as though his body had already chosen for him.

Eventually, he felt puffed, had a stitch in his side and was forced to stop. He crouched down, rested his hands on his legs and tried to catch his breath. Too late to worry about being caught now, he thought. If I go back it will take me so long that the nightwatchman is bound to be back at his desk. He felt frightened yet exhilarated at the same time. *I'm having an adventure!* He started running again and carried on until, just as he thought the corridor would never come to an end, he saw in the moonlight that he was approaching a sharp bend. He came to a halt just before it and leant his back against the wall. His breathing was fast and noisy and he realised that, because he had not seen anyone since leaving the dorm, he had become careless about making noise. He tried to breathe more quietly as he straightened up, ready to move on.

Then he heard a shuffling sound. He froze and held his breath.

It was coming from around the corner. His muscles felt paralysed. His heart felt like it would hammer its way out of his chest. Just as he was beginning to think he had imagined it, he heard the noise again – a rustling, like someone rearranging their clothing or turning over the pages of a book. *By the gods – what if it's another nightwatchman!* Whoever or whatever it was, it was plainly only a couple of feet away, just out of sight. Tazmand did not know what to do. He realised that he could not run back the way he had come. The corridor was too long to reach safety before whoever it was might chase after him. He decided that he would have to brave it, take a look. If it was another nightwatchman well, he would just have to make an excuse and take his chances.

Just as the noise was getting more frenzied it abruptly stopped and there was a moment of complete silence. As quietly as possible, he crept close to the corner, ensuring no part of him was yet visible to anyone on the other side, and prepared himself to run for it. His heartbeat was so loud he was sure that anyone nearby must be able to hear it. Then he heard a tapping, scratching noise that he could not figure out at all. He steeled himself and, half expecting to be met by an angry face, he slowly craned his neck and peered around the bend.

Instead of a nightwatchman with an angry face, what he saw was a metal door. It looked firmly closed and, just in front of it, stood the largest bird he had ever seen. It had its back to him, and its head was jerking up and down as it busily, yet carefully, ran its pointed beak through its slate-grey feathers. Tazmand watched, transfixed by the sleek elegance of this beautiful creature. Once it had finished its grooming, the bird stretched its wings and gave them a gentle flutter, before tucking them back against its body. The span of them was so wide that, when stretched out, each tip could brush the corridor walls.

Slowly, its head turned towards Tazmand and its large, blue-black eyes peered at him, blinking rapidly as if it was having difficulty seeing in the moonlight. It turned its body to face him, its razor-sharp talons shuffling and scratching the floor. The bird had a beautiful pale cream colouring to its chest and underside, with bars of darker grey running across the downy feathers. It was at least two feet tall and the feathers covering its head were black, as if it was wearing a skullcap.

Tazmand moved closer and the bird remained totally still as they stared at each other.

'How did you get here little birdie?' he said at last, his voice sounding overly loud in the silence.

At the word 'little', the bird's eyes narrowed in a look

of disapproval and when Tazmand said 'birdie', they closed completely, certainly in contempt.

Tazmand shook his head to clear it. 'Don't be a pronk,' he reassured himself. 'It couldn't possibly understand what I just said. Must have flown down the corridor from the library rafters.' He squatted down and cautiously reached his hand towards the bird as a sign of friendship. 'Poor thing. Are you lost?'

The bird's eyes flashed in the moonlight as it screeched. Tazmand pulled his hand back quickly, sensing it might perceive him as a threat, and worried that he might get a nasty peck from its beak, or slice from its talons.

'Sorry,' he said automatically, immediately feeling foolish for apologising to a dumb animal. Although the bird did appear to calm down before giving Tazmand a disdainful glare and turning its back on him. It faced the large iron door and tapped at it impatiently with its beak as if, far from being lost, it knew exactly where it wanted to go.

'You want me to open the door?'

The bird tapped on the door again and gave annother irritated shriek. Tazmand was astonished. Were he and the bird communicating? He shook his head again. 'Course not, someone's trained it,' he thought, as he turned his attention back to the door.

It looked firmly shut and too heavy to force. It had a heavy iron ring in its centre, in place of a door-handle. Probably just another corridor on the other side Tazmand thought to himself but, I've come too far now to turn back so soon. He reached out both hands and grasped then turned the iron ring. It twisted easily on an oiled spring. There was a click and the door swung smoothly towards him.

#

The door swung open fully, allowing a gentle night breeze into the corridor, brushing Tazmand's face. His mouth gaped in astonishment as before him, instead of yet another boring corridor, lay a handsome garden. This was nothing like the ramshackle, so called yard the grunts had access to at recreation times, all high walls, razor wire, broken stone, dirty gravel and scrubby grass. This was beautiful. Pale pink, white and yellow blossoms caressed by moonlight clung to the surrounding old walls, peeping through a cloak of dark green foliage, drenching him with the scent of perfumes he had never experienced before.

An ancient vine, heavy with purple fruit draped itself across an ornate, sandstone pergola. White statues glowed in the moonlight; half-naked ladies, some carrying baskets of fruit or water pitchers on their shoulders and men who sported horns on their foreheads and had hairy legs like animals and hooves where their feet should be, struck a variety of static poses. Some played musical instruments whilst others danced. They looked life-like enough to wake up and play with the morning sunshine.

A manicured lawn, studded with tiny white flowers that twinkled in the bright moonlight like stars, played host to a set of gold metal bats and an assortment of colourful wooden balls of varying sizes. They lay abandoned by the players, apparently mid-game around a gurgling fountain that splashed into a marble font. The dark silhouettes of animals in a variety of poses showed that someone had been skilfully shaping the box hedges.

Tazmand felt a rush of air as the bird launched itself from the ground at his feet and lifted high into the night sky, almost brushing his face with the tip of its wing. It flapped once or twice and silently glided away into the distance.

'Don't bother to say thank you or anything,' he called after it, immediately taken aback when he heard a distant screech cut through the air as if in response. He shook his head and muttered. 'No. Couldn't be.'

'No turning back now,' he muttered to himself, stepping into the garden and closing the door behind him. Its beauty was astonishing; he had never seen anything like it and wondered whom it could belong to. He wandered around the flowerbeds, feeling the silkiness of various petals with his fingers and soaking in the scents of the flowers and plants. He remained amongst the flowers for some time before eventually tearing himself away to refresh himself from the fountain.

He had just dipped his hands beneath the surface of the water and had started to drink when he felt a jab at his back, like someone had poked him with a sharp stick.

'Do not turn around. Do not move. Do not make a sound,' a voice said. 'I have the point of a dagger pressed at your back, directly in line with a kidney. This blade is as sharp as a razor and if you attempt to move, I shall kill you. In the unlikely event that I do not manage to slay you outright and only give you an agonising wound, I will shout for the guards and they will kill you. Do you understand?'

Tazmand remained as still as one of the surrounding statues; he did not dare respond. Water dripped from his cupped hands.

'Speak now,' the voice commanded.

'Yes,' Tazmand yelped, his body tensing at the sharp prick of the dagger through the material of his dressing gown.

'Say you understand.'

'I understand.'

'Good. Now, I am going to ask you some questions which you will answer honestly and quickly,' the voice continued. 'Who are you?'

Tazmand's mouth felt parched, even though he had just had a drink. 'I'm Tazmand,' he rasped.

'Your full name,' the voice insisted.

Tazmand was confused. 'That is my full name.'

The voice remained silent for a moment as if assessing his answer. 'Where are you from?'

'The library.'

'How did you get into the garden?'

'Through that door.' Without turning, Tazmand waved his arm in the general direction behind him, 'over there'.

'Liar!' the voice hissed, pushing the sharp point of the dagger into the flesh of his back, just enough to cause him to wince. 'You are an assassin!'

'No please, I'm not lying. I left my dormitory to go to the latrines and the nightwatchman wasn't about, so I decided to try exploring. I ran down the corridors and I met a bird and found that door and it was unlocked and I just walked through and-' He stopped babbling when he ran out of breath. 'I'm really, really sorry. If you just let me go, I promise I'll return to-'

'Shut up,' the voice snapped. It was then quiet for a moment, as though contemplating something. 'Do you know the penalty dealt out to escaped slaves?'

'Really, I am not trying to escape. I just wanted to have a look around.'

The voice was quiet again for a moment then it gave a low chuckle. 'He is no threat, Your Highness. Only a weak little boy,' it said to someone else then continued back to Tazmand. 'Turn around slave and let us look at you properly.'

Tazmand felt the point of the knife leave his back. The muscles of his neck and shoulders relaxed as he turned slowly to see two sumptuously dressed women standing in front of him. One had a black, silk veil obscuring the lower part of her face. Above the veil a pair of bright eyes, surrounded by wrinkles, scrutinised him. On her head she wore an intricately folded headdress made of starched silver and black satin with stones of amethyst woven into it. A few wisps of white hair stuck out from underneath it. She held a long, metal dagger with an ornately carved ebony handle, set with deep-red garnets. The blade glinted in the moonlight and the woman was careful to keep it pointed towards him.

The other had no headwear and Tazmand was shocked to see that she wore no veil. She had on a simple shift of pale blue silk and her long, black hair was tied back with a gold cord. Tazmand thought she looked about the same age as him.

'He's looking at me Nana,' she said.

'Look away slave,' the woman in the black veil hissed, giving him a menacing wave of her dagger.

Tazmand immediately looked down at the ground, his long blonde fringe flopping forward to partly conceal his face.

'Oh, Nana he looks so scared. You must have given him quite a fright with your knife,' the younger one said, laughing.

Tazmand peeked at her through his fringe and could see her dark, brown eyes looking him up and down. 'I think I shall ask father if I can keep him. He can entertain me by standing in the garden in his funny clothes.'

He flushed with embarrassment. He had forgotten he was wearing night clothes and threadbare ones at that. This young woman was so beautiful, and fully dressed, apart from having no veil, which was scandalous.

'As you wish, Highness,' the woman called Nana bowed. 'But, bear in mind that if you ask your father for this, there is no guaranteeing that he will grant it and,' she added, 'it is likely that the boy will be severely punished, probably executed, for leaving his sleeping quarters without authorisation. Let alone for breaking into your private garden.'

'I didn't break-' Tazmand tried to speak.

'Oh, what a complete pain in the pangbat!' exclaimed the girl, exasperated, cutting him off.

'Highness, please!' Nana exclaimed. 'Watch your language.' The old woman's eyes flashed a reproach at the girl who took no notice of her and continued to stare at Tazmand.

'Very well, I shall not get you into trouble,' the girl said to him, completely ignoring the older woman. 'I am in a good mood tonight but, I am bored. Nana is perfectly sweet but, she's as old as the mountains and can't play with me.'

'I'm sure I do my best, Highness.'

'Yes, you do Nana, but your best is not really good enough is it? Now you, Desmond,' she said pointing at Tazmand. 'You are about my age. Do you like games?'

Tazmand had to think for a moment. He continued to stare at the ground as he answered. 'My name is Tazmand not

Desmond. I don't know about games. I've never played any.'

'That could not be more excellent!' the girl shouted, clapping her hands. 'I shall enjoy teaching them all to you. I am an extremely good teacher.'

Nana flashed a warning look at her young mistress. 'Highness, what are you talking about?'

'Oh shut-up Nana. He can come to me every day so we can play. No one need know.' She turned to Tazmand. 'Agree or I shall tell my father and you will get into trouble.'

'I can't come during the day. I have to work in the library.'

The girl thought about it. 'Very well. I'm reasonable. You can come every night. Come at the same time as now. What's your name again?'

'Tazmand. What's yours?'

The old woman let out a shocked gasp. 'How dare you question the daughter of Lord Garesh-Far,' Nana snapped, pointing the knife at Tazmand's face. She turned to the girl. 'I knew I should have just killed him and sent for the guards to clear away the corpse.'

'No one's ever dared ask me anything like that before. Especially anyone as common as you,' said the girl, obviously taken aback. 'You're meant to answer when I question you and do what I tell you. Everyone else does.'

'What's wrong with asking a simple question?' retorted Tazmand, looking up from the ground and acting more bravely than he felt. He could see the girl properly now. Her face was proud, and she did not seem in the least bit shy or frightened. Her large, brown eyes studied his face for some time as if determining whether she liked the look of him or not. Feeling embarrassed, Tazmand blushed and looked away, not able to hold her gaze.

'By the gods,' Nana wailed, 'there he goes again. I shall kill him immediately for his impertinence.'

'Oh, hold on to your petticoats Nana.' The girl said, still looking at Tazmand. 'It doesn't matter. It's quite refreshing really. Besides, I think he might have a point. What is wrong with a simple question?'

'But, Your Highness, that is not the point. Firstly, he is a slave and secondly he has broken into your garden. Thirdly he has spoken directly to you and fourthly, and most scandalously, he has looked upon your face! It is unheard of for a slave to even speak to you let alone look.'

Sky crossed her arms, looking bored. 'I can only pray that there isn't a fifthly. I don't think I could take the strain.'

'By the gods, what if he is an assassin! You must take this more seriously! He must be put to death. You must be protected.'

'Don't you think that's a tad harsh Nana? I've never really understood the reason for that law.'

'It is your father's law. It cannot be altered. You are too important for any commoner to-'

'My name is Skylark,' the young girl said suddenly to Tazmand, cutting Nana off mid-sentence, 'and this is Nana. Well, her real name is the Lady Narine but I call her Nana. You should refer to me as Your Serene Highness really but, seeing as we shall be playing together and that could become tedious, you may call me Sky. I have always wanted to shorten my name to Sky but, no one except my father is allowed to use my first name so I have never had the chance before. You are privileged.'

Nana threw her hands up in the air and turned to address one of the nymph statues. 'What am I to do? She won't listen to an old woman who has looked after her and taught her since she was a baby. I may as well talk to myself or to you-'

'Leave us alone Nana. I want to talk to Edmund.'

'It's Tazma-'.

'Highness, that is impossible. What if he attacks you?'

'Do it now!' Sky shouted and stamped her foot.

Nana bowed her head. 'As you command, Your Highness. But, I shall be standing close by. With my dagger,' she added, pointing it at Tazmand and giving him a meaningful look.

Sky started to walk beside a low row of hedges. 'Come and walk with me... what was it again?'

'What was what?' Tazmand asked.

'Your name.'

'Taz-mand,' Tazmand said again, loudly and carefully enunciating each of the two syllables.

'How do you spell it?'

'Spell it? Um, I don't know.'

'You don't know how to spell your own name? That's funny.'

Tazmand looked down at the ground and did not reply.

'Tazmand,' Sky repeated, rolling the name around in her mouth as if trying to get used to it. 'Tazmand, Tazmand, Tazmand. Yes, I suppose it will do.'

He looked at Sky's face and felt himself blush. He had never seen a girl of Sky's age without a veil before in his entire life. All the other female grunts at the library and at the nurseries were expected to wear veils after the age of ten years old. He noticed that Sky didn't seem to mind him looking at her face one bit.

'It's not the best name I grant you but, at least it sounds nice when I pronounce it,' Sky continued. 'I have a beautiful voice. I shall sing for you if the mood takes me. I might dance at the same time. I can do both extremely well. My father loves to see me dance. Now let's walk. Nana will follow at a discreet distance and-', she interrupted herself to raise her voice and turn to stare at the Lady Narine, 'will mind her own business!' She turned back to Tazmand. 'She means well, even though she's a pain in the pangbat. It is her job to look after me, so you won't attack me will you?'

'No,' Tazmand assured her, as they started to take a tour around the garden.

'I do carry my own knife, just in case you had any ideas.'

'I won't attack you,' he promised.

'Good. I was pretty sure you wouldn't.' She looked into his face for a moment as if trying to decide whether she could really trust him then looked away. 'What are you doing exploring at this time of night anyway?'

'Couldn't sleep.'

'Oh, I completely understand, me neither.' Sky paused to break off a small sprig of jasmine from a bush they were passing and put it to her nose. 'Mind you I don't usually get out of bed until two or three in the afternoon. I find the mornings somewhat tedious and tend not to bother with them. I love the night-time; it is so quiet and everything is so beautiful in the moonlight. So, I am absolutely wide-awake now. Which is more than can be said for Nana. She never seems to have any energy.' She looked back to see the Lady Narine still following them.

'Perhaps she gets up earlier than you,' Tazmand said. 'And she is a lot older.'

'Yes, you're right. I should probably swap her for a younger one,' Sky replied, slightly louder to make sure Nana could hear.

They walked along in silence, admiring the different flowers and shrubs that could be seen in the bright moonlight. Tazmand had to ask the names of all of them and Sky delighted in giving him the answers. Eventually he asked, 'who is Lord Garesh-Far?'

Sky gave him an incredulous look. If she did not have the trained poise of a princess, her jaw would have certainly dropped to the floor in astonishment. 'Tell me you are jesting,' she looked at the boy in disbelief.

'No, I'm not. Why would I be?'

'Who is Lord Garesh-Far?' she repeated. 'He is only the most important man in the world. He owns and rules this entire city and all the lands beyond it for thousands of leagues, probably hundreds of thousands. He is completely all-powerful. He is the Kareshian emperor.'

Tazmand's mouth felt dry. He swallowed nervously.

'The Kareshian emperor?' he repeated.

'Yes. He owns you and all the other people who live and work in Karesh and I am his one and only child, Skylark Garesh-Far.'

Despite being shocked by the news that this girl was the emperor's daughter, Tazmand started to feel irked by her apparently unrelenting arrogance. 'Oh, I see,' he said. 'So, I suppose being the daughter of someone so powerful you have lots of importance and power too.'

By now, they had returned to the fountain. Sky leant over the font and tried to see her face in its still water by moonlight. 'Well of course I do silly.' She placed the jasmine sprig behind her ear and admired her reflection.

'Like what?'

'Well,' she thought about it for a moment. 'Let's see. Everyone has to bow to me when I'm out and about. I get carried everywhere on a palanquin with gold curtains-'

'What's a palanquin?'

Sky allowed a flash of irritation to cross her face at being interrupted and started walking again, signalling Tazmand to follow. 'It's a sort of large bed covered in cushions and supported by poles. I lie on it and get carried around.'

'Oh right.'

'As I was saying, it is covered with gold curtains so people cannot see me, although I can peek out at them. People are not, as Nana pointed out to you a little earlier, allowed to look directly at my face, talk to me, answer me back or ask me questions. I have absolutely everything I want. I only have to command it. I have vast amounts of beautiful clothes and jewellery, lots of lovely things to eat, an army of people to do things for me. I have this glorious garden to play in-'

'You must have lots of friends?' Tazmand interrupted again.

Sky went quiet for a moment as if she had to think about the question. 'I have Nana,' she said eventually.

'But you don't have any friends your own age to play with?'

'Well of course not, I'm much too important for other children to be allowed to play with me.'

139

'It sounds lonely.'

'Lonely? No, I told you, I have Nana. I also have tutors who come in every afternoon to give me lessons. I have servants-'

'I see,' Tazmand said, immediately changing the subject. 'It certainly does sound like you are important.'

Sky drew in a deep, satisfied breath. 'Yes, I am,' she said. 'Very.'

'It doesn't really sound to me like you are powerful though.'

The princess looked astonished. 'Not powerful? How dare you! I can do anything I please!'

'I didn't mean to make you angry.'

'Angry? I'm not angry. Don't be ridiculous,' she snapped. They walked on in silence for some time. 'Go on then,' she said suddenly, 'ask me some questions about how powerful I am.' She had apparently been thinking about it.

'What do you mean?'

'You know. Ask me what sorts of things I can do or order people to do. What I can order them to get me. That sort of thing.'

'Um...I'm not sure what to ask.'

'Oh, for the gods' sake. Um, ask me who has to bow to me. Go on.'

'All right. Who has to bow to you?'

'Everyone! Ha! Well, apart from my father, obviously. Ask me another one. Ask me why I don't have to wear a veil like all the other girls and women in Karesh.'

'Why don't you have to wear a veil like all the other girls and women in Karesh?'

'Because I should not have to make the effort to hide my beauty. It is up to everyone else to avoid looking at my face. If they do look at me, they must be punished. As a matter of fact, you should be put to death for looking at me really but, we won't get hung-up on protocol.'

Tazmand felt his stomach turn over at the thought. 'Thank you.'

'Anyway, you get the idea. Ask me some more questions.'

'All right.' Tazmand had to think about it for a moment. 'Can you leave the palace and go out whenever you want to?'

'Um... ask me another one.'

'Are you allowed to talk to anyone you want?' Sky did not answer again. She was starting to look annoyed.

'I know. Can you choose who you want to play with? Are you allowed to go anywhere you want?' Skylark remained silent so Tazmand thought it might be best to stop asking questions but, couldn't help himself expressing an opinion instead. 'It doesn't sound very powerful to me, not for the things that really count.' Still no response. 'You might be able to buy lots of dresses and make people bow to you but, you can't make them like you or want to be with you. It sounds lonely. I am a slave. I realise that now. It means I am owned and must do what I am told. You are a princess. Your father owns you and you must do what he tells you, regardless of your own wishes. It seems to me that the only difference is you have a much nicer prison than me-'

'And what would you know? A mere slave! What friends do you have?'

'Well, I don't have many. Actually, I only have one. He's my best friend. His name is Dharma. We laugh a lot, even while we are working. We tell each other things and share stuff. We protect each other and get each other out of trouble. I don't know what I'd do without him.'

'Shut up!' Sky suddenly erupted. 'I don't care anyway. You're just a slave. A, a nobody. I'm a princess. I have everything I want. Get out of my garden.'

Tazmand looked at her in amazement. Her beautiful face was twisted in rage and she was shouting, stamping her feet and pulling at her hair in a temper that seemed to have appeared from nowhere.

'Get out! Get out! Get out! Nana throw him out! I never want to see him again. He is common and hurtful and he… he smells of wee!'

'I don't!' Tazmand exclaimed, feeling himself turn bright red again.

Nana moved beside Tazmand. She put her hands on his shoulders and steered him gently back towards the door he had originally come through. Tazmand noticed that she had sheathed her dagger.

'Quick now, before the guards wake up and come through to see what the commotion is all about. Don't worry about her, bor. She gets like this sometimes. She may be a princess but, she's got a temper like a fishwife.'

'Was I rude, Lady Narine? I didn't mean to make her angry.'

Nana sighed and shook her head. 'You weren't rude. Just broke the rules and got a little too close to the truth, that's all. It was a shock to me too actually. But, strangely, I'm glad you turned up tonight. I know you didn't mean any harm. She's highly strung and very spoilt. Most of all though, she's lonely.

Thirteen years old and not one friend but me. Certainly no one else of her own age. It isn't her fault. She also isn't used to people talking to her like you just did. No-one's ever told her the truth about herself, not even me.'

'I'm sorry, Lady Narine.'

The old woman took Tazmand's face in her hands and peered into his eyes. 'There's a look about you, bor. I don't know what it is but, you definitely have a look.'

'What do you mean?'

The Lady Narine thought for a moment. 'I've been watching you with Skylark. I don't really know what it is. There is something about you that says more to me than slave. I pride myself on being able to read faces and yours has a future, bor, a destiny. I think it could be a face I might trust too.'

'I wouldn't hurt her Lady Narine.'

'I believe you, bor.'

'Will I get into trouble?'

'Look,' she said. Her eyes twinkled wickedly above the rim of her veil and she pointed to her dagger, 'safely sheathed now.'

'Lady Narine. Why do you keep calling me bor?'

'Do I? I hadn't noticed. Now isn't that interesting. Well Tazmand, it's an expression we use where I originally come from for boys or young men. It is a term of endearment. Do you mind?'

'No, I like it.'

'Well, that's all right then eh, bor?'

'Stop talking to him. Get him out of my garden! He smells! I hate him! Get him out!' Skylark's voice could be heard behind them, screeching. 'I never want to set eyes on him again. Get him out or I'll call for the guards.'

'You go now Tazmand,' Nana said kindly. 'I'll talk to her. She won't turn you in. She's just angry.'

'And tell him to brush his hair. He looks a state,' Skylark's voice continued.

'I can't help my hair,' Tazmand shouted back. 'I've just got out of bed!'

'Listen, bor. Take no notice. You come back tomorrow night about the same time. She will be calm again by then. She likes you really and I know she wants to see you again. She just can't get over the shock of being spoken to like an ordinary human being. I think you might do her some good.'

'I'll try, Lady Narine. But I think tonight was a one-off. The dormitory nightwatchman will probably be back on duty. He might be there now when I get back.'

'Well, just do what you can. If you can come back again then do. If not...well, what is meant to be will be; our fates, as always, are in the hands of the gods.'

Tazmand walked across the garden back to the doorway. He could hear Sky's voice behind him, ranting and shouting louder now that he was walking away. Just before he reached the door he heard a shrill 'squeak' coming from beyond the walls of the garden. He looked over and detected some movement in a tree. The dark figure of a large bird swooped from the top branch and flew off into the night giving another loud screech. He was not sure why but, he felt certain that the bird had been watching him and it had screeched to attract his attention.

He hurried back along the corridors. As he got closer to his dormitory, he started to feel sick with worry at the almost certain prospect of being caught; the nightwatchman must surely be back on duty by now. It was all well and good going off and having an adventure but, now he would have to face the consequences, whatever they might be. What could he say that would sound convincing? He would have to say that he had been bursting and had gone to the latrines when the nightwatchman was not at his post. He would just have to hope that the man had not been back on duty for long.

He got to the dormitory door and found it open, just as he had left it earlier. There was still no sign of the nightwatchman. A massive flood of relief washed over him. He could not believe his luck as he scurried across the room back to his bed. As he was climbing under the covers, he heard Dharma turn over muttering something softly in his sleep about his arm hurting but, he did not wake up. Tazmand lay on his back thinking about the strange turn of events; the missing nightwatchman, the unusual bird, the pretty but spoilt Skylark Garesh-Far, the beautiful garden and the fierce Lady Narine. Life had certainly started to become more exciting since turning fourteen. Tazmand wondered if it was like that for everyone.

A lot had happened and he felt tired. He yawned and, stretching his arms above his head, thought about his promise to the Lady Narine to try and go back to the garden. He had no idea how, or if, he would ever be able to keep that promise. He certainly would try but, he felt pretty sure he would never be able to make it back there again. A thrilling adventure while it lasted. Something he would always remember. Especially Sky. What a spoilt brat! With these thoughts swirling around in his head, Tazmand fell into an exhausted sleep.

Just before his eyes closed, he thought he saw the silhouette of a large bird glide across the skylight.

CHAPTER SEVEN

Salt

Salt's eyes began to well with tears, his nose was filling with snot and the left side of his face was red and stinging. He had just bent forward to receive a slap from an overgrunt. But, he wasn't going to cry because of that; years of abuse and whippings had left him pretty much immune to physical pain. The reason he was on the verge of blubbing was because he did not like people to be angry with him.

He snuffled and wiped his nose across the short, red hairs on his bare forearm. 'S-sorry, Gruntmeister,' he managed to blurt between sobs. He stood before the overgrunt, his shoulders stooped, a look of crushed resignation on his face. His arms, over-developed from years of lifting and carrying buffalo carcasses from the slaughter rooms to the salt pits, dangled on either side of his short, scarlet tunic. He was exhausted from working a triple shift in the meat vaults, deep in the bowels of Lord Garesh-Far's palace. He had not had a rest for over eighteen hours.

Salt was very tall and the overgrunt, who was very short,

had needed to order the boy to lean forward to receive his slap. Now the boy was standing straight, he had to bend his head back at an uncomfortable angle to peer up at him. He looked Salt up and down and noted his bright red hair, which stuck up in tufts giving him the look of having permanently just got out of bed.

'You look like an orang-utan,' the overgrunt sneered. Salt did not reply. A group of young grunts, glad for a distraction from their work and a sneaky break, gathered around to enjoy the sport. The overgrunt, spurred-on by his spectators, continued. 'You don't know what an orang-utan is, do you?'

Salt shook his head. 'No, Sir.'

'Well, if you ever met your mother, you'd get a good look at one. It would be like looking in a mirror.' The newly arrived grunts laughed hysterically. The overgrunt smiled, enjoying the adulation, then waved them away to get on with their work. He looked up at Salt's face and sighed. 'Why can't you stand up straight, and for the gods' sake stop that blubbing?'

'Yes, Gruntmeister. S-sorry,' Salt stammered, trying to stop crying without much success. His blue-green eyes kept filling with tears and just stung more as he wiped them across the back of his arm.

The overgrunt continued to regard him with disgust. 'Why don't you brush your hair? You look a mess.'

'I did brush it, but it sticks up anyway, all by itself.' Salt heard a snigger behind him. Obviously not all of the others had gone straight back to work as instructed. He did not look around and tried his best to ignore it; he was used to the other grunts making fun of him and he was accustomed to being told off in front of them.

Dozens of fresh grunts started to arrive for a new shift; they glanced at Salt as they passed, smirking, relieved it was him again and not them at the receiving end of the overgrunt's attention. As they began their work, they moved back and forth across the vast expanse of the pits, collecting their cargo of quartered buffalo carcasses, then carrying them to designated areas for burial under mounds of salt, moving like dozens of black ants in long lines. They yelled to each other between pits, sang songs and shouted lewd jokes to each other. This, along with the constant thud of cleavers on wooden chopping boards from the butchers' halls and the intermittent, metallic clunk of the slaughterers' killing hammers could all be heard from further away, down the extensive network of corridors. All of it echoed through the cavernous vaults up into the vaulted ceilings that supported the immense weight of the palace and library buildings above their heads.

The overgrunt needed to shout to be heard. He pointed to the deep carpet of white salt that covered the floor. 'I have told you a million times boy that you must lay the carcasses top-to-toe if you want to make the most of the space in the pit.'

'Yes, Sir.'

'What?'

'Yes, Gruntmeister, Sir,' Salt shouted louder, straining his voice to be heard over the commotion around them.

'Why can't you remember? It is so simple. Top...to... toe.' The overgrunt reached up and poked Salt's massive chest slowly and deliberately with his index finger to emphasise each word. 'Top' – poke – 'to' – poke – 'toe' - poke. 'I tell you again and again and again and nothing sinks into that thick head of yours. Where are your brains? In your pangbat?' He stood on tiptoe and reached up to tap on Salt's forehead with his knuckles. 'Hello. Any brains in there? I know it does not require intelligence to work here but, you really win first prize for being stupid pronk of the year! I swear to the gods these dead buffalo have more intelligence in their rumps than you do in your whole...'

As the overgrunt droned on, Salt let the words flow over him. He stared into the mournful face of the dead animal he had most recently thrown into the pit. The eyes looked back at him, their glassy dullness reflecting the flames from the gigantic fire torches on the cellar walls, giving them an unsettling semblance of life. He had heard it all before a trillion times and he was so used to being shouted at by everyone, not least by the more senior grunts, that he had learnt to let his attention drift and allow the words to melt away to nowhere. He tried so hard to get everything right, do everything he was told. But nothing ever seemed to be good enough. At his age – he had just turned fourteen - he should be well out of the salt pits and learning to be a slaughterer. Nobody else ever stayed as a salter after the age of eleven but, Salt had never progressed far because, as he had been told all his life, he was very, very stupid.

He heard the other grunts starting to sing. They had a song they had made-up about him. It had become so well known that they used it regularly now as a work chant, so he heard it many times every day. It wasn't a poem exactly, just a long, rhyming list of all the names they called him.

Don't get annoyed when you meet Salt,
He might be dim but it ain't his fault,

Just turn to him and sing this ditty,
It's not that great but it ain't half witty!
Brainless, dimwit, dumbo, dimbo,
Goopy, dummy, muttonhead, bimbo.
Bonehead, lamebrain, meathead, lunky,
Gooney, prawn, bozo, flunky.
Knucklehead, pangbat, drongo, pronk,
Gobdaw, dingleberry, dumdum, tonk!

He had heard these terms and many more used about him for as long as he could remember and so, he had come to believe that they were right; he believed what they told him, that he was slow and stupid and useless. But, even though he thought they must be true, the words still hurt and he usually fell asleep at night crying, praying that one day he could be clever enough to become a slaughterer's apprentice. Perhaps, one day he might even be allowed to work with the butchers. But, Salt reckoned, he would have to become very clever for that. So, it was pretty unlikely.

'Are you listening boofhead?' the overgrunt's voice drifted back to him. 'Salt!' the sharp voice snapped out - as did a whip - interrupting Salt's reverie and stinging his arm. 'Stop dreaming you dozy pronk and get that carcass re-buried. I don't want to be here all day. And this time, do it properly. Make sure it is completely covered. We don't want the meat going bad. I'll be back to check on you.'

'Yes, Gruntmeister.' Recognising that he had been dismissed, Salt heaved the enormous buffalo carcass back up from the salt pit and re-positioned it the way he had been told. He then went to the side of the pit, dug both his large, red hands into a wooden barrel and scooped out as much salt as he could hold. He carried it over to the carcass and threw it over the meat to preserve it.

'Better,' said the overgrunt reluctantly, taking a large leather fan from his robes and waving it in front of his face to cool off. 'Now, do that another dozen times or so before you go and get the rest of the carcasses from slaughter room six. There are about thirty to bury before the shift ends. Get a move on!'

'Yes, Sir, Gruntmeister, Sir.' Salt moved off quickly towards the slaughter room, glad to avoid any more reprimands. He kept his eyes firmly fixed on the ground, not wanting to invite any spiteful comments from the other salters either.

The overgrunt went off to have a rest, muttering to himself. 'The gods help me that boy is as thick as the manure of a constipated buffalo.'

#

Nana sat cross-legged on a blanket by the fountain, humming gently and sewing by the soft light cast by a paper lantern. She had taken off her veil and headdress and, as Tazmand entered the garden, he gave a gasp, shocked at seeing her face exposed. She looked up from her work, vaguely startled, then smiled. 'You made it, bor!'

'Hello Lady Narine.' Despite being unsettled by her nakedness he was, nevertheless, interested to see what she looked like: her skin, a beautiful dark brown in colour, was deeply lined with age and her hair was white and braided into a complicated design, close to her scalp. He was surprised, assuming because of her physical agility, that she would be much younger.

Nana put down her sewing. 'I was sure you'd be back.'

'Were you? I wasn't. I didn't think I stood a chance to be honest but, it's really strange, the nightwatchman wasn't on duty again!'

'Ah, you see. I knew the fates were on your side.'

'I went to bed, waited for the time candle to burn down a couple of hour units then got up when I was sure all the others were asleep.' Despite Nana's friendly manner, Tazmand felt uncomfortable and kept his gaze averted from her face, looking around the garden, at the ground. Anywhere, other than directly at her. 'So, I've come back for another visit. I did promise I would try.'

'I'm glad.'

'I might get caught when I go back though.'

Nana patted a space next to her on the blanket. 'Never mind worrying, bor, providence is working in your favour. I'm happy you returned. Here, eat some food.' She indicated an array of bowls and plates laid out on the ground around her.

Tazmand accepted the invitation eagerly, and sat down. 'I wasn't sure if you would still be up. It is very late,' he said, staring at the contents of the dishes in front of him. He did not recognise anything, having spent his life eating little other than bread and bean soup.

'Oh, we are always up late, bor,' Nana sighed, picking up her sewing once more. 'Always up at night; always doing. She can't sleep you see. It's different during the day: she lies in bed all morning, gets up for a bit in the middle of the day to study with her tutors then, when it's too hot and humid in the afternoons, she goes back to bed. She couldn't sleep at night then, even if she wanted to. Mind you, we both prefer the coolness of night-time. Thank the gods I don't need as much sleep as I used to.' Tazmand was not really listening, preferring to stare at the food. Nana gave Tazmand a shrewd look. 'Would you feel more comfortable if I replaced my veil, bor? It must seem strange to you. It's just so nice to not have to bother with it when I don't have to.'

'No!' Tazmand immediately felt embarrassed. 'I mean, please don't feel you have to.' He made an effort to look directly at her, realising that his shyness must have seemed obvious. 'I'll get used to it.'

'Very well.' She handed him a china plate covered in small, pale yellow balls. 'Try one of these, bor. They are lark's eggs poached in saffron broth.'

Tazmand stared at the little objects suspiciously. He moved his nose closer and sniffed. 'They smell sweet.' Nana smiled and urged him to try one. 'They have a touch of honey added'. Tentatively, he placed one in his mouth and his eyes widened in amazement. 'It's delicious!'

'Help yourself, bor, there are plenty.'

Tazmand wasted no time in tasting everything else in front of him: tangy cheeses spread on delicate biscuits flavoured with cashew and basil; delicious fruits straight off the trees in the garden; sticky cakes. Then there were warm things, kept heated on a metal trivet, over candles: hot breads, roasted meats and, best of all, cups of steaming-hot, runny, brown, thick stuff she called shokolade. Its flavour was so sweet and creamy the aroma alone made his mouth water. As he tried each dish, Nana explained what it was and how it was made, although he was only half listening, too busy stuffing his mouth with the food.

Eventually, feeling full and a little bit sick, he started to slow down enough to speak. 'So, Lady Narine.' He looked vaguely around the garden, trying his best to sound offhand. 'Sky not around?'

'Oh, she was here a moment ago,' Nana replied in an overly loud voice, glancing behind her. 'Must be off sulking somewhere. Doesn't want to talk to you it would seem, after your little tiff.' She leaned closer to whisper, 'she's over there,' she pointed her thumb over her shoulder, 'hiding behind the summerhouse watching us. She will come out when it suits her.'

Feeling full and drowsy, Tazmand leant back on the lawn. With nothing to do but relax and digest his food, he nibbled the remains of a cake with one hand. His other hand started to pull blades of grass out of the lawn and twist them around his fingers. Nana continued with her sewing.

'What's on your mind, bor?' she said at last, narrowing her eyes to try and make out her work in the soft light of the lantern.

'Nothing.'

She looked at him, her keen eyes studying his troubled face. 'You have the look of a norther,' she said at last.

'A *norther* Lady Narine? What do you mean?'

'Call me Nana, bor. A norther. I mean you look like someone who comes from the northlands. Pale skin, light hair, blue eyes. Or are they green?' She gave him a closer look. 'Yes, they're green, I think. Tricky to tell in this light.'

'What a strange thing to say Lady Narine – I mean Nana.

I'm from Karesh.'

'Karesh?'. She chuckled. 'Oh no, bor, definitely not.'

'What?'

'You are not from Karesh.'

'Not from Karesh?' He sat up. 'What do you mean? Of course I am. I was sent to the library from the city nurseries.'

'Oh, I don't doubt that. But, what about before the nurseries?'

'Before?'

'How did you arrive at the nurseries? What about your parents? Your mother and father?'

Tazmand looked confused. 'Parents, Nana? What about them?'

Nana put down her sewing and looked at Tazmand kindly. 'What do you know of them?'

'My parents?' he had to collect his thoughts. No one had ever asked about his parents before. 'They gave me to the city nurseries when I was a baby. I don't know much about them.' He shrugged. 'I suppose they were too poor to keep me, so they gave me away to be raised by the city.'

'Is that what you were told by the nursery staff?'

'Yes. Well, sort of. They never told me much, just that they handed me over at the nursery door. I just sort of worked the rest out myself.'

'They lied.' Nana smiled and returned to her sewing.

His eyes widened in disbelief. 'What?'

'They lied, bor. You'll be off one of the wagons.'

Tazmand felt his brain spinning. 'Nana hold on a minute. I'm not with you. What are you talking about, *norther, wagons*? I don't understand. I'm from here. I was given to the nurseries by poor but patriotic Kareshians who wanted me to have the privilege of working in the library.'

Nana looked up briefly from her sewing. 'Oh no, bor,' she said, 'you would have been brought to Karesh as a baby from one of the northern countries conquered by Karesh. Your parents will have given you to the soldiers to bring back here. Or when I say *given*, they might have been encouraged to give you up or, I'm afraid to say, even forced to hand you over.'

Tazmand was dumbfounded. 'You mean I don't come from Karesh?'

'That's right.'

'And my parents come from the north. I come from the north?'

'I'd bet my best silk veil on it.' Nana concentrated on her work again. 'I really must get this mended by tomorrow.'

Tazmand remained silent for what seemed like minutes. His brain was spinning, and he did not know what to make of it all. Was this woman mad? Did she know what she was talking about? Was she just making it up for sport? Could he trust her? After all, he hardly knew her.

'How do you know all this?' he asked at last.

'It's no great secret, bor' everyone knows. Well, I say *everyone*, but I suppose you never got to hear about it because you've obviously never been taught. I know more than a lot of others I suppose because many years ago now, I used to work on the wagons. Infants would be put in large wagons to be brought back to Karesh. My job was to look after them. You know, feed and change them, make sure they were all right. Basically, keep them alive until we got back here.'

Tazmand was dumbstruck. Waggons, babies being

taken. It seemed as if Nanna had seen his dreams. Images came flooding into his head in sharp relief. Images of crying infants being wrested from the arms of screaming parents. Soldiers, rain, blood screaming, fire cages. It could not be possible.

He was about to say something when Sky's voice broke in on the conversation. 'What are you talking about Nana? Are you saying we steal other people's babies?' She had left her place of concealment behind the summerhouse and had obviously been listening. 'It's a lie. Karesh would never do that. My father would never allow it.' She sat down giving Tazmand a cursory glance as if only just noticing he was there. 'Oh, hello. You're back then?'

Tazmand stared at the ground, a half-eaten cake forgotten in his hand and did not reply.

Sky leant close to his ear and shouted. 'I said, Helloooo!'

Tazmand jumped. 'Oh, it's you.'

'Nice to see you too,' she muttered, obviously not at all happy by the lukewarm response.

'I wondered when you might come and join us,' Nana said. 'Not *steal,* your Highness. No, of course not. Karesh doesn't need to steal them. The babies are owed to Karesh as part of the annual duty and taxes the conquered countries must pay. It's all perfectly legal and above board, according to Kareshian law. If you agree with that sort of thing, that is,' she added, after a short pause.

'Oh,' the princess said relaxing, 'that's all right then.'

'Hold on a minute!' Tazmand jumped up, suddenly angry. Images from his dreams still swimming in his head. 'What do you mean 'that's all right then'? Of course it's not all right. You can't just go around taking people's babies away from them and besides, why do the other countries owe duty to Karesh?'

'Because Karesh owns them,' Nana replied simply.

'How can Karesh own other countries? I mean I know there are other countries that are a part of Karesh but, how can it own countries that belong to other people?'

Nana let out a long sigh and stopped sewing. 'Calm yourself, bor and I will tell you.' She waited for Tazmand to sit down. 'Because it wins them in battle. It is the natural way of things. Karesh goes to war with other nations, the nations go to war with Karesh. Those nations invariably lose and Karesh wins their lands and possessions. They then have to pay duty to Karesh, and part of that duty is a quota of infants.'

'It is right that they should pay duty to us,' Sky interrupted. 'And in return Karesh offers them civilisation, peace, education and prosperity. They are all savages before Karesh steps in and teaches them how to behave. Don't you know anything?'

'Well, you didn't know everything either, Highness. You didn't know about the babies and the wagons,' Nana said.

Sky stared into the air in front of her, looking bored. 'So? I'm sure it will be covered in one of my future lessons.'

'But, babies...' Tazmand said, trailing off before finishing his sentence.

'But, babies what?' Sky asked.

'Paying duty is one thing but, live babies taken away from their families. That's awful. Nana says I'm one of those babies. I was probably taken away from my parents when I was little.'

Sky smirked. 'They probably gave *you* up willingly.'

'They wouldn't have done that!' Tazmand snapped.

'There's no need to get defensive. Just joking. How do you know anyway?'

'I just know. I just have a feeling that they loved me and would not have given me away unless they had to.'

Sky raised her eyebrows and rolled her eyes towards Nana. Tazmand looked as though he was going to say more, then thought better of it. Nana put her sewing down, held up her arms and unfastened a row of small pearl buttons on her sleeves, exposing her wrists. Tazmand and Sky stopped bickering and turned to see what she was doing. Tazmand let out a gasp. 'Wristbands!'

Encasing each of Nana's wrists was a shiny, black, metal band.

'You seem surprised, bor.'

'I thought being called 'Lady' that you were important.'

'I am important. Important enough anyway. I am a high servant. There are only a few of us with black wristbands. Perhaps a handful in the entire city. Only a high servant could hold the post of governess to Lord Garesh-Far's daughter.'

'You're like me. You're a slave,' Tazmand said in a shocked whisper.

'A high servant,' Nana corrected him. 'I came myself as a baby on the wagons many years ago, when Lord Garesh-Far's grandfather was still on the throne. I was raised in the nurseries and then worked in several roles as a slave. I have learnt since that I am from one of the eastern countries that was civilised by Karesh a long time ago.'

Tazmand turned to Sky. 'Did you know this?'

Sky took a bite out of a sweet pastry, gave it a look of

disgust and threw the remainder of it back on the plate. She picked up another and did the same thing again. 'Far too much almond paste! Nana, tell the cooks.'

'Sky!' Tazmand snapped.

'What? Yes, of course silly. Well, I knew she was promoted from a slave to a high servant. I didn't know about her being a baby or the eastern things. Well you know what I mean. I suppose I had never really thought about where she might be from originally. Like you, I just thought we were all Kareshian. What's the problem anyway? You look upset.'

'I'm not upset. It's just that...'

'Just that what?'

'It's just that I have been learning so much over the last few days and everything is so different to how I thought it was.'

Sky tried a different type of cake, made a face and threw it back on the plate. 'Really, like what?'

'I can't explain it properly. One minute I was just getting on with my job in the library, working hard for promotion and looking forward to eventually learning to read and then the next thing I know...' Tazmand stopped and stared at the ground.

'Go on,' Nana urged.

'Well...suddenly I'm having strange dreams-'

'Dreams?' Nana looked interested. 'Dreams about what?'

Tazmand shook his head. 'Doesn't matter. I've met both of you and come to this garden. I meet weird overgrunts that tell me all about slaves and how people outside Karesh aren't really savages at all and suddenly my whole world is upside down. Now I find out that I might have parents. I mean proper parents, perhaps a whole family and they come from outside

Karesh.'

'You are better off without them,' Sky said, pouring herself some shokolade and sounding matter of fact. 'Savages I should think. At least here your life has some purpose.'

Tazmand sighed. 'You might be right. All the same, I can't help wondering...'

'Go on, bor, what do you wonder?' Nana prompted him.

'I wonder if they are still alive?'

Nana shrugged. 'It is possible of course. You are still young, so it stands to reason that they won't be old.'

'I wonder who they are and what they are like?'

'Savages I should think,' Sky said again, making a face and tipping her shokolade out on the grass. 'Not enough sugar. Really Nana, you must tell the cooks to-'

The peace in the garden was shattered suddenly by a shrill screech. All three of them looked up to see a shape fly overhead, low enough for them to make out the outline of a large bird.

'That falcon again,' Nana murmured, peering up into the moonlit sky.

'I think that's the bird that was behind the door the other night. The one in the corridor,' Tazmand said.

'How on earth can you tell?' Sky asked.

'I don't know. Well, I can't actually tell but, he just sounds like the same one.'

'You can tell the difference between bird calls now can you?' Sky gave a snort. 'You've only just had your first introduction to botany and cuisine. Now you're an expert on wildlife too?'

'I think he might be right, Highness,' Nana interrupted.

162

'It is unusual for them to hunt at night, while it's still dark. They like to hunt at daybreak and dusk or during the day. It's unlikely there would be more than one around well before dawn. And, just as a matter of interest Tazmand, it's a *she*.'

'What Nana?'

'You referred to the bird as a *he* but, I believe it is a female. She is large, and the females are always bigger than their tercels, their mates.'

'What's a falcon Nana?' Tazmand asked.

'It's a bird of prey, bor. They like to live high up in cliffs, although we also have them living in the city. They nest up at the top of high buildings and swoop down to hunt on other, smaller birds while they are flying. This one is a Peregrine falcon. The most beautiful variety in my opinion.'

The bird flew over their heads again. This time, it flew so low, they could all see its cream and black striped underbelly reflected in the light of the lantern. It wheeled around in the air and came back to swoop so close above them, they could have touched it. It screeched loudly, its shrill voice piercing the soft night air.

'What on earth is wrong with her? She sounds agitated. It's as if she wants to tell us someth-' Nana started to say, when she was suddenly interrupted by another sound. This time it was a man's voice coming from the entrance to the garden.

'Skylark! Skylark where are you?'

Nana and Sky looked at each other then turned to stare at Tazmand, panic in their faces.

'My father!' Sky hissed.

The deep voice rumbled again from the shadows. 'Skylark, where are you? I need to speak with you,'

'Quick, bor,' Nana hissed. 'Roll into that flowerbed. There, under the big rhododendron. Fast, he is coming. If he finds you here, we will all get into serious trouble. Hurry yourself!'

Tazmand had just managed to scurry underneath the bush when he heard the man's voice draw near. Luckily the garden was reasonably dark, as passing clouds now obscured some of the light from the moon. The branches and the heavy flowers of the bush now concealed him from sight. Peeking through the foliage, he could see the man's face reflected in the light of the lantern.

Lord Garesh-Far addressed his daughter. 'Ah, there you are. Well done. What on earth are you doing up at this time of night? I thought you would be abed.' Sky and Nana both stood up. Nana quickly replaced her veil and headdress. She knelt, lowering her forehead to touch the ground in front of the emperor. Sky curtsied, keeping her legs bent and her eyes lowered to the ground until he put his hand under her chin as a signal for her to stand upright and look at him. 'Are my eyes playing tricks on me? I thought, as I approached, that I could see three of you sitting here?'

'No father, just me and Nana doing some sewing and studying a little astronomy. Hence our keeping such a late hour.'

'Astronomy eh? I had no idea that you held an interest in the stars, and the Lady Narine is teaching you, is she? Well done.'

'We teach each other father. It is purely a distraction. Neither of us knows a great deal. We just like to look at them.'

Lord Garesh-Far's eyes scanned the garden suspiciously.

'You are sure no one else has been here tonight?'

'Of course not father. Who else could there possibly be? My tutors only come during the daytime.'

He continued to look around for a moment. 'No one I suppose,' he agreed at last. 'Well done.'

Tazmand considered the man's voice; it was deep, controlled and monotone, although commanding none the less, clearly used to issuing orders and not having them questioned. He risked moving a branch slightly to get a better view through the gaps in the rhododendron bush. The emperor was a tall man, certainly well over six-foot and broad across the shoulders. Muscular, trim and fit, he wore a tight-fitting military riding jacket of red velvet with gold and black braid stitched into an intricate pattern across the chest and down the sleeves. Knee-length leather boots, as shiny and black as the beetles that scuttled around in the library gleamed in the dim light.

Power radiated from Lord Garesh-Far; it was palpable, like heat glowing from an open fire. But, the most striking thing about him was his face. From what Tazmand could make out in the muted light, his skin was extraordinarily pale and completely smooth, as if it had been stretched too tightly over the bones. It had none of the usual lines that a face should have, not even around the eyes and it showed no variation in expression as he spoke. It was a face that was impossible to read, expressionless, giving no hint of either emotion or feeling. One feature alone stood out, a livid scar, appearing deep and angry and purple against his white skin in the dim, silver moonlight. It ran from just under his left ear, across his cheek to the edge of his mouth, twisting the side of his lips into a permanent sneer.

This was the lord of the entire Kareshian Empire, the most powerful man in the world and here he was in this little garden, only a few feet away from one of his lowest-ranking slaves. A slave that he would have killed instantly if he found him hiding in the bushes and think no more about it than crushing an insect under his boot.

Tazmand dared not move. He lay on his stomach and tried not to breathe too loudly. Pinpricks of sweat oozed from his skin and he could feel moisture seeping up from the damp earth beneath him. Both started to soak through his pyjamas and dressing gown. It made him shiver slightly. He had never been so frightened. After a while, his attention was distracted as he started to feel an urge to sneeze, and he held his breath in a desperate attempt to control the impulse. *Not now*, he thought. *Really, not now!*

'Let us talk a moment.' Lord Garesh-Far guided Sky by her elbow to a marble bench. 'Well done,' he said for no apparent reason as they sat down. 'I have some important news and I am glad that the Lady Narine is here with you to hear it, because she will need to help you prepare.'

Sky absent-mindedly waved her hand in Nana's direction. 'You may get up.' Being momentarily intent on her father and his news, she had forgotten about her servant bowing low. A visit from him was a rare occurrence, so he must have something important on his mind, especially coming at this time in the early morning. 'Prepare what father?'

Lord Garesh-Far's mouth stretched sideways into what was meant to be a kindly, paternal smile but, as it was joined to his scar, looked more like a ghastly leer. 'To prepare for your wedding.'

'My wed-. My wedding?' Sky could not keep the shock out of her voice.

Just at that moment Tazmand felt his entire body tense. He pressed his face into the ground then, unable to control it any longer, he sneezed violently without warning into the soft earth, producing a muffled yet unmistakeable mini explosion. His body lurched with the strain, causing the rhododendron bush to shake.

'What was that?' Lord Garesh-Far arose from the bench and looked at the bush.

'Just a small animal rustling about I should think father,' Sky said, trying to keep the panic out of her voice and staring hard at Nana.

'A fox or a badger perhaps, your Imperial Highness?' Nana offered. "We get many here at night.'

'You think?' the emperor muttered.

Sky held her father's arm and pulled at it gently so he would sit again then tried to distract him by continuing to show interest in the proposed wedding. 'So, father, who is my fiancé to be?'

'What? Your fiancé? He's a young nobleman from one of our colonies.' Lord Garesh-Far's attention was still diverted by the disturbance in the bushes. 'A small animal you both think? Yes, I am sure you must be right.'

'Would you like me to investigate Sire?' Nana asked.

'No, Lady Narine. Remain as you are. I believe I shall look myself. I would like to see what sort of a creature it is.'

'Father this is hardly the time for minor distractions. Allow my servant to have a look. I have been told I am to be married. It is momentous news, and I would like to discuss it some more with you.'

'In a moment Sky. I will look for the animal first. You never know, it might be dangerous. It could be a poisonous snake.'

As the emperor approached the rhododendron bush, Tazmand could see the pale, soulless face looming closer, peering into the foliage. Lord Garesh-Far's hand started to pull back a branch for a better view so Tazmand shrank as far back into the undergrowth as possible. He could see Sky peering from behind her father; her face as pale as his, where the blood had drained away with alarm. Nana stood next to her, looking on helplessly. Suddenly, there was a loud splattering noise as a stream of warm, sticky liquid fell on top of the bush. Lord Garesh-Far jumped back immediately, and Tazmand felt the warm fluid drip off the dark green leaves and pink flowers onto the back of his head and trickle slowly down either side of his neck.

'Father! Sky exclaimed, raising her hand to her mouth in astonishment. 'Are you all right?'

Lord Garesh-Far stood back from the bush and examining his clothing. 'It missed me,' he replied without a hint of feeling, looking up into the night sky where the silhouette of a large bird glided silently across the backdrop of the moon. He looked at the rhododendron bush. The near side was covered in a cascade of white bird excrement, which glowed, luminous in the dim moonlight. 'What sort of bird is that? A falcon? What is it doing out at this time of night?'

Neither Sky nor Nana commented. They did not have an answer. Tazmand lay quiet in the undergrowth, his heart banging against the inside of his ribcage so strongly, he was sure it would burst out. He felt the gluey substance trickling through his hair and behind his ears.

'If there was an animal father,' Sky said at last. 'I am sure it will have run off by now.'

Lord Garesh-Far regarded the bush for a few more moments then, again, checked his clothes and boots. Satisfied he had not been hit, he sat once more next to his daughter. 'Yes, indeed,' he said, looking up into the night sky. 'Strange, a falcon out at night-time. Ah well. Back to the business at hand. Well done.'

'I am to be married?'

'You are to be officially engaged, in readiness for marriage. You are thirteen and therefore of age. It is time and you will be performing a great service to the Empire and for your father. You look pale my dear. Not enough sleep perhaps?'

'But, father, I do not know him.'

Tazmand noticed that Sky addressed her father formally, not daring to show him any impertinence or discourtesy. Hardly the arrogant young woman he had started to get to know.

'Of course you do not Skylark, he lives in a far-off land. How could you know him?'

'But, who is he? What is his rank? What is he like?'

'His rank is sufficient and he is of good character. This is a diplomatic matter that has been arranged for many years. I owe his father much and-'

'You misunderstand me father. I do not want to get married. I am not ready. I do not know this man and-'

'Enough Skylark. You waste my time and yours.' Lord

Garesh-Far continued to look at his daughter. His face did not change expression when he interrupted her. 'You are to be engaged and then married. You must prepare your things, ready to leave.'

'Leave!' Sky screeched, her temper and arrogance starting to surface.

'Of course. You will go to his home to be engaged and live there – according to the custom of that land - until the wedding. In two years, when you are fifteen, you will be his wife.'

'But, this is my home. I-'

'You will be silent,' Lord Garesh-Far replied. The words came out of his mouth quietly but, none the less, unmistakably threatening. 'These are the wishes of your father. The wishes of your emperor. You will do as you are told.'

Sky said nothing more. She swallowed hard managing, just, to keep her temper under control. She knew better than to dare argue.

'If my mother were alive, I'm sure she would not make me go and live with savages.'

'Do not be petulant Skylark. You know nothing of your mother. If she were alive, she would do as I bid her, as you will.'

'I know nothing of her because you will tell me nothing. Won't you tell me about her, please father?'

'Lady Narine, I leave this up to you.' Lord Garesh-Far stood, talking to the high servant but, still staring at his daughter, ignoring her plea about her mother. 'Have her highness packed and ready in four weeks. Is that clear?'

Nana bowed low. "Your Majesty. It will be as you command.'

'One month Skylark. Do not defy me over this.'

Sky remained silent.

'I require an answer.'

'Yes father.'

'Yes what?'

Sky swallowed again and forced the words reluctantly out of her mouth. 'Yes father, I shall be ready for departure to my engagement in one month.'

Lord Garesh-Far surveyed the garden, saying nothing and glancing briefly once more at the rhododendron bush. He straightened his jacket. 'Well done,' he said, turning to leave. 'Charming garden Sky.'

'Thank you, father.'

'As a present for your engagement you may take it with you. I shall arrange to have it dug-up and packed for transportation.'

'Thank you, father. Father?'

'Yes.' Lord Garesh-Far turned back to his daughter, his skin gleaming like a white plaster mask in the moonlight.

'May I at least ask where I am going? Where he lives? How far away from Karesh city will I be? How far from you?'

He was silent for some time as he considered his reply. 'No, Skylark. No, you may not ask. It is a matter of political alliance and it is my wish for you to marry.'

'But, father I-'

Lord Garesh-Far raised his hand. 'That is all you need to know. What does it matter who he is or where you are going? You will be well looked after and will have the same rank and privileges that you enjoy here.'

'It is just that I want to prepare myself properly,' Sky said, gritting her teeth.

Her father ignored the remark. 'Packed in four weeks. And fewer of these late nights. You are getting dark patches under your eyes. You should look fresh for your intended husband.' He turned to Nana. 'Lady Narine?'

Nana bowed her head. 'Yes, your Majesty?'

'See to it that she goes to bed early in future. No more of this star gazing.'

'Yes, your Majesty.'

'Well done. Carry on.' Lord Garesh-Far walked away briskly.

Tazmand waited for a few moments to make absolutely sure the emperor had left the garden, before scrambling out of his hiding place. His thick, blond hair, shoulders and back were sticky with bird excrement; his face was covered in damp earth. He looked up into the sky but, there was no sign of the falcon.

'I could start taking this personally,' he muttered, wondering how he would get it off his dressing gown and pyjamas before having to explain it to the laundry grunt who collected dirty clothes from the dormitory.

Sky had sunk into Nana's arms, burying her face into the older woman's chest to be comforted. 'One month Nana. One month and then I leave one prison to replace it with another. One master for another. One nightmare for another. Tazmand is right. I am nothing more than a slave.'

'I know my sweet. I know. I will be with you. I will look after you. Never fear. We will go there together, wherever it is.'

Tazmand was about to say something but, Nana's dark eyes signalled him to stay quiet and leave. She lifted her veil and smiled at him, mouthing that he should come back tomorrow. He nodded to her and left the garden quietly, leaving behind the sound of Sky sobbing.

#

The following day, Tazmand sat in the refectory trying to eat his lunch and waited for Dharma who had been dragged away by Sash to do an extra shift. As he dipped his bread into the tasteless, watery soup, he could hardly bring himself to touch it, thinking about the delicious treats that Nana had let him try on his visit to the garden the previous night. Most of all, he remembered the hot, sweet shokolade. Its flavour was so delicious it made his mouth water just thinking about it.

He had been lucky not to get caught on his return to the dormitory. Once again, and strangely, the nightwatchman was nowhere to be seen so he had taken the opportunity to go to the latrines to wash himself and his night clothes before falling into bed, then into a deep sleep. He had woken up exhausted, if somewhat damp, to start work after what felt like only a few minutes.

'Hello Taz.' Dharma arrived carrying his food to the table. He sat down heavily and breathed an enormous sigh.

'How did it go?'

Dharma looked depressed and on the verge of tears. 'I won't cry Taz. I don't care what he does. I won't give him the satisfaction of letting him see me blub.'

'What on earth is the matter?'

Dharma did not answer immediately. He took a handkerchief out of his pocket and blew his nose loudly, looking around the refectory to make sure none of the other grunts or overgrunts had witnessed him being upset. 'It's Sash.'

'Go on.'

'He's getting worse.'

'Dar, what has happened? Tell me.' Tazmand was concerned for his friend and worried that something serious had occurred.

Dharma put his arm under the table so only Tazmand could see it and pulled up his sleeve. Tazmand looked down and saw several red whip marks. Some of them were still bleeding and they all looked sore.

'By the gods!'

'What can I do? There's no one to complain to. He can do what he likes. Well I know I could complain, although it's a waste of time, who would listen to me? I don't even know why he's being like this to me.'

'I do,' Tazmand said. 'It's my fault. He's bullying you because you're my friend and he knows it will make me angrier than if he did it to me.'

'That's not all,' Dharma continued, pulling his sleeve down. 'I've been promoted. As of next week I am to be a shelver.'

'Oh,' was all Tazmand could think of to say. He knew that promotion was the last thing Dharma wanted as he was convinced that being a shelver was too dangerous and that he would be killed if he had to work up a ladder. 'Promotion arranged by Sash no doubt.'

Dharma nodded. 'What am I going to do? Either Sash will kill me or I'll die on the ladders.'

'Listen to me Dar. Don't give up. I will think of something.'

'But, what can you do?

Tazmand put his arm round his friend's shoulders to comfort him. 'I don't know yet. But, I promise you I will think of something. All right?'

Dharma did not look convinced.

'All right?' Tazmand repeated more forcefully.

Dharma took a deep breath and attempted a half-hearted smile at his best friend. 'All right Taz. I trust you.'

Dharma ate his lunch in silence and with little enthusiasm. Tazmand, having by now completely lost his appetite, sat and looked aimlessly around at the hundred or so other 'slaves' (as he now referred to them), coming and going through the refectory. Then his attention was caught by an older-looking overgrunt with a long, dirty-grey beard, waving at him from the other side of the room.

'Daniel!' Tazmand shouted out loud. Because of the high level of noise and activity in the refectory, nobody seemed to hear him except Dharma. Daniel was facing in Tazmand's direction and giving him a thumbs-up sign.

'Daniel? That old overgrunt from the other day? The weird one? Where?' Dharma said, looking up.

'He's right over th-' Tazmand pointed to where he had seen him but, the old man had gone. He looked around and could not find him anywhere. 'He's disappeared.'

Dharma snorted. 'Just as well. That man was trouble. Forget about him and his crazy ideas.'

'I suppose you're right,' Tazmand replied but, he could not forget about Daniel's 'crazy' ideas, especially the one about freedom. He also could not now forget about Nana and what she had told him about his northern roots and the fact that he might have a real family still alive somewhere outside Karesh. These were things that he now had permanently on his mind: he thought about little else and felt frustrated because he could do absolutely nothing about it.

CHAPTER EIGHT

Slaughterhouses

T azmand was visiting Sky and Nana in the garden every night now. He would wait until late, ensuring Dharma and the other grunts were sound asleep, before creeping out of the dormitory. He was puzzled by the fact that the nightwatchman was never now on duty but, had grown used to it and still ensured he took care not to make any noise and stay alert just in case he turned-up. He also placed a pillow under his blanket before leaving, just in case anyone should check. It did not look that convincing close-up but, at least his bed did not look obviously empty from a distance, and it should pass a cursory inspection, especially in the night-time gloom.

Sky had not seemed in the mood for talking recently; Tazmand realised she must be feeling depressed at the prospect of leaving her home and going away to get engaged. She still appeared to expect, and quietly welcome, his visits even though they were often spent in silence, playing games that required little or no conversation. Sometimes Sky would give him a reading lesson. He was showing promise and coming along quickly. He saw little of Nana, who was busy indoors organising the packing of the princess' enormous collection of clothes, hats, shoes, jewellery and toiletries.

Other items which Sky had also decided to take included her own bed with several dozen sets of silk sheets and fifteen different goose-down stuffed quilts; enough crockery, glassware and gold cutlery to seat a hundred people for dinner; two hundred and fifty rolls of assorted fabrics; her favourite crystal chandelier for her new boudoir (which took three men to carry) along with dozens of her more cherished paintings; several hundred dozen pots of spices, pickles, condiments, sauces and cooking oils ('just in case they didn't have them' wherever she was going); her personal fencing and riding equipment and other items of sports kit. Also, she had commissioned new statues to go in her garden (which was due to be packed for transportation - as her father had promised). The list was still growing.

On his way to the garden each night, Tazmand had started taking detours and was getting to know the layout of some of the rest of the library and palace complex. He had discovered large storerooms heaped with thousands of books yet to be brought into the central chamber of the library for shelving. He crept past dormitories with sleeping grunts, in neat rows like planted seedlings. Latrines, kitchens, bathhouses, infirmaries, food stores, pantries, a dairy, common rooms, uniform closets and workshops all opened up a whole new world of interest and fascination to him. To his relief, he rarely came across guards, probably because they were not considered necessary. What intruder would be mad enough to enter the emperor's palace complex? He remained vigilant just the same, and had become adept at avoiding the few that were around when necessary.

Apart from the rooms currently in use, in older parts of the building he discovered many that were not: vast, grey rooms where white cobwebs fluttered gently in breezes that blew through broken skylights and draped the ceilings and walls like ripped and tattered sheets. These rooms appeared to be long unused and deserted. Cockroaches clicked and scuttled across the broken, marble floors whilst rats nested in holes gnawed out of the horsehair padding of the furniture.

As Tazmand spent more time each night discovering further areas of the building, he had time to think. Slowly it dawned on him that there was a reason why he went exploring. It was because, even though he had not yet truly admitted it to himself, he was thinking more and more about escaping and finding his family. He no longer believed, as Sky suggested, that they were savages, after all as Daniel had said, how could savages write books?

He felt himself getting angry and was not sure why. Then he realised, like someone had just lit a blazing bonfire in his brain, he wanted to punish Karesh. If it was true that he had been taken from his mother and father and put to work as a slave in the library, then he wanted Karesh to be taught a lesson that it could never forget. Karesh must be stopped. No more babies stolen and an end to slavery. He had no idea how he would do it, he was a slave, he was powerless, he was nothing. But, even as he thought these things about himself and knew them to be true, a small seed of certainty and knowledge was starting to grow deep inside him; a small seed of courage that told him he must at least try.

He started to focus his mind on escape, wandering the rooms and corridors of the library and palace, looking for a way out. Night after night he looked and with each night that passed, his escape seemed less likely. All of the windows were too high; even if he were to get up and through one of the broken ones, there would be no safe way down to ground level outside. All the doors he had come across were made of heavy, black iron and most were locked. Any he had found open and had gone through just led to more rooms or corridors. A couple had led him outside but, only to high-walled courtyards. Escape seemed impossible.

One area that Tazmand had so far avoided was the long corridor that ran past the kitchens. It was the one place in the building he had noticed where grunts stayed up all night working so, there was a higher danger of him being discovered. But, if there was a possibility of finding a way out, he reasoned, then he must take the risk.

The next night, he left the dormitory as usual. Realising that he would look odd in pyjamas if he did meet anyone, he went into the latrines and changed into his day clothes before heading straight towards the kitchen quarter.

The first part of the journey proceeded without incident: he got as far as the huge kitchens and managed to slip past the doors unobserved. The grunts working there were too busy to take much notice but he didn't dare enter their noisy domain in case he was questioned. Instead, he stuck to the main corridor and continued along it to investigate where it might lead. It soon dawned on him that he was going downhill as the floor began to slope sharply and the walls were getting higher.

As he descended further, the corridor became lighter; there were no windows to let in moonlight but, fire torches had been placed in wall brackets at regular intervals. Tazmand realised that if torches were being maintained, then he was likely to bump into people but, he had come too far to stop now so, reckless as it might be, he kept going determined to see where the corridor might lead.

He was past the kitchens and just skirting a bend when he came face-to-face with three young grunts, a girl and two boys, coming up the slope from the opposite direction. Tazmand knew meeting people had always been a likely possibility but, it still gave him a shock and he stopped and froze in front of them, not knowing what to do next.

Despite their youth - they could not have been more than nine or ten years old - each looked physically strong beyond their years and this was just as well Tazmand thought, because each of them had an extremely large quarter of animal carcass slung over their shoulder.

'Evening,' one of the boys said. All three of them stopped and stood still, taking the opportunity to take a rest. They blinked in the brightness of the torches, as if not used to the light.

'Hello,' Tazmand replied. His voice sounded hoarse and squeaky, not having spoken for some time. His mouth felt dry and he tried to summon some saliva, as he coughed to clear his throat. Noticing their red wristbands, he placed his hands behind his back ensuring his own gold ones were out of sight.'Actually, it's morning really. Early morning.'

'Is it?' The boy looked vaguely surprised. 'That's the trouble with working down in the salt pits. Never know what time of day it is. *Morning* then.'

'From the kitchens?' the girl asked.

'Er no, not exactly, Tazmand replied. The three grunts stared at him blankly.

'Where from then?' the second boy asked.

'From the.... from the department of meat research,' Tazmand said, cringing inwardly at the ridiculous sound of his own lie. *Why didn't I have a story ready?* 'I am doing a project on...on...on,' he glanced at the carcasses over their shoulders. 'On meat and...and how to best, erm...to cook it.'

'Oh righty-ho,' the second boy said.

Tazmand looked incredulous. 'You have heard of the department of meat research?'

'No.' The grunt shook his head. 'I just saw your posh golden bands and knew you weren't from down the pits, so reckoned you must be some sort of fancy kitchen bloke.' The other two grunts muttered in agreement. 'Anyway, must be off. These buffalo won't get up the hill to the kitchens by themselves eh? End of our shift now. Deliver these and then off to bed. Can't wait. Tata.'

'Tata, I mean goodbye,' Tazmand replied cheerily as the three of them went on their way. He let out a sigh of relief; surprised that they had not appeared suspicious.

He carried on down the slope until, eventually, he reached a banister rail at the top of a stone spiral staircase. Cautiously, he leant over the rail and peered down, expecting to see a face, or faces, staring back up at him. Thankfully, there was no one around that he could see. The steps were lit by torches and he could see they were well worn in the middle from what must have been years of usage, so he started to make his way down.

He walked and walked, round and round until he started to become dizzy and his legs ached. He had no idea how deep he had gone and, as he continued on his journey, he considered the three grunts he had met and realised he needed to think up a better cover story. He did not feel confident that anyone else he met would be as gullible as them. But, before he had time to come up with anything half-decent, the steps ended and he emerged into a cave-like vault.

Tazmand stood still for a moment, giving himself time to get his breath back and for his head to stop spinning, then looked around and was amazed by what he saw. He was surrounded by dozens of square pits, each at least thirty strides square full of what looked like snow. No, obviously not snow he realised, salt. Hundreds of tons of pure, white salt. The walls were immensely high and supported by vast, arched beams that towered above him supporting a massive stone roof.

He looked more closely into the nearer pits and, by the light of the flaming wall torches, he made out the darker outlines of hundreds of animal carcasses. He assumed they must be piled there for storage.

'Who are you?' a deep voice said from behind him.

Tazmand spun around in alarm. Standing there was a giant of a boy with spiky red hair and an open, friendly face covered in freckles. Amazingly, he had an entire buffalo carcass slung across his shoulders. His scarlet tunic was covered in slime and gore.

Tazmand was too surprised by his appearance to answer immediately but, the boy waited patiently. 'My name is

Tazmand,' he managed to say at last, his voice rasping through a dry throat.

'Hello Tazmand.'

'Friends call me Taz,' he continued, coughing to loosen up his vocal cords and holding out his hand for the boy to shake it. 'What's your name?'

'Salt,' the boy said. 'Like the white stuff in the pits. I've never had any friends so I had better call you Tazmand.' Salt looked baffled at the hand being offered to him as if he did not know what to do with it. He suddenly let out a gasp of amazement. 'Your wristbands,' he shouted. 'They are golden!'

'Yes they're gold,' Tazmand said, considering his lie about the meat research and deciding, as he did not have a better story anyway, to take a chance and tell Salt the truth. 'I work in the library.'

'Library,' Salt repeated out loud. 'What's that?'

'The library? It's where we store all the books.'

'Oh!' Salt said nodding knowledgeably, then remaining silent for a moment, as if thinking. 'What's that then?'

'What's what?'

'Books.'

'What are books?'

'Yes.'

'Everyone knows what books are.'

The tall, ginger boy looked sad. 'I don't.'

'Oh. Really? All right then. They are. Um. Well it's difficult to say. I've never been asked that, never had to describe one before.' Tazmand stopped to think for a moment. 'Well, they are bits of paper all attached together with writing on them. If you can read the writing then you get to know what information they have in them and they-'

'Gosh you must be important,' Salt interrupted, seeming to lose interest in Tazmand's description and staring at his wristbands. 'I've never seen golden ones before.'

'Golden? Oh my wristbands. I'm not important. I'm just a grunt like you.'

'Really?' Salt seemed astounded by this piece of information.

'Yes of course. They are just a different colour, that's all.'

'Oh.' Both boys stood silently for a moment, shuffling their feet.

Tazmand broke the silence eventually. 'So, how did you get a name like 'Salt'?'

'Dunno. Sometimes people use my name but, most of the time I just get called 'pangbat', 'pronk' or 'dumbo'.'

'That's a bit rotten.'

'Yes it is but I'm used to it,' he said, tears forming in his eyes.

'You look upset.'

'Do I? Yes I think I am but, I don't always notice because I'm used to that too. I'm a bit stupid you see and a bit slow and I have got to load all of these buffalo carcasses into the salt pits before morning and I don't think I'm going to get it all done and then I'll get punished. Everyone else has already finished and gone to bed but, they didn't have as many to do as me.'

'I know the feeling. We get punished in the library too.'

'Do you sometimes get hit over the head with a large dead animal?'

'Erm no, I can't say that's ever happened. I get whipped though.'

'Oh. Me too.'

'Don't you have any other name?' Tazmand asked. 'Salt just seems lazy, like no one ever bothered to give you a proper one.'

'No, that is the only name I've got. I was never given any other one,' Salt replied, tears welling-up in his eyes again.

'Well Salt is a perfectly decent name.'

Hearing this, the tall boy's face immediately brightened. 'You think so?'

'Yes, of course.' Tazmand replied, deciding he would change the subject. 'Would you like some help?'

'What?'

'Some help, with the carcasses?'

'Help?'

'Yes. Would you like me to help you so you don't get punished?'

'What's 'help'? I don't know what it means.'

'You don't know much do you.'

'No. I don't.'

'It means that you have got all this work to do so would you like me to do some of it too? Together we can get it done much faster. Then you won't get into trouble.'

Salt stared at Tazmand. He looked as amazed as if he had just told him he had two pangbats. Then, he burst into tears, sobbing loudly.

'Salt be quiet. Someone will hear and you'll get us into trouble.'

'No one has ever' – sob – 'wanted' – sob – 'help me' - sob – 'before.'

'Well I'd be glad to but, you must stop crying.'

'You are so nice,' Salt wailed, wiping his snotty nose on his bare arm.

'Please stop crying. If we get caught we will be in trouble.'

Eventually, Salt stopped crying and his face lit-up into a big smile. Without warning, he dropped the carcass he had been carrying, put both his arms around Tazmand's neck and gave him a tight hug. Tazmand did not want to cause offence but, he was aware that Salt had just wiped his nose on his arm, and stank badly of animal guts and blood.

'I've got a friend!' Salt yelled, still holding on tightly to Tazmand, squeezing him hard.

'Yeah,' Tazmand wheezed. 'A friend who now has a snotty neck and clothes that smell of rancid buffalo. Salt, you can let go now. I can't breath. Salt, let go. Get off!'

'Sorry.' Salt took his arms away immediately and starting to sob again.

'Don't cry again, please. I am not angry with you. I just couldn't breathe properly because you were hugging too tight.'

Salt brightened again straight away. 'Really? You're not angry?'

'No. Not at all. Of course not.'

He gave a big smile. 'All right then. Let's get to work.'

Tazmand had never been so exhausted in all his life. Carrying piles of books was heavy but, carrying dead meat carcasses was nearly impossible. He could not manage to get a whole one or even a half one over his shoulder but, by getting a firm grip of hooves, he was able to drag a few quarter carcasses to the side of the pit for Salt to then throw them in and bury them. Tazmand managed to move seven carcass pieces and

Salt did all the rest. The boy's strength was phenomenal: he was able to lift entire carcasses, fling them over his shoulder and then carry them to the pits by himself.

Tazmand was just about using up his last ounce of strength on dragging his seventh part carcass to the side of the pit, when he noticed that it looked an odd colour and did not smell like the others. He mentioned this to his new friend who bent down, stuck his nose right into the chest cavity of the dead animal and inhaled deeply and noisily.

'Uh oh, bad meat,' he said out loud to himself. He straightened-up and lifting the carcass up to his nose, he took another deep breath to confirm his first conclusion. 'Stinks a bit, this one. Bad meat can't eat,' he chanted slinging it over his shoulder and skipping across the salt pit. 'Come with me my friend Tazmand,' he called behind him. 'Bad meat, can't eat.'

Tazmand did as he was asked and followed the big skipping ginger boy out of the salt pits and into another large vaulted room lined with steel butcher's tables. Each table was covered with a collection of knives, cleavers, saws and other cruel-looking metal instruments of every conceivable size and shape. They gleamed in the torch light, all scrupulously clean and mercilessly sharp.

Salt carried the carcass, carefully negotiating the tables with their skinning, carving and sawing implements, to the far end of the room where he stopped at the far wall, by a metal door. Tazmand, who had followed closely behind, peered around Salt as he opened the door to reveal an empty cupboard, into which he dumped the carcass. It landed on the small floor with a squelching thud, then he closed the door, turning a lever to lock it shut with a click.

He put his finger to his mouth and cocked his ear towards the door as a signal to Tazmand that he should be quiet and listen, which he did. There was a moment's silence then, they heard a slight thump and rattle at the other side of the door followed by a soft rumbling noise, like pieces of oiled metal rubbing against each other under thick-padded leather. Salt then opened the door to reveal that the carcass had disappeared. He beamed at Tazmand as though he had just performed a majik trick. Tazmand could still hear the soft rumbling.

'Where has it gone?'

'Bad meat can't eat,' Salt replied laughing.

'Yes you've already said that but, where has it gone?'

'Outside. Up the chute, outside. Gone away with all the other rubbish.'

Tazmand looked at Salt for a moment. 'You mean it has gone outside the building?'

Salt scratched his head. 'Dunno. Gone to the rubbish. Savages eat it.'

'Savages? But, don't savages live outside the city.'

'Oh yeah. Outside the city then I suppose.' Salt turned and started to walk back to the salt pits. 'Come on. More buffalo to finish moving.'

Tazmand went back to have another look at the cupboard. He opened the door and saw that the interior appeared sturdy enough: a ceiling, a back wall and two side walls, with the door itself forming the fourth, all of which he gave a thump with his fist, hearing a reassuringly solid thud from each. When he closed the door, there was a moment's silence and then the faint sound of something sliding and then a humming, whirring sound before the rumbling started. He opened the door again quickly just in time to see the rear wall of the little room sliding back into place.

Salt's voice was calling from the afar end of the chamber. 'Come on my friend Tazmand. Lots to do.'

'Coming!' Tazmand felt the kernel of an idea start to germinate in his head.

#

Later that night, Tazmand was once again in the garden with Sky. He was preoccupied, his thoughts elsewhere. He had helped Salt move the remaining carcasses then left him in the slaughterhouse vaults, beaming with delight after receiving a solemn promise from his new, and only, friend to return soon for another visit. Tazmand had then made his way straight to see the princess.

Sky was getting bored. 'You're quiet tonight Tazmand. You look exhausted.' They both sat on the lawn drinking shokolade. Nana was indoors, still organising her young mistress's ever-growing list of things to pack.

'Hmm? Oh yes, I'm just thinking about things.'

'Anything in particular?'

'No.'

'Oh,' the princess paused for a moment. 'I wondered perhaps if you were thinking about me having to go away to get engaged?'

'Hmm?' Tazmand murmured, not really listening.

'I thought perhaps you were thinking about the fact that you would never see me again and were going to miss me.'

'No.'

'What!'

Sky's outburst made Tazmand jump. 'I mean yes, I have been thinking about it. Of course I have but, I just wasn't thinking about it at that precise moment.'

'I seriously can't believe you! I am going away to the gods knows where to marry the gods knows who. My entire life is being turned upside-down, on its head. I haven't slept for days. I have a constant headache from worry, which, I might add is doing my looks absolutely no favours. We will never see each other again – not that that's such a great loss to me actually,' she added, giving him a sideways, angry glance, 'and you don't even seem to care!' Tazmand remained quiet while Sky pulled-up tufts of grass with both of her hands and threw them at him. 'You can be such a pronk! I hate you and won't miss you one bit,' she said.

'I'm going too,' Tazmand said quietly, looking directly at her, bits of grass stuck in his hair.

'What? Going where?

'Leaving.'

'I'm not with you.'

'I'm leaving too.'

'Have you been transferred? Where to?' Sky's temper was momentarily calmed as she was distracted by this piece of news.

'No I haven't been transferred,' Tazmand said, pausing for a moment and then continuing. 'I am going to find my parents.'

Sky stared at him, her eyes wide with disbelief. He had never seen her look so lost for words. 'What? How?'

Tazmand hesitated for a moment. He shrugged his shoulders, not wanting to tell Sky that he might have found a way out. 'I don't know yet.'

'You don't know yet?' the young princess immediately burst into peals of laughter. In fact she laughed so much that she had to lie on her back, tears running down her face. It was the first time in ages that Tazmand had seen her look even vaguely amused. Now she looked on the verge of hysterics. 'Oh, I think I'm going to wet myself that's so funny.'

Tazmand remained stony-faced. 'I don't think it's so funny.' He wished he had not said anything about it.

'Of course it is,' Sky said, still chuckling.

'Why exactly?'

'Well, let me see.' She sat up. 'You, a slave,' she said, 'and a mere boy,' she added, looking him up and down, 'are going to escape from a fortress-like building, built to house an emperor and his priceless library. Built to keep intruders out and people in. And, not only that, you are going to escape from Karesh itself to cross vast terrains of burning-hot desert, impenetrable forests and high mountains that even the Kareshian army finds difficult to negotiate, to go and find some parents you know absolutely nothing about and who are most probably not even still alive.'

'Yes.'

Sky looked at him for a few moments. He was looking hurt and sullen. Her laughter died away and she calmed down. 'Tazmand, you are mad. You are wasting your time. There is absolutely no way out.'

'Yes there is.'

A flash of irritability shot across Sky's face. 'No there is not!'

'I said yes there is. There is a way out. I've found one.'

Sky looked briefly interested then made a huffing sound. 'Liar.'

'I'm not a liar!'

'So what have you found then? A way out of the city?'

'Well no, actually I'm not sure. It might be a way out of Karesh but, I'm pretty sure I have found a way out of the palace. At least I think it might be.'

Sky stared at Tazmand as if he was raving. 'I don't believe you. You are just showing off.' She let out a big sigh and looked at the ground. 'Face it Tazmand, there is no way out.' Then added, 'for either of us.'

'I have found a way out I said and I don't care if you believe me.'

Sky studied Tazmand's face. 'You're really not joking are you?'

He could have kicked himself for telling. 'No, I'm really not joking.'

There was a long, tense pause until Sky, eventually, broke the silence. 'Take me with you.'

'What?' Tazmand was truly surprised. He had not reckoned on this. 'Wha-?'

'Take me with you. We can escape together.' There was an edge of urgency to her voice, of desperation.

'Hold on Sky, you're right. I was just showing off.' Tazmand panicked. He was losing his confidence and backtracking. 'It's only an idea actually. I'm not sure if it really is a way out. I don't know if it will work. If we do get outside the library or even outside the palace or the city, I have no idea what is out there.'

'I don't care. I'm coming with you. I would rather die by the hands of savages in the desert than be sent off to marry some ghastly prince I have never met.'

'Stop being so dramatic. Anyway I'm not sure I am brave enough. All I have ever known is the library. I don't know what is out there. I don't know if I will be able to look after you.'

'Look after me?!' Sky looked furious. 'Don't be ridiculous. I can look after myself, and you for that matter.'

'But-' Sky put her finger to Tazmand's lips to silence him. She looked serious, her petulance and anger gone. Tazmand thought she looked older and suddenly tired.

'No 'buts' Taz. This is our only chance for freedom. We must do it or die trying. I know I am spoilt but, I have grown up a lot recently. Since meeting you I mean. I have learnt – from you and from Nana - about Karesh about slavery and about,' she paused for a moment and then continued, 'about my father, the emperor.'

'But-'

'Tazmand, we must go. I am as much a slave as you. You have taught me that. I must do what my father says, just as you and the hundreds of thousands of other people in this city must. I am no different. Tazmand, I cannot stay.'

'Sky, I-'

'Please don't say 'no'. This is difficult for me to admit but, well, you are really the only friend I have ever had. The only person I have ever been able to really talk to anyway. I mean about anything important.'

Tazmand looked nonplussed. 'Really?'

Sky nodded. 'And - I am sorry to do this - but, either take

194

me with you or I will tell my father what you are planning and you will be arrested and executed.'

Tazmand stared at the princess with undisguised shock. He had been starting to warm to her unusual frankness and affection but, realised that he really should have known better.

'It is your choice,' Sky continued. Tazmand peered closely at her to see if she was joking. The look on her face indicated that she was not. 'I know you want to go Tazmand. I know you've got it in you to do it,' she said, encouraging him. 'And I really, really do not want to get you into trouble, let alone executed but what else can I do?'

Tazmand was quiet for a long time. Then at last, he gave his answer. 'Looks like we are both going then,' he said, feeling stunned, partly by Sky's ruthlessness and partly at his sudden decision.

Sky's face lit up with an enormous smile. 'Yeeeees!' she shouted. 'Yes, yes, yes, yes, yes!'

The noise brought Nana out of the building. 'Highness, please, you must be quiet. The guards will hear and come to investigate.'

Sky ignored her servant. She put her finger to her lips and said quietly, 'our secret Tazmand. We have two weeks left to prepare. Two weeks until I am meant to leave for my engagement. Must be gone before then.'

Tazmand buried his face in his hands. 'By the gods. What have I got myself into? What have I agreed to?' He was brought to his senses by a sudden cry of fear from Sky.

'Who are you?' she shrieked, her eyes wide with alarm, looking over Tazmand's shoulder. 'Nana!' She screamed. 'Nana!'

Nana rushed immediately to where Sky was pointing, wielding her dagger dangerously. She had a wild gleam in her eyes.

'No. I'm a friend of Tazmand's. Honestly I mean no harm!' a familiar voice wailed.

'Dharma?' Tazmand was amazed as he took his face out of his hands and turned to see his old friend lying on his back a few yards away on the lawn. Nana was sitting on his chest, her dagger positioned at his throat.

'Who are you? Nana shouted at him. 'Answer me or I will slit your throat like a squealing pig.

Tazmand ran towards them. Dharma was indeed squealing with fear. 'Nana. No, he is my friend. Don't hurt him please. He means no harm.' Tazmand looked down at Dharma's round face peeping up at him from between Nana's knees. 'What, by all the gods?'

'Hello Taz. Please don't let her kill me. Hello,' he said again, looking at Sky who had run after Tazmand and was standing next to him.

'Hello,' she said back, no longer frightened.

'Nana,' Tazmand entreated. 'It is all right. I promise. He is my friend. He won't hurt Skylark.'

'You vouch for him, bor?' Nana said, a dubious look in her eyes, as she scrutinised the young man on the floor.

'With my life Nana.'

'Very well then,' she said, getting up and re-sheathing her dagger. 'But, I will be watching you my chunky little friend,' she continued, looking directly at Dharma. 'Don't try any of your tricks.'

'Dharma. What on earth are you doing here?' Tazmand

asked.

'I'm not chunky,' Dharma muttered, looking at Nana through narrowed eyes.

'Dharma?' Tazmand repeated, firmly.

'Hello Taz. Oh, I think that old woman has put my back out.' He raised his voice on the word 'old', just loudly enough for Nana to hear him as she went back into the building to continue with the packing.

'Dharma?' Tazmand insisted, getting annoyed.

'Well I could ask you the same question 'Mister I sneak out of bed at all hours and go wandering off around the place without bothering to tell my best friend.'

'Oh I see. Look, I know I should have told you but, I didn't want you to get into trouble. How long have you known?'

'A few days. At first I thought you were just going to the latrines but, then you didn't come back for ages and ages, and then you started putting your pillow under your blanket in what I can only describe as a miserably improbable attempt to fool anyone checking the dorm. So, the night before last I waited to see how long you were away and then I got up and found the nightwatchman missing – strange that don't you think? I wonder where he's been going? Anyway, you were away for hours. It explains why you have been looking so peaky and tired during the day. So, last night I was prepared. I stayed awake but, pretended to be asleep to see if you would go off again. When you did I decided to follow you. I trailed behind you all over the place, quite wore myself out. Eventually you came here to this garden and I hid in the bushes and watched you with this girl.'

'Hello, I am Skylark Garesh-Far.'

'Oh, how do you do Miss. My name is Dharma.'

'I have heard of you Dharma. Tazmand says you are his best friend.'

'Really?' Dharma raised his eyebrows, looking pleased. 'Anyway, tonight I thought by the gods I'm not wandering half way around the library and wearing myself out. I decided to come straight here and wait for you. You have been ages.'

'Where have you been waiting?' Skylark asked.

'Over there in those bushes. It was very damp and I am sure my lumbago is coming on as a result.'

'Dharma you should not be here,' Tazmand said.

'Neither should you.'

'Well, I suppose that's true but-'

'No buts Taz. I want to come too.

'What?!'

'You heard. I've been listening and I want to come too. I am not staying here without you and besides which Sash has been getting more and more unpleasant with his whip. I can't take the bullying and I won't last a week when I get promoted to a shelver. You know I won't. I have to escape Taz. I absolutely have to.' Dharma's voice was now pleading.

Tazmand let his body slump down so he was kneeling on the grass. He looked bewildered and at a loss about what to do next.

'Look,' he said at last to his friends. 'I do want to leave. I want to go and find my parents, my family and... and I have some other reasons for going too. And yes, I have found a possible way out of this building and I stress it is only *possible*. But, I don't know if it will work. I don't even have a proper plan. It will be dangerous; in fact the whole idea is lunacy.

It is almost certainly doomed to failure and anyone trying it will probably end-up being killed – if not by Kareshian soldiers then by the savages outside the city walls. Going by myself is a stupid enough idea but, with three of us...I am not willing to let either of you take that risk.'

'Not willing to let me?' Sky said. She looked furious. 'How dare you. I will be the one to decide what risks I take.'

'Me too,' said Dharma, looking less confident than Sky.

'And besides which,' Sky added, 'you have already agreed to take me. You made a promise.'

'I can't stay here Taz,' Dharma whined. 'Sash is going to get me killed. It is only a matter of time.'

'Do you really want to try this by yourself Tazmand?' Sky asked, calming down.

'I don't really want to try it at all. By myself or otherwise.'

She sat next to Tazmand on the grass and took his hand in hers, looking around to make sure Nana had not come back to eavesdrop. 'Listen, let's be reasonable. I do not want to go and get married. Dharma doesn't want to be bullied or promoted and you want to find your family. If you think about it, what sort of life do you have – do any of us have - here anyway? This could be our only chance to get away. Let's take the risk. Let's do it.'

She looked deep into his eyes, willing him to have the strength to make the right decision. Tazmand glanced at Dharma, who nodded his agreement, then stared at the ground still thinking and let out a deep sigh.

'All right then,' he said at last. 'Let's do it.' He sounded anything but convinced.

'Yes!' Sky shrieked evidently relieved, purposefully

ignoring Tazmand's reluctance and sounding more than a little triumphant. She let go of Tazmand's hand. 'It's agreed; we are all going. We'll meet here tomorrow night to plan it all out. Oh and Tazmand, one other thing.' He looked at her to show he was listening. 'Please have a wash before then and put on some clean clothes. I don't know what you've been doing today but, you look and smell disgusting!'

CHAPTER NINE

Plans

The following night, Sky, Tazmand and Dharma held an escape meeting in the princess's garden. Tazmand and Dharma had left the dormitory together. As had become usual the nightwatchman was not on duty and they had crept out, Tazmand with his usual stealth, Dharma less so, bumping into beds and grumbling too loudly about bruising his shin. Tazmand was forced to shush him several time but, surprisingly, nobody woke up and, luckily, they met no-one during their journey to the garden.

They sat cross-legged on a blanket spread across the damp grass. Dew glistened on the lawn, a carpet of miniature diamonds glinting in the thin moonlight of early morning. Dharma, ignored by the others, warned of the dangers associated with sitting on damp grass and complained about the likelihood of developing a chill.

'So let me get this right,' Sky said. 'The three of us have to get from here,' she indicated the garden, 'past the kitchens, deep down to the palace vaults where, apparently, there are large salt pits full of meat. Then, we all cram ourselves into a tiny metal cupboard with a false floor-'

'Uh, wall is what I think you'll find Taz actually said,' Dharma corrected her. 'It was a wall.'

The princess closed her eyes momentarily then flashed Dharma an irritated look. 'Wall then. And this wall will open and we will be carried by a moving conveyance – with a load of rotting, stinking meat and offal – to the gods know where; it might be outside the palace or, it might be outside Karesh city. In which case, we will most certainly be attacked by savages and probably murdered!'

'Possibly eaten by them,' Dharma added, helpfully.

'Yes,' Tazmand mumbled. 'Although, unlikely about the being eaten part.' He looked at the ground and twiddled wet grass between his fingers. He felt embarrassed: he had explained his plan to his friends and Sky was now busy picking it to pieces, with good reason. What insane impulse ever made him tell Sky that he would be able to get them out of Karesh? What had possessed him?

'I see. What a completely brilliant plan!'

'There is no need to be sarcastic Sky.' Tazmand said, feeling defensive. 'It may not be perfect but, it could work.'

'Not perfect! I don't believe this! When you said you had a plan, I assumed it might be something that might have at least a slender chance of being successful.'

'I told you I didn't actually have a plan at all. I told you it was just a possibility and that it still needed to be worked out. You were the one that insisted on coming before hearing the details.'

'I didn't realise at the time that your escape route

was some half-baked possibility explained to you by a ninnyhammer who works in the meat vaults.' Sky's voice was starting to rise in pitch and volume.

Tazmand held his temper and took a deep breath. 'You heard what you wanted to. I didn't force you into it.'

Sky lay back on the grass, indifferent to the damp. She took a deep breath, making an effort to calm herself. 'Well how do you know the conveyance chute machine thingy leads outside?' she snapped. 'What if it goes…I don't know…to an incinerator or… grinders or something?'

'An incinerator or grinders?' Dharma echoed, rising panic evident on his face.

'Salt told me-'

'Oh yes Salt! From what you have told us about him, he has the mental capacity of pondweed! You want us to trust what he says!'

'Sky, he has worked there all his life. He has heard from others that the bad meat goes outside…somewhere.'

Sky sat back up, she looked tired. 'Tazmand, even if it does go outside, we know nothing about the location or geography of the area. I have never been allowed to roam the streets and I know even less about outside the city walls except that it is all desert. Where will we head for once we are out? Where will we sleep? What will we eat?'

Tazmand clenched his teeth and spoke slowly, as if to a small child. 'That is why we are meeting now. We know what we are going to do, that is escape. Now we need to organise how we are going to do it and when.'

'But -'

'Listen princess.' Tazmand was losing his patience. 'You

convinced me to go ahead with this. You said that you have no choice; it is either escape or go off and get married to someone you have never met. I never said this escape route was perfect and if you have any better ideas I would like to hear them.'

Sky made a sound similar to a buffalo snorting and threw herself back on the grass. The only sound audible for several minutes was that of Tazmand's teeth grinding.

At last Dharma broke the silence. 'Well I for one can't stay here. I trust you Taz. I'm with you whatever your plan is.' He turned to Sky. 'Come on. What choice do we have?'

She did not reply immediately. She stared at the waning moon, her eyes glistening in the silver light. She was holding back tears. Whether of anger or sadness Tazmand could not tell. Probably both he thought. Eventually, she took in a deep breath, sighed and sat up. She looked at the others for what seemed a long time, as if trying to weigh things up in her mind.

'All right,' she said at last.

Tazmand looked at her, surprised. 'Really?' he said. 'That's gr-'

'I suppose I will have to go along with you, although-'

'Go along with me?' Tazmand shouted. 'How pig-headed can you get? I wasn't keen to go ahead with any of this anyway.'

'Oh don't start arguing again you two-' Dharma groaned.

Tazmand ignored him. 'It was your idea princess. You were the one who went on at me to escape. You convinced me-'

'Convinced you of what? To be a stupid pronk with some great scheme that will get us killed-'

'Hey, hey, hey. What is all this now?' Nana said emerging through the silk curtains of Sky's bedroom windows. She walked towards them across the lawn. 'I have told you all countless times to keep the noise down or the guards will think there's a problem and come into the garden to investigate.' She leant on Tazmand's shoulder as she lowered herself onto the grass. 'By the gods this grass is damp with dew. You'll all catch your death.' Reminded of his chill, Dharma pressed his hands into his lower back, screwed up his face and gave a moan. He was about to comment but, Nana continued. 'Now, you two. Squabbling again? You never stop. What is it about this time?'

'Oh Nana,' Dharma said, standing up and stretching. 'They're arguing again about the escape plan! I think the meat chute sounds like it might work quite well but, Sky is moaning abou...' His voice trailed off as he noticed the other three staring at him in stony silence: if Sky's mouth had dropped open any further in astonishment her jaw would have been scraping the ground; Tazmand was shaking his head and mouthing the word 'no' at him whilst Nana just looked stern, her face as rigid as granite.

'Escape plan?' She enunciated the words slowly. Her eyes were glued to his, like a snake hypnotising its prey before swallowing it whole. 'What escape plan?'

The three budding runaways remained silent, each holding their breath, hoping in vain that Nana had, by some miracle, not heard Dharma properly. Unfortunately for them, she had hearing keener than a dog's.

'What escape plan?' she repeated.

'What?' Sky asked, widening her eyes innocently.

'Please do not make me say it again, Your Highness.'

'Oh the escape plan,' Tazmand said, interrupting and laughing a little too loudly. 'We have been playing a game about running away from the palace. Just a bit of harmless fun.'

Sky and Dharma both nodded, joining in with Tazmand's laughter. Nana voice was as brittle as glass. 'Really? 'Harmless fun? And who precisely is going to escape – in your game I mean?'

'Well all of us of course,' Sky said.

'Escape to where exactly, Your Highness?'

'Oh, you know. Here or there. Somewhere else...other than here I mean.'

'And in your game, have you made plans for your escape route?'

'Oh yes,' Dharma said, nodding enthusiastically and then faltering as Tazmand stared at him. 'I mean, in theory of course.'

'Of course. And have you, in theory, decided what you need to take with you, where you will go once outside the palace, how you will eat, where you will get water, what you will buy things with-'

'Buy?' Tazmand interrupted, puzzled.

'Yes, you need money, precious metals or jewels to purchase things. People will not give you food or shelter for free. People will not hide you for nothing in return.'

'Oh.'

Nana looked round the three of them. 'Perhaps you would let me join in the game. You never know, I might be a good player.'

Tazmand and Dharma glanced at each other apprehensively then shrugged their shoulders. Sky looked at the elderly woman who had been her nanny and governess all her life. 'You know it's not a game, don't you Nana?' she said. 'I've never been able to hide much from you.'

Nana nodded slowly. 'I guessed as much by the looks on your faces. Now what is this all about? You had better tell me everything and don't leave anything out – not if you want me to help that is.'

'Help?' all three of them exclaimed at once.

'Well you don't think I'm going to let my beautiful princess go off and marry some foreign pronk of a nobleman that she's never met before do you? Not if I can do anything to stop it.' Nana looked directly at Sky. 'I'm surprised, Highness. I thought that you would trust me with something this important.'

'Of course I trust you Nana. You have always been a faithful servant. I just didn't want you to worry that's all.' Sky sounded haughty but Tazmand, who was watching her face, thought she looked a little ashamed.

'Well,' Nana said, 'that's good then. Now, tell me your plan and I'll see what I can do to assist.'

'Hold on Sky,' Tazmand said. 'I've just thought. If Nana helps us she could get into serious trouble.'

'Yes, bor, I could,' Nana interjected before Sky could answer.

Tazmand looked intently at the old woman. 'I don't want to see you get hurt.'

'Me neither,' Dharma added.

'Listen to me, all three of you. I am an old woman. I have been a slave most of my life and a high servant for the rest of it. I have devoted the last thirteen years to the care and safety of Skylark Garesh-Far. I cannot stand by and watch her throw

207

the rest of her life away by being sold into a marriage just to cement a political alliance. It would break my heart.'

'But Nana, I don't want you to be in trouble,' Sky said.

'My dear, if you had disappeared without telling me, I would most definitely have been punished. Your father would have been bound to suspect that I had helped you. Now tell me your plan. If it has a chance of working I will tell you and, if we plan well together, I think I can ensure that you will all get away and I will not get into any trouble at all.'

The three of them then told Nana the whole plan – as much as there was of it. They explained about getting down to the slaughterhouse vaults and into the meat chute then trailed off as they had no idea what they would do after that. She listened quietly. When they had finished, she remained silent, thinking.

'This Salt, she asked after some time. 'Do you reckon he's telling the truth?'

Tazmand, being the only one who had met him, thought for a moment. 'I believe he is honest Nana. Whether his information is correct, that I don't know.'

'And you know how to get back down to these vaults?'

'Definitely.'

'And when are you going?'

'In ten days.'

'Ten days eh?' The old woman remained silent again for a few minutes and stared in front of her at the grass. The others stayed quiet as well, waiting for her to speak. 'You will need rope,' she said at last.

'Rope?' Tazmand repeated.

'Yes, or something like it - and lots of it.'

'What for?' Sky asked.

'I haven't been out of the city in quite a few years,' Nana continued. 'Although, I remember when I used to work on the baby wagons, and we used to return to Karesh from our trips abroad. We would arrive tired and filthy after weeks or sometimes months of travel. My wagon, full of its fresh infant cargo, would have trundled through the snow and ice of the high mountains, across windy and wet grasslands then, getting closer to home, across the rough stony tracks and sands of the scorching deserts of Karesh.

'As we approached the city, if we were coming in from the north, we would eventually have the relief of the narrow strip of arable lands close to the Grand Canal and, finally the wagon would heave itself up onto the smooth granite tiles of the city roads. Oh what bliss to my aching bones after a long journey!'

'Yes, I'm sure that's fascinating Nana,' Sky said, butting-in, 'but, is this really the most appropriate time for reminiscing? And, what about the rope?'

'All in good time, Highness.'

'Nana, we have important business-'

'Sky, let her finish,' Tazmand said. 'If you closed your mouth for five minutes and opened your ears you might learn something.'

Sky was furious. 'How dare you. You, you-'

'Highness,' Nana interrupted. 'Listen to my story, there's a dear. It is important.'

Sky was about to say something else to Tazmand, then thought better of it. She decided it could wait until later. 'Carry on Nana.'

'Thank you, Highness. As I was saying, we would arrive back tired and dirty after a long journey. The babies would be squalling – those that had survived the journey that is – and I would be aching for a soak in hot water and desperate for some fresh clothing. Now, it would be customary for us to go through the main gates of the city where crowds would gather and wave and cheer us in. It would not have done to arrive looking untidy so we would generally go round to the back of the city first to wash and change. The horses would be groomed, the wagons cleaned and its cargo,' Nana paused for a second as if trying to consider how to phrase it, 'freshened-up.'

'Freshened-up?'

'Yes, Highness.'

'What do you mean?'

'Well,' Nana looked awkward. 'You must understand that these were often long journeys of many months duration over hard terrain with harsh weather conditions-'

'Yes Nana, we get the picture. Please get on with it,' Sky snapped.

Nana flashed an angry glance at the princess, before continuing. 'Well, there were never enough nannies to look after all the infants individually and, try as we might, some of the poor little things didn't survive the journey and well, not to put too fine a point on it, some of the cages would have to be emptied.'

'You mean some of the babies would be dead?' Dharma exclaimed.

'I'm afraid that's so yes. The cages would have to be emptied.'

They all went quiet. Nana broke the silence eventually.

'Anyway,' she continued, wiping a little moisture away from her eyes. 'The live babes would be washed and changed and then we would go back round to the main gates and into the city. But, to get to my main point: when I used to go round to the rear of the city it was to get to the Scavenging Grounds.'

'Scavenging Grounds?' Dharma asked.

'Yes. It's just outside the west side of the city walls. It's where the city population's rubbish gets dumped. Oh it was a ghastly place and I shouldn't imagine it has changed. As we went there in the wagons, the smell was atrocious, all sorts of waste and refuse all mixed-up together in vast heaps; mountains of it. Large bonfires would be burning day and night and the smoke would choke you like you were trying to swallow a spiny hedgepig.'

'But, why did you go there?' Sky asked.

'We went there because the people who live and work there - the 'scavengers' we used to call them - would do all the cleaning up on the wagons and well, they would take away the dead infants for us.'

'What did they do with them Nana?' Tazmand asked.

Nana went quiet for a moment before answering. 'I'm not sure Tazmand, to be honest. I believe there is some sort of burial ground somewhere nearby and they would take them there for us. Anyway, we would pay them and they would give us fresh water to wash in and groom the horses but, that's not what I wanted to tell you about. Now listen, what did you think I saw there?'

They all shook their heads.

'I saw holes.'

'Holes?' Dharma echoed.

'Yes, holes. Lots of them. Small ones high up the city walls, where bundles of rubbish were coming out and falling down into the Scavenging Grounds. These are the waste chutes from the city and I'll be an elephant's grandmother if one of those holes isn't the end of a chute coming up from the meat cellars.'

Tazmand looked at Sky. Excitement and hope made his stomach flutter madly, as though a small, winged insect was trapped in his gut.

'Why are they called the Scavenging Grounds Nana?' Dharma asked.

'Well Dharma, I'm not absolutely sure but, I think it's because the scavengers go there to pick through the waste and steal it. In other words they go scavenging. The city authorities tolerate it because it helps clear away some of the rubbish.'

'How far up the city walls were the holes Nana?'

'They varied Tazmand, although I would guess some of them to be at least thirty metres above the top of the largest rubbish heaps – and those heaps are big – perhaps fifteen to thirty metres themselves. Some of them are permanently kept on fire to incinerate the rubbish.'

'Well,' Tazmand said, 'at least we now know where the meat chute comes out. Most probably anyway. And we now know it will get us outside Karesh city!'

'Yes,' Sky replied. 'Outside the city and thirty metres up the side of a sheer wall, suspended above a flaming mountain of stinking rubbish!'

'Well, Highness, that is why you will need rope,' Nana said, 'to climb down from the holes.'

'Sky, why are you always so negative?' Tazmand burst

out, finally losing his temper. 'May I remind you – again – that you are the one who pushed for this escape and no-one ever said it would be easy. What do you want? An open door, a carriage and a kiss goodbye from daddy? It will be difficult and dangerous and it might not work at all: we might get caught and we might be killed!'

Sky's eyes bulged; she looked as if she was about to explode with rage. Her mouth opened and closed like a fish desperate for air, although no words came out. Dharma held his breath, waiting for a torrent of abuse but, she looked so shocked, she seemed incapable speech.

'Well,' Tazmand mumbled, feeling embarrassed now his temper had subsided, 'it's true.'

Sky battled for breath, eventually managing to gulp down a lungful. 'How dare you talk to me like that!' she whined. 'Nana did you hear?'

'Yes, Your Highness, I did of course, although he does have a point.'

'What? He has a what?'

'Well you are the one who wants to get away. It will be a big risk but, you have to decide if you would rather play it safe and go off to get engaged or-'

Sky looked furious. 'You're on his side!'

'No. I am on no one's side. I think this plan may stand a chance but, you have to decide to commit yourself to it or stay here and do your father's bidding. It's quite simple.'

'But-'

Nana ignored Sky and changed the subject. 'Rope,' she reminded them. Neither Tazmand nor Dharma said anything. 'Rope!' Nana said again, firmly.

Tazmand shook himself as if just emerging from a sleep. 'Of course, I see now,' he said, giving Sky a sideways glance. 'Rope. We'll need it to get down from the holes, but, where can we get some Nana?'

'I don't know bor, that's up to you. One of those obstacles you just mentioned I suppose. But, you are going to need quite a bit of it if you want to climb down to the Scavenging Grounds alive.' The elderly servant stood up and started to go back to Sky's bedroom. 'Oh well, work to do. Can't hang around here chatting all night. Now listen to me you three. If you want this plan to succeed you are going to need to be well organised. You already know when, and now you have to think carefully about the how. Decide between you what supplies you are going to need for the journey, who is going to obtain them, how and where from. I'll go over the list with you, once you've compiled it, and check it through.' She went back through the curtains and disappeared.

Tazmand turned to Sky uncertainly. 'Nana said we will need money. Can you get us some?'

She said nothing at first; she looked deflated. 'Nana has never spoken to me like that before,' she murmured.

'Sky? Money?'

'Money?' she repeated.

'Are you in or out?' Dharma said. 'Come with us or stay; it's your choice.'

'All right Dar,' Tazmand said, 'I'll deal with this. 'Sky, I didn't mean to get cross but, Dharma and me are going. Are you going to come with us? It will be dangerous but, even Nana thinks we stand a chance.'

Sky said nothing, just nodded slowly.

'Does that mean yes?'

'I don't suppose I have much choice; engagement or certain death by stinking rubbish. Either sounds like a dream come true.'

'Er, good, that's good, I think. So, money, can you get some?'

Sky gave a shrug. 'I can bring jewels and precious trinkets to sell I suppose. I've got lots.'

'Excellent,' Tazmand said trying to sound enthusiastic. 'That's a great start. Just remember to keep whatever you choose small and transportable. It needs to be easy to hide and keep safely.'

Sky just smiled slightly. She looked depressed.

Tazmand continued. 'I'll get rope.'

'Where from?' Dharma asked.

I don't know where yet but, I'll find some somewhere. I'll try and get some food as well.'

'Oh I can get some food for us,' Sky added, seeming to brighten up a little. 'After all, it's better to die on a full stomach'.

'Please stop going on about dying Sky,' Dharma pleaded.

'And a little less sarcasm might be more helpful,' Tazmand added.

Sky shrugged her shoulders.

'All right. That's good. Just enough food for the start of the journey though Sky, we can't carry too much. We'll worry later about how to feed ourselves.'

'What shall I get Taz?' Dharma asked.

Tazmand thought for a moment. 'We will all need new clothes Dar. My robes are so badly worn they wouldn't keep out a light breeze. I'm not due new robes for another six months so I can't go to the uniform depot but, you have to go and get your new shelver uniform.'

'Oh I have numerous clothes,' Sky interrupted him, seeming to get excited by the subject of apparel. 'Capes, cloaks, dresses, petticoats, furs. What on earth shall I take? I shall have to get Nana to re-pack for me. Practical and hard wearing – what to wear? I could take one of my riding costumes. Now let me see the forest green with the ermine trim or the cherry red with sky blue moleskin jodhpurs?'

'And discreet,' Tazmand continued.

'What?' Sky said, momentarily distracted from her train of thought. 'Oh discreet. Well naturally. Perhaps then I should go for the forest green. I could always change into browns and russets later – you know, autumnal colours. I could blend right into the background.'

Tazmand ignored her. 'Dar, when you go to the depot to get your new uniform, you will need to sneak out robes for all three of us.'

'All three of us!' Dharma looked dismayed. 'How am I meant to do that?'

'Forgive me,' Sky interrupted. 'Did I hear you say *all three* of us?'

Tazmand ignored her. 'Use your initiative Dar. I've got to get hold of rope and I haven't got a clue where to get that. Clothes should be easier.' He placed a reassuring hand on his friend's shoulder. 'You can do it. Be brave and just try and think it out for yourself.'

Despite looking terrified, Dharma let out a long breath then squared his shoulders. 'All right Taz. I'll do my best.'

'Make sure whatever you get is warm. Although it's likely to be hot during the day, we don't know what the weather will be like or what shelter we might be able to get at night time.'

'Tazmand. Would you mind explaining something?' Sky said, reverting to her most imperious tone.

'Yes Sky, what is it?'

'You said three uniforms.'

'Yes I did.'

'I am assuming one of those is for me?'

'Yes it is.'

The princess was silent for some time as she stared at Tazmand in disbelief. He waited for her to say something but, as she would not, he decided to break the silence. 'All right Sky, what is the problem now?'

'The problem? The problem Tazmand is that you cannot possibly expect me to wear one of those, those awful robes. I've seen the grunts running around in them.'

'Why not? What's wrong with them?'

'Well for a start they are shapeless. They look hideously scratchy and the material looks like it is just common sheep's wool – not even vicuna. I am used to silks and the finest linens. I just couldn't possibly. I would come out in a rash.'

'Sky, if you want to get out of here you won't get far wearing silks and finest linens. If we bump into anyone while we are travelling through the palace, you are less likely to get stopped and questioned if you can blend in with us as a slave. Oh that reminds me, Dharma?'

'Yes Taz.'

'You will need to make sure that the robes have long

sleeves to hide our slave bracelets once we're outside.'

'I'll do my best.'

'Oh and Sky, you will need to wear a veil.'

'A veil! Don't be ridiculous. I won't do it.'

'All right then. Dharma?'

'Yes Taz.'

'Just two robes. We are going alone.'

'What? Wait a minute. You can't do that,' Sky said, panic rising in her voice.

'Course I can. Watch me. Come on Dar let's go. Bye Sky. Good luck with your marriage. Make sure you have lots of children.'

The princess looked on in evident disbelief as the the two boys started to walk out of the garden. 'Where are you going?'

'Off to get ready for our escape of course,' Tazmand called back. 'Good luck, and all that.'

'Wait!'

Tazmand turned his head but continued walking. 'Yes, Your Highness?'

'If you don't come back and take me with you I shall tell my father about your escape and you will both be executed.' The boys stopped and Sky gave a triumphant smile. 'Good. Now, you will come back in ten days' time and we will all go together. I will wear what I like and you will do what I say.'

'All right then.'

'Really?' Sky said, seemingly surprised that Tazmand had seen things her way so easily. 'Well, I'm glad you're seeing sense.'

'By 'all right' Sky I mean go ahead and tell your father.

218

I would rather die than stay here and be a slave all my life. Goodbye.'

Tazmand turned and continued walking to the door. Dharma's face displayed the fact that he was not so sure he agreed with his best friend about preferring to die, but he followed regardless.

'What?' Sky wailed.

'You heard me,' Tazmand shouted back over his shoulder. 'Tell, your father if you want. I don't care anymore. You're negative all the time. You cause problems at every turn. You would end up being a liability.'

Tazmand and Dharma were just getting to the door when Sky screeched out. 'I hate you!'

'Suits me.'

'All right, all right, stop!'

Tazmand ignored Sky and continued walking. Dharma started to turn around but, Tazmand pulled him along.

'Stop!... Please?'

Tazmand winked to Dharma, who breathed an enormous sigh of relief and wiped off the cold sweat that had formed on his forehead. Tazmand turned back to the princess. 'What do you want Sky?'

'I will do what you said. I will wear the robe of a slave. And a veil.'

'Why should we agree? You argue with everything I say. You find fault with all my plans at every turn. You are getting to be a complete pain in the-'

'I have to come. I won't argue any more. I promise. I will do what you say. I won't notify my father. Take me with you... please?'

Tazmand thought about it for a moment. 'All right. Get the things you agreed to: the jewellery and food. Be ready in ten days' time. Me and Dharma will be back then and we will all go together.' The princess took a deep breath then let it out. 'Good. That's good.'

As the boys walked towards the garden door, Dharma whispered. 'Do you really think she will do all those things she promised? You know, behave, not argue, be more positive?'

'What do you think?'

'I don't think she will Taz.'

'I think you're right. I reckon she will be a complete headache. But, we can't leave her behind.' Tazmand turned to his friend. 'Can we?'

Dharma shrugged his shoulders. 'Can't we?'

Tazmand thought about it briefly then shook his head. 'Tempting but no, she doesn't deserve that. Besides which, we won't get far without money or food. And I reckon the Lady Narine might talk some sense into her. Hope so anyway.'

Dharma shrugged. 'All right Taz. Whatever you say.'

CHAPTER TEN

Chotzo

As it turned out, getting three sets of uniform was easier than Dharma had anticipated. After the escape meeting in Sky's garden, he and Tazmand managed to get back to the dorm without any problems and, after a quick wash, he had rushed to the refectory for breakfast. Then, before his first shift started, he went to the uniform depot. He felt nervous as he pushed open the door; a small bell tinkled above his head, making him jump. He immediately calmed himself and attempted to look less furtive.

Before him stretched a long, highly polished copper-plated counter behind which stood a thin man with an overly large, bald head. The man was slouched forwards, both of his bony elbows on the countertop, his sharp chin balanced in his hands. Dharma was surprised the man wasn't wearing a turban and couldn't help thinking that he resembled a boiled egg, resting in an eggcup.

A small wooden and brass placard rested on the counter

in front of him, identifying the man as *'Wardrobemeister Fudgel'*. Dharma noted that, although he had the word 'meister' in his title, he was dressed as an ordinary grunt, not an overgrunt. The man was facing the doorway and had his eyes closed.

Dharma coughed loudly hoping to gain his attention. The egg-like head did not move at first but then, one eye opened slowly, its eyebrow rising into a disdainful arch. The eye studied Dharma for a full thirty seconds before two thin lips snapped apart and spoke.

'I did hear the bell you know.' The voice was thin and squeaky, like the sound made by pieces of wet rubber rubbing together. 'There was no need for all that affected coughing.'

'Sorry, I thought you were asleep and I only coughed once, actually.'

'Asleep!' The egg rose from its cup as the man stood. 'I never sleep. Been doing this job for forty-seven years and never been asleep on the job yet. Who says different?' he moved his face close to Dharma's.

'No one says different. I didn't mean to imply anything,' Dharma stammered, taken aback by the man's sudden aggression. 'It's just that you looked like you were asleep.'

'Looks can be deceptive.' Wardrobemeister Fudgel eyed Dharma up and down. 'What do you want?' he snapped.

'A new uniform please.'

'A new uniform? Oh that's a good one that is. Did you hear that?' he said, turning behind him to speak to somebody. 'He wants a new uniform.'

Dharma glanced towards where he was talking but, there was nobody there. The Wardrobemeister then had a coughing fit. He leant forward slightly, his eyes and mouth screwed up, and his body heaved up and down. Small dry whimpering noises emanated through his nose. After what seemed to Dharma like a long time, the Wardrobemeister stood straight again and Dharma realised that he had not been coughing. He had, in fact, been laughing.

'That's a good one. If I had a bowl of soup for every time someone had come through those doors and asked me that, I'd be able to take a swim in it.'

Dharma looked confused. 'I only want a new uniform.'

The man stopped laughing and leant across the counter menacingly.

'Wouldn't we all? I would like a new uniform myself young man but, you won't find me traipsing through my own door every five minutes making unreasonable demands.'

'It is not unreasonable. I have to have one because I have been promoted to shelver.'

'Well bully for you.'

'This is the uniform depot isn't it?' Dharma asked.' Where you come if you want a uniform?'

The man crossed his arms over his chest and closed his eyes. A whole minute went by without either of them talking. At last Dharma broke the silence.

'Well?' he said.

'Well what?'

'Well, can I have one?'

The man opened his eyes and looked at him. 'A promotion eh?'

'Yes.'

'Well we would all like one of those, wouldn't we?' He

leant forward again across the counter suddenly, sounding angry. 'Forty-seven years I've been here fitting you lot - grunts, overgrunts, underlibrarians, even the divines themselves - the whole lot of you with new uniforms like, like they grow on trees! No thought of me though, oh no, no thought of me. Forty-seven years doing the same job and look at me, still a grunt. Overlooked, never noticed, just here to provide nice new clothes and take away the old ones for reattribution. Well, I'm completely sick and tired of it!'

Dharma wasn't sure what to do. He noticed the man's extensive scalp was turning purple with anger; thick veins were standing out at his temples. He took a piece of parchment out of his pocket. It was a form that Sash had stamped, authorising the uniform collection.

The man's eyes flicked to the note, widening in alarm. 'What's that?'

'It's an authorisation form.'

'Noooooooooooo!' the man screeched, throwing himself across the counter and beating it with his fists. 'Noooooooooo!' he sobbed again.

Dharma was taken aback. He felt sorry for the man, who was obviously distressed but, he did feel that the reaction was excessive. He was also nervous about what Wardrobemeister Fudgel might do next.

'Um,' Dharma offered tentatively. 'You seem upset.'

The man stopped sobbing and sat up. He blew his nose into a large handkerchief. 'Oh you don't say.'

Dharma started to feel irked at the man's attitude. 'You don't have to be so sarcastic all the time you know.'

'Why not? I have little else to keep me fulfilled.'

'Is there anything I can do?'

'Obviously not. Not if you've got an authorisation slip. Nothing I can do to stop you. Go on. Help yourself. Denude the entire store. I don't care anymore.' He slumped across the counter top again.

'I don't want to denude the store. I just want my new uniform,' Dharma said, knowing that this was not strictly true.

'Forty-seven years and no one has ever come to visit me. You know, for a chat or just to pass the time of day. No one else for company. Just me, by myself, alone. Forgotten. My only companions have been rolls of cloth, robes, jackets, buttons, metal fastenings, nightwear, vests, shoes, socks and underpants. All great conversationalists they are.'

Dharma was not at all surprised that people left Wardrobemeister Fudgel alone, considering his negative attitude and violent temper but, he thought it best not to share this opinion. 'It sounds lonely,' he offered instead.

'Go on and get your new uniform for your new promotion and then go away, enjoy your new life and leave me alone to wallow in my old one.'

The Wardrobemeister snatched Dharma's authorisation slip. He brought a large rubber stamp savagely down on top of an inkpad and then even more savagely down on to the parchment. The counter shuddered under the attack. He then held the parchment by its edge with the tips of his fingers, as if it were an infectious thing and, opening a drawer, he dropped it inside with piles of other, similar papers.

'Fourth row down on the left.'

'Sorry?'

'That's where the shelver robes are kept. Don't make any noise, don't make a mess, no eating, and no drinking, no pets, hurry up, don't leave anything unfolded that you found originally folded and don't expect any help from me. I'm on duty and cannot leave the counter.'

'Thank you,' Dharma said.

The wardrobe master did not reply. Preferring instead to turn and take up his original position, chin resting in his hand, elbows on the counter top, eyes closed, facing the door.

'No wonder he doesn't have any friends,' Dharma muttered to himself as he walked down to the fourth row on the left.

Sure enough, displayed in front of him he found a long row of new, black shelver robes hanging in order of size along a rail. Below the rail were shelves of non-slip boots designed for working up ladders and above the rail were heaps of neatly folded vests and underpants. He looked around him and, finding the area empty of people, he started at the far end of the row. He pulled his own grey robe off and hurriedly pulled on four pairs of underpants, two large ones for himself and two mediums for Tazmand. The medium-sized ones were a tight fit over the ones he had on already. He realised that he could not possibly fit on anything small enough for Sky but then, he reckoned, she would be making her own underpants arrangements.

After putting on some extra vests, he selected a thick shelver's robe in a smaller size that would do for Sky. It was far too small for him, so he folded it into a kind of a belt and tied it round his waist. He managed to just about squeeze into a medium one for Tazmand. He then threw his old, grey pusher robe back on over the top of it all. With all the new clothes underneath, his old robe felt, and looked very tight. He selected a new pair of boots, a large, black shelver's robe and some more underwear for himself and carried them back to the counter. He had to concentrate on making his walk appear natural; the bulk of the clothes he had on was causing him to waddle.

The wardrobe master stood up unenthusiastically and inspected the items.

'One robe large black shelver's, one pair boots large, one pair underpants large, one vest also large.' He looked Dharma up and down, noting the tight fit of his current uniform. 'They certainly feed you lot well. Do you think large will be big enough?'

'Of course,' Dharma said, blushing slightly.

'All right, suit yourself. Just remember there are no returns. If it doesn't fit, you can't bring it back.'

'I won't need to bring anything back.'

'I'd lose some weight if I were you.'

'Well you're not me. How rude!'

'Bags are over there,' the wardrobe master said impassively, pointing without looking to the far end of the counter.

Dharma threw his new clothes in a bag and stomped out of the depot.

#

Dharma waddled inelegantly along the corridor that led to his dormitory. The rule was that grunts should always run to get to and from working appointments as quickly as possible.

227

The stiff, new material of all the uniforms he had on made it hard to walk comfortably let alone run, not to mention the extra underpants and vests he wore underneath which had started to chafe in some embarrassing places. On top of all this, he was beginning to sweat heavily. He prayed that no one would recognise him and comment on his strangely bulky appearance.

The corridors were busy and noisy with staff running to and from various jobs: so different from the deserted moonlit silence of his late night and early morning travels to Skylark's garden with Tazmand. As his thoughts drifted to the garden and the events of that morning, his step lightened, and he allowed himself to enjoy the exquisite thrill of fear running up his spine at the thought of escape. This was also accompanied by the more negative sense of foreboding brought on by the thought of it all going wrong. He did his best to ignore his stomach turning over and threatening to empty its contents, preferring the former, more positive, thrill option.

Without warning, a voice hissed in his ear, a hand grabbed his upper arm and he felt himself being pulled roughly into a secluded alcove.

'Not so fast my sluggish little friend,' Sash whispered, his hot breath tickling the sensitive skin around Dharma's ear. 'You seem cheerful for someone who is about to receive a promotion that is akin to their worst nightmare.'

'Do I?' Dharma responded weakly, his arm becoming numb from the pressure exerted by Sash's fingers. 'Let go Sash, you're hurting my arm. I'll get bruises.'

'Bruises? Good. All the more to remind you of who is boss.'

Sash squeezed tighter, pinching the thick material. Catching a piece of flesh between his thumb and forefinger he twisted it hard.

'Ow!' Dharma squealed, pain shooting down his arm. 'Stop it.'

'Feels like you have put a bit of weight on. They must be making the soup too rich in the refectory.'

Still pinching, Sash used his other hand to grab Dharma's wrist and twist his arm up behind his back. Dharma thought he would pass out from the pain, if his arm did not snap first.

'Leave me alone you bully. Why are you picking on me?' Dharma cried, tears of pain welling up in his eyes. Some other grunts looked over in their direction as they jogged past but, carried on quickly when they saw that Sash was an overgrunt.

Sash did not hurry, obviously enjoying his captive's discomfort and taking time to think about his question.

'Why am I picking on you? Well obviously it's because I can,' he replied eventually. 'And besides, I get bored pulling wings off flies, sticking pins in cockroaches and practicing whiplash on rats.' He put more pressure on Dharma's arm and laughed as the boy squealed louder. 'Moreover, I miss dropping books on pushers' heads and I can thank your great friend Tazmand for that.'

'Sash, stop it please. I think I'm going to pass out.'

'Go on then. Pass out and I'll kick you in the pooks.'

Dharma could feel the pain now like a numbing cold through his arm and round his shoulder. Sash, obviously unaware of the extra robes worn by Dharma giving him some protective padding, seemed dissatisfied that the boy was not in more discomfort, so gave an even harder twist and Dharma, instead of squealing, finally lost his temper.

'I don't care. Go on, do what you like,' he shouted. He had reached a threshold of pain where he no longer worried about what he said or what Sash might do to him. 'I won't have to put up with your bullying for much longer any way – I won't be here!'

Sash, surprised by this sudden and uncharacteristic burst of aggression, let his arm go. Dharma collapsed on to the floor and knelt in front of the overgrunt. Feeling flooded back into his shoulder socket and he rubbed his arm to get the life back into it, wincing as he felt the bruising.

'Won't have to put up with my bullying? Won't be here? What on earth does that mean you ridiculous little pronk?'

Dharma went quiet and looked at the floor.

'Well,' Sash asked, prompting Dharma with a swift kick in his lower back. 'What do you mean you won't be here?'

'Ow! I don't know,' was all Dharma could think of to say. He could have kicked himself for giving such a lame answer, or for saying anything about leaving in the first place.

'You don't know. What an inspired response.'

'I just said it so you would let me go,' Dharma mumbled.

Sash remained quiet for a moment, staring at the young grunt who continued to cower on the floor. 'Maybe true,' he said at last. 'In fact, probably true. I mean to say, what could you, of all people, possibly do to interrupt my fun? Won't have to put up with my bullying! Ha, ha, ha. Won't be here. That is really very funny.' Sash spent a good minute laughing. Tears rolled down his face and his stomach heaved up and down under his long robe, so it looked like a large jellyfish, bobbing around in rough water. Dharma continued to look at the floor. Eventually Sash calmed down. 'Very good. You've made my day.'

Dharma took this as his cue to leave and started to get up off his knees but, he was finding it hard to stand with the bulkiness of the extra clothes. Sash rested the hilt of his whip across his shoulder and pushed him back down to the floor.

'Just before you go.'

'Yes Sash.'

'Gruntmeister!'

'Sorry Sash. I mean yes, Gruntmeister.'

'I shall be watching you.'

'Yes, Gruntmeister.'

'I mean,' Sash continued, his eyes narrowing - no sign of mirth remaining in them, 'I shall be watching you closely. And your little friend Tazmand too. If you or he are up to something, rest assured that I shall find out about it.'

'Yes, Gruntmeister.'

'And rest assured that I will put a stop to it.'

'Yes, Gruntmeister.'

'And rest very much assured that you will wish you had never been born once I decide what sort of punishment to give you.'

'Yes, Gruntmeister.'

'Good, we understand each other. Now get away from me. I'm sick of the sight of you.'

Dharma did not need to be told twice. He stood up with difficulty, picked-up his bag of new clothes and waddled off down the corridor as fast as he could manage, still massaging his injured arm. Sash continued to watch him suspiciously until he was out of sight.

'You two!' Sash pointed the hilt of his coiled whip at two grunts who were walking slowly, watching him. 'Run! There will be no walking in these corridors. Run I said! Get to work.'

The two grunts started running immediately, narrowly avoiding the tip of Sash's whip, which cracked harmlessly on the stone floor. Sash looked meditatively once more in the direction taken by Dharma.

'Won't be here, eh?' he said out loud. 'Now I wonder what those two are up to?'

#

To say that Tazmand was on tenterhooks would be an understatement; now that he knew they were definitely going ahead with the escape he was excited, edgy, nervous, anxious, happy, worried and frightened, all in the same measure, all at the same time. On top of this, he was tired after so many late nights in Sky's garden. Exhausted would be more accurate, He had been shelving books in the wrong places, taking ones down that had not been ordered and directing Dharma to completely wrong sections of the library. He had even been nodding off and taking quick naps while he was on duty up the ladder. Dangerous to say the least but, he had managed to keep this fact from Dharma - thank the gods, or he would have never heard the end of it.

He had been doing his best not to arouse suspicion by any obviously odd behaviour: he had been getting on with his work as best he could and watching all the other grunts around him getting on with theirs. It was hard to believe, now that he knew he was about to break the law and escape, that no one else was aware of it. His whole life was about to alter fundamentally and yet, for everyone else, everything would remain the same. The library looked smaller to Tazmand and so did the people in it.

He could think of little else other than their plans. Dharma had already returned from a successful mission to get clothes, which were now safely hidden under his bed but, Tazmand still did not know where he was going to get rope.

He also found himself spending time considering Sky and her behaviour. Every time he thought about her he got angry. She had been a complete pain in the pangbat. Why should he let her come with him and Dar? She had been difficult about everything. She was argumentative, arrogant, demanding and vain. She had no idea about taking anyone else's feelings into consideration and was the most self-centred person he had ever met. Just totally spoilt. Maybe he should leave with Dar and not go back for her at all. It would be just what she deserved.

To top it all, she was a princess. The daughter of the emperor, Lord Ganesh Far himself! He had got to know her so well, he tended to forget who she was. If two slaves disappeared there would be a quick search and a small bit of fuss but, for the princess to go missing…the resulting mayhem was too awful to think about. The whole Kareshian army would be sent out and they would never stop looking. What was he thinking?

He stopped shelving for a moment and leant forward onto the rungs of his ladder for a rest. A mental image of Sky sitting in her garden on the appointed night, waiting in vain for him and Dar to turn up and then having to go off and marry someone she didn't know made his stomach churn with guilt. No, he thought, he had promised to go back for her and so he would. No matter how awful she might prove to be or how terrible the potential consequences. A promise was a promise after all.

The rest of the day proved uneventful and Tazmand did his best to think about getting rope and think less about how difficult Sky was. He continued to work with Dharma who pushed the ladder with his usual skill and whispered up the tube constantly about what he termed his 'daring adventure' at the uniform depot that morning.

That night, Tazmand told Dharma to stay in bed and get some rest, as he was not going to the garden. Instead, he got up and made his way to the slaughterhouses to see Salt. It seemed like a good idea to do a trial run before all three of them had to do it for real. He also wanted to warn Salt to expect him in a few nights with some friends.

This time he did not meet anyone on his way. He passed empty corridors, darker than usual, as there was only a partial moon mostly obscured by cloud. He knew the corridors well enough by now, however, to feel his way along the darker parts. He passed the kitchens without incident, pausing momentarily to listen to the noises of grunts working and to sniff the cooking smells. Not the most pleasant aromas but, he was hungry and his stomach rumbled all the same as he thought of the delicious treats he could have if he went to visit Sky.

He descended further towards the vaults, helped now by the bright, burning torches along the walls of the lower corridors. Eventually he reached the deep spiral staircase and ran down them until he reached the salt pits. As he stood at the bottom of the steps, feeling dizzy and trying to regain his balance, two grunts walked towards him with large pieces of meat carcass slung over their shoulders as casually as a couple of Sky's silk shawls.

'Hello there,' they both said together. 'Do you mind if we just squish past? Got to get these upstairs or the cooks will have our guts.'

They were both girls of about Tazmand's own age. Neither wore headdresses and both had short, cropped, hair and the same bushy black eyebrows peeping over their veils. Tazmand thought they might be twins. They both looked strong.

'Oh sorry,' he said as he moved away from the steps to give them room to pass.

'Oh I know who you are,' one of them squealed.

'You do?' Tazmand said, alarmed.

'Yes, so do I,' the other one said. 'You're that posh grunt with the gold wristbands doing the survey from the meat department. Nabby told me about you. She bumped into you outside the kitchens the other night.'

'Nabby? Oh urm, yes that's right,' Tazmand agreed quickly, relieved as they seemed friendly and not at all suspicious.

'Would you like to take down my particulars?' the first one said, raising her eyebrows and giving Tazmand a wink.

'I beg your pardon?'

'For your survey I mean.'

'Perhaps,' continued the second girl, 'you might need me

to fulfil your quota.'

The two girls burst out into peals of laughter.

'No thank you but, I will bear you in mind for the future,' Tazmand said, somewhat stiffly.

'Ooh 'bare' me in mind. Does that mean I need to take my clothes off?'

'No, of course not!'

'Shame.'

'I'm looking for Salt,' Tazmand said, deciding to ignore their comments.

'Well,' the second girl said, jerking her head in the direction of the salt pits, 'you've come to the right place. There's plenty of it down here.' Both girls burst into peals of laughter again, obviously amused at their own joke.

'No, I mean the grunt, Salt.'

'You mean Gingernut? What do you want that pronk for?' the first girl said.

'Erm, he is helping me with the survey.'

'What use would he be?'

'He is useful actually. Do you know where he is?'

'No, not really. He'll be around here somewhere. He always is. Come on Dumpa,' she said to her companion, losing interest in Tazmand. 'Let's get these delivered to the kitchens.'

As they both walked up the stairs, Dumpa looked back longingly at Tazmand over her carcass.

'Hullo Tazmand.' Tazmand turned round to find Salt standing right behind him. He looked tired and had a red cut down the side of his face.

'Salt! How are you?'

'I don't know.'

'Oh. Why not?'

'Because no one ever asks me usually so I don't normally think about it.'

'Well, why not think about it now?'

'All right.' Salt closed his eyes and thought about it. 'I'm happy,' he said at last, opening his eyes and smiling as if he had just discovered a new mood. 'I'm happy because you are here. My friend Tazmand has come to see me.'

Tazmand smiled back. 'So am I Salt. I am happy too,' he said and meant it. 'Salt, how did you get that cut down your face?'

'I got whipped.'

'On your face?'

'No, on my back but, I turned round at the wrong time and caught the whip on my face.'

'It looks sore. Have you seen a physician?'

'No. I put salt on it. It stings but, it will heal fast.'

'Why did you get whipped?'

'Oh, you know.' Salt took a deep breath and let out a gulping sigh as though he might cry. 'Not working fast enough.'

'But you always work really fast.'

'Yes I do but, not fast enough.'

'I'm sorry.'

'Thank you. But, it doesn't matter now I have a new friend,' Salt said beaming.

Friend, Tazmand thought suddenly feeling horribly guilty. *Not much of a friend and not for much longer. Once I escape Karesh, I'll be gone for good.* 'Erm, yes. New friend,' he said out loud. 'Listen Salt. I've come down to see you-'

'Yes I know you have. It's wonderful.'

'I have come to see you,' Tazmand repeated, 'to let you know that I will be coming back with a couple of other friends next time.'

'More friends?'

'Yes, more friends. Two more friends to be precise.'

'Two more friends,' Salt echoed, smiling dreamily and getting excited.

'They want to come down and meet you and look round the meat vaults. But-,' Salt was about to interrupt him but, Tazmand held up a finger and stopped him. 'But, I also have a favour to ask of you.'

'A favour? Favour, favour, favour.' Salt rolled the word round on his tongue as if he could discover its meaning through taste.

'A favour,' Tazmand said again. 'It means I would like you to do something for me because we are friends.'

The large ginger boy thought about this for a moment, then smiled. 'Yes, all right!'

'I don't suppose you have any rope?'

'Is that so?' Salt replied in an awed tone.

'Sorry? Is what so?'

'You don't suppose.'

'Salt I don't understand you.'

'You just said that you don't suppose I have any rope.'

'Oh I see.' Tazmand realised that he had to be much clearer in the way he posed questions as Salt had a literal way of interpreting them.

'Let me try again. Do you have any rope?'

'Yes.'

'You do have rope?'

'Yes. Hide rope.'

'Hide rope?'

'Yes. Do you want to see?'

'Er, yes please.'

Salt walked back along the flagstone path that passed the salt pits and led through an arch to the butcher rooms. Once there, Tazmand saw the tables he remembered from his last visit. This time there were buffalo carcasses lying on some of them. Salt approached one of the dead animals and untied something that was keeping its four legs bound together. He brought it over and presented it to Tazmand.

'Hide rope,' he said.

Tazmand examined the material he had been given. It was a thin, flexible cord that appeared to be made from strands of leather that had been twisted and stuck together.

'Hide rope,' Salt repeated. 'Made from animals. From skin.'

Tazmand pulled the rope between his hands. It seemed strong enough.

'Can't break it. Even me. Too tough.'

'Can you get me a much longer piece?'

'How much longer?'

'About thirty metres?'

Salt looked at him blankly. Tazmand looked around the room to find something he could use as a guide for the boy to understand the concept of length.

'Salt.'

'Yes Tazmand.'

'See that table over there, about half way down the

room?'

'Yes.'

'I need some hide rope that will reach from all the way down there to all the way here. As far as where I am standing.'

'All right.'

'Can you get that for me?'

Salt looked from the table back to where Tazmand was standing and then back to the table again.

'Yes Tazmand.'

'I need it for when I come back with my friends in a few nights' time.'

'All right. I can get lots of shorter pieces from the tanning rooms and glue them all together. I will get glue from the boiling rooms. It's made from animals too.'

'It needs to be very strong. Strong enough to take my weight.'

'Yes. It will be very strong. It will take your weight and mine together. Easy.'

'Salt that is wonderful!'

'That is all right Tazmand. You are my friend.'

Tazmand felt a sick feeling in his stomach. He thought he was not as much of a friend as Salt deserved and he hated lying to him and not telling him the truth about why Sky and Dharma were coming to visit. That in fact they would all be piling into the meat chute and leaving forever. As he was thinking this, Salt put his hand in his pocket and pulled out a short strip of something that looked like dark brown leather. He stuck it in his mouth and started chewing and sucking it noisily.

'What's that?' Tazmand asked.

'Chotzo.'

'Chotzo? Is it food?'

'Yes food. Tasty. Do you want some?'

Salt took another piece out of his pocket and handed it to Tazmand. He took it. It was hard and dry to the touch. He put it to his nose and took it away again immediately. The smell was strong and unappetising.

'Eat it. Good for you.'

'Ugh. No thanks.'

He handed it back to Salt who put it back in his pocket.

'What on earth is it made from Salt? It smells disgusting.'

'Meat. Dried meat. Some carcasses go in the salt pits and some get chopped-up into little pieces and go in the drying rooms. You want to see?'

Tazmand was not sure that he did want to but, he heard himself say 'yes'. Salt took his hand and pulled him between the tables and out of the butcher rooms through a side door. As they walked along a long, straight corridor, Tazmand felt a warm breeze blow towards him carrying a rich, salty smell to his nose. At last they reached a door and Salt opened it with a flourish.

'Drying rooms,' he said.

Tazmand entered an enormous circular chamber. His robes blew gently around and between his legs and his hair blew about on his head as a dry breeze swept through the room.

'Look up,' Salt said and pointed towards the roof.

Tazmand looked up and saw, suspended above his head; row upon row of brown, wrinkled chotzos pegged to wooden poles all swaying in the downdraught.

'Dried by the wind,' Salt said, obviously proud he had some knowledge to share.

'There are thousands of them.'

'It's for the soldiers. You can keep it in your pocket for as long as you like. Eat it when you want.'

'Where does the breeze come from?' Tazmand asked.

Salt shrugged. 'Smells nice,' he said.

Tazmand held his nose between his thumb and forefinger. 'Smells horrible.'

Salt, who thought this was funny, laughed and slapped his hands on his thighs. He went over and untied one of the many leather strings knotted to metal pegs attached to the wall. He let the string out and one of the poles descended from the high ceiling.

'These ones are ready. Take one.'

Tazmand reluctantly took a piece of the dried meat off the pole. It felt smooth and leathery. Holding his breath, he bit off a small piece and chewed it delicately. It did not taste as bad as he expected; it was rich and earthy. Then he had an idea; it would be perfect to take on the journey for emergencies.

'May I take more?'

Salt shrugged. 'Yes. Take lots.'

Tazmand unpegged all the pieces on the pole and pushed them into his pockets.

'Tazmand is hungry.' Salt laughed.

'Famished,' Tazmand replied also laughing, although still feeling guilty.

The next morning at breakfast, Tazmand was trying to eat some dark brown porridge. The firm, gluey consistency now made him feel nauseous as he was getting used to the taste of the finer foods provided by Sky at their nightly feasts. He stuck his spoon in the thick mixture and noted how it easily stood to attention, supported securely by the thick sludge. As he watched it stand rigid, waiting to see how long it would take to fall sideways, he sipped some water.

'Taz!' Dharma sat on the bench heavily.

'Hello Dar-'

Dharma rolled up his sleeve to reveal deep purple bruising around his bicep. 'Look what he's done now. That's twice in two days. He pinched the same bit of arm yesterday!'

'Yesterday? You didn't mention it.'

'Well I don't tell you every instance you know. It wouldn't leave time to talk about anything else!'

'It looks awful. Is it painfu-'

'Don't worry about me. How long until we get out of here?' Dharma was curt and visibly agitated.

'Shush! Dar, keep your voice down.' Tazmand looked quickly around the room. Some other grunts were looking over towards them. 'I can see that you're upset but, for the gods' sake be careful.'

'Careful! How can I be careful-'

Tazmand cut Dharma off with a warning look.

'Sorry.' Dharma took a deep breath to calm himself and started whispering. 'How can I be careful when Sash just grabs me and hits me, or tortures me whenever he feels like it? I can't do anything about it. I wouldn't be surprised if he kills me before we get away from this...this...' he let out a sigh as he trailed off.

'Listen to me.' Tazmand whispered back, looking around once again. 'We are meeting in the garden tonight to finalise arrangements. I will tell you tonight what the escape route is and how we are going to do it. We will succeed in this. It will work. We've got time. You only have to put up with Sash for a few more days and-'

'Make way. Make way. Rotund Gruntmeister carrying tray laden with food coming through. Make way,' a loud voice boomed towards them.

Tazmand and Dharma both looked along the length of the table to see who was making all the noise. It was Daniel coming towards them carrying a tray. He was pushing between two tables of seated grunts. His knees poked into the grunts in front of him, making them fall forward, whilst his ample backside pushed the grunts behind him straight into their food.

'Pardon me. Excuse me. Oh I do beg your pardon. Make way. Hungry overgrunt coming through.'

Of course none of the grunts dared complain as Daniel was an overgrunt but, there were a few furtive looks of annoyance, and more than a few disgruntled comments from a couple of seated overgrunts. Tazmand and Dharma stared at his progress in undisguised amazement. Daniel eventually made it to their part of the table and sat down in front of them, giving them a sunny smile. Without a word, he lifted a bowl of porridge to his mouth and, using his spoon as a form of spade; he shovelled the brown paste in and gulped it down. He rolled his eyes at the two boys as if to suggest an agreed mutual appreciation of the food, and then wiped his beard clean with his hand.

'Well boys, how lovely to see you both again,' he said at last. Then, catching sight of Tazmand's full breakfast bowl, he added, 'are you not eating that?"

Tazmand shook his head, too astonished to say anything. Daniel took the still erect spoon out of Tazmand's bowl, licked it clean and then demolished the porridge in the same manner as the previous bowlful.

'Oh that was simply gorgeous!' he said, putting his hands behind his neck and stretching his elbows up towards the ceiling. This effort at gentle exercise resulted in the escape of a long rumbling fart. 'Oh I do beg your pardon.'

'Don't mention it,' both boys replied automatically.

Several grunts in the nearby vicinity started to giggle but, went silent when Daniel stared at them. He turned back to Tazmand and Dharma and, leaning across the table so only they could hear him, spoke under his breath.

'So boys, how are the escape plans going?'

Dharma let out a loud yelp. The sound was like something half way between the start of a laugh and a response to sitting on a pin. Tazmand just stared blankly at the overgrunt. He felt his skin go clammy. Chilly beads of sweat oozed sluggishly out of his pores as fear and nausea gripped him. His head started to swim and his eyes went out of focus. His mouth felt parched as if all his saliva had turned to dust. At last he forced himself to speak. Words lumbered out of his mouth sounding slurred and clumsy. 'I have no idea what you mean.'

'Hey now boys. No need to worry. My goodness you've both gone pale as ghosts. Well, Tazmand you've gone white I'd say Dharma you have more of a green tinge. Neither of you looks healthy at any rate. I'm not here to frighten you. I'm here to help.' He smiled at them and winked. 'Seen any nightwatchmen in your dorm lately?'

Tazmand stared at Daniel for a long time trying to determine how he could know these things and waiting for his mouth to regain the ability to form coherent speech.

'How can you know about the nightwatchman?' Dharma asked, his jaw dropping in astonishment.

'Who are you Daniel?' Tazmand asked at last. 'And how can you possibly-?'

Daniel stared back at Tazmand. 'I am a friend,' he said. His clear eyes twinkled in the morning sunshine streaming through the skylights high above.

'But, how do you know?'

'Know what Tazmand?'

'Things. How do you know about the nightwatchman? As a matter of fact why haven't we seen any recently? Is it something to do with you?'

Daniel paused again before answering. 'I will tell you everything when the time is right. Until then both of you, I am here to help. Trust me.'

'No Taz! Say nothing. It's a trap.' Dharma gripped his friend's arm.

Tazmand stared at Daniel for what seemed a long time then, finally making his mind up said, 'we meet tonight to make final arrangements-'

'No!' Dharma yelped in horror. 'You mustn't tell him.'

'Why not Dharma?' Daniel responded calmly, turning to look at him. 'You have already as good as told Sash.'

Dharma blushed a deep crimson. 'How? What?...It was an accident.'

'You did what?' Tazmand hissed, turning to his friend.

'I didn't tell him Taz. Well not in so many words. He is suspicious that we are up to something but, he doesn't know what.'

'What exactly did you say?'

'He was hurting me Taz. He had my arm twisted up my back. I thought he was going to break it; I could feel the bones almost snapping-'

'Dar, just tell me what you said to him.'

'I said I wouldn't have to put up with his bullying for much longer.'

Tazmand stared at his friend in disbelief. He was dumbfounded. 'Are you losing your mind? What do you think Sash will have taken that to mean?'

Dharma went quiet and went back to rubbing his arm. 'Well, it might not be too bad I suppose. That could mean a whole load of different things-'

'Tell him the rest Dharma,' Daniel prompted.

'The rest?' Tazmand asked.

Dharma looked sheepish. 'What rest?'

'About not being here much longer - remember?'

'Oh, that *rest*.'

'Dharma. What in the gods' names is Daniel talking about?' Tazmand was losing his patience.

'Oh yes, I forgot. It is conceivable that I may have possibly given him the impression that the reason I wouldn't have to put up with his bullying is because I wouldn't be here for much longer.' Dharma pointed an accusing finger at Daniel. 'But Taz, that just proves Daniel is a spy, otherwise how could he know about it?'

Tazmand looked astonished. 'You did what?'

Several grunts and one or two overgrunts looked around at them, curious about the trio and surprised to see a grunt shout in the close presence of an overgrunt. Daniel stood up, reached across the table and slapped Tazmand across the face, hard. Tazmand and Dharma were both stunned into immediate silence.

'How dare you raise your voice in my presence! You shall attend me later and receive a severe punishment you filthy book rat!' Daniel pronounced in a voice loud enough for those at nearby tables to hear, at the same time winking at Tazmand.

The nearby grunts and overgrunts, seemingly satisfied with this display of authority, went back to their breakfasts and Daniel sat down again.

'Sorry about that Tazmand. Had to make it look realistic,' he said under his breath.

'Um, that's all right. I suppose,' Tazmand replied uncertainly. Then turning to Dharma he continued under his breath, 'when did this happen. When did you tell Sash we might not be here for much longer?'

'Yesterday, on my way back from the uniform depot.'

Tazmand stared at Dharma in disbelief, gingerly massaging his cheek to ease the stinging from Daniel's slap.

'Now listen carefully,' Daniel said to both of them. 'I can't sit here much longer or people will guess something is up. Sash suspects your escape attempt, although he has no idea how, or when, you are going to do it.' Tazmand shot Dharma an angry look. 'He still only half believes it because he says that no one would dare to try, especially you two,' Daniel continued. 'But, he is amazed that you could even be thinking about it and intends to watch you closely and catch you in the attempt.'

'Daniel. How do you know about all of this?'

'I know about it because... well let's just say I am friendly with Sash.'

'What?' both boys gasped together.

'Well, I have got to know him quite well recently and we talk a lot. He tells me everything.'

'But, if you are his friend-'

'I didn't say I was his friend. Just that he and I are friendly. There is a difference. Listen boys. I have no time to explain everything now. Please, you just have to have faith. You will see me again I promise. Until then, trust me. All right?'

Tazmand and Dharma looked at each other then turned to Daniel and nodded. What choice did they have?

'Good. Very good. Now I have little time. We must not be seen together by Sash or he might get suspicious. I will do my best to put him off the scent of what you are doing but, you must be careful. You must watch out for him and you must go quickly. Stick to your plans but, I repeat, leave quickly.'

'So you know what the escape plan is then?'

'Pretty much.'

'How? How do you know?'

'All in good time Tazmand. I will tell you all in good time. Now heed what I tell you. Leave soon. Leave tonight.'

'Tonight! That's impossible. We have another eight days before we are planning to go. Sky won't be ready and Salt won't have had time to make the ropes.'

'The longer you delay the more chance that Sash will be ready for you and will catch you. You must leave tonight!'

Tazmand and Dharma both nodded again. What else could they do?

'Good,' Daniel said. 'And one more thing, the high servant. She is planning to help you I believe?'

Both boys nodded in amazement that he could possibly know so much of their secret business. 'The Lady Narine you mean?' Tazmand said.

'If that's her name. Are you sure you can trust her?'

Tazmand and Dharma looked at each other again and Dharma shrugged his shoulders. This was not something they had considered.

'I don't know Daniel. I suppose so. Hadn't really thought about it,' Tazmand said.

'Be careful, she is an unknown quantity. Remember that she is a high servant. Her status was given to her by Lord Garesh-Far himself and that sort of promotion commands loyalty. She has much to lose – she was once a slave and will fear being one again. She will also be risking her life to help you and that is a great deal to risk.'

'Don't you trust her Daniel?' Dharma asked.

'I didn't say that. I'm just saying be careful. She might be loyal to Sky she might not. I just don't know yet.'

'She is devoted to Sky. I don't think she would do anything to put her in danger,' Tazmand said.

Daniel thought about this. 'Perhaps you're right. We shall see but, in the meantime, bring your plans forward and leave tonight. I will see you again soon. Away from Karesh.'

'Away from Karesh? But, how will you escape?'

'All in good time Tazmand. You will see me again and I will explain everything then.' Daniel stood up without another word and left the refectory.

'Tonight?' Tazmand whispered to Dharma.

Dharma raised his eyebrows and gave his shoulders a shrug. 'Tonight.'

Both boys felt their stomachs turn over.

CHAPTER ELEVEN

Gifts

T azmand lay in bed, on his back, hands behind his head. It was late; three candle marks after lights out and, despite being tired and needing sleep, he had been wide awake the entire time. Escape plans ran around and around in his head, back and forth, over and over again. He wanted to make sure there was as little room for error as possible but, he realised that this was pointless as his plans were woolly at best, and downright disastrous at worst. The only thing they could do was go for it, hope for the best and really, really trust to luck.

He was plagued by doubt. Was he doing the right thing? He and Dharma had been slaves since leaving the nurseries; they knew nothing of the world outside. They would be leaving with Skylark Garesh-Far, daughter of the emperor himself. What if they were caught and accused of kidnapping? A painful execution would be the best they could possibly hope for. What if they never even made it past the kitchens, let alone outside Karesh city? After all, Sash was now suspicious and would definitely be tightening-up security.

And, what if they did escape? What then? Would that be any better? Being eaten by savages didn't appeal. Neither did starving to death in the desert.

What was the alternative though? The continued bullying of Dharma by Sash and his imminent promotion to shelving (and certain death)? Sky's forced marriage. What about Tazmand himself? He would never find and meet his real family. He would remain a slave for the rest of his life. Wasn't it worth the risk?

He tried to push the fears out of his head and started running through the plans for the hundredth time. Stage one; him and Dar get out of the dormitory undetected and back to Sky's garden.

Stage two; meet-up with Sky and trust she would be able to get away earlier than originally planned. Well, if she wanted to come, she would just have to get herself ready. Arrange with Nana to cover for them while they get down to the Salt pits. And that's another issue, Tazmand thought. Can Nana be trusted? Would she risk her position as high servant and her life to help them? They had no way of knowing for sure but, Sky trusted her so that would just have to be good enough.

Stage three; get to the salt pits.

Stage four: get the rope off Salt and get into the meat chute. That is, of course, if Salt had had enough time to prepare the rope. Not worth thinking about now. They would just have to go without it and pray to the gods for a bucket full of luck. There was also another aspect to stage four, which Tazmand did not want to think about at all. It was coming to terms with lying to Salt and leaving him behind. Salt was obviously fond of Tazmand and he had given them so much help.

He let out a deep sigh. That was it; that was the whole plan so far. Not very thorough – they had not had time to consider the finer details – and not likely to succeed: more likely impossible, in fact. What was he thinking? It was madness! As to what they would do if they were ever able to get outside the city and to the Scavenging Grounds – stage 5 – well that was not worth thinking about just now. Our fate lies with the gods, as Nana liked to say.

The gods? If he knew how to pray to the them he would do it now gladly but, he had never been taught. Gods were something preserved for the rich, not for slaves like him. He knew nothing about them at all - just a phrase everyone used, 'by the gods' or 'gods help us', 'it's in the lap of the gods', that sort of thing. Maybe Sky knew more about them. He would ask her sometime. Certainly no time left to ask Nana.

Dharma was sleeping soundly a couple of beds away, his gentle snoring interrupted now and again by angry groans and mumblings. These Tazmand recognised as Dharma talking in his sleep. He was unable to distinguish the words but they sounded angry. Dharma also had the habit of running in his sleep; occasionally his feet would kick back and forth furiously for several seconds under his blanket. Tazmand could only assume that he was having dreams about pushing. At the moment Dharma was making no noise at all and Tazmand started to go over the plan one more time in his head.

'Taz? Taz, are you awake?' Dharma's voice whispered a little too loudly. 'Taz? Are you-'

'Yes! I'm awake. Keep your voice down or everyone else will be wide awake as well. I thought you were asleep.'

'No way! Asleep? How could I sleep on a night like this? I have been pondering in silence.'

'Oh right. So it wasn't you that was snoring a few minutes ago then?'

Dharma ignored him. 'Is it time yet?'

'It's been time for over an hour.'

'Well why haven't we-'

'Dar, we've got a problem.'

'A problem?' Dharma caught his breath.

'Don't get your pooks in a twist. We will be able to sort it.'

'What is it?'

'I went to the latrines about an hour ago and...'

'Yes,' Dharma urged, 'and what?'

'The nightwatchman's back on duty.'

'No!' Dharma squeaked.

'Keep it down!'

'Sorry.'

'Listen, it's not a problem. Obviously we can't get out while he's there because he will come looking for us if we are away for too long. Also we can't get past him fully clothed – he will want to know why we're not in nightwear, and we can't wear pyjamas and smuggle clothes past him as they are too bulky.'

'What are we going to do?' Dharma had a note of rising panic in his voice. 'Why has he come back now? He hasn't been on duty for ages.'

'I don't know. I guess his being away may have been something to do with Daniel. His coming back...well, I hope not. It might be something to do with Sash tightening up security and keeping a closer watch on us.'

'Oh Taz it's all my fault. I should never-'

'No point worrying about that now. Anyway, he can't stay there all night. He will have to go off at some point, even if it's just to empty his bladder. We will have to be ready to move as soon as he does. Now get dressed – as quietly as possible. I'm already in my new robe.'

'What are you going to do Taz?' Dharma asked as he struggled to change his clothes under the blanket.

'I'm going to watch him. You will have to watch me. As soon as I give you the signal, be ready to grab your stuff and follow me.'

Tazmand climbed quietly out of bed. He pushed the rag pillow down under the covers and did his best to make it look like a sleeping body. He kept low, crouching on his haunches and turned to Dharma.

'I'm going to squat by that bed over there,' he whispered, pointing. 'Watch me carefully and when I give you the signal, do the same as I did with your pillow and move quickly and quietly straight to the door. And don't look back. All right?'

Dharma nodded that he had understood, so Tazmand crawled cautiously across the moonlit floor. Staying low, he stopped and knelt by a bed where he had a good view of the nightwatchman's desk. As Dharma could not see the nightwatchman from his bed, he watched Tazmand's dark, crouching silhouette intently, terrified that if he took his eyes away for a second he might miss the signal. As time passed, Dharma's eyelids drooped and he had to fight to stay awake. Just as he thought the signal would never come, Tazmand raised his hand into the air then moved off quickly towards the door. Dharma felt a jolt go through him as his eyes flicked open and he became instantly alert. He took a deep breath and scrabbled out of bed.

The boy in the bed next to him suddenly sat up and Dharma stopped moving, frozen to the spot. He did not dare breathe. The boy muttered something groggily in his sleep, turned over and lay down again seeming to return quickly to his dream, so Dharma continued in silence. He pushed his pillow down under the blanket, grabbed a bundle from under the bed and scuttled on his hands and knees towards the dormitory exit. The door was open and the nightwatchman was not at his post. Dharma entered the corridor and could see the recognisable figure of Tazmand already in the distance. Dharma picked up speed and rushed to follow his friend. As he passed the latrines, he could hear the sound of splashing water.

#

Tazmand and Dharma burst through the door to Sky's garden at a run. Breathless and giddy with the excitement of their escape from the dormitory, they fell on the grass, panting and giggling in nervous exhilaration. Once they had caught their breath, they looked around and found the garden deserted. It was dark; the only light being the cold glow of a thin fingernail clipping of moon. There were no lanterns lit and the fountain was turned off. Sky's bedroom window was slightly ajar but, there was no light showing inside.

The boys looked at each other nonplussed. They had not expected this. Sky and Nana were always up late at night and into the early morning, despite the emperor's orders to the contrary; this was highly unusual. Tazmand tiptoed to Sky's bedroom window and listened for sounds from inside. He heard nothing and shrugged to Dharma who was standing close behind him.

'Try calling very quietly,' Dharma suggested.

Tazmand nodded and knocked on the glass gently, hardly making any noise and calling Sky's name softly through the open gap in the window. There was no response.

Dharma peered over his friend's shoulder. 'Knock a bit louder?' Tazmand knocked harder on the glass. Still there was no response. 'Should I go in do you think?' Dharma nodded and started moving forward, pushing Tazmand through the gap in the window. 'I said I not we,' Tazmand whispered, pushing Dharma back out into the garden. 'She'll have a fit if she's asleep and wakes up to find us both in her bedroom.'

Dharma signalled his apologies whilst Tazmand moved through the curtains and entered Sky's bedroom. The room was cool and scented with roses and from what he could see in the dim light, it was not as big or grand as he had expected. Soft carpets yielded under his boots and everywhere he looked, he could see the outline of what looked like heaps of dresses piled up over furniture and strewn across the floor. At the far side of the room, he saw the outline of a large bed. It had four tall posts – one at each corner, which held silky curtains suspended between them to form a canopy. These stirred in the mild breeze coming from the window. He took care stepping over the heaps of clothes and moved cautiously towards the bed.

'Sky,' he whispered. 'Sky, wake up.'

He took one last, large stride over a high pile of clothes, bringing him right next to the bed and felt his foot come down onto something soft. Without warning the soft thing sprang up from under his foot and Tazmand felt himself flung backwards. The next thing he realised was that he was lying on the floor, on his back. Something heavy was on his chest and something tight was around his throat.

'What is it Nana?' Tazmand heard Sky's soft, sleep-drenched voice come out of the darkness, and the sound of her scrabbling around lighting candles. Once some light appeared, he could make out the outline of Nana's unveiled face looking down at him, as she sat on his chest with one hand around his throat and the other holding the sharp point of her dagger towards his left eye. Her own eyes were glassy and intense. Sky was peering down at him from behind Nana. She carried an ornate, golden candelabrum from which wax was dripping over her servant's shoulder and onto Tazmand's upturned face.

'Tazmand!' Sky exclaimed. 'What on earth are you doing in my bedchamber?'

Tazmand tried to reply but, found Nana's tight grip stopped any sound coming up through his throat. He thought about Daniel's warning and started to panic; perhaps she was going to kill him.

'I think he's choking,' Dharma said, his face coming into Tazmand's field of vision.

'Oh hello Dharma,' Sky said. 'I think you'd better let him go now Nana.'

'Oh right, of course.' Nana's eyes cleared. She released her grip from Tazmand's throat and, re-sheathing her dagger, got off his chest.

'Nana has a tendency to go into automatic assassin mode whenever she senses danger. It's her training.'

Tazmand rubbed his throat and sat up giving Nana a suspicious look. 'What was she doing on the floor?'

'She sleeps there. Next to my bed to make sure I'm safe. It's her job.'

'I am here you know,' Nana interrupted. 'I'm not a piece of furniture. Just in case anyone would like to talk to me directly?'

'What are you both doing here anyway? I wasn't expecting you for a few more days. Has something happened?' Sky asked, choosing to ignore her servant's impertinence.

Tazmand and Dharma looked at each other.

'What is it?' Nana asked. 'What has happened?'

Tazmand frowned. 'We have to leave tonight.'

'What!' Sky started to shout but, stopped as she thought of the guards. 'What?' she repeated more quietly, although no less shocked. 'Tonight! Why?'

'Something's happened that means our plans need to move forward. Sky you will just have to get ready as we haven't got much time. I will explain on the way.'

'Well excuse me Tazmand, tonight is not convenient.' She placed the candelabrum on a table and moved both her hands to her hips. 'As you can see I was having a sleep and also as you can see,' Sky indicated the heaps of dresses and clothes strewn about the bedroom, 'Nana is only half way through my packing. I have nothing ready for the journey.'

'Sky you don't need anything except a simple veil. Dharma has your robe.' He turned to Dharma. 'Give her the robe. And all you need to take is a small bag with jewellery that we can sell and a bit of food. We have to travel light or we will never get away.'

Sky looked at Tazmand as if he was mad. 'I don't need anything? I don't need anything?' Her mouth gaped as she seemed at a loss as to what to say. Eventually she recovered herself. 'Of course I need things! I need changes of clothes. I mean all right, I agreed to wear the slave uniform until we get out of the palace but, I will need clothes to change into once we get away. Just how long are you expecting me to wear that... that thing?'

'I don't know. As long as necessary I suppose,' Tazmand snapped, getting irritated. 'Besides, how do you think you are going to carry all this stuff?'

'Me carry?'

'Yes.'

'Well you and Dharma are carrying most of it of course. I can't carry it.'

Tazmand glanced at Nana.

'Don't look at me, bor. I am her servant. She won't listen to me. I just do what she tells me. She said pack for the journey. I packed what she told me to.'

'Sky I don't have time to argue with you. Put on the robe, find a veil – something plain - grab some jewels and come on. Dar and I will wait out in the garden while you get changed. You have got five minutes then we go – either with or without you.'

'I-' Sky looked at Nana for support.

Nana shrugged her shoulders. 'It's not my escape, Your Highness. You must sort out your own arrangements with the boys.'

Tazmand and Dharma went out into the garden and stood on the lawn. Tazmand had his arms crossed over his chest and was tapping his foot fiercely on the turf. His brows were knitted into a tight frown and he was grinding his teeth noisily.

'What do you think she will do Taz?'

'Bluntly Dharma I don't care anymore. She has got five minutes then we are gone. She can come, she can stay. I'm sick to death of her. It's her choice.'

Nana emerged through the bedroom window and came to them on the lawn. 'She's having a little bit of a tantrum. Throwing her clothes around the room, ripping things up – the usual. At least she's doing it quietly. The guards won't come,' she continued calmly. 'Tazmand I'm terribly sorry about your throat. Are you all right now?'

'I'm perfectly well, thank you Nana.'

'Good. Good.'

Nana looked over to Sky's bedroom window where everything had gone quiet. Tazmand and Dharma followed her gaze.

'Do you think she will come with us Nana?' Dharma asked.

'I don't know. I really don't,' she sighed. 'Now, down to our own business. You have only a couple of minutes before you set off and I want to give you a couple of things. Dharma, this is for you.' She reached deep into a pocket in her robe and pulled out a small, velvet bag. She handed it to him. 'I have a feeling you will use this well.'

'Thank you Nana. What is it?'

'Open it up and have a look.'

He opened the bag and pulled out two small bottles of cut crystal. Both had gold stoppers fitted tightly into their necks. One was filled with a red liquid and one with green.

'They are healing ointments,' Nana told him. 'Red for cuts and wounds and green for stomach and internal disorders and poisons. It is easy to remember – red for blood and green for bile. That's how I remember them anyway. Use them sparingly; they are potent. They are also valuable so you can sell them if you need to. But, make sure you do that only as a last resort; I have a feeling their real value to you will be in using them.'

Dharma looked at the bottles in awe. 'Thank you!'

The old woman nodded then turned to Tazmand. 'Now, I have a gift for you also.' She handed him another pouch. This one was slightly bigger than the one she had given to Dharma and made of old, well-used leather. Tazmand undid the thong holding it closed and pulled out a plain silver disk, about six inches across. 'Push the clasp on the side.'

Tazmand pushed in a small metal button on the rim of the disk and the whole thing popped open like a clamshell. Tazmand looked inside and saw that one half contained a mirror and the other half was a dial with figures and marks all around its perimeter. A golden arrow was suspended at the centre of the dial, which wobbled and spun round pointing at the different marks.

'Do you know what it is?'

Tazmand shook his head. 'It is beautiful.'

'Ay, it is, bor. I bought it from a nomad trader many years ago when I was out on the wagons. It is a scope.'

'Scope?'

'Yes. See that arrow? Wherever you are, whatever time of day or night it may be it will always point north. So you can never get lost.'

Tazmand stared at the brightly painted dial. 'North, where I come from.'

'Yes, bor,' Nana nodded, 'where you come from.'

'How does it work?'

'It's all to do with magnetics. Don't you worry about that just at the moment. All you need to know is that the arrow points north at all times.'

'Which is north Nana?'

'Look at the marks Tazmand. I know you cannot read well enough yet but, look at the colours. See the four big symbols at quarter intervals around the edge of the scope?'

'Yes.'

'Those are the pointers. North – where the arrow is pointing – is represented by a black diamond in the shape of a star. The letter above it is 'N'. South is the one directly on the opposite side which is a deep red ruby, just above the letter 'S'. East is the green emerald right of the letter 'E' and west is the letter 'W', left the blue sapphire. Just remember the colours and you will know where to go.'

Tazmand continued to stare at the scope. 'Thank you Nana. It is beautiful. North black, south red, east green and west blue,' he repeated out loud.

'If it helps, bor, just remember the different terrains of the land. The north is the black lands where it is mountainous and rocky and rains all the time; the east is green because it is temperate and crops and greenery grow abundantly; the south is red hot desert - that's where we are in Karesh - and the west is towards the blue waters of the sea.'

'So I come from the north, where it rains?'

'Yes. It's a long way off. Very different to the heat and dust of Karesh. It lies way across the southern Kareshian deserts, over the Great Plains then through huge forests and dangerous swamps. The northlands lie way up past these and on the other side of a high mountain range. It is a long journey. When I went there, many years ago now, it took us over a sixmonth to get there and the same plus half the time again to get back. So, whatever you do never sell the scope. It will be the one thing to guide you safely on your way.'

'I won't. I promise. Thank you.'

'You are welcome, bor. Turn round in a circle and see how the arrow always remains pointing in the same direction. See how it always points towards your real homeland.'

Tazmand looked at Nana as tears welled-up in his eyes at the thought that he might one day find his parents – his real mother and father. He turned round as instructed, as did Dharma and Nana, only to come face-to-face with Sky. She had been standing behind them and she was dressed in the robe Dharma had stolen for her.

'You have decided then?' Tazmand said, wiping his eyes with the back of his hand.

Dharma turned to Tazmand and whispered, 'she looks pretty angry Taz.'

'What's new?' Tazmand whispered back.

'Let's get going shall we?' the princess hissed at them between clenched teeth.

'Got everything?' Tazmand asked with more than a hint of sarcasm in his voice.

'Of course,' Sky replied, jerking her head stiffly sideways to indicate a small brown, leather knapsack slung over her shoulder.

'Food?' Dharma asked hopefully.

'No food. I wasn't expecting you tonight so no time to prepare.'

'Not to worry. We have a little bit and I know where to get hold of some more,' Tazmand said, thinking of the chotzo drying on the wind racks in the vaults. 'You've got the jewels and things to sell?' Tazmand asked.

'Yes!' Sky snapped. 'Of course I have. Now shut up and let's get on.'

'I almost forgot,' Nana said, 'these are for you.' She handed Tazmand and Dharma two of the same small, leather knapsacks that Sky was wearing. 'To carry your things in.'

'Thank you Nana,' both Tazmand and Dharma said together, taking the bags. Tazmand carefully stowed his scope into his bag and Dharma wrapped his healing bottles up in the spare underwear he had been carrying and put them in his.

'And one more thing,' Nana said, taking a battered leather bottle from the folds of her dress. 'A water bottle. It won't hold a great deal but, it will keep your thirst at bay when you are desperate.' She handed it to Dharma who placed it in his knapsack. 'Now, listen to some advice from an old woman. When you get outside Karesh there is only desert to the east, south and west of the city. You need to head northeast where there is a narrow strip of arable land, which follows the course of the Great Canal. This is the only direction where you will find food and water for leagues. Do not go directly north as it is only desert. Follow the canal. Tazmand, you have the scope in case you get lost.'

'Yes Nana but, if we stick to the canal route, surely it will be too busy. Won't we be at risk of being caught?'

Nana thought for a few moments before replying. 'Yes, bor, it will be busy. There is a main road to and from Karesh following the canal. It will be a great risk and you must find a way not to get caught. The alternative is going into deep desert. If you do that then your deaths are a certainty.'

Tazmand and Dharma both started to ask questions at the same time, until Nana raised her hands to signal them to be silent.

'Enough talk,' she said. 'It is time for you to leave.'

Tazmand and Dharma went quiet and looked at each other.

'All right. Tazmand. Bang me on the head,' Nana said.

'What?'

'Come on, no time to argue. Tie me up and then hit me on the head, hard. We must make it look authentic.'

Nana handed Tazmand some pink silk cord, which had been hanging next to Sky's bedroom windows as curtain ties. He held the cords loosely in his hands and looked bewildered. Dharma looked shocked. Sky kept her arms crossed over her chest and remained expressionless, refusing to communicate any reaction at all.

Tazmand started to speak. 'Nana I don't-'

She raised her hand to signal silence. 'Come on, we will go inside. There's a perfect chair just inside the windows. It's extremely heavy. You can lash my legs and arms to the frame so I can't move or get away.

Nana marched back into the bedroom and the others followed her. Sky had lit more candles. The dull sheen of pale pink damask wall coverings glowed with a soft radiance.

Crystal and mirror sconces twinkled in the gentle amber candlelight and Tazmand noticed, amongst the discarded piles of clothing, small objects and details that surprised him. Little toy dogs and cats made of wools and cottons sat on every available surface. The pictures on the walls were of little boys and girls in different settings which reminded him of stories he had heard when little – *fairy tales* they had been called, and every piece of furniture had delicate cloths of intricately embroidered, snow-white lace adorning them. Everything, that is, except a large throne-like chair which Nana now occupied.

The chair was dark and heavy with elaborate carvings of gargoyle-like faces, weaponry and strange animals. It had sumptuous, velvet upholstery, plush and deep black. It seemed gloomy and oddly out of place in the otherwise young and feminine style of the room.

'This belongs to Lord Garesh-Far,' Nana said, as if reading his thoughts.

'I can have nothing that is truly just my own,' Sky said, thinking out loud.

'I would normally be punished for using it,' Nana continued, her hands rubbing the richly polished wood nervously. 'But, if I am forced and tied onto it against my will, I suppose I will not be.'

'Nana I can tie you up but, I can't hit you,' Tazmand said.

'Nonsense! You will do what is necessary. This is your only opportunity to get away and my only chance to help Skylark. It must look as though you overpowered me and tied me up. A blow to the head will give me the excuse I need to say that I was unconscious and could only undo my bonds and call for assistance when I awoke.'

'But, Nana, what if I do knock you out.'

'You won't. It merely has to be hard enough to look real not actually be real. It will take me about an hour to get out of the chair. I will show you how to tie knots that I can work open within that time. Now, Dharma get the rest of the curtain ties, you can help Tazmand do the tying. We will leave the head hitting until the end.'

Under Nana's direction, the two boys gathered all the curtain ties and successfully tied her arms, legs, wrists and ankles to the heavy chair.

'Good lads. I can hardly move. That will give me a few cord burns, which will look better when they question me later. Highness, would you be kind enough to put my veil on for me – thank you. I don't want the soldiers to see my face. Right all of you, time is running on and the morning is getting closer. Are you ready to leave?'

The three escapees looked at each other briefly then nodded.

'Tazmand – you know what to do. Take my dagger and hit me over the top of my head with the pommel. Do it as hard as you can. I can take it. Don't worry; my head is as hard as old stone and I've had much worse knocks.'

Tazmand took the dagger from Nana's scabbard and wrapped a scarf he found on the floor around the blade.

'Go on, bor. Do it now,' Nana said, closing her eyes.

Tazmand raised the dagger and walked close to the chair. He was about to bring the pommel down on Nana's head when he felt a hand restrain his arm. He turned and found Sky looking at him.

'I will do it,' she whispered calmly. 'She is my servant.'

She took the dagger and moved forward as Tazmand stepped back. Holding it firmly she swung it down sharply on the top of Nana's head. The old woman let out a muffled grunt and slumped forwards.

'Pangbats!' she said loudly, raising her head again. 'That was a mighty blow young Tazmand. She looked up and saw Sky holding the dagger. A small trickle of blood ran down her forehead.

'Highness?' You hit me?'

'Yes Nana. If anyone is going to hit you it will be me and no one else.'

Tazmand noticed Sky's eyes mist with tears.

'Thank you, Highness. You are a good girl.'

Sky started to sob. 'Oh Nana, what shall I do without you? Please come with us.'

Nana smiled. 'No child. I am too old. You must go now. Go to meet your fate and leave me to mine. I shall miss you Skylark Garesh-Far. You are like a daughter to me.'

Sky bent forwards and kissed Nana on the forehead. 'Good bye then.'

'Goodbye. Now, before you leave, you know your pretty little orange scarf with the pale blue trim?'

'Of course.'

'Well I need you to tie it around my mouth. Get a small Hankie to put in my mouth first then tie the scarf over afterwards. Then light that candle over by the bed, the one with the hours marked down the side. Once that's done you must all go. I shall watch the candle and wait one hour while I loosen my bonds. Then I shall call the guards for help. You must be in the meat chute within one hour.'

Sky got a small cotton handkerchief and, lifting Nana's veil, placed it gently into her mouth. She then tied the scarf across the lower half of Nana's face, over her veil. While Sky was doing that, Dharma lit the time candle. Nana nodded that she was all right and indicated with a jerk of her head that they must leave quickly.

The three escapees wasted no more time. They hurried through and out of the garden without looking back.

CHAPTER TWELVE

Boozak

Tazmand was out of breath. 'So far so good,' he panted. He had come to a halt and was peering cautiously around a corner. Dharma and Sky waited close behind him, both also breathing heavily. They had run along several long corridors without stopping, being caught, or yet attracting attention. It was dark and quiet; the only light being that cast by the moon through the high windows, the only sounds the soft pad of their boots on the stone floors and the rasp of their own breathing.

Dharma wiped some sweat from his forehead with his sleeve. 'How much further Taz?' he managed to wheeze, struggling to gulp a deep lungful of air.

'We just need to get past the kitchens and then we can start the descent to the vaults. It will be better lit there, although there's also more chance of bumping into grunts that might be working late. We'll have to be prepared. So, remember both of you, if anyone asks, we are grunts from the department of meat research conducting a survey about the most effective cooking methods for buffalo meat.'

Dharma nodded unnecessarily in the darkness, still panting. 'Right you are Taz. Buffalo meat - research - cooking. Got it.'

Sky remained silent.

'All right Sky?' Tazmand asked. The princess did not respond. 'Sky, did you hear what I said?'

'Yes!' she snapped at last. 'I said I would follow your plan, didn't I? You don't have to keep asking if I'm all right or if I agree with every little thing.'

'Well it's hard to tell how you might be feeling; I can't see your face under that veil. Actually I can't see your face at all in this gloom.'

In response, Sky manoeuvred herself into a weak patch of moonlight and lifted her veil. She gave Tazmand a fake smile. 'I'm fine, all right?'

Tazmand decided to ignore the sarcastic tone of her voice and just nodded. 'Good, well come on then. It's all clear ahead.' He moved off around the corner at a fast jog, Dharma and Sky following close behind then, just as they rounded a wide bend, they came to a large iron door which was firmly shut.

'What the-' Tazmand halted dead in his tracks. Dharma and Sky both stopped behind him as he tried the handle. 'It's locked,' he said, surprised.

'Well how did you get through it all the other times?' Sky asked.

'What other times? It's never been here before.'

'Well it can't have just appeared by itself.'

'No I don't mean that Sky, I just mean it's never been

closed and locked. I've never even noticed a door being here before.' Tazmand ran his fingers all over the smooth metal surface, as if he might be able to feel for a way through.

'I reckon it's Sash again, tightening-up security,' Dharma suggested.

'Well that's just great!' Sky said, slumping down to sit on the stone floor.

Tazmand continued to feel the door. 'I could do with some help Sky.'

'Oh yes, I know, I'll bash it down with sheer brute strength or just rip through it with my teeth.'

'She'd have more success with her tongue; it's sharp enough,' Dharma murmured to Tazmand under his breath. Both boys couldn't help suppressing a snigger and Sky, who had heard, was furious.

'Go ahead, laugh all you want. I'm not the one who's got us stuck before our escape has even started. I'm not the one who said he'd be able to get us down to the vaults. I'm not the one-'

'Oh give your jaw a rest,' Dharma snapped, his sudden and uncharacteristic show of irritability surprising the other two. 'We are all in the same situation. Let's remain positive and try to find a way round-'

'Round! That's it!' Tazmand said, interrupting his friend. 'Look, we're not going to get through the door but, I do know another way past the kitchens. Or, at least, I'm pretty sure I do.'

'*Pretty* Sure?' Sky queried. "You don't sound very confident.'

'Well, I've always come this way before but, I have seen another route.'

'Well what are we waiting for Taz?' Dharma said, doing his best to sound enthusiastic. 'Just give me a second to get my breath back. Then let's go!'

'Yes all right, although there is just one little thing.'

'What?' Sky and Dharma asked together.

'The particular passage I'm talking about. Well, I think it goes straight past some soldiers' quarters. When I've started to go along there before, I've heard voices down the passage. Not quiet and restrained like young grunts but older, grown-up voices all laughing and talking loudly in the distance.'

Sky and Dharma did not reply for some time, each deep in their own thoughts.

'All right then,' Dharma said eventually, rallying himself. 'We will just have to get on with it and take a chance.'

Tazmand turned to Sky. 'What do you think?'

She shrugged her shoulders and gave a brief nod, which the others could just about make out in the dim light, but said nothing. Tazmand decided to take the shrug as a yes. He knew she was still angry with him. That much she was making apparent. Although, he also thought she looked and sounded scared and worried, despite her bravado. He reckoned the reality of the escape was starting to dawn on her. This was dangerous - they all knew that. They could be caught and severely punished, even executed, for what they were doing. Well, Tazmand and Dharma would definitely be executed. Tazmand was not sure at all what Sky's father might do to her but, whatever it might be, it would not be pleasant. What she was doing constituted high treason after all.

The three of them turned and set off back along the corridor. Rather than head towards Sky's garden, however,

Tazmand led them around a sharp bend to the right, under an elaborately carved stone archway and down a shallow flight of broad, well-worn granite steps. A narrow corridor stretched before them. Shafts of ashen moonlight seeped through the gloom at regular intervals along its length, coming through small windows high up, just below the vaulted ceiling. Because of their height, they illuminated only the upper parts of the opposite wall.

Tazmand whispered to the others as they went. 'This runs in roughly the same direction as the previous corridor. It goes past the kitchens anyway and should eventually get us down to the vaults. There are no torches lit along here so it's dark at floor level, which will help hide us.'

'Looks quiet enough,' Dharma managed to pant, between gasps for air.

'What's that?' Sky hissed suddenly, pointing down to the far end of the corridor. They all stopped and peered through the gloom. They did not see anything straight away, until a tiny flicker of light appeared for an instant in the far distance, before quickly disappearing again.

'That! Did you see it?

'Yes I did,' Tazmand whispered.

Another flicker appeared moments later, and then another and then they both disappeared.

'What is it do you think?' Dharma whispered. 'Glow worms?'

'People,' Tazmand replied. 'Or, more specifically soldiers. I think they are walking in and out of doorways or passages at the far end of this corridor. They must be carrying torches to light their way.'

'What will we do?' Dharma asked, a nervous edge to his voice.

'Well Dar. If you want to give up and go back, now is your chance. Otherwise, I suppose we had better go down there and see how we can get past.'

All three remained silent, thinking. Only the sound of their nervous breathing could be heard in the cold stillness of the passageway. Then without a word of agreement, they found themselves moving forward once more, careful not to let their footfalls sound on the hard floor, like noiseless ghosts in the dark. They proceeded cautiously along the corridor noticing the occasional, yellow lights continue to appear, flicker then disappear in the distance.

As they got closer to the end of the corridor, the flashes of light became more distinct. They could now see flaming torches being carried above the heads of tall figures in army uniform. When they were close enough to see clearly, they stopped and crouched down, making sure they were still effectively concealed in the shadows. They had reached an intersection where another corridor crossed theirs and there was a fair amount of activity going on as soldiers moved to and fro in front of them. It seemed most were coming from the left and continuing straight down the right-hand turning, which was exactly the direction Tazmand, Sky and Dharma needed to take to get past the kitchens.

They remained as still as statues, watching and listening. The soldiers walked, singly and sometimes in groups, unaware of the three young runaways, crouching only a few feet away from them in the gloom. Torchlight reflected tired faces and dark uniforms. The glint of hard steel reflected ominously from well-polished sword hilts. All the soldiers, mostly men but also a few women, seemed to be in a good mood talking and joking loudly; discussing the gargantuan amounts of food they were going to consume; boasting about the amount of alcohol they would put away over the next few hours and commenting lewdly on the types of company they were hoping to meet.

Muffled sounds of laughter and singing were coming from around the right-hand turning. As soldiers disappeared from view, these sounds briefly became louder, as if a door was opening into a room full of people then closing again. While the door was open, they heard voices roar out in welcome to any new arrivals. A woman was singing a sad song about a pretty girl, a soldier, the soldier's best friend, a horse, a bag of gold and something about love, betrayal and death. She was singing badly and was accompanied by a set of pipes that were being blown out of tune. No one seemed to be taking much notice of the song, as glasses clinked together and occasionally smashed, accompanied by loud applause. Women screamed with raucous laughter and feet stamped in rhythmic dancing. These noises became muffled again when the soldiers went in and the door closed.

'They must be on a rest break,' Tazmand whispered to the others.

'We'll never get past them,' Sky hissed.

The door opened again and Tazmand waited until it shut once more before replying. 'We have to. It will be risky but, we will just have to wait until the traffic dies down. When there's a gap we will make a run for it-'

'Not more running please,' Dharma interrupted. 'I'm

done in.'

'Come on Dar. It isn't much further. We just need to get around this corner and past that door then it's all downhill to the vaults.'

Dharma let out a sigh. 'I'll do my best.'

'What if we get caught?' Sky asked.

'We won't,' Tazmand replied sharply.

'You can't be sure,' Sky persisted. 'There must be another way round. This is too dangerous. The place is swarming with soldiers-'

'We won't get caught Sky. Think positively. There is no other way around, not that I know of anyway. Look, this is brilliant timing. These soldiers are all in a great mood. They are coming off duty, having a bit of rest and relaxation. There will be fewer of them passing soon – once they all arrive. So, we will wait. Wait until they have all gone in to the party and they are all drunk, then we will just slip round the corner and race down to the kitchens.'

Sky snorted. 'Easier said than done.'

'We just need a bit of nerve. Now, keep quiet and hold my hand.'

'What?'

'Grab my hand and Dharma's hand as well. When I reckon it's time to move off, I will squeeze your hand and you will immediately squeeze Dharma's. As soon as you feel the signal, we all run round the corner as fast as possible. No talking. No stopping. No looking back. Just run. Is that clear?'

They fumbled for each other's hands in the dark and waited. It seemed a long time. They heard the door open and close a few times as more soldiers joined the revelry although, eventually, the flow eased to a trickle and fewer seemed to be arriving. Sky and Dharma waited for the signal from Tazmand. It had been several minutes since the last group had walked down the corridor but, still he watched and waited. After a few more minutes, Sky felt Tazmand's hand squeeze hers and sensed his body move from a crouch into a standing position. She squeezed Dharma's hand in turn as she stood and felt herself being pulled round the corner by Tazmand. All three of them let go of each other, moved quickly in the dark round the corner and started to run as fast as possible in the direction of the kitchens. The floor felt smooth and even and was starting to slope gently downwards, which helped to accelerate their speed.

Sky ran as fast as she could, one hand gripping her veil to stop it flying up over her eyes. Tazmand and Dharma were already well ahead of her; she could hear their footsteps pattering down the corridor. She noticed the door to the party room coming up on her left, or rather, she saw where the light emanated from underneath it and she could hear the singing and shouting coming from behind it more clearly. Then, without warning, the door flew open and the next thing she knew, she was lying flat on her back, her head throbbing badly where it had hit the floor. She felt dizzy, sick and disoriented.

'So what have we here,' a deep male voice boomed above her. She screwed up her eyes as the harsh light of a burning torch was pushed towards her face and the blurry image of a darkly bearded face peered down at her. 'Got lost dearie? The party's in there,' he said thrusting the torch in the direction of the mess door, which was now wide open, noise, alcohol fumes and tobacco smoke billowing out into the corridor.

'What is it Shazek?' a woman's voice shrieked from inside the room. Piercing and shrill, it cut through the rest of the din like a metal nail scraping down a glass window.

'Oh just one of your girls out here in the corridor,' the soldier answered her. 'I was just coming out to go to the lavs when she crashed into me. Went flying and hit the back of her head on the floor. Think she's had a few too many.'

'Well don't leave 'er out there you great oaf, bring 'er in to the warm. Who is it anyways?'

'Dunno. She's wearing a veil. Who are you,' he said, his hand coming down to move Sky's veil aside.

'Wearin' a veil?' the woman's voice shouted out again. 'How can she be one of my girls if she's veiled? We don't wear none, not when we're workin' anyways.'

'Well Boozak. She's definitely got one covering her face.'

A scream of guttural laughter came from another woman inside the room. Sky thought it sounded like a seagull being strangled. This was followed by the loud crash of a table overturning and the smashing of many glasses.

'Dazmin! I've told you before about holdin' your liquor!' Boozak screamed. 'That lot will 'ave to be paid for straight out of your wages. And no more dancin' on the tables! Your feet are too big.'

'She's getting up off the floor Boozak,' Shazek shouted as Sky started to stand up. She was still feeling nauseous, although less dizzy, and she was aware that she must have crashed into Shazek as she was running. She felt the back of her head. There was a tender lump but no blood as far as she could tell.

'You can't get decent girls no more,' Sky heard

Boozak muttering aloud. 'They just don't appreciate the old profession. Think they don't need no trainin'.'

'Are you all right?' Shazek asked Sky, still clumsily attempting to move her veil away from her face with his big, rough fingers and staggering as he tried to maintain his balance.

'Leave my veil alone,' Sky snapped, slapping his hand away. 'You're drunk and reek of alcohol.'

'Aw aren't we posh dearie. Too good for old Shazek eh?' He grabbed Sky's veil and gave it a hefty tug. It ripped away and Shazek stared at her face in the torchlight. 'By all the gods dearie you're a gorgeous bit of fluff you are.'

Sky tried to push past him but, Shazek grabbed her arm and swung her round so her back was pushed against the wall and the full weight of his body was pressing against her, pinning her there.

'Get off me immediately you common lout!' Sky shouted in her most haughty tone of voice.

'Ere, what's all the commotion?' Boozak's voice shouted from the room.

'She's trying to get away from me Boozak. I thought your girls was trained better.'

'Trying to get away! Flaming cheek. None of my girls try to get away. I'm comin' out to 'ave a look. Hold on to 'er and don't let 'er move an inch!'

'With pleasure,' Shazek replied, giggling drunkenly and leering down at Sky as he pressed his stomach against her so she could hardly breathe, let alone move or escape.

Boozak emerged from the room. With the light behind her, her silhouette looked like a bull seal that had been squeezed into a tight, sleeveless dress. Mounds of flesh hung over the top of her low collar like foam spilling over the rim of a beer glass. As she moved, Sky could hear muted snapping sounds, like the muffled cracking of a whip as the bones forming the corset she was strapped into clicked against each other and groaned in protest. Sky could not see the woman's face clearly until she moved into the glow of Shazek's torch.

'Well, well what 'ave we 'ere,' the woman murmured to herself. Her voice sounded hoarse, like gravel crunching under a heavy, wooden wheel. She took a deep pull on a black clay pipe and smiled, allowing Sky to see a row of brown teeth peeping out between sticky, red, painted lips. 'Well you certainly are not one of my girls. But-' she interrupted herself to let the pungent smoke out in a steady stream, 'I certainly wouldn't mind if you was.'

Sky did not reply.

'A grunt is it?' Boozak continued, her eyes meandering over Sky's robes. Sky still did not answer and just concentrated on trying to breath. 'Get your great bulky belly off the poor girl and let 'er breathe,' Boozak shouted at Shazek, prodding him in the shoulder with the stem of her pipe. He moved back unsteadily. 'And move that torch nearer so's I can get a better look.'

The soldier did as he was told and Boozak brought her face close to the princess's. Sky guessed that the woman was seventy years old at least, if not well over. It was hard to tell under the layer-upon-layer of stale cosmetic powder and paste that had been applied and, apparently, never washed off. Her skin looked like the surface of a mud pond, baked for so long in the sun that every ounce of moisture was eradicated and only dust and cracked clay remained. Her hair was bright orange and as brittle and elaborate as icing on a wedding cake.

Boozak took another deep drag on her pipe. 'So, grunt, who are ya? And what, exactly, are you doin' round 'ere on my patch,' She exhaled a cloud of toxic-smelling smoke into Sky's face before continuing, 'at this time of night?'

Sky could contain herself no longer. 'I am Skylark Garesh-far!' she barked in her most imperious voice. 'Daughter of Lord Garesh-Far, Emperor of Karesh and you are both in enormous trouble. Not only have you looked at my face, you have touched my person and talked to me without permission. My father will have you executed for this outrage!'

Boozak did not respond immediately, continuing instead to peer at the girl in front of her through the thick haze of pipe smoke, her thin, painted-on eyebrows raised in vague amusement. Shazek, who was glassy-eyed with alcohol and had not heard a word Sky had said just stared at her, an inane grin now spread across his face. Suddenly, Boozak burst out into the loudest, coarsest laugh Sky had ever heard. Shazek joined in, not sure what the joke was.

'By the gods girly, I have heard everything now!' the woman screeched, her cackling chuckle echoing down the passageway. 'Shazek, bring 'er into the mess. I think I'll keep 'er – mad or not – I'll get the paperwork sorted tomorrow. That face alone could make me a fortune and besides which she's a great laugh.'

'Get your paws off me! How dare you! I am Skylark Garesh-Far. You will take me nowhere-'

'Excuse me?'

All three of them turned towards the voice that

suddenly came from behind Shazek. It was Dharma. He was standing in shadow and they could not see him clearly.

'Who are you? Boozak demanded.

'Oh I am Dharma. I have come back to retrieve my colleague.' He indicated Sky and gave her a little wave. 'We work for the department of meat research and we were on our way to the kitchens to conduct a survey with night-worker grunts about cooking buffalo meat and-'

'Shove off,' Boozak grunted, closing her eyes and turning away from him as she would from an irritating insect. 'She's mine now.'

'I beg your pardon?'

'You heard her,' Shazek said. 'Shove off.'

'I must protest. My overgrunt will want to know where she has gone when we report back in the morning-'

'Listen you little shrimp,' Boozak turned back to him with a threatening glare. 'I don't know who you really are or what you are doin' 'ere at this time of night when you should be tucked up in beddy-byes, and I don't care. I do know that if you do not back off and go away, I shall get Shazek 'ere to arrest you. That meat department thing might fool some of the other little grunts you bump into on your nocturnal wanderin's but, I am too long in the tooth to be taken in by your pathetic fibs. I am pretty sure you are out of your dormitory when you shouldn't be and that you, and your little mad friend 'ere,' she indicated Sky, 'are up to no good, and that you will be in big trouble if I dob you in. So, just go away quietly little boy and leave 'er 'ere with me, and we will say no more about it.'

'You can't just take her.'

'Yes, as a matter of fact I can.' Boozak replied, a wide

grin on her face. 'You don't get to be my age in my profession without making some pretty influential friends. I'll find out who she belongs to and get 'er transferred over to me. I always get what I want.' She stopped for a moment to slap Shazek around the back of his head, before turning and walking slowly back into the mess. 'Come on Shazek, you old soak; bring 'er inside.'

The soldier dutifully grabbed Sky tightly by her wrist and started to drag her in behind Boozak. His eyes widened as soon as his hand touched skin instead of metal.

'Boozak!'

'What is it now?'

'Wristbands Boozak. She's got no wristbands.'

'Don't be daft. What would a free citizen be doin' wanderin' round the palace corridors in the middle of the night in a grunt's robe?'

'Look for yourself then if you don't believe me,' he replied, holding one of Sky's wrists up to the light of his torch. Boozak looked at Sky's wrist then grabbed her other one, feeling it with a spongy, damp hand. She brought her face close to Sky's; who turned immediately to avoid the overpowering, mingled odours of stale tobacco, cheap wine and ancient food rotting between her teeth.

Boozak looked stern, as if she would tolerate no messing about. 'Who are you really Dearie?' she demanded.

'No, leave me alone. Dharma help me! Don't just stand there! Do something!'

Dharma shrugged his shoulders and started to give Sky a helpless look when, all of a sudden, Shazek tumbled forward, ending up sprawled on his front on the floor, dragging Sky underneath him. He lay motionless on top of her and blood was seeping out of a gash in his forehead where he had hit it against the wall. Boozak was backed-up against the wall and screeching as Tazmand sprang up off the floor, disengaging his arms from around Shazek's legs where he had tackled him to the ground.

'Who's this one?!' Boozak shouted, looking shocked and angry and not at all frightened. 'What's goin' on?'

Tazmand did not answer as he and Dharma grabbed Sky's arms and pulled her from underneath the heavy, unconscious soldier.

'Is he dead?' Sky asked trembling as she emerged from underneath the limp body and stood, shaking. They heard Shazek give a loud snore.

'No, he's not dead, Dharma said, stating the obvious.

They started to move away when Sky felt sharp nails dig into her shoulder.

Boozak's gravelly voice hissed into her ear. 'And where do you think you're goin' my little chicken?'

Sky turned to face her. 'As far away from you as possible!' she shouted, stamping on the fat woman's foot as hard as she could. Boozak immediately loosened her grip and screeched so loudly, they all thought the roof might come down on top of them. They began to run as Boozak shouted into the room for help.

'Quickly get after 'em. They are getting' away!' she screeched but, no one took any notice of one more howling voice amongst the many. She kicked Shazek in the side of his stomach. 'Get up you great, lazy pig. Get up and arrest them!' Shazek did not move; he just snored louder.

Sky, Tazmand and Dharma raced as fast as they could along the corridor until they ran straight past the kitchens. Pretty soon it started to descend sharply and, as they turned a bend, they found a short passageway lit by sconces that Tazmand recognised as leading to the steps down to the vaults. They stopped for a moment and lent forward resting their hands on their thighs and breathing heavily.

Tazmand turned to Sky. 'Are you all right?'

Sky nodded, catching her breath. 'Yes, yes…I'm fine.'

'Why on earth did you tell them who you really are?'

'I, I don't know. Force of habit I suppose. It was stupid. I panicked.'

'Don't worry about it, although we'd better get a move on. It's only a matter of time before that woman raises the alarm and they all find out that you weren't actually mad after all.'

'Thank you for coming back… both of you. You didn't have to. You could have left me.'

'No we couldn't Sky,' Dharma smiled at her. 'We are in this together.'

'Thanks,' she repeated, a begrudging smile touching her lips.

'Hurry up you two,' Tazmand hissed from further along the corridor. 'We are running out of time. Nana will call for the guards and raise the alarm any moment now. We have to get to the meat chute.'

They set off again, running faster than ever.

#

Tazmand hurried his friends down the spiral staircase, fortunately meeting no one else along the way. Arriving, at last, at the bottom, they found the pits to be deserted, apart from a few grunts dotted about in the distance, hefting heavy buffalo carcasses and burying them under their snowy blankets of salt. Dharma and Sky gaped wide-eyed at the vast squares of white stretching away into the distance.

'Is one of those workers Salt,' Dharma asked, pointing.

'I don't know Dar. They are too far away to tell but, I don't think so. He's much taller than most people so I should be able to tell him apart from the others.' He screwed up his eyes and peered into the distance. 'He doesn't seem to be around'

'So where is he then?' Sky demanded.

'How should I know? He's always been here before.' Tazmand continued to look around the huge chamber. 'Come to think of it, I haven't got a clue where to find him if he's not here.'

'Well you know where the meat chute is so I suppose we will just have to leave without seeing him,' Sky said.

'No, I won't leave without saying goodbye. He's my friend and anyway, we can't go without the rope.'

'Even if we do find him though Taz, he probably won't have made it yet. He won't have had enough time,' Dharma pointed out.

Tazmand ignored his friend, continuing to look around, now with a real sense of urgency. 'And I want to get some more chotzo off him as well.'

'Some what?' Sky asked.

'Oh never mind, you'll understand when you see it.'

Sky was just about to ask another question when a voice

boomed out behind them.'Tazmand!'

The three companions turned to see who had called and there, emerging through the entrance from the butcher halls was Salt, the entire trunk of a buffalo slung around his broad shoulders, as if he was casually carrying an enormous towel out of the shower.

'Salt!' Tazmand shouted and waved, breathing a massive sigh of relief.

The tall, ginger boy strode straight towards them grinning and, ignoring the carcass, wrapped his huge, muscular arms around Tazmand, giving him an enthusiastic hug.

'Tazmand my friend. I am glad to see you.'

'M-too-alt-bt-pse-put-th-anmal-don.' The sound of tazmand's muffled voice came from somewhere between the salter's armpit and the buffalo's rear end.

'What?'

Tazmand managed to push himself away slightly and took a deep breath, 'I said me too but, please put the animal down.' Salt looked bemused. 'The carcass. Put it down, I'm covered in buffalo juice... again.'

'Sorry Tazmand!' Salt looked grief stricken as he pulled away and saw the mess he had made on the front of Tazmand's robe. He started to rub it with his hands, only managing to spread it around and make it worse.

'Salt, listen to me. It doesn't matter. It's fine.'

'Really?'

'Yes of course. Please, just leave it alone. Here, meet my friends. This is Sky.'

Sky nodded, smiling nervously and backing away just in

case she got the same treatment. Salt took in a deep breath and clamped his free hand to his mouth.

'What is it? Tazmand asked, suddenly feeling alarmed.

Salt pointed at Sky, his eyes wide. 'It's a girl!'

'Yes.'

'Salt went bright red and turned to Tazmand to whisper in his ear. 'She has no face covering.'

Being so relieved to get away after the scuffle upstairs with Boozak and Shazek, and because they were so used to seeing Sky without a veil, none of them had considered the fact that it had been ripped off.

Tazmand kicked himself for not picking it back up off the floor. And thank the gods we didn't bump into anyone else, he thought to himself.

'Yes Salt. Sky doesn't wear a veil,' he said at last, recovering himself. He had discovered that with Salt, it was usually best not to complicate things with unnecessary explanations.

'No veil?'

'That's right. She doesn't wear one.'

'Never?'

'No Salt, never,' Tazmand confirmed.

'Oh,' Salt said nodding wisely, as if he now understood completely. He shrugged his shoulders, seemingly happy to accept this as a simple fact, 'all right then.'

'And I am Dharma,' Dharma announced, stepping forward with his hand out.

Salt immediately grabbed his hand and shook it violently. 'Tazmand taught me about shaking hands. We are friends now yes?'

'Um, yes I suppose so,' Dharma replied, taking his hand back and looking down at it before wiping it on his robe.

'I thought you were coming later,' Salt said, turning to Tazmand.

'Yes, we were Salt but, we had a change of plan. Um, do you remember about the rope I asked for?'

'Yes.'

'I don't suppose you have got it ready by any chance?'

'Don't you?'

Tazmand remembered Salt's tendency to respond literally to questions.

'I mean, have you got the rope ready that I asked you for?'

'Yes I have.'

'You're joking!'

'Am I?'

'No, I mean that's wonderful!' Tazmand jumped over to Salt and gave him (and his dead buffalo) a big hug, ignoring the slime and blood. Salt beamed with pleasure as Tazmand let go of him. 'Salt, please get rid of that meat.'

'Oh yes sorry, just a moment.' He wandered off to bury the buffalo carcass in a nearby salt pit. The others watched him for a moment, marvelling at his strength.

'That is excellent news,' Dharma said. 'About the rope, I mean. Taz, perhaps this is a good time to review all our resources. You know - all the other things that we need to take with us.'

'Good idea Dar. Come on, let's sit down and go through our stuff. We will have to be quick. There is no telling how soon that large woman upstairs might raise the alarm.'

'Or Nana for that matter,' Dharma added. 'If she hasn't

already.'

Both boys lowered themselves to the ground and started to open their packs

Sky, looking bemused watched them for a moment before asking, 'erm, hang on a minute Dharma. What do you mean about Nana and *if she hasn't already*?'

The boys stopped what they were doing and Dharma opened his mouth to answer but, did not seem sure what to say. 'I, erm, well-'

'Why would she do that? Nana said she would give us a full hour.' Tazmand and Dharma looked at each other guiltily, but said nothing. 'Oh I get it. You don't trust her do you?' They still said nothing as Sky continued to stare at them. 'Well,' she said at last, letting out a sigh, 'I don't suppose I can blame you. You don't know her like I do but, if you will take my word for it, I can assure you both we can trust her completely. Really, we can.'

'All right Sky. I suppose we don't have much choice,' Tazmand said, not looking completely convinced before adding, 'it's just something someone said, that's all.'

'What? Who said something? When?'

'Never mind. It's all old news. Now we really need to get on.'

'Wait a minute, who-?'

'Sky we haven't got time for this,' Tazmand interrupted, pulling open his pack. 'We do trust Nana, don't we Dar?'

'Yes,' Dharma said then added, changing the subject, 'equipment Taz. Let's go through it now.'

'All right. We've got the rope organised,' Tazmand said, 'and we have a bit of chotzo. I will go to the drying rooms and get some more – it's a type of dried meat we can use to keep us going if we can't get decent food,' he explained to Sky. 'At least it will keep us alive.'

Sky sat down cross-legged, joining the boys on the floor. She was listening to them talking as they undid their leather packs and went through the contents. She started to open her bag then stopped suddenly, closing it again quickly.

'I've got changes of clothes and the healing medicines that Nana gave me,' Dharma said. 'Oh yes.' He added, rummaging, 'I've also got the water bottle.'

'Good,' Tazmand said. 'And I've got the scope.'

The boys turned towards her. 'And what about jewels and stuff to sell-' Tazmand broke off suddenly. 'Sky what's wrong. You look completely grey. What is the matter?'

Sky was silent for a long time before she spoke. 'I've forgotten them,' she mumbled.

'Hmm, what was that?' Tazmand asked. 'I didn't hear you.'

'She said she's forgotten them,' Dharma said, before turning to the princess. 'What have you forgotten?' he demanded.

'The jewels. I forgot to pack them.' Silence followed as the impact of her news sank in. 'In the rush and confusion, I just had so much to do and too much to think about.'

'I reminded you before we left the garden. I asked if you had packed them.'

'I know Tazmand but you hurried me. I wasn't expecting to have to go for a few more days yet and I was upset and then we had to hit Nana over the head and then-'

'All right, all right don't get all bothered. It was an

oversight. An accident. I know we rushed you. No one is to blame-'

'Yes they are! Her!' Dharma shrieked, pointing at Sky who glared back at him. 'What are we going to use out there?' He motioned with his hand vaguely around him to indicate the world at large. 'We will starve if we can't buy things. No one will give us shelter or hide us. We have to have money. Nana told us. It's essential for our survival!'

'Look I am really, really upset about it. I can't say any more than that-'

'Well upset isn't enough-' Dharma snapped at her. 'I can't believe-'

'That's enough both of you!' Tazmand shouted over their raised voices. 'It is no one's fault.'

They all went quiet when they heard a sob behind them and turned round to see Salt staring at them. He looked miserable and shocked and had tears in his eyes. 'Why are you shouting? Not friends anymore?'

Tazmand looked at the others, who both glanced at the floor, embarrassed, before responding. 'Yes Salt we are friends. We just had a slight disagreement but, it's all right now. Isn't it?' he said, glaring at Sky and Dharma. They both nodded and did their best to smile at Salt so he would not get any more upset. He did not. In fact he dried his tears immediately and beamed at them.

'I will go back and get them,' Tazmand muttered to himself, after some quiet consideration.

'What?' Sky and Dharma both exclaimed together.

'I will go back to Sky's garden and pick them up. Sky, where did you leave them? I assume they were packed-up and ready to go?'

'Taz, you can't go back,' Dharma started shouting, immediately lowering his voice to a harsh whisper as he noticed Salt starting to look upset again. 'It's much too dangerous. We are lucky to have made it this far. You will be arrested and killed. Besides which there's hardly any time left before Nana raises the alarm.'

'I will go and get them,' Sky said. 'It was my fault and I will remedy it.'

'You'll get caught,' Tazmand said.

'Possibly. So if I am not back within the time we've got left, you must go without me.'

Dharma looked horrified. Tazmand studied the floor as he considered the situation quietly for a moment.

'No Sky,' he said at last. 'It makes no sense for you to go. You are a girl with no veil. If you get stopped there will be too many questions. Besides which, that Boozak woman will be looking out for you.'

'I-' Sky started to respond.

'You have no wristbands. How can you explain to anyone who stops you what you are doing in the library or palace complex?'

'I could go,' Dharma volunteered half-heartedly, looking terrified at the prospect. Tazmand smiled.

'Thanks Dar, it makes more sense for me to go. I'll be faster and I know the corridors better if I have to take a diversion.'

'Wait a minute,' Dharma said, getting everyone's attention. 'What are we all arguing about? This is madness! None of us can go back. Whoever goes back is bound to be caught and killed. It makes no sense. We will just have to go on without the jewels-'

'Dar,' Tazmand interrupted. 'You said it yourself. We need to be able to buy food. We have to have the jewels or we will die out in the desert. Our escape attempt would be hopeless without the means to purchase help and food.'

'Tazmand, listen to your friend,' Sky said. 'He's right. I know it was my fault and it is not worth the risk-'

'I will be fine. Trust me both of you. I know I can do this. I know the corridors well. I know where to hide when I need to. But, on the slim chance that I don't make it back, then the same one-hour rule applies. If I don't make it back in that time you must go without me and just trust to luck and take your chances. Leave sooner if the soldiers come.'

'Well how much of the hour have we got left before Nana raises the alarm?' Sky asked.

'Enough,' Tazmand replied.

Dharma looked pale with shock. 'We won't go without you.'

'You have to Dar.'

'If you don't get back in time then none of us will go. You just said yourself that without the jewels the attempt would be hopeless.'

'Dar, listen to me. You have to at least try. It might be impossible without the jewels but, you will have to try, otherwise all this will have been in vain. Promise me you will go on without me. You and Sky. Promise!'

Dharma was quiet. He chewed the side of his mouth as though he was fighting with something inside himself that he did not want to let out.

'Promise me Dar. Promise you will go without me... if you have to.'

'Go where?' Salt asked.

In the sudden panic, they had forgotten that they had not told Salt they were planning to escape. Tazmand did not want to upset Salt but, equally, he did not want to lie to him.

'Listen Salt, I can't explain everything now. I have to go and get something. I won't be long and when I get back I will explain everything to you. Will you wait for me?'

'Of course I will wait,' Salt replied, shrugging his shoulders.

'Thank you my friend. In the meantime I need you to get the rope ready and give it to Dharma, along with as much chotzo as you can cram into a small bag.'

'All right Tazmand.'

Tazmand turned to Sky and Dharma. 'Remember, if I'm not back in time, leave without me. Salt will show you the meat chute.'

Dharma gave Sky an angry glance.

'Well, whatever you decide to do. I must try and get the jewels. Dharma, take my knapsack and look after it. Remember you've got the scope in there.'

Tazmand smiled at his friends. Then, before any of them could say another word, he ran up the staircase.

CHAPTER THIRTEEN

Arrest

Nana shifted in Lord Garesh-Far's throne-like chair, attempting to ease the aches and pains in her back. This piece of furniture was certainly not built for comfort. Her eyes scanned the bedchamber, resting from time to time on objects that, once trivial, seemed somehow suddenly significant, now that Skylark had truly gone.

A brush lay on the dressing table with strands of dark hair still clinging to it where only that morning, Nana had assisted with her young mistress's toilet. The ebony eyes of a threadbare toy dog made of silk and wool, stared up at her from where it had fallen to the floor. Nana remembered Skylark playing with it as a young child. For months she had refused to let it out of her sight, carrying it around with her all day and hugging it in her bed at night.

Nana removed the gag from her mouth and used it to dab at her eyes. The pink cords that had bound her hands and legs already lay by her feet in a discarded heap on the floor. Her wrists felt sore where the cords had chaffed her skin while she worked them loose. She rubbed them to ease the stinging and let out a deep sigh. Her thoughts were consumed by Skylark; she was thankful that she had aided her young mistress's escape but, was saddened by the thought that she was never to see her again. Also, the worry that the plan might not work and that the three youngsters would not get away safely gnawed like a hungry rat at the edge of her mind.

She glanced across the room at the time candle that had been lit before they went. It burned steadily in its holder by the empty bed and the honey-coloured beeswax had melted down very nearly to the first hour mark. Nearly time to call for the guards. She wondered what would happen to her when she reported that Skylark had been kidnapped and that she, the princess's body servant and body guard, had failed to protect her. Lord Garesh-Far was not famed for his leniency and she would not be at all surprised if she were condemned to burn in a fire cage.

Another deep sigh escaped her lips. Looking through the window she noticed the first tinges of a pale pink dawn above a line of trees, beyond the wall in the distance. She was surprisingly calm and felt vaguely surprised that she had no fear for her own safety.

'As fate decrees, so shall it be,' Nana murmured aloud. She eased herself slowly out of the chair. The ancient wood creaked in vague protest as she rested her weight on its arms. She felt tired and her bones ached. 'I am an old woman,' she thought, suddenly surprised by the fact. 'When did I become old?' she wondered. She walked to the open window and took a deep breath of air. Then she began to shout for help as loudly as she could.

The garden remained silent for only a matter of seconds before she heard the sound of boots crunching at speed over gravel. A guard appeared carrying a flaming torch. He seemed young to Nana and worried. He bowed before her.

'Lady Narine. What is the matter?'

'The princess-' Nana murmured, pretending to find it difficult to talk. She pressed the back of her hand to her forehead and swayed slightly.

'Lady Narine?' the guard repeated, looking anxious. He moved towards her, worried she might collapse.

'The princess-,' Nana repeated more loudly, leaning against the window frame, her eyes closed 'get help immediately. Skylark Garesh-Far has been abducted.'

The young man's face drained of colour. He stared at Nana with his mouth hanging open. 'Abduct-' he started to echo. The word died on his lips as the significance of Nana's statement struck home, not least of which would be him in a fire cage unless he roused the duty captain immediately.

By the time Nana opened her eyes the young guard had gone and his torch lay scorching the grass where he had dropped it. She heaved a sigh of relief. It has started and there is no going back now, she thought. Within minutes she heard harsh voices shouting orders and the stomp of many more hurrying boots. She saw the gleam of torches coming to her from across the garden and watched as Kareshian military, soldiers of the Shadokin, ran in her direction, crushing underfoot the delicate flowers she and Sky had planted together over the previous weeks. Out of the corner of her eye, she thought she saw a shadowy figure crawling into a thorn bush. Intrigued, she tried to get a closer look but, was

301

distracted by a shadokin captain who was shouting out orders to his soldiers.

'Secure the exits! You two get round to the back of the summerhouse. You three follow me into the princess's chambers and the rest of you patrol and secure the perimeter walls!'

'Here, Captain,' Nana croaked as she stepped through the window, pretending to stagger as if drugged or having just woken from being unconscious. She kept her voice weak and feeble. 'I am over here,' she whimpered and then sank to the grass in a dead faint. Just before she hit the ground, she lifted her head briefly and peered into the thorn bush. Her eyes widened in shock; Tazmand was crouching right in front of her, in the bush. As she watched he moved further into its shaded centre to conceal himself from the view of the standing soldiers. She raised her eyebrows and he placed one finger up to his lips to signal her silence.

'Over here cap'n!' one of the soldiers called out as he came to Nana and knelt beside her. Nana saw it was the young guard who had answered her original cries for help. She closed her eyes quickly, praying he would not glance towards the thorn bush. 'Sir, it's the Lady Narine.'

'Where's the princess?' asked the captain, crossing over to have a look at what the soldier had found and peering down at Nana's expressionless face.

'Dunno, cap'n. Haven't seen her. It was the Lady Narine who told me she had been abducted.'

'I wasn't talking to you. I was addressing the lady.'

'Sorry, Sir. I think she's passed out, Sir.'

'Well wake her up then.'

The young guard started tapping Nana's face gently with the tips of his fingers. 'She won't come round, Sir.'

The captain pushed the young guard out of the way. 'Get looking for the princess and fast. I'll deal with her.'

'Yes, Sir!' The guard jumped up quickly.

'Nothing in here, Captain,' another guard shouted out through the bedchamber windows. 'It's empty.'

'I want this entire area scoured from top to bottom. Turn over every leaf in this garden. Uproot every plant, bush and tree if you have to. I want the princess found and I want her safe. Now get to it! You,' he shouted, pointing at another young soldier, 'get over to the barracks and get every available person out and searching the entire palace complex, including the library. Sound the general alarm. I want all staff rounded up, accounted for and questioned. Go and warn Commander Garrand that Lord Garesh-Far will need to be disturbed; he will have to be told that his daughter has gone missing. This is a full alert – top priority.'

The guard stood looking at his captain, his face white with shock and seemingly paralysed.

'Get to it now!' shouted the captain, obviously affected by the gravity of the situation himself.

Nana, her eyes tight shut, could hear the urgent stamp of heavy boots running around the garden then she felt the captain kneel beside her and a place a warm, calloused hand on her forehead. She desperately wanted to open her eyes to see if Tazmand was really hiding in the bushes or if she had imagined it.

'Lady Narine? Lady Narine can you hear me? Lady Narine?'

She felt her shoulder being shaken and she opened her eyes gradually to peer up into the face of the captain.

'Wha-? Who? Oh, where am I? I can't...' she said, feigning grogginess and disorientation. She prayed to the gods that the captain of the guards, who was relatively new and did not know her well, would assume that being an old woman, she was weak enough to be in this condition.

'Lady Narine, what has happened here? Who has attacked you and where is Princess Garesh-Far?'

'Princess Garesh... oh by the gods!' she shouted, as if all of a sudden recalling what had happened. 'Skylark! She has been taken. They hit me on the head. I was tied up and... and they took her by force!'

'Lady Narine. Who has taken her?'

Nana signalled that she was weary and needed a glass of water before she could continue. A guard was sent to bring her some. She raised her veil slightly and slipped the glass underneath. Taking a sip of the chilled water, she sneaked a look towards the thorn bush. Sure enough, deep in the shadows she saw the dark outlines of a boy's shape keeping very still. Close to black in colour, the leaves on the bush had long white thorns sticking out of them. Chosen by Sky for their ornamental appeal, Nana knew from experience that these thorns were extremely sharp. With any luck, this would deter any of the guards from looking too closely. Also it was highly unlikely that anyone would have been able to get deep into such an inhospitable bush; she wondered how Tazmand had managed it.

'Lady Narine, please continue. Who has taken her?'

Nana handed the glass back to one of the guards with a

nod of thanks.

'Young men. They were dressed like grunts,' she replied, tearing her eyes away from the bush and hoping nobody had noticed her staring.

'How many young men? What did they look like? What colour robes?'

'Well, I don't know. It all happened so fast. I was asleep. I heard Skylark scream and I jumped up from the floor to see what was wrong, little expecting intruders. I saw them standing next to her bed. Two of them I think, maybe more. I think they were male although, they might have been female. Very hard to tell. They were in shadow. Then, they hit me over the head. The next thing I knew was that I woke up bound to a chair and gagged, with a thumping headache and them and the princess gone!'

'Lady Narine, you must remember something more. How did they get here into the garden? What colour wristbands did they have on? Which way did they leave?'

'I don't know I tell you. It was dark. I saw them dimly by the bed. One of them had their hand over the princess's mouth to stop her screaming. Another came towards me and before I could draw my knife, I was plunged into darkness. Then I came to with a splitting headache and managed to untie my bonds. I could only call for help once my hands were free to take off the gag.'

'How tall were they? Were they fat or thin? Even in shadow, you must have been able to get some overall impression of their physical type.'

'Well young man I will try,' Nana answered, capitalising on her age and the tiredness in her voice. 'You know, it was dark and it all happened so incredibly rapidly. Also my memory is not what it used to be. I am nanny and personal high servant to the princess, I do not have the sort of training you soldiers receive in observation of detail.'

'Please Lady Narine, just do your best.'

Nana peered into the distance, as if attempting to recall the events. 'They seemed of average height with, well you know… regular builds.'

'Average height and builds.' The captain looked pained. 'Did they wear turbans?'

'Erm, I can't be sure. No, now I think of it, I am pretty sure there was no headwear.'

'What about their hair length then?'

'Sort of ordinary really.'

'Hair colour?'

'Um-'

'Wait. Don't tell me.' The captain interrupted. 'Let me guess. Average.'

'No actually. I would say more… you know, run of the mill colouring.'

The captain of the guard let out an exasperated sigh. 'How long ago did this happen?'

Nana was quiet for a moment as if trying to calculate. 'I'm afraid I can't guess. It was the middle of the night. It was dark. It could have been hours ago. I don't even know what time it is now. I have been unconscious.'

The captain looked towards the bedchamber window. 'There is a candle burning in there. When did you light it? Was it after you came 'round?'

'Er, no actually. It wasn't. They must have lit it after they knocked me out.'

'Can you stand?'

'Yes I think so.'

'Good, come with me please.' He gave Nana his hand and helped her to get up. As he led her back towards Sky's bedchamber, Nana took one more glance towards Tazmand's hiding place. A guard was poking through the foliage and peering into the bush.

The captain led Nana into the bedchamber, through the still open window. There were soldiers milling about all over the room, opening drawers and wardrobe doors. Looking behind racks of clothes and generally creating a mess.

'Well that's a piece of good fortune,' the captain said as they walked in.

'What is, Captain?'

'The candle, Lady Narine. They lit a fresh candle with hour marks down the side. The wax has melted just a quarter past the first hour which would indicate that they have only been gone for that amount of time.'

Nana could have kicked herself; she felt furious at her own lack of forethought. 'Why didn't I blow it out before calling for help,' she muttered to herself, her teeth clenched so tightly that she could feel her jaw muscles start to numb with the pressure.

'What was that?' the captain asked, turning towards her.

'Oh nothing, Captain. Just thinking what a stroke of luck. You know, the candle.' She jerked her head towards it.

'Yes, Lady Narine. Yes indeed. Quite fortunate.'

As she looked around the room, she noticed a small bundle on the table by the window. It was a velvet pouch, which Nana instantly recognised as the pack of jewels Sky had prepared to take with her on the journey. So that's why he's back in the garden, Nana realised immediately; Sky had forgotten the jewels and Tazmand had returned to get them! Oh that foolish girl, Nana thought. And foolish boy for risking his neck. Without drawing attention to herself, Nana moved to the table and stood for a moment with her back to the rest of the room. She leant her hands on the table as if taking a rest and smoothly scooped the bundle of jewels into her pocket.

'Are you well Lady Narine?' the captain asked. He was standing directly behind her. Nana gave a small start.

'Oh, yes, Captain. Nothing serious, a little dizziness. That is all.'

'Then let us go back outside for some air.' Nana gave a nod and they both walked through the window. 'They can't have got too far in that time.'

'I beg your pardon, Captain?'

'One hour and a quarter. The candle?'

'Oh yes of course, the candle.'

'You must not worry. This is a big place Lady Narine as you well know, and there have been no reports of anyone unauthorised leaving the building complex either via the library or palace exits, as far as I am aware anyway. So, they must still be in here somewhere. And, if they are, then we, the Shadokin House Guards, will find them.'

'Thank the gods!' Nana gasped, doing her utmost to sound enthusiastic.

One by one, soldiers approached the captain to report that they had found nothing. He nodded as if satisfied and turned to Nana. 'Thank you Lady Narine, for your help,' he said, bowing his head and clicking his heels together.'

'You have finished here?' Nana asked, hopefully.

'Indeed we have Lady. The garden is empty and we have found no useful clues other than an unlocked door leading into the palace complex.'

'Really, Captain? An unlocked door you say?'

'Yes Lady. A door that would usually require no guard as it is internal and has no access to outside the palace. A low-level risk, as long as it remains locked of course.'

Nana nodded, showing she understood. 'Locked, yes. Fair reasoning, Captain.'

'Most likely then an inside job, so we now need to concentrate the search on the rest of the building.'

'Inside job! My goodness, Captain. Shocking!'

The captain smiled and gave a shallow bow. 'A physician should arrive soon to tend to your wounded head and,' he paused momentarily to glance down at the red marks on Nana's wrists, 'any other injuries you may have incurred.'

'Thank you, Captain, I have no need of a physician. I just want the princess back safe and sound,' Nana replied bowing slightly in return. Relief washed through her now that the soldiers were leaving.

'Have no fear of that Lady. She will be found and her abductors will be severely punished. I guarantee it.' The captain signalled the soldiers to leave the garden and move indoors.

'Captain!' the guard standing next to Tazmand's hiding place shouted. She was leaning over the bush and poking her sword down into it, between the leaves and branches. The captain turned towards her, signalling the others to wait.

'What is it, Private?'

'Captain, I'm pretty sure there is something or possibly someone here in this bush.'

The captain instantly went over to see what the guard had found. Nana was about to follow him but, he pushed her back gently.

'Please stay here, Lady. It may be dangerous.'

Nana remained rooted to the spot. She felt her stomach turn over and cold sweat broke out on her forehead. The captain went over to the bush and drew his sword. He and the guard hacked away at the bush with their weapons until most of the thorny leaves lay around them on the grass like autumn had come early. The squatting figure of Tazmand could now be seen clearly through the denuded branches.

Several other guards came running towards the spot as the captain called to them for assistance. They encircled Tazmand, holding up flaming torches in one hand and pointing their swords towards him with the other.

'Come out and stand in front of me,' the captain shouted at Tazmand. He did not move. 'Come out now. You will not be harmed but, I am placing you under arrest.'

Nana looked on in horror as Tazmand slowly crawled forwards out of the bush, his already badly-torn clothes catching on the branches and any remaining leaf thorns. He stood in front of his captives appearing dirty, vulnerable and frightened. Nana could see in the torchlight that his black robe was shredded and bloodied and his face, hands and other areas of exposed flesh had scratches and cuts from the vicious thorns. The guard who had first discovered him put down her sword and torch and stood behind Tazmand, twisting both his arms painfully up behind his back.

'Who are you?' the captain snapped. Tazmand said nothing in reply and stared at the ground. 'Where is your tongue boy? Speak up. What is your name and what, by the grace of the gods, are you doing here? How did you get in?'

The Lady Narine watched Tazmand as he continued to hang his head and say nothing. What could he say and what would it matter, she thought? He would know his life was forfeit now anyway. A slave hiding in the garden of Skylark Garesh-Far. It was unheard of; let alone the fact that she had been kidnapped. She could tell by his face that he was resigned to his fate. He could think of nothing to say. Nana tried to get his attention by coughing. *Don't give up Tazmand. I will find a way. Look at me.*

'He is a grunt; a shelver from the library – or at least he was! His name is Tazmand!' a voice shouted suddenly. Everyone turned to see a bulky figure limping towards them across the lawn.

'And who exactly are you?' the captain asked irritably, pointing his sword in the figure's direction as if this new arrival posed a fresh threat to state security.

'I am Sash, overgrunt to this miserable creature, the person replied moving into the light of the torches and pointing at Tazmand.

'Another servant in the wrong place,' the captain said, raising his eyes. 'What are you doing here?'

'I have come to lend my help, Sir,' Sash replied, bowing. 'I am in charge of this grunt and have suspected for some time that he, and a thoroughly disreputable colleague of his called Dharma, were planning something-'

'So you are to blame for all this!'

'Blame!' Sash suddenly straightened up, his face starting to redden in a mixture of anger and fear. 'Absolutely not. I cannot possibly be held responsible for what is going on-'

'You say you knew that they were planning something. Did you report it to security services?'

'Well no I-'

'Why not?'

'Because grunts are always up to something or other. Little scams. Trying to bunk off work, you know that sort of thing. How could I possibly ever suspect that something this huge was likely to happen?'

'So why haven't you been watching them?'

'I have been keeping an eye on them. I even tightened up the watch on their dormitory and had a few of the nearby corridors sealed off to put a stop to their tricks. And, tonight I was in my common room and heard the general alarm and heard about the princess. Well of course I did not for a moment believe that Tazmand or Dharma could be involved but, just in case, I went to check their dormitory and was astounded to find that they were not there! Just a coincidence I thought but, I decided to report it and was directed to come here to see you. I did not think it relevant or of any real consequence. They are mere grunts.'

'You did not think that either the safety, or even possibly the life, of Princess Garesh-Far were of any relevance or any real consequence?'

Sash had turned bright red with frustration and embarrassment. He was flustered. 'No. I mean yes! No, of course I do but, what I mean is that they are just library grunts. I did not think for one moment they could possibly be planning anything this serious. You are twisting my words and distorting their meaning.'

'Well we will just have to see what Lord Garesh-Far thinks of all this won't we?'

Sash's face tuned from bright red to pale grey as every drop of blood drained from it. 'Lord Garesh-'

'Well of course. He will want to personally interview anyone involved in the abduction of his daughter.'

Tazmand seemed amazed to witness Sash speechless for the first time ever.

'I, I ca-, can't see Lord Garesh-far.'

'Too bad,' snapped the captain. Because he will definitely want to see you. Seems to me that you are responsible for all this mess. If you had been keeping a proper eye on your staff, none of this would have happened.'

'Hang on just a minute, Captain. You can't blame all this on me. You are in charge of looking after the princess's safety. Where were you and all your men when this happened?'

'Do not be impertinent. Me and my men were doing our duty...'

The Lady Nadine was only half following the the argument between the fat overgrunt and the captain. She realised this Sash person was in charge of Tazmand and, judging by Tazmand's expression, there was no love lost in their relationship. She looked up at the sky. A pale blue strip was cresting the horizon with light yellow and gold clouds. The sun was rising fast now. She could also hear lots of noise and commotion coming from inside the surrounding buildings; people were ringing bells, lights were being lit and people could be heard shouting and moving about.

She worried that Tazmand had given up and tried, by sheer force of will to get him to look at her. *Here Tazmand, here. Look at me. Look over here!* Eventually, he did. She stared back at him. She pulled the bag of jewellery out of her pocket and held it low down by her side. She looked down at it. He looked at it too. He looked back at Nana's eyes and gave an imperceptible shrug. *The jewels Tazmand. It's Sky's jewels.* She looked down again and, with her other hand, pointed to one of her rings. She saw understanding instantly flood his face. The jewellery! He looked round at the guards. All of them, even the one holding his arms, were watching the argument between Sash and their captain.

Again, making sure he was watching her, Nana looked directly at him then moved her eyes purposefully to the door leading back into the palace. She then walked slowly across the grass to where he was standing. As she approached him she kept darting her eyes towards the door. She moved over in his direction until she was right in front of him. Suddenly her face filled with rage and, screaming as loudly as she could, she slapped Tazmand around the face, hard. As she did this, her other hand dropped the bundle of jewels at his feet, before she then used both hands to beat him on the chest. Everyone turned to look, too engrossed in the spectacle to witness her drop the bundle.

'Why? Why? Why?' she screamed repeatedly. Then she reached for her dagger and, raising it high above her head, looked as though she was going to stab him through the heart. Sash, distracted from his argument, looked on gleefully, seemingly excited by the prospect of witnessing Tazmand's imminent murder.

'No!' the captain screamed in alarm. 'We need him for questioning!'

The guard holding Tazmand's arms let go of him and reached forward to grab the knife from Nana's hands.

'Now!' Nana shouted to Tazmand, indicating the open door once more with her eyes. Tazmand did not need to be told twice and, as soon as the soldier had released him, he grabbed the bundle off the ground darted sideways and ran for the door. The guard reached for Nana's wrist and gripped it firmly. Nana, quick as a flash, twisted around so that the guard was behind her and, pulling another dagger from her robes with her free hand, stabbed her in the stomach. The guard let go and fell backwards onto the ground, writhing and groaning in pain.

Tazmand stopped to look behind him. He was greeted with the sight of Nana surrounded by several of the other guards running her through with their swords. 'No!' he screamed, hurrying back.

'No Tazmand! Run, save Sky!' Nana moaned out loud as she collapsed to the ground.

Tazmand, tears staining his filthy, bloodstained cheeks turned once again towards the door but, he had hesitated just a moment too long as, without warning, he was tackled to the ground. His face hit soft turf. He felt his legs pinned together by strong arms and the packet of jewels flew from his hand. He twisted himself around and found Sash now kneeling behind him, looking triumphant.

'Didn't think I could run that quickly did you Taz?' he gloated as he looked down at his victim. 'Not since my injury.'

315

Tazmand could see the guards racing across the garden towards him. He knew with certainty that, at this point, it was all up when suddenly, in the rapidly lightening sky a blue-grey shape swooped down and brushed past Sash's head at incredible speed. Sash screamed with rage as small drops of blood spurted from his face and spattered across the grass. At the sudden sight of blood, Tazmand's surroundings immediately started to turn hazy, as if he was being sucked down underneath the surface of a body of warm water. The noises around him receded and he realised he was entering another dream.

'Not now,' he shouted aloud. 'Please not now. I have to be awake. I have to stay here. I have to escape, get back to the others.'

As if someone, or something, heard his plea, his head cleared. He started to re-emerge from the waters; he felt himself break through the surface and come back to the garden. He gulped air into his lungs with relief and looked up amazed to see Sash ducking and flailing his arms wildly at a screeching falcon. It was assailing him pitilessly as it hurtled from the early morning sky with wings neatly folded into its sides like a pebble let loose from a slingshot. Suddenly, its wings expanded to full span to halt its descent and its yellow talons flashed in the air breaking skin and slicing through flesh before it flew up quickly, out of reach once again. Sash screamed and swore and punched at the empty air.

Every time Sash tried to seize Tazmand, the bird swooped again and viciously attacked him. The overgrunt's face was covered in angry scratches and had been sliced open in several places, as had his hands and wrists where he had tried to protect his face. Blood seeped from the wounds and mingled with sweat, creating a grotesque mask through which the look of rage in Sash's eyes still penetrated. His mouth twisted into a grimace of forbidding determination as he desperately tried to hold on to Tazmand.

The falcon circled above their heads making piercing screeches and diving at Sash whenever it had an opportunity. The sounds it made seemed urgent and, for some reason, Tazmand felt they were directed at him, as if telling him to get a move on. He needed no more encouragement; the guards were nearly on top of him. While Sash was forced to loosen his grip on Tazmand as he fended off yet another attack from the falcon, Tazmand seized his opportunity. He jumped up, grabbed the package of jewels and ran as fast as he could for the door.

His legs carried him swiftly and he did not turn round. Voices shouted from behind to halt. Sash screamed incoherently and the falcon screeched its encouragement. Just as he reached the doorway, he felt the point of a sword slash dangerously a hair's breadth from his back: the guards were closer than he thought. He barged through the doorway and used his shoulder to push the door shut with a resonant clang.

There was no key in the lock so they would have it open again in a moment. He rushed along an empty corridor and, sure enough, heard the door crashing open behind him only seconds later. Voices were shouting, ordering him to stop. He did not stop and he did not look back; he just kept running. Tears and blood now coursed freely down his filthy cheeks, stinging the deep scratches from the thorn bush and blurring his vision. Without noticing, he reached the end of the

317

passageway and continued to run round the corner. Before he could stop himself, he barged headlong into a crowd of people.

CHAPTER FOURTEEN

Meat Chute

Nana is dead! The words echoed inside his skull. Nana is dead! I didn't trust her and she saved me and now she is dead! Dead because of me! Tazmand could think only of the Lady Narine but, any grieving would have to wait. He had to get to the meat chute now, as quickly as possible.

People stared in horror and disbelief at the dishevelled, bloody figure suddenly appearing amongst them with its gore-smeared face and filthy, torn clothes. It had been a strange start to the morning for all of them; alarms going off, being jostled by soldiers and herded into rooms for counting and questioning. Gossip was rife about the disappearance of some princess or other. All the senior staff had heard of Skylark Garesh-Far of course, although many of the lower ranks, such as the grunts in the library and palace complex, had not. They didn't even know the emperor had a daughter.

Tazmand wiped the blood and sweat from his eyes and looked around him at the varied assortment of soldiers, grunts

and other people crowding the corridor. No one tried to stop
him immediately as he snarled and spat like a cornered wild
animal. He pushed through the startled crowds, knocking
people out of his way, and continued to run. Frightened,
most people stood aside to let him through, although a few
overgrunts coming to their senses, shouted for him to stop and
tried to use their whips. They looked thoroughly astonished
when he refused or did not seem to hear them. The pursuing
soldiers, their swords drawn shouted at him to halt but, could
not get close enough through the press of people.

Using a strength and determination born of
desperation, Tazmand continued to run, knocking to the floor
anyone rash enough to get in his way. As he rounded a
corner, he noticed vaguely that all the human traffic had come
to a standstill; grunts and overgrunts of all classes stood to
attention at either side of the passageway as a senior librarian,
a divine, was proceeding with her retinue of underlibrarians
in great pomp, on her way somewhere. Tazmand smashed his
way right through the lot of them, caring little for their petty
hierarchy when only a day before he would have been too
terrified to move a muscle and would have stood aside meekly
with all the others.

The shock of this strange apparition, giving no heed to
even a divine gave rise to the belief that Tazmand was some
sort of inhuman apparition or wild animal that had got into
the library complex; no member of staff could possibly behave
in such a way. This belief was lent further plausibility by
the fact that soldiers with unsheathed swords and a rather
overweight overgrunt suddenly appeared round the corner
chasing it.

Tazmand was progressing through the crowded corridors well and had made it nearly as far as the kitchens, when three soldiers appeared and blocked his path. *Nana is dead and it was my fault!* was the only thought going through his mind as he recklessly charged towards them. He no longer cared if he died as long as his friends got away and Nana's death actually counted for something. The three soldiers raised their swords ready to strike but, out of control now, Tazmand charged at them at full speed.

'That's 'im! That's one of the little pangbats what hurt your comrade Shazek while he was trying to save the princess!' Tazmand recognised the voice of Boozak, the crone who had wanted to take Sky and make her work in her brothel. 'Yes,' she continued screeching loudly to someone else in the crowd, making sure everyone could hear her. 'Shazek and me, well we knew it was the princess straight away. She was screamin' and trying to get away from these two louts. So Shazek goes and grabs her off 'em in an attempt to save the poor little girl and they attack him and me. Shazek's got a great big cut on his head for his trouble and I was lucky to get away with my life! And my honour,' she added coyly.

'You sure that's him Boozak?' one of the three soldiers asked, gripping his sword tightly.

'Well of course I'm sure you pronk. How many grunts do you get racing around early in the morning covered in blood, with their robes in tatters? Kill 'im. Get 'im quick so's we get a reward,' she screamed, her voice getting hysterical with excitement at the prospect of seeing a kill.

'No!' a voice behind Tazmand shouted. 'He must be caught alive. We need him to tell us where the princess is!' It was the captain of Sky's guard. The three soldiers immediately dropped the points of their swords and attempted to catch Tazmand in their arms when, all of a sudden, Daniel sprang up from nowhere behind them and, knocking the turbans off two of the guards, he grabbed both of their heads and bashed them together like coconuts. The third guard turned to see who it was behind him and what had happened to his two comrades, only to have Daniel give him a hefty punch in the stomach. Boozak screamed in rage and frustration and flung herself at Daniel, kicking and pulling at his hair and beard.

'Keep going boy. Run!'

Tazmand felt confused. He stopped momentarily and stared at the elderly grunt. 'How?'

'No time for explanations now. Keep moving! Run!' Daniel shouted, pushing Boozak away. Tazmand kept going and, reaching the stone steps that descended to the vaults, flew down them like the wind. When he got to the bottom he shouted hysterically for Salt, Sky and Dharma. They were nowhere to be seen. Soldiers and overgrunts were everywhere, rounding up the salter and butcher grunts from dormitories around the perimeter of the room, herding them like cattle into corners to be questioned and counted. Tazmand kept running, successfully dodging the soldiers who tried to catch him.

The guards were still close behind him on the staircase shouting to everyone and anyone to capture Tazmand. Running close behind them was Sash, who was huffing and puffing and looking blue in the face from the unaccustomed exertion. The scratches and cuts on his face from the falcon looked livid and sore.

Tazmand continued to run as fast as he could through the butcher rooms, which were now empty but, he was starting to slow down as he was reaching the limits of his energy. His legs felt numb and wobbly and burning all at the same time and he could hardly catch his breath. He continued to shout for his friends, able by now to manage only a hoarse whisper. He received no reply. He was not sure what time it was and realised that the agreed hour must certainly have been up some time ago and that they would have gone without him. He sank to his hands and knees on the hard floor and tried to catch his breath. He was glad, he thought; at least they would have a chance, even if he did not. Now, he would just stop and let the soldiers catch up with him. Nana was dead, his friends had got away and there was nothing else he could do.

'Tazmand!' Someone was shouting his name. He looked around. His vision was blurred from sweat, tears and blood but, he could dimly see a face floating in front of him, peering from around a door.

'Tazmand run. Don't stop. Quick, this way. Faster, they are catching-up!'

Tazmand wiped his face and his eyes with the back of his hand.

'Your Highness!' Tazmand heard the captain's voice shout from behind him. *Your Highness?* thought Tazmand - Sky!

'Taz, quick get a move on.' It was indeed Sky peering at him from behind the door of the meat chute. 'Quick we have been waiting. Jump in. Hurry!'

Tazmand stood up with some effort and ran towards the vision. He reached the door of the meat chute and sure enough,

Sky and Dharma were crammed inside with Salt.

'Salt! What are you doing here?' Tazmand panted.

'Hello my best friend Tazmand,' Salt said, beaming with relief and pleasure as he reached out and, grabbing what was left of Tazmand's tattered robe front, effortlessly pulled him into the little, metal cupboard.

'Explanations later,' Dharma snapped as Tazmand fell in amongst his friends and Dharma pulled the door shut. 'I hope to the gods that this contraption works.'

Just as the door was swinging closed, they heard a terrible scream of pain. There was a gap in the door where it would not shut properly. Salt leaned forward and helped Dharma by giving the door a heave. It was no good, it would not shut. There was another scream of agony. Something was jamming it. They all looked down and, at the base of the door, a foot was stuck. Sky bent down and grabbed the foot with her hands. Another screech of pain emanated from the other side of the door.

'I would recognise that boot anywhere. It has kicked me enough times,' Dharma said. 'It's Sash.'

'Open it, please! I think my foot is broken,' they could hear Sash squeal from the other side of the door.

'Get that door open Corporal, the captain's voice could be heard. They have got the princess in there.' Then, to them he shouted. 'It's no good you scoundrels. You can't stay in that cupboard forever. We will have you out soon, Your Highness, never fear.'

'I don't want to come out!' Sky shouted back and gave Sash's foot such a mighty push that he was able to pull it free. The door then clanged shut and Salt, using all of his phenomenal strength, twisted the inside door handle out of shape so that it could not be opened again, either from the outside or the inside. Salt, Tazmand, Sky and Dharma sat in total darkness. Muffled pounding could be heard from the far side of the door.

'No going back now,' Sky said out loud as they all waited in the dark for something to happen. Nothing did.

'I got the jewels,' Tazmand said, noticing that the package was still gripped securely in his hand.

'How was Nana?' Sky asked. Tazmand did not reply and Sky had to repeat the question. 'Tazmand? Nana? How was she?'

'Fine,' Tazmand replied eventually, his voice thick with emotion. 'She was fine.' He cleared his throat and changed the subject. 'Dharma?'

'Yes Taz.' Dharma's voice answered out of the dark.

'Have you got my knapsack?'

'Yes of course.'

'Good, then put this in it for me.'

They both fumbled in the dark until Dharma felt Tazmand's hand and took the package of jewellery from him and stowed it in the leather bag. They could still hear muffled banging and shouting from the other side of the door as the guards tried to get it open then, without warning, there was a soft whirring noise, the floor gave a slight vibration and the rear wall of the room slid open.

The floor suddenly tipped up and they were all thrown backwards onto a flat platform. The wall closed again with a soft thump and they found themselves in intense blackness and silence on the other side of it. Dharma felt around on the floor in the dark, his fingers encountering lumps of squidgy, spongy, wet things. There was an overwhelming, rotten stink. 'What's all this?' he asked, already knowing the answer, and wishing he did not.

'Meat,' Salt's voice answered in the darkness. Dharma's stomach turned over. 'And blood,' Salt added matter-of-factly. 'And bits of-'

'I think I'm going to be sick,' Sky moaned, interrupting him. 'The stench is unbearable.'

A low hum started somewhere deep underneath the platform. This was followed by a gentle rumble and a metallic clunk as the platform jerked and started to move. It tipped up at an angle of forty-five degrees so they all had to adjust their sitting positions and hold on to each other (or whatever came to hand) as they started to be conveyed upwards.

Sky let out a scream as something heavy fell into her lap, pinning her legs down. She warily felt with her hands to see what it was and recognised a head and shoulders. 'What?' she began to say out loud, feeling panic rise in her chest as she thought a body had been thrown with them into the chute when she realised that she could only hear Salt and Dharma's voices asking what the matter was.

'Tazmand?' she shouted. 'Tazmand, are you all right?'

There was no response. He lay across her legs, motionless.

'Tazmand!' Sky screamed, shaking his shoulders. 'What's wrong?'

He did not move or respond.

The captain was shouting at one of his guards. 'Well it can't be that difficult to get the door open!'

'Sorry, Sir, we've tried everything. It's completely jammed.'

'Go and get some equipment so we can prize it open. The princess could have suffocated to death in that cupboard by the time we get to her.'

'She said she didn't want to come out, Sir,' the guard reminded him.

'I know what she said you pronk!' the captain said, his voice harsh with anger. 'She is not in a fit state to make any sort of decision for herself. She is distraught and in the power of those... those, depraved monsters. She realises she needs to say anything to survive.'

'Yes, Sir, of course, Sir.'

'Find some tools immediately and get this cupboard open!'

'Yes, Sir!' The soldier saluted and ran off at double-quick time.

Sash sat on the floor, groaning and massaging his mangled foot. 'I must have a physician.'

'Oh shut up!' the captain snapped, not one ounce of sympathy forthcoming. 'This is entirely your fault. You should have kept a better eye on those two grunts of yours. As a matter of fact, who was the third one in there with them? The ginger one?'

'No idea. Never seen him before.' Sash groaned again, holding his broken foot.

'Don't lie to me.'

'I'm not. I have never seen him before. Please get me some physic aid. My face needs stitches and my foot is unusable.'

The captain smiled. 'You can get treated when we get the princess out of there. Then you can join her captors in a fire cage. In the meantime, shut up.'

'A fire ca-' Sash was about to screech his innocence, when a young voice piped up from behind them.

The captain turned to see a young girl of about nine. She stood in front of him, one hand supporting a buffalo leg balanced on her head, the other cramming a piece of chozo into her mouth. 'They won't come back out of there you know.'

'What are you doing with that, that thing?' He pointed at the buffalo leg. 'That animal limb?' he asked her.

'It's my job, Sir. I'm a salter,' she replied whilst chewing.

The captain had no idea what the girl was talking about and did not care, so asked for no further explanation. 'What do you mean they won't come out?'

'It's the meat chute, Sir. We put all our bad meat in it and it gets taken away to the rubbish.'

'What? You mean the room leads somewhere else?'

'Uh huh.' The girl nodded and fished another piece of dried meat out of her pocket.

'Where does it go?'

The girl shook her head. 'Don't know.'

'Don't lie to us you diminutive piece of vermin-infested filth,' Sash joined in, fondling the hilt of his whip. 'Tell us the truth or you'll get a taste of leather.'

The little girl, obviously used to the strong-arm

methods employed by overgrunts did not even blink at his threat. 'I am telling the truth, Gruntmeister. No one has ever told me where it goes. I just know it goes.'

'She's telling the truth,' Sash said to the captain, letting out another groan as he remembered his foot, then another as he delicately probed one of the newly-forming scabs on his face.

The captain turned to another guard. 'Go and find out where this chute thing leads, then report back to me on the double.'

'Yes, Captain,' the guard responded before running off, just as a new messenger arrived.

'Sir?'

'Yes, Private what is it?' The messenger took a deep, nervous swallow. 'Get on with it man, can't you see I am busy?'

The messenger swallowed again, obviously uneasy. 'Our great and mighty emperor, the Lord Garesh-Far commands your presence immediately, Sir.'

The captain closed his eyes and swore under his breath. 'By the gods, so soon.'

'Ha, you're in for it now pangbat face,' Sash said, smiling despite the cuts giving him terrible pain when he moved any of his facial muscles.

'No, Sir,' the messenger continued. 'You are both to attend him.'

Sash's mouth dropped as the captain managed to raise a smile to his. 'Come along then, Gruntmeister. We cannot keep His Imperial Majesty waiting. After you.'

Sash tried to stand but, found it impossible on his broken foot. He gave a shrill squeal and collapsed once more to the floor.

'Guard!' the captain addressed one of his men.

The guard snapped to attention. 'Yes, Sir!'

'Pick this bag of pig's giblets up off the ground and assist him to walk.' He looked down at Sash. 'Drag him if you have to.'

#

Lord Garesh-Far, Despot of Karesh, Potentate of the Desert Lands and rightful emperor of the known world, stood before a full-length mirror in the retiring chamber behind his throne room. He scanned his reflection, from the pomaded lustre of his black hair, along his immaculately tailored white uniform, down to his black leather boots which gleamed like highly-polished jet. His grey eyes betrayed no hint of feeling, thought or opinion - good, neutral, bad or otherwise. He simply stared at his mirror image, like an ant might stare at another ant.

As it happened, his reflection pleased him, so he decided to attempt a smile. The two corners of his mouth stretched out sideways, in opposite directions so that his already thin lips compressed into an even thinner line. The line joined up with his purple scar, giving his otherwise immobile face a grotesque, lopsided look. He gave-up on the smile and allowed his eyelids to blink once, just to remind himself how to do it.

Turning from the mirror with military precision, he walked across the sparsely furnished room, his boots clicking on the hard stone floor, to a plain wooden shelf attached to the wall by a couple of chains at knee height. This was his bed. The emperor sat on it for a moment, before deciding to lie down and rest. His eyes remained open wide, like a fish, as he stared at the ceiling wondering whether his daughter had been truly abducted or whether she had, in fact, run away. Doubtful, he thought but, possible.

He considered the situation dispassionately; she would, of course, be captured eventually, returned and a suitable punishment would need to be administered. Then she would perform her expected duty and be bundled off to be married as planned. The noble in question, the intended spouse, was not strictly high-ranking enough but, he had made a deal with the man's father many years ago and had no choice except to honour it. A pity but, there we have it. Also, the groom's father was essential to the emperor's future plans, as was the son; Sky's new husband would be in eventual control of one of Karesh's wealthiest provinces, one with potential access to extremely lucrative trade routes, once the emperor allowed their ports to re-open that is.

He shifted his position making a slight grunt of discomfort; his breathing was otherwise so shallow that, to an observer, this would have been the only indication that he was, in fact, alive. 'Well done,' he mumbled briefly, then continued to lay on his back as still and pale as an alabaster statue allowing thoughts of his daughter to drift through his mind, staring at the ceiling and listening to the sound of a fly buzzing overhead.

His rest was disturbed eventually by the gentle tinkling of a small bell. He stood up abruptly and moved to a curtain on the opposite side of the room.

'Yes?' he enquired stiffly.

'Your Majesty,' a muffled voice from the other side of the fabric answered, 'the persons involved with the disappearance of the princess are arriving now for an audience.'

'Very well.' The emperor clicked his fingers and three valets appeared from discreet corners of the room where they had been waiting. One straightened his jacket, another smoothed his hair down at the back where the wooden bed had disturbed its perfect symmetry. and the third adjusted his belt then handed the emperor his sword, which was swiftly placed in its scabbard.

Freshly re-arranged, he moved through the curtain, which was lifted for him by an unseen servant, and entered a magnificent assembly room. Early morning sunlight streamed through two-dozen multi-coloured crystal windows each fifteen metres high and five wide, illuminating the deep red, purple and gold of the interior. As soon as the emperor stepped through the curtain a gong was sounded. Instantly, the several hundred people gathered in the space, hoping for an audience, went silent and bowed low, touching their foreheads to the floor. Lord Garesh-Far took his seat on a great, gold throne raised high on a dais, facing the crowd.

Looking across the room, he saw before him a sea of turbans. He made a signal with his hand and the gong struck again. The turbans rose from the floor, revealing beneath many men with tired, anxious and hopeful faces. Lord Garesh-Far made another signal and an usher shouted to those assembled to clear the room. The faces of the men before him crumpled with disappointment (many had been waiting for days, some for weeks, others even longer). Obediently, they shuffled silently out through an enormous pair of highly-polished, brass doors.

When the room was empty the gong sounded once more

and two tiny figures appeared from a side entrance. As they approached, the emperor could distinguish that one walked erect like a military man, dressed in the uniform of a captain of the personal household guard. The other was an overgrunt who hobbled painfully with the aid of two sticks.

The two men stopped before the dais and knelt, bowing their heads until their foreheads touched the floor. Lord Garesh-Far noticed the practiced ease with which the military one bowed. The tubby one with the walking sticks had more difficulty. Lack of habit in deep bowing, along with disability would seem to be the obvious reasons, the emperor thought. He watched with amusement, as the servant before him eventually managed to prostrate himself before his emperor, quivering with fear, his buttocks wobbling like two large jellies.

He allowed the two men to maintain the discomfort of the pose for some time before eventually speaking.

'You are both responsible for the loss of our precious daughter,' he intoned at last, his voice flat and dispassionate, his face blank. 'How is this so?'

Sash raised his head. His face was badly swollen. Scars and encrusted scabs covered the skin like sun dried tomatoes baked into the crusty surface of a loaf of bread. He was sweating profusely and could not stop shaking. 'Your Majesty,' his voice quivered, sounding loud as it reverberated around the vast, empty chamber. 'I am aghast at what has happened but, I would just like to say that it was not my fault. I-'

'And you, Captain? What do you have to say?' Lord Garesh-Far interrupted.

'Your Majesty, I am at a loss. Obviously I knew nothing of the plans by this man's grunts to abduct your daughter or of the disloyalty of the princess's body servant until it was too late. I-'

'Yes, the Lady Narine. Her body will be fed to the rats in the city sewers.'

The captain lowered his eyes. 'I beg your forgiveness.'

'You are responsible for my daughter's safety, Captain.'

'My Lord I... Yes I am. I do not know what to say. It is my fault.'

'Yes. You have failed in your duty. You know what to do.'

Sash looked sideways at the captain wondering what it was he had to do. The man had gone pale and looked like he might throw-up.

'Yes my Lord,' the captain answered and, without further delay he drew his sword, turned it so that the hilt was resting on the ground and the point was facing his stomach. He then threw himself forward on to it. The deep red of the thick carpet camouflaged the man's spurting blood. Sash, in shock, wondered if the choice of colour for the carpet was made with this in mind.

Lord Garesh-Far regarded the dead body slumped motionless before him. 'Well done,' he muttered dispassionately.

Sash flung himself fully on the floor; he lay face down and pleaded for mercy, his cries muffled by the thick floor covering. Tears sprang from his eyes and streamed down his cheeks, mingling with snot from his nose. Lord Garesh-Far said nothing until Sash had calmed, and lay sobbing and panting quietly before him.

At last the emperor spoke. 'And what shall I do with you?' he said. 'You should of course also die.'

'Spare me oh Great Lord,' Sash screamed. 'That's what you should do, since you're asking. Spare me and I will do anything I can to put things right. Anything!'

Lord Garesh-Far studied the miserable creature before him. *You will do anything?* He thought to himself. *You should die but, maybe you could be useful yet. Yes, perhaps you might be able to put things right. You must hate these grunts that have caused you so much pain and embarrassment. You have good reason to want to catch them and punish them. Better reason than anyone else. You have a strong motivation – revenge. You would never give up. Never stop, even where paid soldiers would have had enough, you would continue. I know you, Gruntmeister. I have met your type many times before. So, we will not dispose of you yet – quite the contrary in fact.*

'Our daughter and your two library grunts-'

'May they rot for eternity in the afterplace, Your Majesty.' Sash started shouting. 'Filthy rats, they-'

'Silence!' The usher boomed, striking his gong for emphasis. Sash shut up immediately and lay on his front quivering.

The emperor continued. 'I am informed that the princess and her captors have entered a rubbish chute with another grunt from the kitchen slaughterhouses,' he said aloud. 'Even as we speak they are travelling by mechanical conveyance through and up the chute to the outer walls of the palace. As this lies to the western edge of the city, it is also the outer wall of the city of Karesh. In a short time, they will be disgorged through a hole in the city wall, out into the rubbish heaps of an area known as the Scavenging Grounds. Are you listening to me, Overgrunt Sash?'

335

Sash, realising that Lord Garesh-Far was talking to him and had not, so far ordered him to kill himself, stopped quivering, raised his head and listened harder. 'Yes, Your Majesty. Every word.'

'Well done. You are to go and find them and bring them back. Our daughter - if she has survived the experience of her abduction - must be returned to me, unharmed. The others may be disposed of as you see fit.'

Sash knelt before his ultimate master and wiped his nose on his sleeve. He stared at the emperor open-mouthed. 'You mean you are not going to kill me, Your Majesty?'

'On the contrary, Overgrunt Sash. You know these boys and you are the best person to track them down and bring back the princess. Now, take that badge,' he pointed to the silver braided knot on the dead captain's shoulder. Sash reached over and pulled the badge away from the corpse. It was sticky with his blood.

'You are now officially made captain of the Shadokin House Guard. Well done. Unusual circumstances call for even more unusual measures. You are authorised to take as many men, horses and supplies as necessary to retrieve our daughter. Do not disappoint us, Captain Sash.'

Sash was flabbergasted. It was unheard of for a grunt to be promoted to an army position. He stared at the silver braid and then up at the throne.

'Your Majesty, I will not fail.'

'If you succeed you will be a free man and a wealthy one. You will be given riches beyond your wildest dreams.' Sash glanced down at his gold wristbands. Lord Garesh-Far noticed where Sash was looking. 'Those will be removed for the time being.'

'Thank you, Your Majesty.'

'Do not thank me yet. If you fail, you will be found
– wherever you run and attempt to hide – tortured, flayed,
disembowelled and then put to the fire cages. You will die
slowly and in a great deal of pain.'

Sash swallowed, his tear-swollen eyes hardened and he
tried to smile as he thought of taking his revenge out on
Tazmand but, the deep cuts and scabbed, dried blood made
smiling too painful. Instead, he summoned up the image of
Tazmand squirming and wriggling on the point of a sword like
a maggot at the end of a pin and smiled inwardly.

'I will not fail, Your Majesty.'

'Good. You may go. Well done.'

Sash hobbled out of the room, enjoying the
unaccustomed deference shown by the guards who saluted
him as a new shadokin officer.

CHAPTER FIFTEEN

Maggot, Pyg, Tripe

T he platform continued to shudder on its steep ascent of the meat chute. Dharma did his utmost to hold on. He could feel spongy lumps of – he decided he would rather not think what of - soaking through his robe. He spread his hands out onto the metal floor to steady himself, and to find something to hold on to. His round face grimaced in the darkness as his fingers closed round what felt like a large, bony finger and it did not take him long to figure out, once he had felt further around the area, that it was actually a rib bone attached to the remains of a large animal. He had no choice; he gripped it as best he could. It felt slimy but, it was sufficiently anchored to the weighty remains of the carcass to prevent him from sliding about so much.

As the angle of the chute became steeper, the noise increased, becoming significantly louder and louder until, eventually, it sounded like the entire population of the library refectory bashing their cutlery against tin plates whilst at the same time stamping their feet. Dharma found it unbearable and he tried to calm his nerves by distracting himself; focusing on calculating how long they had been in the chute. *How long since we escaped? Seems like ages but, probably only minutes.*

His calculations went straight out of his head as the platform suddenly gave a mighty judder. It was not the first one. His chest tightened and panic threatened to overwhelm him. *What, by all the gods, have we done? Where are we? Stuck in the dark, in a narrow, stinking, carrion-infested chute, going the gods know where; probably to a hideous doom! Perhaps I should have stayed at the library? Stayed safe, got fed, kept my comfy bed well, maybe not 'comfy' but, better than here. Who knows, maybe I would have been all right as a shelver, got used to heights? Perhaps I could even have faced whatever Sash had planned for me?*

His eyes started to sting and he could feel himself about to cry when Sky's voice brought him back to his senses. 'Tazmand, what's wrong?' she shouted over the din. 'Wake up!'

Tazmand was still unconscious and someone, Dharma decided, had to take charge of the situation. He took several deep breaths and calmed himself. 'Taz? Taz, can you hear me?'

'He's collapsed Dharma and I can't wake him up. He's lying across my lap. I think he might be dead.' Sky had to shout over the noise, through the darkness. 'I don't know what has happened.' She sounded terrified.

'Sky!' Dharma shouted. 'Sky can you hear me?'

'Yes.' Her voice was tinged with the early signs of panic.

'Good, then listen to me. Firstly, are you secure on the platform? Have you got something to hold on to?'

'Yes, I can't move. Tazmand's head is lying in my lap. I'm pretty much pinned to the floor.'

'Salt, are you all right?'

'Yes, thank you Dharma. I'm very well.' Salt's calm voice could be heard over the noise. 'Is Tazmand all right? He's my friend.'

'Yes Salt, I think so. Sky?'

'Yes.'

'Is Taz breathing? Can you feel?'

'Oh I hadn't thought.' She went quiet for a moment. 'Um, yes. Yes he is,' she yelled. 'I can feel his chest going in and out and his breath on the back of my hand.'

Dharma let out a sigh of relief.

'I can see something,' Salt said.

'I think he's all right Sky,' Dharma continued, ignoring Salt. 'This has happened before, in the library. He just sort of passes out and lies like he's in a dead faint. All we can do is leave him until it wears off and he wakes up.'

'Has he been doing it for long? Is he ill?'

'Not long and I don't think he's ill. Don't know really. He just has these funny turns now and again.'

'How long have we been in here?' Sky shouted.

'I can see something,' Salt said again.

'I, I don't know,' Dharma said. 'I've lost sense of time. It seems ages. I think we have gone up a long way. It might be half an hour or it could be three hours. I haven't got a clue.'

'I can't believe we're doing this.' Sky sounded on the verge of tears. 'How in the gods' names are we going to get out without breaking our necks?'

'Light,' Salt said. The others were too wrapped up in their own concerns to hear him.

Dharma thought about what to say. And, in the end had to admit the truth. 'I don't know how we'll get out Sky.'

'Light!' Salt shouted as loud as he could.

'What?' The other two said together, startled.

'Light, light, light. Look. Up there, a little dot.'

Dharma and Sky both looked in the direction the platform was travelling and squinted. Sure enough, in the distance a tiny pinprick of white was clearly visible.

'End of the chute,' Salt said, stating the obvious. 'We can get out. Hurrah!'

Sky started shouting and slapping Tazmand's face as hard as she could. 'Tazmand, wake up! You have to wake up! Wake up!' Tazmand continued to sleep. 'Dharma he won't respond. What can I do?'

'Just keep slapping and shouting. Do whatever it takes. Just get him awake - now!'

'Tazmand please wake up we haven't got much time. We have to get the rope ready. Wake up.' But, he still did not respond.

'Sky,' Dharma shouted, 'you have to rouse him! Now! I don't think I can hold on much longer. I'm starting to slip backwards.'

'I am trying Dharma.' She gave Tazmand several more slaps across his face, hitting him much harder than she meant to, out of mounting panic.

The white pinprick was getting bigger and was no longer above them: it lay straight ahead as the platform had stopped travelling upwards and was now moving along on the level. They could see each other faintly in the new, dim glow and the groan and clatter of the machinery was, thankfully, quieter. Dharma felt stable enough to let go of the animal carcass. Tazmand still lay unconscious in Sky's lap. She continued to slap him and shout his name. Salt was squatting, balanced nimbly on the platform as if he had done it a thousand times before.

"What's that noise?' Dharma asked suddenly.

'What do you mean?' Sky said. 'It's this infernal machine we're on. It's been clanking and clattering for ages!'

'Sky, shut up for a minute. I can hear something. Something else I mean.' He got on to his knees and listened intently. Sky went quiet too and they all concentrated.

The illumination from the far end of the chute was getting brighter and they could see each other more clearly. They could also see the platform stretch out in front of them in a long strip, all the way to the exit. The smooth tunnel walls gleamed, displaying a gap at either side of the platform big enough for any of them to fall through. The new noise was sharp and metallic with an underlying crunch. Similar to the mechanical grinding earlier but, harsher – like the sound of a sharp knife trying to slice glass. There was another noise too, like the flat sides of two sharp swords rasping together.

'It sounds like a giant grinding his teeth,' Dharma said, having no idea just how accurate his description was until they got still closer.

Bright flashes of sunlight now streamed through the exit and reflected on the dirty metal walls, making them squint. Something was moving across the hole with a regular, relentless rhythm every few seconds, briefly blocking the sunlight. As they got closer, it became clear what it was: serrated sheets of metal moved up and down and from side to side across the mouth of the chute. They cut and chopped through meat and bone and anything else that came through their path, with no more effort than someone biting through celery.

Dharma felt his body go rigid. Terror gripped him, paralysing every nerve in his body. Sky screamed and started slapping Tazmand's face even harder to try and wake him but, he continued to sleep, oblivious to the approaching danger.

'It's like teeth made of metal!' Salt said, excited and pointing. 'Look!'

#

Tazmand is floating, suspended in warm, smoky air. He feels safe and comfortable, insubstantial, dried out, like a leaf wafting at the whim of a soft breeze. 'Nice here.' He stretches, enjoying the sensation of weightlessness, then roles on his side and places his hands under his head, like he is in bed. 'Just a little nap.' He yawns. 'Then I'll get up.'

Just as he is drifting into a relaxing sleep, his rest is interrupted by a loud blast on a trumpet. The sound is discordant, harsh and tuneless. He sits up reluctantly and covers his ears with his hands as the trumpet blasts another few crude notes.

'What the-' Feeling still half asleep and disorientated, it takes him a few moments to notice that the smoke has cleared and now, rather than floating, he is sitting on a damp rock surrounded by glaring, white sunshine, rushing winds and the frenzied roaring of water.

He feels cold, despite the sunshine and is badly missing the comfort of the warm smoke. 'Where am I?' Looking around, he is alone. 'Hello!' His voice is drowned out by the sound of huge waves crashing against the rock, which then shatter into rivulets of pale green and foaming white, spraying his feet. 'Hello!' he tries again, louder. 'Anyone?!' No response.

He shakes his head, trying to clear it. 'I'm sure there is something I'm meant to be doing. Somewhere I've got to go. Can't remember.' He peers into the distance but, all he can see is an ocean of black. 'The sea!' he gasps. 'This must be the sea!' Having never seen it before, its immensity awes him.

'This is no good!' He takes a deep breath, attempting to calm down. 'Right Tazmand, come on, take hold of yourself. Think!' He covers his face with his hands, rubs his eyes, punches his forehead a few times for good measure, then takes several more deep breaths, gulping the fresh sea breeze.

Now, images flash into his mind like tiny birds fighting a strong wind but, disappear too quickly for him to net and inspect them. 'Strange. No books anywhere. Hang on, books? Why am I thinking of books? And a garden. Statues. Oh, and a library?' The images start to rush at him faster, take on a more substantial and lasting form: long dark corridors, a falcon, animal carcasses, a tall ginger boy, a dead rat, a princess... and then it all floods back in a mad torrent, with the last memory being him jumping into the metal meat chute with his friends. And Salt is there. 'Dharma, Sky, Salt!' His heart sinks. 'Am I dead? Perhaps we didn't make it. Maybe this is the afterplace?'

His mind clears a little more, then it suddenly hits him. 'Dreaming! I'm dreaming. Another bloody dream!' He feels like screaming. Instead, he takes another deep breath and calms himself. 'Fine, fine, think it through. If that's the case, I really need to wake up. But I can't. Why can't I wake up? Don't know.' He scratches his head. 'Pangbats, I don't know.'

He looks out to sea, hoping for inspiration and desperate for a clue as to what he should, or could, do next. On and off, when his view is not obscured by a towering wave, he glimpses a distant horizon. At first, there is nothing to see except a straight line where sky meets water but then, as if out of nowhere, he catches sight of a speck. Initially, he cannot make it out. Just a tiny object. Not particularly significant. But, each time there is a break in the waves and he catches another sighting, it becomes bigger and potentially more interesting. Slowly, it dawns on him that it is getting larger because it is moving closer and, it is not just one object, it is three; three figures are walking steadily towards him over the surface of the churning water with no more difficulty than treading on solid ground.

The figures have the shape of people clothed in white robes that reflect the brilliant sunshine and billow and whip around their bodies in the breeze. Bent forwards against the strong wind, they are hurrying, yet each turns frequently to look back, as if concerned about pursuit. The trumpet blasts again; another series of jarring notes and the figures lurch forwards, picking up speed.

When they are close enough, Tazmand tries to make out their faces. To his amazement, and horror, he sees that they do not have any; no human features show, no eyes, just smooth, white skin with ragged holes where their mouths should be. Holes that gape like rips in a sheet that flap incessantly in the wind.

The figures come to a halt eventually, then remain standing on the water in front of Tazmand's rock. 'Who are you? What do you want? Where am I?' No reply is forthcoming. In fact, no sounds at all come from the holes that resembled mouths. Tazmand supposes though, from the gesticulations they are making with their arms, that they are trying to tell him something. He does not feel afraid, which surprises him; if anything, he feels sorry for them, as they themselves appear nervous, frightened.

'This is a dream, isn't it?' The figures turn to each other, as if communicating with one another but, offer no response. 'How do I wake up? Tell me – I must wake up!'

Still no response. Instead, each figure, in turn, reaches inside its robe and pulls out an object. The first figure stretched out its arms, holding a large green egg. Tazmand squints to get a better look. No, not green, now it is red. No, no it is still a green egg but, it is dripping with red liquid like blood, oozing through the pale fingers of its bearer, making Tazmand feel queasy. He recognises it straight away; it is like the stone from his dreams that the man called Osmand wears in his turban.

The second figure stretches its arms high above its head. Clasped in its hands is a golden chalice bearing the mark of a star, outlined in silver. Then, upturning it, a great stream of blood cascades over the figure's white head and down its featureless face onto its shoulders.

Tazmand is horrified. 'What the-? What is wrong with you people? What do you want? Why are you doing this?' The figures remain impassive and do not respond, continuing their grizzly pantomime. The trumpet sounds again, much louder now. Much closer. The figures turn to look towards the horizon then back towards Tazmand, signalling to each other that they need to hurry.

The third figure, having waited patiently for its

companions to display their items, holds up a looking glass. It steps across the water onto the rock, and hands the mirror to Tazmand before returning to its two companions. All three figures point to the mirror so, puzzled, he holds it up and looks into it. Expecting to see his reflection, he is surprised to see instead the inside of a room with bare, stone walls; it is as if he were peering through a glass window. A woman sits in the room, richly dressed although not in the Kareshian style, for she wears no veil. She looks beautiful and sad. She sits between two babies' cradles, both of which are empty. Again, Tazmand thinks he recognised her; is it the woman Iphigenia, from his dreams? Could be. He is not sure. His memories are hazy.

'I don't understand,' Tazmand shouts at the figures above the sound of the crashing waves. 'Why are you showing me these things? What do you want from me? None of this means anything. I want to wake up!'

The trumpet sounds again. This time harsher, as if angry. The three figures fall trembling to their knees, half sinking under the water as a shrill, clear roar of fury pierces the howling of the wind. A new figure is moving swiftly towards them, striding across the water from the distant horizon. Each tread results in the escape of hissing steam from the surface of the sea. As it gets closer, Tazmand can make out the dark shape of a man. Like the other three, it has no discernible facial features but, it radiated an unmistakeable impression of anger and menace. Within its forehead a dim, crimson light pulsates like a small beating heart. Again, Tazmand remembers this figure from in his dreams; it is the creature that Osmand had summoned.

Cowering, the three white figures sink further below

the surface of the waves. 'Wait! You haven't answered my questions!' All to quickly they disappear completely and Tazmand feels a mounting dread as the shadowy figure advances towards him and steps from the sea onto solid ground. He feels a tremor as the rock beneath him shakes with its first footfall.

#

'Not a bad livin' this scavengin' eh Tripe?' the larger of the two men pronounced. The wooden shaft of his spade gave a splintering squeak of protest as he leant heavily on it, bending down to run his calloused fingers through some loose clumps of sand and debris, his practiced eyes scanning the ground for anything of interest or, more importantly, value.

Tripe nodded his head and sucked noisily on a clay pipe. 'Not a bad livin' at all, Pyg. Not if you've got the stomach for it.' He shifted his weight to adjust his position and sit more comfortably on a broken stone pot.'

Well, you've certainly got that,' Pyg said standing back up straight, slapping his leg and laughing.

'Eh? Got what?'

'The stomach; you've got loads of that,' Pyg continued, laughing.

Tripe looked annoyed. 'You can talk,' he said peering up and shielding his eyes from the blazing midday sun.

'Oh I suppose so,' Pyg said glumly, glancing down at the mound of flesh straining against his belt.

The two men were taking a break from their work. They had arrived at the Scavenging Grounds before daybreak, to make sure they got the best pickings from the morning rubbish. They chatted constantly but, rarely did either of them take their eyes off the ground, just in case they missed anything. Every now and again a rushing, rumbling sound alerted them to new refuse tumbling out of the holes set high up in the sheer city walls nearby. It landed in great heaps on top of the already enormous mounds of rubbish below. They would only bother moving their pitch for the day, however, if the debris fell reasonably close by or if the smoke from one of the many bonfires shifted direction in the breeze and choked them.

'You need the talent too mind,' Tripe continued, tearing his eyes from the ground for a moment to give his companion a challenging look. 'It's not an easy livin' by any means,' he continued. 'All this diggin' around, tryin' to find stuff to sell.'

'Oh yeah, 'course you've got to 'ave the talent. Goes wivout sayin'. You'd never find anythin' worth anythin' without the knack. It's an 'ard livin' this. Not easy at all.'

Pyg continued to lean on his shovel and scanned the perimeter of the city wall through screwed up eyes. A vista of hills and valleys made of refuse, rotting in the strong sun, spread into the distance for as far as he could see. Bonfires resembling mini volcanoes belched black, sticky smoke. Stray dogs fought over scraps and barked at scavenging birds whilst rats swarmed through intricate holes and gaps where they had built their nests. A thick blanket of flies crawled over everything.

'Got to find the stuff first,' he continued. 'All that fossickin' in piles of rotten rubbish 'till you find somethin' good. Then there's all the travellin' abroad to try and flog it. My missus never likes it when I'm away for too long and I often am away for an age an' an half, me.' He stopped talking and peered into the distance, noting the shifting smoke from the bonfires with a professional eye. 'Not that I don't enjoy it mind,' he added at last, 'but, it is 'ard work.'

The two men remained silent. Both were happy and satisfied with what life had given them; the opportunity to make a living at what they did best by scavenging through piles of other people's waste for things that those people deemed worthless. Their eyes scanned the surface of the mounds, looking for the tell-tale sign of the glint of metal, a colourful scrap of material, a piece of broken furniture capable of being 'done-up' or even (as happened more often than one would think) the flash or sparkle of a precious jewel, slipped off the finger of a careless city-dweller throwing their leftovers out. With his mind on jewellery, Tripe at last broke the silence.

'Even harder than thievin' from the necropilops...erm, I mean necraplips, neprocalips... oh you know what I mean, the grave-robbin'. Now there's somethin' that's worth the risk. Dangerous but, worth the risk. At least with that you're almost always guaranteed to get a few decent trinkets. If you don't get caught that is.'

Pyg put his finger to his lips and looked around anxiously. 'Shush you pronk. Do you want to get us arrested?'

'Wha's the matter? Arristid by who? There's no one around to 'ear us.'

Pyg looked over towards a young, skinny boy who was grubbing about through a pile of rubbish nearby. The boy took no notice of them as he concentrated on his search. His dark eyes squinted and darted about, looking for anything significant that his thin, mud-caked hands might dig up. His fingernails, split and torn from barehanded digging, snagged in his long, black hair as he continually flicked it away from his eyes.

'Oh he's all right. That's only Maggot. He's always around,' Tripe said, stuffing more red leaf into the bowl of his pipe with a large, rough-skinned thumb.

'I know who 'e is'. Pyg said. 'But, you can't be too careful.'

Both men went quiet again. Tripe sucked on his pipe and Pyg continued to lean on his shovel. They watched the skinny boy digging industriously. Every now and again he would find something in the dirt, examine it, wipe at it with his sleeve then put it into a sack.

'All right, lad?' Pyg shouted over to the boy, giving him a wave. Maggot did not respond, preferring instead to continue with his work. 'Suit yourself then if you don't wanna talk.'

'He's a young one ain't he?' Tripe commented.

'No, not that young. He must be at least twelve. I've been at this game since I was six.'

'Oh yeah, I know that of course,' Tripe nodded. 'I mean we all started young I s'pose, just like my father and his father before 'im. It's just that he looks so weedy like, all scrawny. Much younger than twelve. Don't look like he's really up to it if you know what I mean.'

'Who, Maggot? He does all right does Maggot.'

'Who's 'is family then?'

'Family?' Pyg stopped to take off the cotton turban he was wearing and scratch the short, grey stubble on his head. 'Well, now you mention it I don't believe 'e 'as any. Used to be looked after by that old woman who died a few years back.

Can't rightly remember 'er name. You know the one. She lived by the metal 'eaps over by the north end. Long grey 'air and a big nose. She was from an old scavengin' family I think, although Maggot weren't her own, by all accounts.'

'Well what's he doin' 'ere then? Not allowed on the scavenge if you don't belong to an established scavengin' family. My family - the Potents – well as you know yourself Pyg; they've been scavengin' for nigh on three 'undred years. There's always been Potents 'ere abouts. Just like your family, the Pygals.'

'You're right there Tripe, although I've seen 'im around for so long now, I've got used to 'im. Let 'im be. There's no 'arm in it.'

The two men were quiet again as they watched Maggot do his work.

'Don't matter 'ow long you've been at this lark. There's still somethin' new to learn every day,' said Pyg at last.

'Quite right. Quite right. Yep, somethin' to learn every minute of the day as a matter of fact. Every minute of the day.' Tripe paused to take a long suck on his pipe then addressed himself once more to his friend. 'So… what have you learned today then?'

'What?'

'Today, what have you learned?'

Pyg appeared slightly taken off guard then quickly changed the subject. 'Just shut up and 'elp me dig. I found a load of old horseshoes and bridle bits 'ere last week, we'll see if there's more and we can sell 'em to a blacksmith. Honestly the things those city folks throw away. They must be made of money in there.' He indicated the other side of the wall with a jerk of his head.

Pyg straightened himself up and pulled his shovel out of the ground. Tripe hoisted himself up from his seat, grunting with the effort, stuck his pipe into his top pocket and went to pick up his crowbar. Just then a loud roaring sound heralded a new delivery of rubbish crashing down the side of the walls. This time, it emerged from one of the higher holes close by.

'Quick, fresh pickin's. Come on.'

The two men ran towards where the rubbish was vomiting out of three holes and showering down like rain. They were surprisingly fast and nimble for two such large men as they skipped and leapt over the obstacles in their way, carefully avoiding any of the rubbish mounds that were smoking or on fire. They arrived at the site at the same time as Maggot.

'Phew this lot stinks,' Pyg gasped, out of breath after his run.

'I'm puffed,' Tripe said, taking deep gulps of air. 'Getting' too old for all this runnin' about lark. Still,' he looked around him, 'there's no rush today eh. No one else about. Don't know why it's so quiet.'

'No one 'cept Maggot there.'

'Oh he won't get much. We can afford a bit of a rest before we do any serious diggin'. Let's just have a gentle fossick about before we get properly stuck in.'

Maggot was ignoring the two men and had already started rummaging around energetically, like a dog digging for a bone.

'I wish they wouldn't throw all their stuff out at the same time.' Tripe shouted to no one in particular. 'Look, it's all mixed up now. We've got rotten old food mixed in with the good stuff.' He started picking through some of the loose bits on the surface of the new heap.

'Look here Pyg. There's an old feather mattress that's still got some good wear in it but, someone's gone and thrown out a load of old vegetables with it, and they've gone rotten and soaked right through. Useless now. What you got there?'

'Cat.'

'Dead?'

'Course it's dead. Either that or it's very good at 'oldin its breath. Don't know if it came out with the rubbish or got caught in the downpour from the 'oles just now though.'

'Poor little thing.'

'Come on. Mornin's half gone and we ain't got much to show for it yet. Wife'll kill me if I don't bring nothin' decent back home.'

The two men started sifting through the rubbish in earnest.

#

The wind has calmed and the sea has become as flat as the surface of the hand mirror, which now lay discarded next to him on the ground. The three white figures have disappeared without trace under the surface of the sea. Tazmand sits on the rock and peers up at the dark figure looming over him. The pulsating, red light in its forehead glows like a burning ember in the ashes of an otherwise cold and lifeless fire. The demon, as Tazmand had decided this creature must be, stands in front of him, its arms folded over its chest. Although it has no eyes,

Tazmand knows it is staring down at him like a man might study an insect, deciding whether or not to crush it under foot.

The only sound now discernible is Tazmand's own breathing. Now, he cocks his head to listen, there is another noise; he can just about hear something; a soft vibration in the air, like someone dragging a stick across velvet-covered railings fast but, far away. The sound becomes louder and Tazmand looks down to see a fat ginger cat with greasy fur materialise from behind the demon's right leg. It peers up at him as it rubs its sticky body against the demon's leg, all the time purring loudly. Close behind the cat another sound follows; the rustle of silk, as a man also emerges from behind the demon. He is tall, exceptionally thin and wears the largest turban Tazmand had ever seen. He is dressed from neck to toe in a tight robe of purple silk. The man looks down at Tazmand with great interest then addressed the demon. 'Can he see us?' The demon nods slowly and the man raises his lip in a sneer. 'Good. Hear us?' The demon nodded again.

As Tazmand stares at the man, images and fleeting memories of previous dreams flicker once more across his mind.'Who are you?'

'All in good time boy.'

Tazmand catches his breath. 'Of course! I've seen you before, in other dreams. I'm sure I have. And your cat.'

'Yes, indeed.'

'Well, I don't suppose it matters much.'

'Really?'

'Yes. I've figured out this is a dream.'

The man makes a high-pitched noise through his nose like air escaping from an inflated pig's bladder, which

Tazmand takes to be a laugh. The cat purrs louder then disappears out of view behind the man's back.

'Yes boy, a dream. Let's call it that, if that is what you want it to be. A dream.'

'Well what else could it be?'

The man stares at Tazmand. His pale, grey eyes search the boy's face as if attempting to figure out his level of knowledge and capacity for understanding. His upper lip curls again into a sneer as he speaks. 'Well let me think. It might, perhaps, be a vision.' He moves closer, 'or a nightghast.'

'Yes, a nightghast perhaps. It has been strange, not to mention frightening.'

'Did you see the objects the white spirits showed you?'

'Yes. Is that what they were then – spirits?'

The man ignores the question. 'Did you understand what you were shown?'

'No.'

'No, of course not, simple boy,' the man makes the high-pitched noise again. 'All in good time.'

The cat comes back into Tazmand's view and, without warning, leaps at his foot. Its claws flash and its jaws open wide to reveal its sharp, metal teeth, which it sinks into his boot. Tazmand feels nothing as the teeth pass straight through his foot like a row of tiny silver daggers through mist. The cat gives an irritated snarl and its face contorts with feral anger as it swipes its claws at Tazmand's leg. Again, they pass through his clothes and body as if they are made of nothing but air. Frustrated, the cat gives the impression it does not care and sits with his back to the boy, licking its belly.

'Well whatever this is, a dream or a nightghast,

whatever, I need to wake up.'

Osmand nods slowly. 'I agree.'

'You do?'

Osmand nods again. 'Your sleeping body is in more danger in life than you are in dream. I need you alive boy. I want you whole – at least for now. You have a task to perform and you must come to me. You must come to Cardemont.'

'How? I've tried to wake up and I can't and… I'm afraid of this demon.'

'Demon?' Osmand laughs. 'Good word boy. Not far off I suppose, although not quite correct.' He fixes the boy with a disdainful stare. 'How can something so pathetic be so necessary to my future plans,' he murmurs to himself. Then, turning to the demon he issues an order, 'wake him.'

The demon bends forward, bringing his featureless face close to Tazmand's. As he feels the heat from the red glow in the demon's forehead, Tazmand recoils and falls back to lie on the ground.

'Come to Cardemont. Remember that name – Cardemont,' Osmand croons. 'Now wake up!'

The dark shadows on the lower half of the demon's face contort and shift until they form the semblance of a mouth. The mouth opens and expels a rush of hot, fetid air directly into Tazmand's face, who sits up immediately, gagging and choking. He thinks he is going to be sick.

CHAPTER SIXTEEN

Danger of Death

'Funny time to go to sleep,' Pyg said.

Tripe rested for a moment, leaning on his shovel. He wiped some sweat off his forehead. 'Yeah, funny place too.'

They were watching Maggot who was lying, not far away, face down on a small mound of rotten fruit.

Tripe scratched a particularly troublesome flea bite on his backside. His other hand shaded his eyes from the sun, as he tried to get a better look. 'Do you think he's awright?'

'Well... he's prob'ly tired, bless 'im.'

'Don't think he might be, well you know, dead or nothin'?'

'Don't be soft Tripe, look he's all twitchin' and movin' about. Can't be dead. He's havin' a dream I reckon.'

'Oh yeah, look. Seems like he's runnin'; his legs are racin' on the spot.'

'My neighbour's dog Bouncy does that.'

'Your neighbour's got a dog then? I didn't know that.'

'He's mumblin' as well,' Pyg added, pointing his ear in Maggot's direction and straining to hear.

'Come on then. Let's go and listen closer. He might need help.'

The two men put down their tools and went over to the boy who had, by this time turned over to lie on his back. He was shouting loudly and squirming about in the rubbish. 'Go away! Leave me alone! Who? No, I don't know him. What are you talking about? What? Just leave me alone. You're always pestering me!'

Pyg looked at Tripe. 'Do you think he's talking to us?' he asked.

'Nah. He can't even see us. His eyes is tight shut.'

Pyg looked unsettled by what he regarded as Maggot's odd behaviour. 'Who's he talkin' to then?'

'How should I know?'

'I don't care what happens to them. I don't know them. Just go back to wherever it is you come from.' Maggot was flailing his arms around wildly as if fighting off a swarm of flies. 'I don't know him. No I won't do it! Why should I?'

'He don't look happy. Must be 'avin' a nightghast,' Pyg pronounced.

'In the middle of the day?'

'I know that but, he's still asleep ain't he? Perhaps he's 'avin a dayghast then. Should I wake 'im up do you think?'

'Dunno. I've heard that's not a good thing. It's dangerous when someone's 'avin a night- sorry, I mean dayghast.'

'That's sleepwalkin' you pronk.'

'Oh, is it? All right then. Give him a gentle nudge and see what 'appens.'

359

Pyg approached Maggot cautiously and squatted down on his haunches. He was just about to shake the boy by the shoulder when Maggot sat upright suddenly and opened his eyes wide. 'Tazmand!' he yelled. The sound of the name rang out across the Scavenging Grounds, bouncing off the sheer walls of Karesh city and frightening a flock of crows that took flight squawking in irritation.

Pyg fell backwards in shock, his ample bottom landing uncomfortably on a broken crate of rotten cauliflowers. 'Taz- what?' he said.

'What?' Maggot asked, looking dazed.

'You was 'avin a bad dream boy. I was gonna wake you up and then you shouted out a load of stuff like you was bein' attacked by someone. Then you shouted out a word.'

'Name I think,' Tripe interjected. 'Sounded more like a name Pyg.'

'All right name then. Taz- somethin' it sounded like.'

'Taz- somethin',' Tripe repeated.

Maggot stood up and started to brush the muck off his clothes with his hands. 'I don't remember.'

'Yes,' Pyg continued. 'It was definitely Taz- somethin'. Heard it clear as day.'

'Me an' all,' Tripe added, nodding.

'It was just a dream,' Maggot mumbled sullenly.

Pyg stood up and massaged his rump where the crate had bruised it. 'Angry type of a dream then. Looked like you was bein' beat up.'

'Like you was at the mercy of evil forces,' Tripe added, moving up close behind Pyg and talking over his shoulder.

'Yes, thank you Tripe,' Pyg turned and addressed his

friend. 'I am handling this. Could you move back a bit? I can smell your breakfast on your breath.'

Tripe moved away looking hurt and grumbling loudly.

Pyg turned back to Maggot. 'As I was sayin'-'

'I told you, I don't remember!' the young boy snapped, standing up. 'I need to get on with my work.'

'Well sorry I'm sure for bein' of any help. Thought you was in trouble and came to your assistance and what thanks do I get? Just a clear off out of it.'

'Yeah, clear off out-' Tripe started to repeat but, stopped at a sharp glance from Pyg.

'Sorry, Maggot said. 'I, just, well I've got a pain in my head and it makes me feel irritable. Really, thanks for the help. I'm fine now. I appreciate it. Thank you.'

Pyg looked slightly less affronted. 'Well, all right then - I s'pose.'

'All right then,' Tripe echoed.

'I'm feeling fine. I need to get on with my work now. Thank you - both.'

'Well if you're quite sure,' Pyg said, sounding reluctant. 'Wouldn't want to leave you if you was goin' to go off on another dayghast and injure yourself with all that runnin' in your sleep. Wouldn't want to be blamed for leavin' you 'ere with no 'elp.'

'I'm all right.'

Pyg gave Maggot one more penetrating look, designed to figure out if he really was safe to be left alone. 'Right you are then. We'll be off.'

Pyg and Tripe moved back towards their patch, although not without a few grumbles. Maggot could hear them arguing as they walked away. Pyg was telling Tripe to stop repeating everything he said and Tripe was denying that he did anything other than try to be supportive in a crisis.

Maggot stood still, calmed his breathing and attempted to collect his thoughts. He had not had a vision like that for some time and never when working in the Grounds. The spirit voices usually only came to bother him when he visited the necropolis and usually only when he was awake. *What was that name they kept shouting? Kept urging me to repeat out loud?* He could not remember clearly. *Pyg was right. It was Taz- something. Anyway what does it matter? They always want something, or for me to do something. Bloody spirits!*

Maggot massaged his forehead and, thankfully, felt the pain slowly begin to ebb away; a headache always accompanied the voices. They had left him alone recently. Until today. *Forget about it. Ignore them. They're bound to give up eventually.* He picked up his sack and went to search for a fresh rubbish heap. Hopefully somewhere more private.

#

'Tazmand wake up!' Sky screamed, her voice verging on hysteria.

'Sky you have got to get him awake right now!'

'Well what do you think I'm trying to do you great pronk?' the princess screeched at Dharma over the growing turbulence in the meat chute. It was getting noisy again. 'Tazmand, wake up! Wake up!' Every time she shouted his name she slapped him across the face. He still would not move.

'We have to move backwards down the platform. We are

getting too close to the exit and those teeth,' Dharma shouted over the rising din. 'We have to find a way to stop this thing or we will all be chopped to pieces.'

'I can't move. If you haven't noticed, Tazmand's lying across my lap. I'm still pinned down!' Sky looked towards the exit. And stared at the metal sheets slicing across the opening. 'How can we stop it?'

'I don't know. We have to think of something. Get him awake - now!'

'Tazmand wake up for the gods' sake!' Sky shouted at the top of her lungs giving him some more extremely hard slaps. She either ignored or failed to notice the blood on her hands; the hard slapping was opening the scars on Tazmand's face received from the thorn bush in her garden. 'How long have we got?' she asked Dharma, her voice hoarse from the continued strain of shouting.

Dharma shrugged. Then, without warning, the platform started to lurch and shake much more violently.

'What's happening now?' Sky screeched. Her face looked sick with terror, her skin bleached by the intermittent light from the exit. 'I thought the platform had calmed down now it's travelling on the level?'

Dharma did not answer; he was too busy holding on and now had his eyes closed tight. Salt, on the other hand, did not appear to be unduly alarmed by all the commotion around him. He was squatting comfortably, managing the erratic rhythm like a seasoned rider of wild horses. Now and again he would effortlessly leap backwards, forwards or sideways to maintain his balance. Dharma, by contrast, was being bounced and shaken about like a stringed marionette at the mercy of an insane puppeteer. He held on with both hands to the large rib with grim determination, although the carcass was itself being thrown about nearly as much as him. Sky found – strangely - that her area of the platform remained reasonably still.

'Everything's bouncing!' Salt yelled.

'Really? You don't say,' Dharma shouted back as he continued to hold on, opening one eye then closing it again quickly. 'That's the greatest understatement of all time. It feels like the whole thing's going to collapse or explode,'

'I'm sure no machine should get this rough,' Sky shouted. 'It must have a fault.'

'I know this sounds weird,' Dharma shouted back. 'But, the last time Taz fell asleep like this in the library, there was a temblor. I think he's doing it. Or, at least, it's something to do with him. Everything around him in the library went berserk. Books flew off the shelves. Grunts fell off their ladders. The floor even cracked but, the area where he was lying on the library floor remained calm and undamaged.'

'Tazmand's doing it? Don't be a pronk Dharma. How could he possibly-'

Just then Salt gave a shout that cut through all the noise. 'Get back! Quick! Everyone must get back!'

Sky looked up from Tazmand's sleeping face as Salt did an athletic somersault over her head and landed perfectly on his feet behind her.

'How did you do that?' she asked, amazed and momentarily distracted from the danger.

'Look. Look forward,' Salt shouted before she could get an answer, pointing towards the exit. She looked forward and the teeth seemed very close all of a sudden, slicing through everything the chute fed it.

'We know Salt. We are trying to get back but, I'm stuck with Tazmand's weight on top of me. Help me move him.'

'Move back!' Salt shouted again.

'Salt!' Sky barked. 'Grab both of Tazmand's legs and pull him off me.' Salt did as he was told and easily moved Tazmand's limp body. Sky moved forwards up the platform towards Dharma. She noticed how the platform's movement became more violent once she moved away from Tazmand and had to be careful not to lose her balance. She reached out her hand towards him. 'Dharma, give me your hand and come back with me.'

'I can't Sky. I can't let go or I'll fall down the side of the platform.'

'You have to let go or you'll get sliced to death. Let go and move back.'

'I can't!'

Sky glanced towards the exit. Dharma was only a few paces from the teeth.

'Dharma!' she screamed.

Abruptly, the platform calmed. The violent jerking and juddering stopped. Dharma was lying on the platform floor, still clutching the rib bone.

'Dharma get back now!'

Without any more hesitation he shuffled back to Sky on his hands and knees then stood up. They both hurried back to where both Salt and Tazmand were sitting up together chatting.

'Tazmand, you're awake!' Sky cried with obvious relief.

'What's all the shouting?' He asked groggily. 'And what's that smell?' He looked around him and noticed all the rotting meat. 'Oh, yuk.' He looked like he was about to vomit. Dharma was too exhausted to reply and Sky was too angry. 'I've had the weirdest dream.'

'You made the meat chute bounce,' Salt said. 'And now we are going to be chopped to pieces by the metal teeth and we will all die. Look.'

Tazmand looked in the direction that Salt was pointing. His eyes widened in alarm.

'Back quickly! We'll all be killed!' he shouted, leaping to his feet.

Scared as she was, Sky rolled her eyes. 'Why didn't we think of that?' she muttered under her breath.

'Are you all right Taz?' Dharma asked.

'Yes I'm fine. Mind you, my face is a bit sore.' He felt his cheeks tenderly. 'It feels like I've been in a fight and someone's punched me in the face.' Sky gave Dharma a fleeting, guilty look. 'I don't know what happened. I must have passed out. I had some strange dreams. They're not very clear in my memory now. I remember getting into the meat chute and that man in a turban again and his cat and-'

'Could we possibly discuss this later,' Sky interrupted, 'preferably at a time when we are not about to face a horrible and painful death?' Her voice started to get louder and higher-pitched, moving once more towards panic as she remembered the danger they were in.

They all continued to shamble backwards along the chute, temporarily maintaining the distance between them and the teeth.

'We can't keep this up for ever,' Dharma panted as he moved backwards, watching his feet and trying not to slip on gore and fall through the gaps at the sides of the platform. 'We have to get through those... those things.'

'One two, one two three. One two, one two three.' Salt started to chant. 'One two, one two three. One two, one two three. One two...'

The others stared at him.

'Salt, what are you-?' Tazmand asked.

'One two, one two three,' Salt repeated staring at the metal teeth.

'Salt, shut up! Just shut up! Shut up! Shut up!' Sky shouted. 'I can't cope with your dull-witted stupidity just at this moment.' The others went quiet at her outburst, so she continued. 'We need to do something. We have to go back. That's it! We have to turn this thing around and go back. We can go to my father and tell him it was all a big mistake. He'll understand. We have to face him and just-'

'Sky stop it!' Tazmand held her shoulders and shouted right into her face. She ceased ranting immediately, looking shocked. He turned to Salt. 'I think I see what he means. You're counting the rhythm of the teeth aren't you?'

All four of them stared at the teeth still inching closer and closer by the second. They moved back a few more paces. No one admitted it aloud but, they all realised that they were probably not going to survive. They stared in horror at the exit. Every time the teeth opened, light flooded into the tunnel along with a blast of warm, desert air. Each time they closed, darkness enveloped them once again. They were all reaching the end of their strength and kept stumbling and slipping over bits of decaying animal flesh and tripping over bones as they continually moved backwards.

Dharma tripped over a buffalo leg and stumbled. He would have fallen down the side if Tazmand had not grasped his arm.

'There's more and more of this stuff coming up from the meat vaults,' Dharma said. 'They must have fixed the door.'

They tried jumping up and down as hard as possible to break the mechanism underneath the platform but, it achieved nothing. Salt found two extra-large buffalo shinbones further back along the platform and, risking his life (or at least his hands), he ran forward to the teeth and wedged the bones between the slicing blades, attempting to jam them. Both bones splintered instantly, as if they were no more than dry twigs. The teeth continued their unremitting slicing and grinding and the platform inched forwards on its relentless course.

'What's that?' Dharma shouted suddenly, pointing back down the chute. They all turned to stare at an entire buffalo carcass coming up behind them.

Tazmand gasped. 'Someone must have thrown it in the chute whole.' The carcass lay there, taking up the entire width and height of the chute, shivering with the movement of the platform and vibrating with the thick buzz of flies. They moved as close as they could to the rotten thing. 'By the gods! We can't get back past this!'

They all turned and stared at the exit. There was no way back now and the teeth were no more than a few metres away. They looked at each other, fear and hopelessness apparent in their faces.

Just then, the platform juddered to a complete halt. Sky and Dharma lost their balance with the unexpected lack of momentum and fell over. Tazmand, without thinking, grabbed hold of the fur on the dead beast's forehead to steady himself.

'Where's Salt?' Dharma said.

They looked around and saw Salt's legs sticking up in the air. He had managed to squeeze himself up to his waist, head first between the edge of the platform and the wall. He pulled himself back up on the platform, a wide grin spread across his face. His hair and arms were covered in thick grease.

'What-?' Sky started to say but, was struck speechless with confusion.

'What have you done?' Tazmand managed to ask.

'I stuck big bones in the little wheels,' Salt answered.

'Little wheels?'

'Yes my friend Tazmand. Lots of little wheels under the platform. I stuck two big bones in. They stopped moving.'

A sudden jolt of the platform alerted them all to the fact that the stationary position might not last for long.

'You jammed them?'

'Yes.'

Sky and Dharma stood up. They all remained silent for a moment, concentrating on the straining vibrations underneath their feet. The mechanics squealed in high-pitched protest and the platform itself, although not moving forward, felt like a large dog, straining on its lead to go for a walk.

'We haven't got much time,' Tazmand shouted over the mounting noise. 'Salt has managed to stall the mechanism. We can't guarantee how long it will hold though, so we have to

369

act now.' Salt had started counting again and Tazmand joined in. 'One two, one two three. One two, one two three.Yes I see. Look, they move at a set rhythm. The teeth I mean. The side ones move into the middle twice, and then stay in an open position as the top and bottom ones close three times in quick succession. But, and this is the important part, there is a two second gap before the side teeth move again. We can still get out!'

'What do you suggest?' Sky asked, ignoring her mounting panic by focusing on survival.

'It's the only chance we've got,' Tazmand said and Salt nodded enthusiastically, understanding instinctively what his friend meant.

'Will someone please explain to me what is going on?' Dharma shouted over the mounting noise.

'We go out taking turns one at a time during the two second gap.'

Sky and Dharma both stared at Tazmand as if he had finally gone completely insane.

'We will all jump!' Salt shouted, his face beaming. 'Tazmand will save us.'

'It's not much time I grant you,' Tazmand continued, choosing to take no notice of their astonished expressions and trying to look confident. 'But it is enough. We just have to be coordinated and fast. No hesitating.'

'Are you saying we just throw ourselves out?' Dharma said, dumbfounded. 'We will get killed by the fall. We are probably metres and meters up in the air by now.'

'No falling,' Salt said. 'I will hold the rope.'

Tazmand, Sky and Dharma looked at the tall boy, in his

ripped robe and covered from head to foot in filth, blood and grease.

'How on earth did you figure out the rhythm of the teeth?' Sky asked.

'Good at counting,' Salt said, then thought about it some more. 'Good at counting up to three.'

'But, the rope will be cut by the teeth,' Dharma insisted.

'No cutting. Small gap,' Salt replied.

'What?'

'He's right again,' Tazmand said. 'Look, the teeth don't meet completely. There's just enough room for the rope to fit through even when the teeth are closed. It won't get cut.'

They all looked towards the slicing teeth and, sure, enough, whenever they were fully closed, the friends could see a small gap between the blades where a tiny glint of sunlight continued to shine through from the outside.

'The rope will still fray surely, Sky insisted. 'Those, those things,' she said, pointing at the teeth, not wanting to acknowledge them by giving them a name. 'They look incredibly sharp. Even though there's a gap, the weight of a body hanging will slice the fibre.'

'No way,' Tazmand said, doing his best to give a convincingly reassuring smile. 'This stuff is seasoned buffalo hide. It's as thick and tough as an overgrunt's skin. Isn't that right Salt?'

'Oh yes Tazmand. Very tough. Very strong indeed. I won't let go.'

Sky and Dharma both looked dubious as the teeth looked razor-sharp but, they were running out of options. The squealing of the wheels continued to mount in intensity and the platform gave a sudden jolt, as if about to move forward again.

'Quick,' Tazmand shouted. 'There's no time to discuss it further.'

'But what about Salt?' Dharma asked, close to tears with fear.

'What do you mean?'

'I mean Taz, if Salt is holding the rope in here while we all fling ourselves through that thing. How is he going to get out?'

Taz was silent for a moment. 'You're right. I hadn't thought about that. Sorry Salt. I was being selfish. I just got so excited by the idea. What can we do? I don't-'

Before Taz could come up with an answer, Salt interrupted. 'Easy, I tie the rope to something and then it is my turn.'

'Tie it to what?' Dharma persisted.

'Something very big,' Salt said.

'Like what?'

Salt raised his eyes to the ceiling and thought hard for a moment.

'Um...dunno.'

'Well you had better find something quickly,' Sky interrupted.

Salt looked around in the bright flashes of intermittent daylight.

'That,' he shouted, pointing at the huge buffalo carcass. 'Round its neck.'

Tazmand nodded. 'Right. We do it now! Check your knapsacks are securely fastened. We can't afford to lose anything.' He turned to Dharma, 'you first. Get this rope wrapped around your stomach.'

Dharma did not stop to argue as he wound a length of the cord round his middle and Sky helped to fasten it.

'Thank the gods Nana made us get rope,' she said as she was tying a slipknot. 'I will get back to Karesh one day somehow so I can thank her and make sure she is all right.'

Tazmand felt like someone had punched him in the stomach. The memory of Nana collapsing to the ground as she was slain by several guards, their swords plunging into her body, came back to him in a flood of raw emotion. Neither Sky nor Dharma knew yet that Nana was dead. That she sacrificed herself to help them escape. How was he going to tell them? Should he tell them at all – especially Sky?

'Are you all right Taz?' Dharma asked.

'Of course!' Tazmand snapped. 'Yes I'm fine, just a bit tense.'

Dharma nodded and tried to smile. The blood had drained from his face and his knees looked wobbly.

Tazmand used a supreme effort of will to put Nana out of his mind. Dealing with that would have to wait until later. They had more pressing problems. 'All right,' he said out loud, keeping his voice as strong and even as possible. 'Everybody stand where they are and watch the teeth.'

They all did as they were told, watching the rhythmic chomping of the slicing metal. Tazmand had to shout as loudly as he could now because the grinding and screeching of the teeth was loud enough but, the squealing of the jammed wheels as they tried to free themselves from the bones had become deafening.

'Dharma, when I say go, don't think about it; trust me. I

will do the counting for you. Just throw yourself through the gap.' Turning to the others he yelled, 'you both stay as far back as you can. Give him plenty of room. As soon as Dharma has disappeared through the hole Sky, you be ready. Salt-'

'Yes Tazmand.'

'Whatever you do, don't let go of the rope.'

'No Tazmand.'

'Dharma? Are you ready?'

'Yes,' Dharma's teeth were chattering with fear, much faster than the metal ones ahead of him.

'Now listen. I reckon the rope will be long enough to get you about two thirds of the way down the outside wall. That is if what Nana told us about the height of the walls is correct. You'll get a jolt when the rope reaches the end of its length. You have to release the slip knot in mid air, let go of the rope and then let yourself fall the final few feet to the ground. Salt will feel the rope go slack and pull it up. All right?'

Dharma nodded his head uncertainly.

'Taz?'

'Yes Dar.'

'Um, this is going to work isn't it?'

Tazmand looked at his oldest friend's usually round, open face which was now screwed up with terror and uncertainty. He found that he could not look directly into his eyes. 'Of course it is,' he said glancing down at the floor. 'Now get yourself ready and do not hesitate.'

Tazmand studied the metal blades of the teeth intently and started to count out loud. One two – one, two, three - one two – one, two, three – GO-'

On cue, Dharma threw himself at the teeth as fast as

he could with his eyes tightly shut. Tazmand watched him hurtle through the gap head first to possible death. The last things he saw before the upper and lower teeth came down were the soles of his dearest friend's boots disappear out into bright sunshine, just missing the sharp metal. He held the rope loosely in his hand and felt it slide through his fingers at a terrific speed as it followed Dharma's descent.

Salt and Sky waited by the large buffalo carcass, both holding their breath. The rope went taut, requiring Salt to take up the strain. The tough leather stretched but, did not snap. After a brief moment the rope retracted and went limp. They looked at each other, each forcing a hesitant smile to their lips. They could only hope this meant that Dharma had untied the rope knowing that he only had a short fall left to a safe landing. Salt wasted no time in pulling the rope back up. Tazmand still held it loosely in his hand. As it passed through his fingers he felt a deep groove in the leather where Dharma's weight must have pulled it onto the metal of the lower teeth. He stiffened with anxiety, wondering how many times the rope could take this punishment without finally being sliced through. He said nothing to the others.

'Sky?' Tazmand barked. He had noticed a look in the princess's eyes that usually signalled an argument but, he was not going to allow anything to slow them down now. Salt wound up all the rope and Tazmand tied it around Sky's waist, making sure he secured it with a slipknot. Her face was pale and she looked ill with anxiety.

'We can do this Sky; I know the rhythm of the teeth. I won't let you go through at the wrong time. Do you trust me?'

Sky nodded her head shakily. Tazmand stared at the

teeth. Sky watched his lips move as he counted silently. Without warning he placed his hand on the small of her back and pushed. 'Now!' he shouted.

As Sky was flying through the gap, the upper and lower teeth sliced down just missing her left foot. Tazmand ran back to Salt who was holding the rope tightly. Before too long it became limp and Salt pulled it back through the hole. Tazmand felt it slip through his fingers. The groove was much deeper.

Tazmand turned to Salt. 'You go next,' he said to his new friend.

Salt looked amazed. 'No my friend Tazmand. I must go last.'

'Do what I say. You go. I will hold the rope. There is no time to argue.'

Salt smiled; it was a deep, sad smile. 'Tazmand I am strong. I can hold the rope. You cannot. You go now.'

The platform suddenly gave a tremendous jerk and they heard the unmistakeable splintering of bone. Both boys held on to the carcass as the platform once more continued its interrupted journey towards the exit.

'No time,' Salt shouted, already tying the rope round Tazmand's waist and singing a ridiculous song from the meat vaults so he could not hear what Tazmand was saying. Tazmand gave in. There was no more time to argue, the teeth were getting too close. Then, Tazmand had an idea.

'Salt, bind your end of the rope to the buffalo now. Then, as soon as I untie my end you'll have more time to tie it round your waist.' The boy did not seem to be listening. 'Salt, listen to me!'

'Bye bye my friend Tazmand. You are my best friend.' Salt

was now pushing Tazmand towards the teeth. 'You must go now. Hurry!'

Tazmand started to move towards the teeth, looking back at his new friend. 'Please bind the rope to the carcass. You won't have time to get out. Listen to me!'

'Bye bye Tazmand.'

Tazmand could see Salt waving. He felt tears well up in his eyes. No. Not another one. Not another death because of me! Not Salt as well as Nana. I won't have more blood on my hands. Not for my sake!

'Salt, come now.' he screamed. 'Quickly it's your only chance. There won't be time for you if you wait for me to land. Jump now! Forget the rope! I don't want you to die!'

He turned one more time to see Salt standing by the buffalo carcass, holding the rope securely with one hand, waving with the other. Then, counting steadily, Tazmand gave himself up to fate; he threw himself out into the arid, desert air and the brilliant sunshine.

END OF BOOK ONE

—

Book Two of the Bloodstone of Cardemont series: *'Greef'*
Available to download from Amazon now

www.amazon.co.uk/Greef-Bloodstone-Cardemont-Series-ebook/dp/B008A051HO/

ABOUT THE AUTHOR

Jack Murphy

Contact: jackmurphywriter@gmail.com

www.facebook.com/pages/Jack-Murphy-Author/320843737961295

www.instagram.com/jackmurphywriter/

GREEF (PREVIEW)

https://www.amazon.co.uk/Greef-Bloodstone-Cardemont-Series-ebook/dp/B008A051HO/

Tazmand and his companions have escaped Karesh city. They arrive in the Scavenging Grounds, a vast landscape of rubbish outside the city walls but, now they are free, what's next? Closely pursued by a group of soldiers sent by the emperor and led by Sash, a slave overseer harbouring a personal grudge, they must find safety and, ultimately, decide where they are heading.

Befriended by Maggot, a young scavenger who makes his living trawling through rubbish and Greef, a trainee Coenobite with (erratic) magical powers, Tazmand tries to make sense of the confusing relationship between his dreams and real life whilst undertaking a journey, fraught with danger, betrayal and deceit, that tests the bounds of loyalty and friendship to the limit.

'Greef' is book two of the 'Bloodstone of Cardemont' series.

Printed in Great Britain
by Amazon

28852838R00219